MW00447178

Murders
and other
Confusions

The Chronicles of Susanna,
Lady Appleton,
16th Century Gentlewoman, Herbalist
and Sleuth

Murders

and other

Confusions

The Chronicles of Susanna,
Lady Appleton,
16th Century Gentlewoman, Herbalist
and Sleuth

Crippen & Landru Publishers
Norfolk, Virginia
2004

Copyright © 1999, 2001, 2002, 2003, 2004
by Kathy Lynn Emerson

Cover painting by Linda Weatherly S.

Cover design by Deborah Miller

Crippen & Landru logo by Eric D. Greene

ISBN (limited edition): 1-932009-20-5
(978-1-932009-20-0)

ISBN (trade edition): 1-932009-21-3
(978-1-932009-21-7)

Third Printing, trade edition

Printed in the United States of America on acid-free paper

Crippen & Landru, Publishers
P. O. Box 9315
Norfolk, VA 23505-9315
USA

E-Mail: info@crippenlandru.com
Web: www.crippenlandru.com

Dedication

To my in-house critic and expert on crime, Sandy Emerson, the perfect husband for a mystery writer.

Contents

Introduction   11

The Body in the Dovecote   17

Much Ado About Murder   33

The Rubaiyat of Nicholas Baldwin   54

Lady Appleton and the London Man   71

Lady Appleton and the Cautionary Herbal   85

The Riddle of the Woolsack   103

Lady Appleton and the Cripplegate Chrisoms   122

Lady Appleton and the Bristol Crystals   140

Encore for a Neck Verse   162

Confusions Most Monstrous   180

Death by Devil's Turnip   203

Checklist of Books and Stories by Kathy Lynn Emerson   227

Acknowledgments

Historical short stories take almost as much research as historical novels. My mistakes are my own, but a number of people provided suggestions, inspiration and other assistance. Beth Foxwell, Doug Greene, John Helfers, and the late Cathleen Jordan have my sincere gratitude for convincing me I could write short stories suitable for publication. Five good friends read most of these stories in rough draft and helped make them better: Mary Anne Frounfelker, Sylvie Kurtz, Lynn Manley, Kelly McClymer, and Yvonne Murphy. For details in individual stories my thanks also go to Terry Gerritsen, Susan Tolman, Gretchen Worden of the Mütter Museum, and Luci Zahray. And, as always, I couldn't have gotten far without the help of the Inter-Library Loan system, ably put to work for me first by Janine Bonk and then by Moira Wolohan at Mantor Library, University of Maine at Farmington.

Introduction

The Life and Times of Susanna, Lady Appleton

This volume contains stories connected to the Face Down mystery series featuring Susanna, Lady Appleton, a sixteenth-century gentlewoman, herbalist, and sleuth. At the time of this writing, Susanna has solved murders in seven novels and nine short stories. There will be more.

The remaining mysteries in this collection are investigated by Susanna's friends. In "The Rubaiyat of Nicholas Baldwin," it is Nick Baldwin, her neighbor in Kent, who is the sleuth. In "The Riddle of the Woolsack," I use Susanna's maidservant, companion, and confidante Jennet Jaffrey and Jennet's husband Mark as detectives.

The stories range from the time just before Susanna's marriage in 1552 through the summer of 1577, when she is in her forty-third year and has been a widow for over a decade.

You don't need to read the rest of this introduction in order to enjoy these tales, but for those who are interested in how my characters evolved, I include here brief biographies of my fictional sleuth and the people nearest and dearest to her, together with a few comments on my sources. Additional information on individual stories follows the text of each.

Susanna, Lady Appleton, was born Susanna Leigh in 1534. Her father was Sir Amyas Leigh (d. 1546), a scholar, courtier, and fervent supporter of the New Religion. As several of his contemporaries did, Sir Amyas saw to it that his daughters were well educated. Most Elizabethans, although they might see the point in a woman knowing how to read and cipher (but not necessarily to write, which was taught separately from reading) were suspicious of "learned" females. There are times when Susanna is not so sure her forward-thinking father did her any favors.

Susanna's younger sister Joanna died of eating poison banewort berries when they were children. This influenced Susanna to make an intensive study

11

of poisonous plants and eventually write *A Cautionary Herbal, being a compendium of plants harmful to the health.* When her father also died, in a shipwreck, Susanna became the ward of John Dudley, then Lord Lisle, a real historical figure who was later created Duke of Northumberland. Still later, he was executed for treason when he tried to put Lady Jane Grey on the throne of England in place of the rightful heir.

Northumberland, as part of his duties as Susanna's guardian, arranged her betrothal to Robert Appleton when she was fourteen. After they were married, in October, 1552, he took possession of her family home, Leigh Abbey in Kent. Robert, born in 1525 at Appleton Manor, Lancashire, was the son of Sir George Appleton (1500-1557) by the first of Sir George's five wives. He was nineteen when he entered Lord Lisle's household. In 1553, after backing the failed attempt to put Lady Jane Grey on the throne, he was briefly imprisoned. In 1557, as part of his concerted effort to get back into royal favor, he left England with King Philip's army and fought at Saint-Quentin. This earned him a knighthood. As the wife of a knight, Susanna thus became Lady Appleton.

When Queen Elizabeth ascended the throne in 1558, Robert switched his allegiance to her and took up a new career as an intelligence gatherer for the Crown. *Face Down in the Marrow-Bone Pie,* the first novel in the series, takes place in 1559.

It is Robert's murder Susanna must solve in the fourth book in the series, *Face Down Beneath the Eleanor Cross.* In the sixteenth century, women had few rights. They belonged, like chattel, first to their fathers and then to their husbands. If they had children to provide for they usually remarried soon after they were widowed. Childless, disenchanted by her marriage to Robert, Susanna chooses to remain unwed. From my point of view as a writer, this simplifies matters. Susanna's position as a wealthy widow makes it much easier for her to function as an amateur detective.

Susanna is not averse to male companionship, however. Nick Baldwin, who first meets Susanna in "Lady Appleton and the London Man," was born in London in 1532. His father was a merchant of the staple, which means he traded in wool. After serving as his father's apprentice in London, Nick went to Antwerp at the age of twenty. In 1555, Nick went to what was then called Muscovy as a stipendiary with the Muscovy Company. In 1558, he visited Persia.

Walter Pendennis, born in 1529 in Launceston, Cornwall, is Nick's rival for Susanna's affections. Like Robert, he was sent to the household of Lord Lisle in 1544. He knew Robert there, but did not meet Susanna until 1562. He briefly studied civil law at Cambridge but had a greater interest in architecture. He was wounded at Saint-Quentin. In 1559 he went to France to work for Sir Nicholas Throckmorton, the English Ambassador. His official title was secretary, but he was actually an intelligence gatherer, a job he continued to do after returning to England.

Jennet Barton, later Jennet Jaffrey, started out as Susanna's tiring maid, became her friend and companion, and eventually took over at Leigh Abbey as housekeeper. She was born in Barfreystone, near Leigh Abbey, on January 7,1537. Superstitious but absolutely devoted to her mistress, Jennet is frequently seen lurking behind the arras, or just outside a door, in order to eavesdrop on private conversations—a useful skill for a sleuth's sidekick.

I wouldn't care to live in the sixteenth century, but it is a wonderful place to visit. I've been fascinated by the England of Elizabeth the First and Shakespeare since I was a girl. In college, the focus of my research was on a play, *The Duchess of Malfi*, written in 1613. This was just after the Elizabethan age but the play was undoubtedly influenced by the strong women who lived during the 1500s. Some readers may recall a vivid portrayal of the author of this piece, John Webster, from the film *Shakespeare in Love*. He was the adolescent boy torturing rats and spying on Shakespeare.

The sixteenth century, for all its chauvinist tendencies, was an age that produced some outstanding women. They weren't feminists in the modern sense, but they accomplished a great deal by working around and through the men in their lives. In a time when the laws of the land limited a woman's ability to control her own destiny, a remarkable number of females made their mark on history.

One of them was Bess of Hardwick, a country gentlewoman who was wealthier than the queen by the end of the century. Best known today for the prodigy houses she left behind, in her own time she also managed the not inconsiderable feat of sailing through turbulent political waters without being swamped. With her fourth husband, the earl of Shrewsbury, she had the keeping of the imprisoned queen of Scots. Later, she was guardian to another potential heir to the throne, her granddaughter, Lady Arbella Stuart. Twice she faced arrest and disgrace for seeming to support marital alliances the queen had not sanctioned, but Bess died in her own bed in her eighties—rich, successful, and the head of a dynasty.

Another long-lived and controversial figure was Laetitia (Lettice) Knollys, successively countess of Essex and countess of Leicester. A cousin to Queen Elizabeth on her mother's side, Lettice secretly married the man the queen was said to love, Robert Dudley, earl of Leicester (the duke of Northumberland's son, Lord Robin, in the Lady Appleton novels and stories). At that time, Lettice already had a son by her first marriage, a young man who would eventually become the queen's new favorite. Robert Devereux, earl of Essex, was executed for treason in 1601. Personally, I think Lettice had a lot more to do with her son's downfall and the Essex Rebellion than she's given credit for. Certainly one of her daughters, Penelope Rich, took an active role in the attempt to overthrow Elizabeth. Lettice outlived them all and was in her nineties when she died in 1634.

The Englishwoman with the most political clout during the sixteenth century was, of course, the queen, Elizabeth Tudor, but she wasn't the only one. When Henry VIII went off to war, he left his wife in charge. Catherine of Aragon, wife number one of six, had better success battling the Scots than Henry did against the French.

After the deaths of Henry VIII and his son Edward VI, almost all the heirs to the English throne were females. Mary Tudor succeeded first, before Elizabeth. The other female claimants to the throne included Frances Brandon, duchess of Suffolk, and her daughters, Lady Jane Grey ("the nine-days queen"), Lady Catherine Grey, and Lady Mary Grey. There were also Lady Margaret Douglas, countess of Lennox, Lady Margaret Clifford, Lady Strange, who was said to dabble in witchcraft, and the aforementioned Lady Arbella Stuart. At the head of the pack, however, was, Mary, queen of Scots, queen regnant of Scotland and former queen consort of France. Sadly, almost all of these women forfeited the chance to succeed Elizabeth I by involving themselves with unsuitable men. Elizabeth's decision to remain unmarried may have been unpopular with her counselors, but it was undoubtedly the best choice to ensure a long and successful reign.

Two women who had no claim to the throne themselves were behind an unsuccessful attempt in 1569 to rebel against Elizabeth and replace her with Mary of Scotland. They were the countesses of Westmorland and Northumberland. Contemporary records call them "stouter" than their husbands in rallying the troops, but in the end the attempt failed. Too many conflicting goals—some religious, some political, and some personal—interfered with the success of the Rising of the Northern Earls. One countess went into exile, the other spent the remainder of her life under house arrest.

England wasn't the only sixteenth-century country where women played a vital political role. Most of them were active only behind the scenes, as the wives and mistresses of great men, but a few took center stage. While in religious exile from England during the reign of Mary Tudor, Catherine Willoughby d'Eresby, dowager duchess of Suffolk, served as regent of the Polish province of Samogita (Lithuania) for King Sigismund Augustus. The Netherlands had three successive female regents, Margaret of Austria, Mary of Hungary, and Margaret of Parma. Until her death in 1560, Marie of Guise was regent of Scotland for her daughter. And in France, through several successive reigns, the queen mother, Catherine de Medici, actually ruled the country.

Sixteenth-century girls obviously had role models in high places, but there were also a number of ordinary women who set extraordinary examples for those who came after them. The education given to princesses trickled down through the nobility to the gentry and the merchant class. Books for women were published in increasing numbers throughout the period and female literacy is estimated to have been at a higher level in the 1590s than it would reach again for three hundred years.

The character of Susanna, Lady Appleton, was directly inspired by the lives of four of the daughters of Sir Anthony Cooke, sometime tutor to Queen Elizabeth's brother, King Edward VI. Like the fictional Sir Amyas Leigh, Sir Anthony had his girls educated as if they were boys.

The oldest daughter, Mildred, wed Sir William Cecil, later Lord Burghley, the queen's most trusted advisor, and was mother to Sir Robert Cecil, Burghley's successor at court. Lord Burghley was also head of the Court of Wards and took over the wardships of a number of young peers himself. They were educated in the Burghley household until they were sent away to school, and there Lady Burghley reigned supreme. The second Cooke daughter, Ann, also influenced an eager young mind, her son Francis Bacon.

Mildred, Ann, and their younger sister, Katherine, who married diplomat Sir Henry Killigrew, all wrote poetry and translated Latin and Greek texts, some of which were published. Another sister, Elizabeth Cooke Hoby Russell, became proficient enough in mathematics that university scholars traveled to her home to consult with her on the subject, since women could neither attend nor lecture at Oxford or Cambridge.

I've been fascinated by Lady Russell for a long time. Like many Elizabethans she had a quarrelsome nature. She was involved in several lawsuits and once engaged in a pitched battle with her neighbors over her right to occupy a certain castle. She was also a leading force in the 1590s in keeping the Lord Chamberlain's Men (Shakespeare's company of players) from building an indoor theater in the Blackfriars, the enclosed community in London where she made her home. Too much noise. Too much danger of infection. And the riff raff it would attract! She got up a petition drive and the building of the indoor playhouse was delayed for years.

Some very silly accusations have been made against this lady—her ghost is said to haunt Bisham Abbey, where she lived with her first husband, Sir Thomas Hoby. But her real history is just as compelling. She had two sons by Hoby and two daughters, both maids of honor to the queen, by her second husband, a younger son of the earl of Bedford. Determined to see them all marry well, she became notorious in her own time for meddling in their matrimonial affairs. Once she even used her coach to chase down one of her errant offspring. In addition, she was an ardent letter writer. Most surviving examples are either requests for favors or vitriolic complaints. She wouldn't make a very sympathetic sleuth, but bits and pieces of her colorful history have certainly provided me with plenty of inspiration for villains over the years.

The settings I use in the stories and novels—various locations in sixteenth-century England, Europe, and Persia—play an integral part in the stories. They are carefully researched. My plots, although fictional, are always based on facts. In every way possible, the times, the places, and the characters you will find here are as true to reality as I could make them. I consider it a challenge to create a fictional story but still get the historical details right. If some pesky fact seems to be getting in the way, I contrive to use it, rather than ignore or change it. So, if you like stories that combine history and mystery, here are eleven of them. Enjoy!

Kathy Lynn Emerson
Wilton, Maine
May, 2003

The Body in the Dovecote

May 31, 1552

Delighted with herself at having escaped, if only temporarily, from her duties as a waiting gentlewoman to the duchess of Northumberland, Susanna Leigh slipped into the overgrown garden at Otford and set off at a brisk pace along what remained of a wide graveled walk. She craved solitude and an opportunity to indulge in pleasant daydreams about handsome, charming Robert Appleton, to whom she was betrothed, but she had not gone more than a few yards before she realized she was not alone among the tangled flower beds, knots, and works of topiary.

Anne, countess of Warwick, wife to the duke and duchess's eldest son, danced past on an intersecting path bordered by a low hedge of rosemary. Susanna skidded to a halt and would have turned and fled, but it was too late. The countess had seen her. She reappeared at the point where walk and path met, her expression fierce. "How dare you follow me!"

"My lady, I would never intrude upon your privacy," Susanna protested. "I did not know anyone was here."

Lady Warwick considered that for a moment, then nodded. The two young women were of an age and had both been raised in households that supported the New Religion and believed girls should be educated in the same manner as boys, but Susanna was the daughter of a mere knight. Lady Warwick's father, before his execution for treason, had been duke of Somerset and Lord Protector of England.

"It is a large garden," Susanna offered. "I will stay well out of your way."

The suggestion seemed to amuse Lady Warwick. "Shall we imagine the Picts' Wall down the middle?"

"If you like. I will take the half that includes the dell and the dovecotes and leave to you all the pleached bowers and arbors."

This time the nod of acknowledgment contained a hint of approval. Without further ado, they set off in opposite directions.

For the space of a quarter of an hour, Susanna enjoyed the peace and quiet

17

of a bright morning at the end of May. The only sounds were the gentle stirring of leaves, distant birdsong, and the crunch of her own leather-shod feet on gravel as she strolled beside the dell originally intended to be a trout stream. From the wooden bridge that spanned it, Susanna spent several minutes watching fish flash through the water below. She wondered if the duke meant to restore Otford to its former glory. It seemed a waste to let the manor and its grounds fall to ruin, and yet what need did he have of it when Knole, even more grand, lay less than three miles distant? Both manors had come to him from young King Edward VI when Northumberland replaced Lady Warwick's father at the head of England's government.

Lost in contemplation, Susanna reacted slowly to the sound of running footsteps. By the time she turned, she saw only a blur of brightly colored skirts before the small form wearing them barreled into her. With a sob, Lady Katherine Dudley, aged six and a half, lifted her tear-streaked face to Susanna's and blurted, "There is a body in the dovecote!"

For a moment Susanna wondered if Lady Katherine were playing a prank on her. "Show me," she ordered.

Lady Katherine, youngest child of the duke of Northumberland, blinked rapidly at the command. Then, with a lack of reluctance that both surprised Susanna and heightened her suspicions, she led the way toward the three round brick structures that were home to nearly a thousand pigeons.

The smallest dovecote sat in splendid isolation in a sheltered copse. To lull the doves into taking up residence, their houses were always at some distance from human habitation. But no cooing issued from within this structure, no flapping of wings as birds flew in and out. There should be something, she thought.

There was activity around the larger dovecotes. The inhabitants were foragers, setting off each day to scour the countryside for seeds. She shaded her eyes against the sun, trying to see if the internal shutters were closed, but from the outside she could make out nothing but exterior landing ledges. A protruding stone string course around the outside of the building, designed to prevent vermin — weasels, rats, and martens in particular — from climbing up to the entrances and devouring the birds, further obscured her vision.

"In here," Lady Katherine called.

"Wait." But Susanna spoke too late. Lady Katherine had already opened a low, heavy, wooden door and stepped inside the dovecote.

Ducking her head, Susanna went after her. The height of the entry was deliberate, intended to enforce a slow entrance so that a person's sudden appearance in the dovecote would not panic the residents. No fear of that, Susanna thought. The inside was eerily quiet, empty of feathered inhabitants.

The walls of the dovecote were nearly three feet thick, shutting out both sound and light. The roof, dome shaped and constructed of slates, was topped with a wooden cupola which, when unshuttered, provided air as well as ingress and egress. The shutters, closed as Susanna had guessed they would be, made the interior too dark to see much of anything. As she stood upright, she stepped to one side, allowing in a square of daylight full of dust motes from the earthen floor.

"There," said Lady Katherine. At the far corner of the square, lying atop a thick layer of bird droppings, was a dead dove.

Susanna let out a breath she had not been aware of holding. A bird. Not a person. Relief surged through her.

"I did not mean for it to die," Lady Katherine said in a choked voice.

Puzzled, Susanna squinted at bird and girl as she fumbled for the lever that opened the shutters. She found it after a few frustrating moments but admitting additional light illuminated only enough of the interior for her make out the potence, a revolving wooden pole mounted on a plinth at the center of the dovecote. It rose from floor to roof, its two great arms extending outwards. The ladders at the end of each were used to collect eggs and squabs.

It resembled a gallows, Susanna thought, and shivered.

Rows of nest boxes, each about six inches square at the opening, lined the walls in a checkerboard pattern. They appeared to be empty, but Susanna knew that each nest was L-shaped, about eighteen inches deep and twelve across the back, and fronted with a small raised ledge to keep the eggs from rolling out. Were there more dead doves inside? Or had they all flown away before the cote was shuttered?

Abandoning that question for the nonce, Susanna returned her attention to the body in the dovecote. She could now see that the bird's beak was open. Its dead eyes stared at her, sightless but accusing. She had no difficulty imagining the effect of such a sight on a small, impressionable child. "Come away, my lady."

Instead, the girl knelt by the body, dragging her jewel-toned silk skirt in the dirt. "I killed it."

Startled, Susanna stepped close enough to see that Lady Katherine's tears flowed unchecked. Susanna was uncertain what to say. The doves were raised to feed the household, not as pets. Lady Katherine's despair seemed out of all proportion. Had she been a boy, Susanna suspected, she'd have learned by this age to hunt birds smaller than this with bow and arrow.

Lady Katherine stroked one hand over the ruffled feathers. "It was here, abandoned," she got out between sobs. "It was on the ground, huddled into itself. I collected some seeds to feed it. To make it well." She delved into the dirt beside the bird and came up with one.

Susanna accepted the seed from the child's grubby hand and held it in the light. Black and about the size of a wheat seed, its surface was pitted with small warts. She did not know what plant it came from, but she tucked the seed into the little leather pocket suspended from her waist to study at her leisure. She had for some time taken an interest in the identification of herbs.

"It seems most unlikely that you caused the dove to die, Lady Katherine." Susanna helped the little girl to her feet and dusted her off. "If this bird was left behind, it must have been ill." She stooped, examining the small corpse. "See here? This dove could not fly because its wing is broken."

No doubt being seized by small, determined hands had not helped the poor creature's condition, but Susanna did not say so aloud. Lady Katherine had suffered enough guilt on the dove's account.

"I would have cared for it," the child murmured. "I could have kept it in a cage. Safe from harm."

"Even beloved pets can die, my lady," Susanna said in her gentlest voice, slinging a comforting arm around the girl's shoulders. "Come away with me now. The dove was already mortally wounded. You could not have saved it."

They had just left the dovecote when a man entered the copse. At the sight of them he started and let the rake he was carrying fall to the ground with a dull thump. "Your pardon, mistress. My lady." He tugged on a greasy, chestnut-colored forelock, then remembered to take off his cap, revealing hair full of tangles. "I come to clean out the droppings," he stammered, backing away all the while.

That explained why the shutters had been closed. Bird lime had considerable value as a source of saltpeter for making gunpowder and was collected on a regular basis. Happy to have that minor mystery solved, anxious to escape the pungent smell that clung to his ragged clothes and hobnail boots, Susanna told the fellow to continue about his business.

Forthwith, she escorted Lady Katherine back to her governess, pausing only long enough to suggest that the child might like to have a linnet or a lark in a cage as a pet. That accomplished, Susanna put both the workman and the dead dove out of her mind. She next thought of the latter, and only in passing, when she rose the following morning to news of another death.

" 'Tis Lady Ambrose, mistress," announced Ellen, the tiring maid. Susanna shared both Ellen and the bedchamber with two other gentlewomen of the household. "They say in the kitchen that she woke in the middle of the night in a terrible sweat, then swooned upon rising and suffered terrible pangs and fits, worse than anything she endured when she was ill before, and at six of the clock, she died."

"Poor lady," Susanna murmured as she broke her fast with the bread and ale Ellen had brought.

Throughout the simple meal and while Susanna, Margaret, and Penelope dressed, helping each other with their points, they spoke in subdued tones of poor Lady Ambrose's sudden demise. Penelope seemed to think the duke might consider her as a candidate to be Lord Ambrose's next wife. "He is the most pleasing of all the brothers," she declared.

Susanna doubted that Penelope knew Lord Ambrose well enough to judge. Some years older than Lord Henry, Lord Robin, and Lord Guildford, Northumberland's second son spent most of his time at court with the young king. All the brothers did. Susanna smiled to herself. Although she had once been kissed by Lord Robin and found it pleasant, she had never had any matrimonial interest in any of the Dudleys. Besides, Lord Robin already had a wife and it had been, or so everyone said, a love match. He'd married a girl named Amye Robsart in a quiet, private ceremony one day after the splendid wedding of between the earl of Warwick and the duke of Somerset's eldest daughter.

Inevitably, speculation turned to the cause of Lady Ambrose's death.

"Mayhap her husband tired of her," Margaret suggested with a giggle.

"Certes, 'twas a relapse," Penelope declared.

A month earlier, Lady Ambrose had broken out in spots. One of the duke's physicians had said it was the measles. The other had diagnosed her condition as smallpox. Whichever had afflicted her, she'd recovered in spite of their care.

Ellen turned a face suddenly gone pale to Susanna. "What if it is some horrible plague visited upon us for the duke's sins?"

"You must not say such a thing," Susanna warned her.

But panic made the maidservant careless. Her voice rose. "Some say the duke deserves to be struck dead for all the evil he's done."

"Silence!" Susanna glared the foolish young woman into obedience. "His grace the duke is a good man."

He'd become Susanna's guardian upon her father's death. To ensure that her interests were protected, he'd quickly arranged her marriage to the dashing and debonair Robert Appleton, a gentleman from distant Lancashire. Although Susanna had only met him a few times since their betrothal, he'd charmed her with his manners and a pretty attentiveness. He even professed himself pleased that she was well versed in the classics and had studied mathematics and geography.

Suddenly annoyed by the chatter and speculation, Susanna left the chamber ahead of the others. She thus chanced upon the duke just as he was leaving the rooms allotted to Lady Ambrose. Attended by his chaplain, his physicians, and his steward, Northumberland seemed uncommon agitated. He was not much given to any show of emotion and further surprised Susanna by hailing her.

"Go and keep Lady Ambrose's maid company," he said. "She is in no fit state to wait alone for the women who will wash the body and wrap it in a winding sheet."

Uncertain how to deal with the sobbing servant she found within, Susanna managed a few disjointed words of comfort, but her effort felt inadequate before such a heart-wrenching display of grief.

Tears streamed down the woman's deeply lined face and dripped off the end of a wattled chin. She was of an age to make Susanna wonder if she had been Lady Ambrose's nurse. The deceased had not been a duke's daughter like Lady Warwick, Susanna reminded herself, but came, as Susanna herself did, from wealthy gentry stock. There were many in the household at Leigh Abbey who had served the Leighs for generations. They'd mourned the death of Susanna's father as deeply as she had.

"Lady Ambrose was surpassing sick," Susanna said. "There is naught anyone could have done to predict a relapse." Her illness, whatever it had been, had left her with a lingering cough and a hoarse voice, Susanna recalled. "Mayhap she'd not fully recovered and fell ill again. You must not blame yourself for that."

"She was well." With an angry gesture, the woman dashed the moisture from her cheeks. Her eyes were red with weeping and her lips quivered. "It was not the same ailment that killed her."

Frustrated by her failure to soothe the old woman's grief, Susanna stopped trying to find the right words and fumbled for a handkerchief instead. Taking it, the maidservant mopped her face. The honk when she blew her nose reverberated in the awkward silence.

"The duke says we're all to be kept here," the servant said after a moment. "No one's to leave, he said, until the moon be at the full. His grace's physicians think it may be the sweat, or worse."

Susanna swallowed back the instinctive fear any mention of the sweat aroused. That mysterious disease had devastated England the previous year, killing without mercy or discretion. "Death can come with no warning from a hundred causes," Susanna murmured, more to reassure herself than to ease the maidservant's suffering. She had the best of reasons to know that. Her father had been taken from her in a shipwreck. Her only sibling, a younger sister, had met her death through accidental poisoning.

"Lady Ambrose was sick to her stomach and feverish and giddy," the old woman said. "She grew weak from delirium and pain until she did slip at the last into a deep, unnatural sleep."

Susanna frowned. That did not sound like the sweat. Nor the smallpox nor the measles, neither.

"She was in such high spirits before she went to bed," the maid lamented. "She said she felt herself again at last after so many weeks of illness." A brief and poignant smile showed a flash of yellowed teeth. "She filched three cakes from the high table for a midnight treat. She did love sweets. But she gave one to me." She smacked her lips, as if recalling the taste, and with an absent gesture indicated all that remained of Lady Ambrose's portion, a few crumbs scattered across the top of a small table and a single black seed.

A sick feeling in the pit of her stomach, Susanna rose and went closer. She inspected the seed without touching it, leaning close enough to smell the honey in which it had been coated and to note its deeply pitted surface.

Coincidence, she told herself. Lady Ambrose *must* have suffered a relapse. But she turned again to the maidservant.

"Tell me about your lady's condition when she was ill." During that time, the rest of the household had been kept well away from the sickroom.

Sensible enough to be alarmed by Susanna's abrupt question, the old woman nevertheless complied. "She had a rash and a high fever, mistress. It began on the second day of May, as I remember me, and she was most terrible ill for a week thereafter, but by the twenty-third, she was almost herself again, save for the cough."

"Today is the first of June," Susanna murmured.

Bracing herself, she strode to the bed and threw back the coverlet to inspect the corpse, even turning it over to examine it for spots. It was the duty of every gentlewoman to learn how to lay out the dead. Girls were trained young not to be squeamish.

The only fresh marks were dark bruises between the shoulder blades, an indication that the body had lain on its back for some little time after death. Susanna knew, from her grandmother, who had prepared a good many dead kinfolk for burial in her time, that this often happened, though she did not know why.

Although she could see no outward indication that Lady Ambrose had died of eating poisonous seeds, just as she had no proof the dove had, Susanna took the seed from the cake away with her, determined to discover what plant it came from. If she did not, she feared she would forever be tormented by the possibility that telling someone about the dead dove might have saved Lady Ambrose.

She sought Lady Katherine first. Susanna did not want to alarm the child and racked her brain to think of some reason why she wanted to know where she'd found the seeds to feed the dove. In the end, Susanna's interest in plants – the simple truth, if not all of it – sufficed to broach the subject.

"I hope to make a collection of seeds, roots, and leaves and label them," she explained, "that I may one day identify in an instant, by comparison, any plant that comes into my possession. But I am mystified by that black seed you showed me. Can you describe the plant it came from?"

Lady Katherine, tongue showing at the corner of her mouth, preoccupied with conquering a new embroidery stitch she'd been told to practice, shook her head. If she was disturbed by the death of her brother's wife, she showed no sign of it.

"A pity we are in quarantine," Lady Katherine's governess remarked, overhearing. "There is an old cunning woman at Sevenoaks who is renowned for her knowledge of herbs."

An even greater pity, Susanna thought, that no one had yet compiled a complete botanical reference book in English, one with accurate and detailed illustrations. Only the first volume of Master Turner's *A New Herbal* had so far appeared in print and, as he'd been physician and chaplain to the late duke of Somerset and was out of favor, no copy of his work graced the duke of Northumberland's collection.

"Did you get the seeds from one of the kitchens?" Susanna asked, doggedly pursuing her interrogation of the child. The kitchens were separated from the duke's living quarters as a precaution against fire and were handy to both gardens and dovecotes.

Lady Katherine looked up, frowning with impatience. "They were in a box in one of the dressers."

"What kind of box?"

"A box of seeds!"

When the governess seemed about to interject a question of her own, Susanna retreated. She suspected she'd learned as much as she was going to.

She went next to Otford's kitchens. If they'd been in good repair, they'd have rivaled those at Hampton Court, a dozen or more separate departments from a spicery for storing spices to the confectory that turned out sweets and pastries. At present only two small rooms between the great kitchen and the serving place were in use. There special dishes were dressed and garnished before they were carried into the great hall to be consumed.

A quick peek through the hatch into the first dresser showed Susanna the roast carcass of a peacock. It had been reunited with its feathers for presentation above the salt. In the second dresser, one of the undercooks was glazing marzipan. Forcing a smile, she went in.

She received a glare in return. "What do you want, mistress? I have no time to waste today on idle chatter."

"I need but a moment," she assured him, and produced one of the seeds from her pocket. "Can you tell me what this seed is? It was atop a cake."

He spared only a glance before disclaiming all knowledge. "Not a cake I decorated."

"But where else could it have come from? It was on the duke's table." She bit her lip, fearing she'd let too much slip, but the cook was intent upon his work.

Susanna's gaze roved the small chamber, searching for the box Lady Katherine had mentioned. There were several small wooden containers near at hand, each carefully closed to preserve the contents. She opened the first without being noticed and was disappointed to find ginger within. When she reached for the second she was caught.

"I have told you, mistress. That is not a seed I use." So fierce was his glower that eyebrows like two wooly caterpillars nearly met above his bulbous nose. "Do you think I cannot recognize mine own ingredients?"

Lifting the lid of the second box, she saw that this one did contain seeds, but they were caraways, translucent and slightly curved with pale ridges, not at all like the one in her hand. "Could a few of these seeds have been mixed in with the caraways or some others?"

"I would have noticed," the cook insisted, but she saw the flicker of doubt in his eyes. In the rush of preparing a meal for hundreds of people, such a mistake might be made.

"There were cakes last night, topped with seeds in honey." Once they were coated, would anyone have noticed the difference? Honey would hide any unusual taste, too.

"Caraway seeds," the cook insisted. "Look you, there is naught else in the box."

'Twas true. If any of the other seeds had ever been there, they were gone now, used up, Susanna was certain, on one or more of the cakes. Mayhap it was fortunate only one person had died!

She had been thinking that Lady Ambrose had been poisoned by accident. It was common enough to mistake one herb for another with fatal consequences. Her own sister had consumed banewort berries thinking they were cherries and died a terrible death. But accident, she realized with a sudden, sickening lurch in her stomach, was not the only possibility. What if the seeds had been put in the box deliberately, by someone who knew what their effect would be? A second frightening conclusion followed hard on the first. Lady Ambrose was unlikely to have been the poisoner's intended victim. She remembered what the old servant had said. Her mistress had filched the cakes because she had a sweet tooth. They had been on the high table, placed there for the duke himself to consume.

Susanna knew then that she must talk to his grace and tell him her suspicions, but she needed a breath of fresh air first. Besides, there was one other person she'd might question about the black seeds.

She made her way through the gardens at a brisk pace, finding nothing soothing about them this day. In a short time she reached the dovecotes. Somewhere nearby, she assumed, would be a keeper.

She found him deep in conversation with the very workman who'd raked out the dovecote. She checked and studied both men. No harm in either, she decided, and neither was likely to have gotten into the kitchens unnoticed and added poison seeds to the cook's supplies. Besides, the workman would have discovered the dead dove in the course of his duties. Susanna saw no point in dissimilating.

"Some of these were given to the dove that died," she told them, once again displaying the black seed. "Can you tell me what this is?"

"Corn cockle," the keeper said at once. "What fool fed those to my flock?"

"A child," Susanna said quickly. "There was no intent to harm. And only one dove died, the one in the shuttered dovecote."

The keeper's brow arched and the workman's face took on a look of alarm but neither said a word as she described, without naming the girl, what Lady Katherine had done the previous day.

"Corn cockle," the keeper said again. " 'Tis dangerous, but rarely eaten. It grows in wheat and oat fields, chicken yards, and waste places."

"Is it only fatal to birds?" Susanna held her breath.

"It will poison cattle if they graze on it, but an animal would have to eat a good many seeds to take in a fatal dose."

"What if it were already ill?" She did not dare suggest a person had ingested the poison. The workman's panic was already excessive, as if he feared he would be blamed.

The keeper scratched the bald pate beneath his cap. "Might take it off the sooner, same as with the dove."

An hour later, Susanna was admitted to the duke of Northumberland's private study. The duke had a formidable glower. Between a forked beard and a jutting nose, his full lips thinned. Finely arched brows crept toward a receding hairline as he studied the young woman before him. "You demanded a private audience?" The sheer audacity of her request seemed to have won it for her.

"Yes, your grace." She fought the urge to break eye contact, determined to convince him that the request had not been some foolish whim on her part. "Someone tried to poison you last night," she blurted. "Lady Ambrose died in your stead."

"Explain," he ordered.

When she had told him what she had guessed as well as all she knew, he studied her in somber silence for a long, unnerving span.

"Your grace? Do you know who might want to kill you?"

A wry smile twisted his mobile mouth. "A great many people, I should think. Today was the day upon which I'd intended to set out for the north. The reason for my journey is no secret. King Edward means to make a summer progress through Sussex, Hampshire, Wiltshire, and Dorset. Rather than accompany his majesty and risk letting the king observe first hand my great unpopularity with the public, I excused myself to inspect border fortifications. The perpetual threat Scotland poses is at times most convenient."

Susanna frowned. "Would your enemies not see your departure as a good thing, your grace? You'll be away from court for months."

"Which means," he explained, "that someone knew they must act now or lose the opportunity. Someone in this household."

"Surely not a servant. They are loyal to you."

"Some are. You knew William Huggons?"

Susanna nodded, puzzled. Until a few months ago, he'd been a permanent part of Northumberland's household. She'd never heard an explanation for his abrupt disappearance.

"Huggons's wife was in service to the duchess of Somerset. When the Lord Protector was executed, Mistress Huggons declared I was better worthy to die. That and other remarks, some of them treasonous, resulted in her commitment to the Tower, where her old mistress already resides." His intense gaze focused on her, colder than she'd ever seen it. "Tell me, Susanna, have you heard any of my household utter similar sentiments?"

She shook her head, but she could not help but think of Ellen. She was grateful when the duke broke eye contact to send one of his men to fetch the keeper of the dovecotes and the workman with the rake.

"We will leave the kitchen staff for the nonce," he mused aloud. "You say the cook denied any knowledge of the corn cockle?"

"He did not recognize the seed. Nor did I. It is a weed." Once the keeper had given it a name, she'd been able to call it to mind, tall and spindly with pink flowers. It was a very common plant. Anyone could get seeds and keep them as long as necessary. That made her wonder if someone had planned the duke's murder for many months or acted on impulse.

It was then that she remembered the exact words the cook had used.

"What do you want, mistress? I have no time to waste *today* on idle chatter," she repeated aloud. "Did he mean he wasted time yesterday? With someone else who did not ordinarily visit the kitchens?"

Approval writ large on his countenance, Northumberland sent another henchman to ask who had been in the kitchens the previous day. The answer was not long in coming. The undercook had been twice interrupted, once by Penelope Stilton, one of the gentlewoman who shared Susanna's bedchamber, accompanied by a maid, and the second time by Lady Warwick, soliciting scraps of gingerbread for her lap dog.

Northumberland's eyes narrowed. When the messenger left, he said, "Lady Warwick has good reason to wish me dead, if she blames me, as others do, for the death of her father."

"But she is married to your son," Susanna objected. "To harm you hurts him as well."

Northumberland's laugh sounded bitter. "If I die, Warwick succeeds to all my titles and estates. Scarce a hardship for him or his wife. But I doubt Lady Warwick cares what happens to her husband. Her father and I arranged their marriage without consulting either of them."

"But she agreed. She swore to —"

Northumberland waved aside her sputtered protests. "I have seen no outward sign of hatred toward me, but who can tell what rage, what desire for revenge, seethes inside her?" He sent Susanna a sharp look. "Do you have some reason to think Penelope Stilton a more likely suspect? Or the maid?"

Again, Susanna denied it, but she remembered Penelope's desire to marry the new-made widower. And Ellen's talk of the duke's sins. There must be some way to find out the truth, she thought.

"Your grace," the duke's henchman announced, entering with the keeper of the dovecotes in tow, "the workman you sent for has fled."

Susanna felt a surge of hope. Mayhap her suspicions of the women of the household were unfounded.

"Fellow's been stealing bird lime." The keeper sounded indignant. "I knew naught of it, your grace, till the gentlewoman here mentioned that the small dovecote had been shuttered."

Not murder, then, Susanna thought. Only theft.

"Send out a search party," Northumberland ordered.

As he gave further commands, Susanna slipped from the room. There might be a way to prove guilt or innocence. If she pretended to know more than she did, she might shock one of the three suspects into revealing herself.

She found Ellen in the bedchamber, mending a smock.

"I know what you did," she said in an accusing voice. "You were seen in the kitchens yesterday."

Bristling, Ellen glared at her. "I only do what I'm told, madam."

"Is that your excuse?"

"I am expected to obey all three of you." Ellen's agitation grew so great that she accidentally stabbed her thumb with her needle. She stuck it in her mouth, sulked a moment, then added, "Mistress Penelope gave me a shilling to do as she asked."

Distraught, Susanna left the maidservant without saying more. She had been wrong. Lady Ambrose had been the intended victim all along. Penelope had been serious about wanting to marry the widower.

Her duty was clear. No one should be allowed to get away with murder. She must return to the duke's study and tell him what she had learned, even though doing so would result in arrest and execution for Penelope and dismissal, at the least, for Ellen.

But as she passed along an outer passage that overlooked the gardens, she noticed Lady Warwick sitting on a stone bench under an oak tree. She appeared to be weeping. Susanna hesitated, then went out. A few moment's delay would not matter to Ellen and Penelope.

"My lady?" she asked in a tentative voice. "Are you unwell?"

"Go away," Lady Warwick said on a gusty sob. "I grieve for my poor sister, cruelly taken from us by the sweat. And for all the others who may yet die of that dread disease."

"Lady Ambrose's death was caused by something she ate," Susanna said, thinking to ease the countess's distress. "The ailment is not contagious."

Lady Warwick stiffened and lifted her bowed head. "What do you mean? What caused her death?" There was such agony in the question that Susanna felt she had to answer.

Moving closer, she opened her hand to reveal the two black, pitted seeds nestled in her palm. "This is what killed her."

The sudden loss of color from Lady Warwick's face betrayed her.

Susanna swallowed hard. "Do you recognize them, my lady?"

"No. How could I? I know naught of herbs."

Susanna did not believe her. "These are the seeds of the corn cockle. They are poisonous. Somehow they got into a glaze used to ice cakes and these cakes were taken to the high table. Anyone there might have eaten them, but as it happened, only Lady Ambrose did.

"No." As if the idea were too terrible to contemplate, the noblewoman's eyes abruptly lost their focus.

"Where did you get the seeds, Lady Warwick?"

A moan answered her. Susanna had to seize the countess by the shoulders and shake her to get a proper response.

"From my father! From my poor, dead father! He gave them to me the last time I was allowed to see him and told me how to use them. But I never meant for anyone else to die. Only the duke."

"Are there more? Do you mean to try again?"

"No! No! They are all gone. And I thought I'd failed. I thought I had done all I could, and I was glad nothing happened. I did not know she'd eaten the cakes." She'd grasped Susanna's arm with painful force as her voice rose.

"You tried to kill the duke of Northumberland." With an effort, Susanna broke free, rubbing the bruised forearm.

"No. Yes." She was sobbing now. "I had to obey my father."

She broke down completely then, and had to be helped to her bedchamber. Susanna sent for a soothing posset to sedate her and stayed with her to make sure she drank it.

"I swear I will never attempt such a thing again," Lady Warwick vowed. "You must not tell anyone what I did." Her eyes pleaded with Susanna.

"I wish I could promise that," she said with genuine regret, "but the duke already suspects you."

Lady Warwick turned her face to the wall.

Only when she was certain the other woman was deeply asleep, did Susanna leave her. She went first to her own chamber and once more confronted Ellen.

"What did you do for Penelope?" she demanded.

Ellen blinked at her in confusion. "I thought you knew."

"Tell me." Her tone left no room for refusal.

"She wanted a potion to bring down her courses," Ellen grudgingly admitted. "My aunt is the old cunning woman of Sevenoaks. I know what ingredients to mix. Mistress Penelope distracted the cook while I searched for wormwood and rue."

Susanna was both relieved and dismayed. An ounce of dried wormwood mixed with a pint of boiling water and drunk three times a day could bring down a woman's courses, but wormwood and rue, especially in combination with myrrh and lupines, were more commonly used only when one wished to expel a fetus. She did not ask Ellen for any further details. She did not wish to know.

Still reeling from all the revelations of the afternoon, Susanna made her way back to the duke's study. Northumberland sat behind a table littered with papers, leaning on his elbows, his fingers steepled under his chin as he listened to her account of Lady Warwick's confession. He was silent for a long time afterward, as late afternoon sun filtered in through the mullioned window behind him, making a hatchwork pattern on the rich red velvet of his doublet.

"Lady Ambrose's death has already been attributed to the sweat," he said at last. "That verdict stands. Once you leave this room, you will never again speak of what you know, not even to me."

"Do you trust Lady Warwick to keep her word?"

"Both reward and punishment must be apportioned." His eyes bored into Susanna, as if he would bend her will to his own. "My son's wife must be ... watched, lest she lapse again into ... mental derangement."

Susanna held her breath. Did he mean to imprison the countess? Would he send her to the Tower, where her mother was already housed?

"I am pleased with you, Susanna. You have served my wife well as a waiting gentlewoman. 'Tis time you had more responsibility. From this day forward, you will serve Lady Warwick as her chief lady. Sleep in her chamber. Provide soothing possets as necessary."

"From this day forward?" Numb, she repeated the phrase. She found it difficult to distinguish her reward from Lady Warwick's punishment.

"Your coming marriage need be no impediment," Northumberland continued. "You'd have remained part of this household afterward in any case."

Susanna wanted to object. Her daydreams had included blocks of time spent with her new husband in their own house. But Northumberland's attention had already shifted to his preparations for the journey north. With a sigh, Susanna let herself out of his study.

In the future, she resolved, she would try harder to ignore any mysteries that came her way. She was certain she'd have no difficulty doing so.

A Note from the Author

This is the earliest story featuring my series character, Susanna, Lady Appleton. Susanna is a fictional creation, but in order to write the first book in the series, *Face Down in the Marrow-Bone Pie*, I had to develop an extensive biography for her. I decided that Susanna would be just a little younger than Elizabeth Tudor, who ruled England from 1558–1603, and that she would be trained as a gentlewoman in the household of a real person, John Dudley, duke of Northumberland. In the story you have just read, Susanna is seventeen years old and not yet married to Robert Appleton.

Most of my stories and novels use a combination of fictional characters and real people. "The Body in the Dovecote" was inspired by a letter from the duke of Northumberland to Sir William Cecil in which he described the death on June 1, 1552 at Otford, of his daughter-in-law, Lady Ambrose Dudley. There is no mention, of course, of poison.

After the events in this story, the duke attempted a rebellion that would have placed the Lady Jane Grey on the throne of England. He failed, was tried for treason, and was executed. Northumberland's eldest son, John, earl of Warwick, was released from the Tower of London in 1554 but died soon after. His childless widow, Anne, daughter of the duke of Somerset, remarried and lived until 1588. By 1566, however, rumors of "mental derangement" had already begun to spread. That, too, inspired me.

Much Ado About Murder

"The vii day of March began the blazing [star] at night and it did shoot out fire." Diary of Henry Machyn, 1555/6

An ominous portent first appeared in the sky over England on the same evening Robert Appleton brought Lord Benedick and his wife to Leigh Abbey. It was a blazing star with a long tail. Half the size of the moon, it much resembled a gigantic torch burning fitfully in the wind.

"A sure sign of disaster," muttered a maidservant, casting her baleful glance at the comet high above. She sent an equally suspicious look toward the new arrivals dismounting by rushlight in the inner courtyard.

Ignoring her tiring maid's comment, Susanna Appleton wrapped a wool cloak more closely around herself and went forward to greet her husband and his guests. Jennet could find evil omens and harbingers of impending doom in the twisted branches of a bush or the discolored grass beneath a mushroom. She relished dire predictions, though she always professed herself well-pleased when they came to naught. No doubt she imagined her own warnings had somehow prevented catastrophe.

The visitors were a richly-dressed young couple traveling with two elderly servants. As Susanna watched, the husband lifted his wife out of her saddle and set her gently on her feet on the icy cobbles. He lifted her gloved hand to his lips, then held it tight as he slipped the other arm around her waist to steady her. He was rewarded with a smile of such radiance that Susanna felt a twinge of envy. True devotion between spouses was rare and it was sadly lacking in her own marriage. Robert would always love wealth and position more than he cared for any woman.

"Lord Benedick comes to England from Padua," Robert said after he'd presented Susanna to that nobleman. "Padua is part of the powerful Venetian Republic, where he is held in great regard. And his wife here is niece to the governor of Messina."

33

Titles impressed Robert more than they did Susanna, but she was as well informed as he on the subject of various political alliances. He did not need to tell her that Messina was part of Sicily, or that Sicily was under Spanish rule. So, some would say, was their own land, ever since Queen Mary's marriage to King Philip.

Robert's reason for inviting Lord Benedick to visit his home was just as clear – he hoped a friendship with this well-connected young sprig of the nobility would ease him back into favor at court. He'd made the mistake of backing the Lady Jane Grey's attempt to take Mary Tudor's throne away from her and had spent several uncomfortable months in prison before being pardoned and released.

Susanna had also supported Queen Jane. Now her loyalty was to the Lady Elizabeth, Queen Mary's half sister, although it was not wise to say so. These visitors, she decided, must be looked upon as the enemy, a danger to certain clandestine activities practiced at Leigh Abbey during Robert's frequent absences.

Forcing a smile, Susanna gestured toward the passage that led to the great hall. "If you will come this way, Lady –"

Impulsively, Lord Benedick's wife took both Susanna's hands in hers. She spoke charmingly accented English. "Let us be comfortable together, Beatrice and Susanna. What need we with formality when we are destined to be great friends?"

"Destined?"

Beatrice laughed. " 'Tis written in the sky." She gestured toward the comet. "Under another such dancing star was I born. How can any doubt this new one is a sign of good things to come?"

With great ease, Susanna thought.

As she led the way into the house, she realized that Beatrice's "dancing star" must have been the one that streaked across English skies in 1533. Susanna had not been born until the following year, but she had heard the stories as a child. That particular portent, it was said, foretold the divorce of Henry VIII from Catherine of Aragon. To those of Susanna's religious upbringing, putting aside both Queen Catherine and the Church of Rome had been cause for rejoicing. Catholics viewed the matter in a different light.

The divorce of her parents had been one of the first things Queen Mary set aside when she came to the throne. Now it was her sister, Elizabeth, daughter of Anne Boleyn, who was accounted a bastard. And those who would not renounce the New Religion and return to the Roman Catholic fold faced arrest, even martyrdom, on charges of heresy. The plight of many of Susanna's late father's friends had driven her to devise a way to help them escape persecution.

When wine and cheese and dried fruit had been served, Robert spoke. "We have been granted permission to hunt in the royal deer park on the morrow," he announced. "We will retire early to be up betimes."

Seated before the fire in the great hall, Susanna shifted to allow the warmth to reach more of her. Because Robert wished to impress their guests, he kept them in the largest and draftiest of the rooms instead of retiring to one of the smaller, warmer chambers. While beads of perspiration formed on her forehead from the heat, her back felt cold as a dead man's hand.

"Do you go with them, Beatrice?" she asked.

"I take no pleasure in killing." Beatrice sipped from a glass goblet containing a Gascon wine.

"She prefers slow torture," Lord Benedick commented, *sotto voce.*

Ignoring him, Beatrice remarked upon the color of the claret. "Bright as a ruby, as it should be."

Susanna could not resist. "I am told that if a claret wine has lost its color, one may take a pennyworth of damsons, or else black bullaces, and stew them with some red wine of the deepest color and make thereof a pound of more of syrup, which when put it into a hogshead of claret wine, does restore it to its original shade."

One foot resting on the back of a firedog, Robert stirred the fire with a poker. "The study of herbs," he confided to Lord Benedick, his manner implying a shared masculine indulgence of female weakness, "is my wife's little hobby."

"A very proper occupation." Lord Benedick lounged on a bench with a low back, his legs stretched out in front of him with the ankles crossed. He lifted his goblet in a toast to both women. "Mine delights in devising new uses for holy thistle."

"A universal remedy," Beatrice said with a smug smile. The twinkle in her eyes and the quick exchange of glances with her husband alerted Susanna to the play on words.

"*Carduus benedictus,*" she murmured.

Belatedly catching on, Robert laughed.

Jennet hovered close by, ears stretched to catch every word, but she did not understand the pun. Beatrice's companion, an old woman named Ursula, also seemed oblivious, or else she'd heard the joke too many times before to find it amusing. She sat near the hearth, placid as a grazing cow, her gnarled hands busy with a piece of needlework.

"If you have an interest in herbs other than the one that shares its name with Lord Benedick," Robert said to Beatrice, "you must ask my wife to show you her new storeroom."

Concealed by her skirts, Susanna's hands clenched into fists. Trust Robert to focus attention on the one thing she wished to hide. "I fear it is most noisome," she protested. "I have been conducting experiments to determine which herbs are most effective for killing fleas and other vermin." She'd intended the pungent smell keep Robert at bay. Now she must hope the odor was also strong enough to deter curious visitors.

"Poison would never be my wife's weapon of choice," Benedick remarked. "No more than the bow. She prefers a blade."

"He means I speak poniards and every word stabs." Beatrice gave her husband a playful swat on the shoulder.

This couple bandied words like tennis balls, Susanna thought, and yet each one was served with affection. She glanced at Robert, then away.

Benedick grinned at his wife before returning his attention to his host. "I cherish the hope that this visit will allow me to gain some small understanding of English women, for I do find my wife a most puzzling creature."

"*Your* wife, sir?"

"Did you not know? Beatrice was born in England."

"My mother," she explained, "was Spanish. She came to these shores in the entourage of Queen Catherine of Aragon. But she married an Englishman."

"Have you family here, then?" Susanna asked.

"Alas, no. When both my parents died, Ursula there was obliged to take me back to Spain to be raised by my mother's sister."

Hearing her name, the old woman glanced their way. She sent a fond smile winging toward her former charge, then took up her embroidery once more.

The conversation turned to the delights of travel in Spain and Italy. To Susanna's relief, there was no further mention of the new storeroom she'd caused to be built in an isolated spot beyond her stillroom and herb garden.

†

Before dawn the next day, Susanna rose to watch the hunting party depart, then made her way to what she privately called "the mint room." It was well, she thought, that the three "heretics" she'd had hidden at Leigh Abbey a few days earlier had left before Robert and his guests arrived. And a great pity that another had turned up right on their heels.

She glanced over her shoulder as she turned the key in the lock. No one was in sight and the sun had yet to burn off a concealing early morning mist. With luck, she could spirit the fellow away before Beatrice or her servant rose from their beds.

About the members of her own household she had no concerns. None would betray her. They had been loyal to her father in his time and they were loyal now to her. Further, they regarded Robert as an interloper and doubtless always would. He'd gained legal control of Leigh Abbey only because he'd married her.

The near overwhelming scent of mint rolled out of the storehouse the moment Susanna opened the door. Inside the small, brick-lined, stone building were great bales of garden mint, watermint, and pennyroyal. Taking a deep breath of fresh air first, Susanna plunged inside, skirting the bales to reach another door, this one concealed by a panel in the back wall.

She did not see the body until she tripped over it.

Susanna knelt beside a man sprawled face up on the floor, an expression of agony on his face. She knew even before she touched him that she was far too late to render aid.

As her fingers found a lump on the back or his skull, her own head began to swim. Startled by her find, she'd forgotten to hold her breath.

Was this how he'd died? In fear of suffocation, his heart failing under the strain of trying to take in untainted air?

Eyes streaming, coughing fit to choke, she fled the storeroom. In the yard, doubled over, she inhaled in great gulps, all the while fighting for control of a roiling stomach. When someone took her hand to guide her to a nearby bench, she let herself be led. She assumed Jennet had come to her rescue, but it was Beatrice's voice that spoke, in calm, well-modulated tones.

"I have heard the odor of pennyroyal attracts fleas, then smothers them, but I'd not have thought it would work so well on a man. Was he your particular enemy?"

Susanna stared at the other woman in shock and horror. "I did not kill him!"

"He is dead." Beatrice looked distraught, as who would not, having come upon such a scene.

"A tragic accident."

"Yes," Beatrice murmured. But she did not sound convinced.

What else could it have been? Susanna buried her face in her hands, although she had no intention of giving way to tears. For just a moment, she needed to hide from Beatrice's too-perceptive gaze.

The odor in the mint room had been well nigh overpowering. If he'd dropped the key she'd given him, then panicked as he tried to find it and could not, confusion and the struggle to breathe could have caused him to stumble and fall, striking his head. On what? She had no notion, but she'd felt the lump. The blow alone might have killed him. Or, as she'd first thought, he could have had a weak heart and been snuffed out by sheer terror. She was certain of only one thing. The pennyroyal alone was not to blame. As Beatrice had implied, a man was a great deal bigger than a flea.

"Inconvenient, no matter how he died," Beatrice remarked. "If he is found here and can be identified as a heretic, his presence will endanger your efforts on behalf of the Marian exiles."

Startled, Susanna sat bolt upright. She felt a chill that had naught to do with the cold, damp morning. "What do you know of the work we do here?"

The calm, composed countenance above a sable-trimmed cloak of red velvet inspired confidence, as did Beatrice's words. "Benedick and I have many friends in the English community at Padua."

Susanna's head pounded, an after-effect of her coughing fit. She found it difficult to order her thoughts. Did she mean Benedick had befriended men driven into exile by Queen Mary's religious policies? Or that he was acquainted with Englishmen already there before Mary took the throne? The University of Padua had long drawn students from England, in particular those with an interest in medicine, but not all of them were followers of the New Religion.

"I see I must be blunt with you." Beatrice glanced around to make sure they were unobserved. "Some of the most recent arrivals reached Padua only because of your efforts on their behalf." She named three men Susanna had hidden at Leigh Abbey on their way out of England. "What you do here is of vital importance, Susanna. Benedick and I may not share your faith, but we approve of saving lives."

"Robert would not, if he knew." The bitter words slipped out before she could censor them.

"I am glad to hear that you have kept your ambitious husband in the dark."

"He is a loyal subject!" She stood up too fast, making her head spin.

"Aye, so loyal and so bent on advancement under your present monarch that he might be tempted to betray his own wife. There would be a risk. He might be blamed for your folly. But if you alone were found guilty, he would benefit from your downfall."

That Beatrice spoke the truth did not make her observations any more palatable, but her words also reminded Susanna that she had a more pressing problem. "I dare not call in the coroner. He would ask too many questions."

"Then we must remove the body from the premises at once," Beatrice said, "before anyone else comes along and sees it. Have you a barrel or a buck tub to hide him in while we transport him?" She glanced toward the dark interior of the storeroom, as if considering the dead man's size. "Or mayhap an empty wine butt?"

Susanna rejected Beatrice's more colorful suggestions in favor of a plain blanket to wrap him in. "There is one in the stable," she said. After closing and locking the storeroom door, she led the way there. "He rode in on an old bay mare. We can use her to carry him away again."

"Is there a river or stream nearby?" Beatrice asked. "If we leave him in the water, it will appear that he was thrown when he attempted to ford it and drowned after hitting his head on a rock."

"And the rushing water will wash away the smell of the mint." Susanna had to admire Beatrice's quick thinking. In spite of a tendency toward the over-dramatic, she had a practical bent.

"But what was he doing in your storeroom? Why did he come out of hiding?"

Susanna covered her hesitation by fumbling with the stable door. Beatrice appeared to be an ally. She knew Susanna smuggled heretics out of England and that one of them was dead. But she might not realize that the storeroom had a secret inner chamber concealed behind its back wall. She had no need to know of its existence, Susanna decided.

"You must have told him to remain out of sight," Beatrice persisted.

"When do men ever do what they are told?" Susanna felt a wry smile twist her lips when she heard the asperity in her own voice. "Had it been Robert, he'd have risked venturing out at night to make sure his horse had been cared for." He doted on Vanguard. "That, I think, is the most logical reason for the stranger to have been wandering about in the dark."

"Why go into your storeroom?"

"Curiosity?"

"Do you know his name?" Beatrice fired questions in a barrage and Susanna volleyed answers back.

"I never ask for names."

"Then how —"

"A password."

The system had been devised with the help of Sir Anthony Cooke, a dear friend of her father's. He was himself in exile now, but one of his daughters had remained behind to maintain a station along an escape route for fellow "heretics" similar to the one at Leigh Abbey.

"Saddle the bay and two other horses," Susanna instructed Mark, one of the grooms. When he hurried off to do her bidding, she turned to her companion. "You must not involve yourself in this, Beatrice."

"You cannot manage the body alone."

"Mark will assist me. All else aside, you are scarce dressed for the task. And you can better serve me by staying here. It will help allay suspicion. You can pretend to be closeted with me in my study while I am gone."

Common sense warred with an overabundance of zeal, but in the end Beatrice agreed to Susanna's suggestion.

†

"Does he appear to have struck his head on a rock?" Susanna asked. Although the brook flowed fast and deep with spring run-off, a strong man in good condition, such as this one had been, might have been able to pull himself out if he had not been knocked unconscious.

Even with her stalwart young groom's assistance, it had been no simple undertaking to move the body. The deceased had been dead weight.

"He'll do, madam," Mark said, "and we must away before anyone comes upon us."

"Free his horse," she ordered. "Set her wandering in the woods." She was tempted to order Mark himself to "find" the bay and instigate a search for its rider, but she was loath to do anything to call attention to Leigh Abbey.

Had she thought of everything? She wondered as they rode home. Belatedly, she remembered that he'd had a pack with him when he arrived. That might contain some clue to his identity. All she knew at present, from his appearance, was that he had seen more than forty winters. The better to go unnoticed on his journey, he'd worn plain clothes that gave no hint of his occupation, but he'd had the speech of a gentleman.

The ride back took less than a quarter hour. She'd not dared transport the body any farther now that it was full daylight.

"Go you to the kitchen and dry off," she told Mark. He'd gotten soaked positioning the body.

Susanna went straight to the mint room, pausing only long enough to collect a lantern. When she'd locked herself in, she hurried to the inner door, her key at the ready. A moment later, she was safely inside the second room and had shut out the overpowering smell.

No one had disturbed the hiding place she'd had purpose-built to conceal refugees from Queen Mary's religious persecution. Long and narrow, it took up one end of the windowless storehouse and contained sleeping pallets, a chair and table, and a supply of food and drink stored in a tall, free-standing cupboard.

Suspicions had begun to nag at Susanna as soon as the initial shock of discovering a body had passed. In the aftermath, transporting it and throwing it into the brook, she'd had no time to ask herself questions, but now that she had leisure to consider them, she discovered a disconcerting dearth of answers.

Susanna contemplated her surroundings. The dead man had arrived with a pack. She remembered seeing it. Brown leather, of good quality. The type of bag that hung over a saddle. It must be somewhere.

So, too, should there be a key, a duplicate of the one she'd just used.

She began a methodical inspection of the chamber, end to end, floor to ceiling, but she reaped no more reward for her pains than a splinter in one thumb and sore knees.

No pack.

No key.

Covering her mouth and nose with a cloth, Susanna conducted a quick but thorough search of the storeroom before she emerged into the crisp afternoon air. There was nothing in the mint room but mint.

The hairs on the back of her neck prickled as she made her way to the stable. She glanced over her shoulder, certain someone was watching her, but there was no one in sight. Had he felt this way? She wondered. For all that Mark and the other grooms slept in the room above, the dead man could have gotten into the stables unseen and unheard. Then what? She studied the neat rows of stalls. Had he merely checked on his bay? Or had he come to hide something? More to the point, had he feared some enemy, someone who had, indeed, caught up with him?

As long as the duplicate key to the mint room remained missing, Susanna was forced to consider the possibility that the stranger had been murdered, that someone had trapped him in the storeroom, struck him on the head, and left him there to die ... locking the door on the way out.

"Oh, there you are, madam!" Jennet exclaimed, rushing into the stable. "Mark said you were back."

Beatrice arrived a moment later, closely followed by Ursula.

"Can she be trusted?" Beatrice demanded, glaring at the tiring maid. "She got the whole story out of your groom before I could prevent it."

"I am obliged to trust you both," Susanna told her. "There is no time to waste. It will not do for Robert to return and find me here. I have never shown an interest in the horses before."

"Why *are* you in the stable?" Jennet asked.

"To search for the stranger's missing pack."

When she had described its appearance, they spread out. Beatrice spoke in rapid Spanish, giving Ursula instructions. The reminder that both women were foreigners, for all that Beatrice had been born in England, gave Susanna pause. It seemed odd to her that Beatrice was so determined to help.

For a short while, no one spoke. Susanna inspected the stall where the old bay mare had been kept, the one in the darkest corner, where its occupant had stood the best chance of escaping notice. Stabling the refugees' horses was the riskiest part of her enterprise. Robert paid little attention to people, but he was devoted to his cattle. There had always been a chance he'd notice unauthorized additions.

Mare's droppings aside, Susanna found nothing in the stall. She moved on to the next one.

Jennet's cry of triumph brought them back to the center aisle of the stable. She had found the missing pack in the tack room. She hurried toward Susanna, carrying it in one hand and waving a paper in the other.

"A letter!" Beatrice cried, intercepting Jennet and plucking it from her fingers. "This must be destroyed before it can be used against you."

"Wait!"

But Susanna was too late. Beatrice had opened the nearest lantern and thrust the parchment into the candle flame. By the time Susanna reached her, the paper had been reduced to ash.

"Now, then," said Beatrice, pulling at the pack, "we must do likewise with this."

Jennet tried to keep hold of her prize, but Beatrice was a strong woman. She tugged it free and, giving Susanna no chance to protest, swept out of the stable with it. Ursula trailed along in her wake.

"Is she mad?" Jennet asked.

"It is my hope that she is only overzealous. I intended to destroy the pack myself, but I had planned to examine the contents first."

"It is the fault of the star with the long tail," Jennet muttered darkly. "An evil omen. Did I not say so? Death and destruction. Terror and –"

"Enough! Nothing supernatural caused that man's death, or Beatrice's actions, either." She fixed Jennet with a commanding stare. "What did the letter say?"

"Oh, madam, how could you think that I —"

"What did it say, Jennet?" Susanna tapped her foot and waited. All Leigh Abbey servants were taught to read, and if Jennet had one besetting sin, it was an abundance of curiosity. She'd been caught more than once hiding behind an arras to listen to the private conversations of others. Susanna had no doubt that she'd skimmed the letter before announcing her discovery, or that she'd found it in the first place by searching the pack.

"It was a letter of introduction. I did not have time to read the whole of it." Jennet's affronted tone spoke volumes.

"Repeat the words you did see, exactly as you remember them."

"To Sir Anthony Cooke, Strasbourg. I recommend unto you Master William Wroth."

"Go on."

"That is all I saw, madam."

"What of a signature? Who sent it?"

"I could not make out the name, but the letter was written from Staines on the second day of March. Where is Staines, madam?"

Susanna frowned. "It is some fifteen miles west of London, along the way to Salisbury." Of more importance was the identity of the person in that place who'd sent William Wroth to Leigh Abbey.

"Fetch Mark," she instructed. "I've a message to dispatch. Then find quill and ink and paper and write down every item you noted in Master Wroth's pack."

✝

"The dead man had no mark of violence upon him." Robert paused to refill his goblet with a sharp white wine from Angulle.

He and Lord Benedick and their servants had been stopped on the way home from the hunt by the coroner, who had been called in as soon as the body was discovered. Robert had been asked if he could identify the deceased. He claimed he'd never seen the fellow before.

"No mark at all?" Susanna asked as she and Beatrice exchanged a worried glance. Had no one noticed the lump on his head? This was a complication they had not foreseen.

"The fish had nibbled him," Robert said.

"He must have drowned, then," Beatrice murmured. "Will your coroner declare the death an accident?"

"He is reluctant to do so without knowing the identity of the victim. And he has some suspicion that the fellow may have taken his own life. He cannot be buried in hallowed ground if that is the case."

"What's to be done then?"

"The coroner has persuaded the justices to look more deeply into the matter."

Susanna's fingers clasped her wine cup so tightly that her knuckles showed white. They suspected murder. She was sure of it.

Beatrice did not seem to share her fears. "Officials are wont to fuss and fume and make themselves look important," she declared with a little laugh. "This will all turn out to be much ado about nothing."

†

The next morning, when Robert and Lord Benedick had left for a second day of hunting, Susanna, Beatrice, Jennet, and Ursula gathered in Susanna's study, a pleasant room full of books and maps, with windows that overlooked Leigh Abbey's fields and orchards to the east and the approach to the gatehouse on the north.

"The man's name was William Wroth," Susanna announced.

Ursula gasped, made the sign of the cross, and fumbled for her rosary.

"You know this man Wroth, good Ursula?" Susanna had not expected any reaction. She'd brought up Wroth's name as a preliminary to a discussion of how to convince the authorities his death was an accident.

The old woman's deeply-lined face crumpled further and her eyes, filmed with age, sought her mistress, but she did not speak.

Beatrice laid a hand on her arm. Her voice was gentle. "You must tell us if you know who this man was, Ursula."

"He was evil, mistress," Ursula answered.

Or, rather, that was what Beatrice told Susanna and Jennet they had said. She and Ursula spoke in Spanish, a language the others did not understand.

"Why does she think he was evil?" Susanna demanded.

Their incomprehensible conversation resumed. Beatrice asked questions and paused now and again to translate when Ursula answered, but it seemed to Susanna that the waiting gentlewoman took a great many words to convey very little. She began to wonder how much Beatrice was holding back.

"She knows nothing of help to us," Beatrice said at last, "only that when she was in my mother's service here in England, there was a man by that name who was well known for his hatred of all things Spanish. This was many years ago, for I was still a small child when my parents died."

"Did she ever meet William Wroth?" He'd have been a young man in his twenties then.

"She knew him by reputation. She says he was wont to pick fights with the servants of Spanish merchant families in London. And their sons."

"And no one stopped him?"

"Why should they, once Queen Catherine had been set aside? I remember a little of that time myself, for all that I was so young. My mother would cry herself to sleep over what had happened to her mistress. Once King Henry divorced her, men who felt as Wroth did had few restraints on their behavior. It was a popular belief that the only good Spaniard was a dead Spaniard."

"That must have made things difficult for your parents."

A great sadness clouded Beatrice's countenance. "Since I have been back in England, I have felt their loss the more, but when they were alive they knew great happiness. My father loved my mother as much as Benedick loves me and she returned his feelings tenfold."

Through the north-facing window, Susanna caught sight of an approaching rider. She knew him by his bright green cloak and dappled horse. By the time her neighbor, old Sir Eustace Thornley, who had served as a justice of the peace since Susanna was a girl, had been shown to the study, all four women were seated in a circle, applying their needles to a large piece of tapestry work.

"I am sorry to trouble you," he apologized after he'd been presented to Beatrice, "but I seek information about a man seen in the area of late." He gave particulars of William Wroth's appearance but did not say he was dead. Susanna suspected that Sir Eustace, who had never married, clung to the quaint notion that women should not trouble their pretty little heads about such matters as sudden death and coroner's inquests.

"That is a passing general description, sir," she said with flutter of eyelashes and a pout. "Has he no distinguishing characteristic?"

Flustered, Sir Eustace mumbled, "A faint smell of mint clung to his clothing and beard." He cleared his throat and pressed on. "It is not, I think, a common perfume."

"Mint has many uses." Susanna's voice was level but her heart raced triple time. She could scarce deny knowledge of the herb. Every woman received some training in the stillroom. "I steep the leaves of garden mint to make an infusion. Drinking one to two cups of this daily, but not for more than one week at a time, is an excellent remedy for sleeplessness and helpful to the digestion, as well. Mayhap the gentleman spilled his medicine."

"I prefer to distill mint," Beatrice said. "One must use freshly cut, partially dried plant tops, cut just before the plants come into flower. An over-mature plant produces an oil with a sharp, bitter aroma, but if the process be done aright, it yields a hot, pungent aroma."

The justice's eyes began to glaze over.

Taking her cue from Beatrice, Susanna launched into a detailed description of the preparation of a stimulant using mint and other herbs. She gave up all pretense of stitching. She was not much of a needlewoman in the best of circumstances.

"Well done, Susanna," Beatrice said when Sir Eustace took his leave a few minutes later. "How quick men are to lose interest in domestic matters!"

"A pity. I so wanted to tell him that some mints are cultivated as an aid to love. Why pennyroyal, given to quarreling couples, is even supposed to induce them to make peace."

"It is also a protection against evil," Beatrice remarked.

"Well, then," Susanna said with a smile, "we have nothing to fear. With all the mint we have stored at Leigh Abbey, 'tis certain we are safe from further trouble from Sir Eustace."

†

The next day Susanna and Beatrice rode with their husbands to Canterbury to visit the cathedral. On the way back, Robert stopped at Sir Eustace's manor house, sending the others on ahead without him. Susanna had no opportunity for a private word with him until they retired to their bedchamber for the night.

"Do you hunt again tomorrow?" she asked.

"Aye." He sounded disconsolate. "Lord Benedick cares for naught but hunting, hawking, and dallying with his own wife. He has no intention of attaching himself to the court."

Concealing a smile, Susanna made a sympathetic sound and continued to take pins out of her hair.

"You are a clever woman, Susanna. Can you find a way to give Beatrice a dislike of you?"

She fought a sense of disappointment as she brushed her long, thick hair. Robert believed it was a waste of his time to entertain Lord Benedick any longer, but he did not want to be the one to offend him, just in case Benedick turned out to have some use, after all. Robert expected Susanna to do his dirty work for him.

"I see no reason to discourage her friendship. Beatrice is most pleasant company."

"What do you know of her family?"

The question surprised her. "Her mother was in the household of Queen Mary's mother. I'd think such a connection would be helpful to you."

"Any benefit is overshadowed by what happened afterward. Beatrice's mother killed her English husband, then took her own life."

Aghast, Susanna put down her hairbrush and demanded details.

"Their family seat was at Staines," Robert said. His voice was muffled as he settled himself for the night. "That is all Sir Eustace told me." Their neighbor was well known for his long memory and love of gossip. If he'd had more information, he'd have repeated it.

Susanna crossed to the bed and pulled aside the bright blue damask hangings to glower at her spouse. Staines. The location could not be a coincidence. "Did Wroth come here because of Lord Benedick and his wife?"

Just before his eyes shifted away from her unrelenting gaze, she read the truth in them. He recognized Wroth's name. Had he known all along who the dead man was?

The belligerent jut of Robert's jaw warned her he did not intend to answer questions, but two could play at that game. She did not intend to explain how she'd discovered Wroth's identity. She perched on the foot of the bed and deftly began to braid her hair.

"I am as anxious as you that you regain favor at court." How else could she hope to continue her rescue efforts? "But if I do not know as much as you do, Robert, then I may make some mistake or say the wrong thing. If this dead stranger, for example, is the same Wroth who had such a reputation for hating all things Spanish —"

"God save me from meddling females!"

"He sounds the worst sort of extremist." She could not regret that Wroth was dead, knowing the sort of man he had been, but neither could she continue to ignore the possibility that he had been murdered. "He brought no credit to the cause he claimed to espouse."

"Nor was he faithful to it."

"What do you mean?" Her hands stilled in her hair.

"When last I was in London, I heard a rumor that Wroth, who had been in prison under sentence of death, had agreed to do some service for Queen Mary in order to save his own skin."

The possibility that Wroth had come to Leigh Abbey as a spy made Susanna's blood run cold, but she did not dare ask Robert any more questions for fear of arousing *his* suspicions. Beatrice had been right. Susanna's husband would turn her in himself if he saw any profit in it.

†

Mark returned to Leigh Abbey the next day, bringing a reply to the message Susanna had sent to Sir Anthony Cooke's daughter. The verbal questions had been accompanied, as proof of the sender's identity, by a sprig of rosemary. Margaret Cooke's answers came back with a bit of rue. She sent word that no one in Staines should have known what went on at Leigh Abbey, but that Wroth himself owned property there. He'd bought the estate of a man – Margaret could not remember his name – who had been murdered by his wife.

"Good news," Mark added, unaware that his mistress had been obliged to take a tight grip on the arms of her favorite carved oak chair to quell the sudden trembling in her hands. "When I passed through the village, I heard that Sir Eustace took another look at the body and this time noticed the lump on the dead man's head. The death will be ruled an accident. No more questions will be asked."

"Good news, indeed," Susanna murmured, giving Mark a reward for his services and sending him back to his usual duties.

Sunk deep in thought, it was some little time before Susanna realized that Jennet, who had come into the study with Mark, had remained when he was dismissed. She had a talent for disappearing into the woodwork when she did not want to be noticed.

"What did Beatrice do with the dead man's pack?" Susanna asked.

"Cut it into small bits and burnt them."

Trust Jennet to know. The list she'd made had been helpful, too. Wroth's pack had contained only clothing. No papers. No key.

"Why do you think she did that, Jennet?"

"To protect you, madam?"

"I wonder."

"Madam?"

"Yes, Jennet?"

"It is possible I missed seeing a key in Master Wroth's pack." At Susanna's start of surprise, she rushed on. "I do not know how else she could have got hold of it."

"Beatrice?"

Jennet nodded. "She must have been the one who sent old Ursula to get rid of it, since metal will not burn. I saw it clear when I followed Ursula to the fish ponds. The key caught the sun as she threw it in."

†

Susanna found Beatrice and Ursula in the small parlor. Beatrice had pulled the Glastonbury chair close to the window in order to read by the light streaming in through the panes. Ursula sat close to the fire, mending a stocking.

"Did you arrange to meet Master Wroth here?" she asked. If Robert wanted her to give the other woman a dislike of them, an accusation of murder should suffice.

Beatrice's demeanor remained calm. She marked her place in *Liber de Arte Distillandi* and met Susanna's eyes before she answered. "No."

"But you recognized him when you saw him?"

"No," she said again.

Susanna believed her, but she felt certain Beatrice was hiding something. "If you sought to trap Wroth in the mint room, intending to hold him there until Lord Benedick could deal with him —"

"Why all these questions?" Beatrice asked. "I thought you deemed Wroth's death an accident, even if Sir Eustace does not."

It was on the tip of her tongue to correct Beatrice, but at the last moment, she decided to keep the justice's most recent conclusion to herself. "Someone must have struck Wroth down, then locked him in the storeroom afterward," she said instead. "If he simply fell, I'd have found the key. Tell me, Beatrice, what is the connection between William Wroth and the death of your parents?"

With an abrupt movement, Beatrice rose from the chair and went to stand by the window and stare out at the bleak landscape. Her view encompassed the ornamental gardens, but at this time of year they showed no sign of life.

"You recognized Wroth," Susanna said in a voice she hoped conveyed her sympathy. "You locked him in, doubtless meaning to fetch Lord Benedick to deal with him, but by the time you returned, Wroth was dead."

"Benedick knows nothing of this!" As soon as the words were out she looked stricken, but it was too late to call them back.

If Benedick had seen the body, Susanna realized, it would have been long gone by morning. But if Wroth had not been locked in to await interrogation by Benedick, then Beatrice must have meant to kill him. Unless …

"Ursula," Susanna whispered. "Ursula was the one who recognized Wroth. She locked him in."

With obvious reluctance, Beatrice nodded. She returned to the chair. "I see I must tell you everything. Yes, she locked him in. Then she came to me. It took some time to sort matters out. It was the middle of the night. She had to extract me from my bed without waking Benedick, then explain who Wroth was and what she'd done and why. I had been told my parents were carried off by a fever. It was a great shock to learn that my mother had been accused of killing my father and of taking her own life. Ursula insisted that Wroth was to blame for both deaths."

"Has she any proof?"

"No. My mother took her aside one night at Staines, gave her money, and told her she must take me back to Spain without delay. Then she led Ursula to a window and pointed to a man – Wroth – and said we must avoid being seen by him when we left, that he was dangerous. Within the hour, Ursula and I were on our way to Calais. It was there that word reached us that my parents were dead."

"And Ursula did nothing?"

"What could she do? She knew Wroth's reputation. She was sure he had killed them, but she feared for her own life and mine if she remained on English soil long enough to accuse him. But now – now she is old. She no longer fears death." She smiled faintly. "And because she is old, her bones ache, preventing sleep. She was up in the middle of the night and chanced to look out a window. She recognized Wroth at once, for the situation was much as it had been when she'd seen him all those years ago. She went out for a closer look, followed him into the storeroom, caught him by surprise, hit him on the head, and took the key to lock him in. She reasoned that, together, she and I might be able to persuade him to confess to his crimes, but by the time I heard her explanation and dressed and went with her to the storeroom we were, as you have guessed, too late. He was dead."

"But why just leave him there? You must have known he'd be found."

"It was too close to sunrise to do anything else. As it was, I scarce had time to lock the door again and return to my bed before Benedick woke. I meant to go back and dispose of him as soon as Benedick left on the hunt, but you were there ahead of me."

Susanna wanted to believe her. If Wroth's death had been an accident, the matter was closed. And she'd had a narrow escape, for had he lived to be accused, the existence of the inner room and its purpose would have been exposed. She'd have ended up in gaol alongside Will Wroth. And although he might well have been acquitted, she'd have been certain to be executed for treason. She swallowed hard.

"We will say no more of the matter."

Beatrice frowned. "Benedick and I plan to return to Padua soon, where we will be safe from English law, but the smell of mint made Sir Eustace suspicious of you, Susanna. What if he continues to investigate? What if he discovers that Wroth died in your storeroom?"

"I am confident he will not." Had the return of the hunting party not interrupted her at that moment, Susanna would have gone on to share the verdict on Wroth's death with Beatrice.

†

"I thought they meant to leave this morning," Robert complained the next day. "What is Beatrice doing in your storeroom?"

"Stillroom, Robert. She's preparing her secret recipe for *aqua vitae* as a parting gift, using pennyroyal to add protective properties to the distillation."

"Do we need protection?" He sounded suspicious.

Susanna smiled. "No, my dear, but Beatrice took note of the way Jennet carries on, fearful of evil in the wake of the star with the long –"

She broke off, beset by a vague sense of alarm as she remembered that, as far as Beatrice knew, Susanna also had need of protection – from Sir Eustace. First they'd been distracted by the arrival of their husbands and then the bustle of preparations for Beatrice and Benedick's departure had occupied the rest of the afternoon and evening. Susanna's intention to tell Beatrice there was no longer any need to worry had completely slipped her mind.

Robert failed to notice Susanna's distraction. "She will not be at it much longer," he said after a few moments of consideration, "not with the goodly fire she had Benedick build for her in your storeroom."

"Stillroom," Susanna corrected. "And a stilling pot must be heated over a soft fire. Be patient, Robert. The day is young."

"Storeroom," Robert insisted, "and this was no temperate blaze."

Susanna felt her face drain of color. *Aqua vitae* had another name. It was called "burning water" because it so easily turned into flame.

"Storeroom?" she whispered.

No one heard her. The explosion drowned out all other sounds. It blew the storeroom walls outward as the fire, in one bright flash, consumed the incriminating bales of mint. It did not spread, nor was Beatrice harmed. She'd taken care to avoid both consequences when she planned this parting gift for her hostess.

"The fire was too rash." Benedick's cheerful wink told Susanna that he was now in his wife's confidence. His generous offer to pay for the damage mollified Robert and prevented him from asking awkward questions.

Beatrice, Susanna thought, had also been too rash, but only because she'd believed she owed it to Susanna to protect her from Sir Eustace's suspicions.

✝

"Will you rebuild your storeroom?" Robert asked as they watched their guests ride away a few hours later. Jennet had come out too. And Mark.

"There is no need." From now on, she'd hide escaping heretics in the stable with their horses.

"But where will you store pennyroyal?" Jennet asked. "Won't you need a great deal more of it to keep Leigh Abbey safe from the star with the long tail?"

"No, indeed," Susanna assured her, "for Beatrice had the right of it all along. Your ominous portent, Jennet, is in truth a dancing star, and a sure sign of all the good things to come."

A Note from the Author

The idea for this story came out of a visit to the Celestial Seasonings "mint room," a side trip during Historicon II in Boulder, Colorado. As many mystery writers before me have observed, the strangest things can inspire someone to say "What a great place to hide the body!"

Although Sir Anthony Cooke and his daughter Margaret were real people, there is nothing in history to indicate that Margaret was part of a conspiracy to smuggle heretics out of England. She married a London merchant in 1558 and died soon after. Her four sisters, Mildred (Lady Burghley), Anne (Lady Bacon), Elizabeth (Lady Hoby and later Lady John Russell – she campaigned to keep the Queen's Men from building a playhouse in Blackfriars), and Katherine (Lady Killigrew), were far more famous, in part because of the men they married and in part for their learning. The education they were given provided me with a model for Susanna's schooling.

Several contemporary descriptions survive of the "blazing star" of 1556. Both Henry Machyn and John Stow described this comet, which could be seen over England in early March, 1555/6. The "double dating" stems from the fact that in those days the new year still began on March 25.

As for Beatrice and Benedick, they are the protagonists of Shakespeare's *Much Ado About Nothing*. This story was originally written for an anthology of mystery stories using Shakespearean characters as sleuths. Since Shakespeare gave no specific dates for his tale, there is no reason it could not have taken place in the sixteenth century, and there is no textual evidence in the play to disprove the possibility that Beatrice's father might have been an Englishman.

The Rubaiyat of Nicholas Baldwin
(A Tale of Murder in the Year
of Our Lord 1559)

A woman screamed.

A cat hissed.

Nick Baldwin forgot he was in a foreign land with strange customs and looked for a way over the wall that separated him from those sounds of alarm. Finding no convenient gate, he clambered up one side and dropped into a private garden lush with flowers and foliage, but he'd arrived too late. No more than a foot away from the spot he'd landed, lay a crumpled female form. The blood pooling beneath her head was as vividly red as the roses on the bush beside her.

Nick surveyed the quiet, sun-drenched enclosure for some sign of the person who had attacked her. He caught a glimpse of white out of the corner of one eye, but it was only a small animal darting into a doorway. He turned back to the victim.

She was the first female he'd seen since arriving in Qazvin who had not been completely enveloped in the light-colored robes Persian women wore when they ventured out of their homes. The knife that had slashed her throat had cut right through the lacework veil meant to shield her face and neck from masculine eyes.

Nick knelt beside her, moved to pity, regretting that he'd not been in time to save her. He had no warning, heard no approaching footsteps, before he was roughly seized and jerked to his feet. Exclaiming in horror and rage, apparently convinced Nick was the murderer, three men hauled him away from the body.

In the loudest voice he could manage, Nick bellowed a desperate demand for justice: "Let me plead my case before the Great Sophy!"

That he spoke their language gave his captors pause. Two released him and backed away. Nick glowered at the ruddy-faced young man who still clung to his arm. He repeated the demand. This was not how he'd envisioned obtaining a royal audience, but Nick felt certain Shah Tahmasp, known in other lands as the Great Sophy of Persia, would honor his plea. The only question was whether that powerful ruler would bestir himself to save Nick's life.

The young man did not loosen his grip.

A debate ensued. Nick stopped trying to break free and concentrated on translating the barrage of heated words exploding over his head. He'd begun to study the language four months earlier, when he'd resolved to journey to Qazvin and persuade the Persian king to open trade with England. Nick had a gift for foreign tongues, possessing the happy facility of learning to speak them with ease, but in the heat of strong emotion some of what he now heard was well nigh unintelligible. Nick comprehended only enough to know that Bihzad, the fellow with the terrier's hold on his arm, argued for his immediate dispatch.

"He must have killed her," Bihzad declared. "There is blood on his hands."

"And on your own." Nick pointed to the gore and noticed that a streak of red also marred the robe worn by another of his captors. "Where is the weapon? How did I slash that woman's throat without a knife?"

"Search him, Hamid," Bihzad ordered.

The man with the stained sleeve hastened to obey.

Concealed inside a series of hidden pockets in the elaborately slashed and puffed doublet that marked Nick as a foreigner, was a small fortune in gemstones – pearls, sapphires, and rubies – portable trade goods Nick had brought with him from Muscovy. He resisted Hamid's efforts until the third man rejoined the fray.

Their rough, inefficient probing missed the valuables, but Nick was relieved of his eating knife and his dagger. Neither showed any sign of recent use and both were free of bloodstains. It was only then, when he considered asking his captors to produce their own weapons for inspection, that he realized none of them seemed to be armed. A scar blemishing the third man's cheek might have been made by a knife, but Nick saw no other indication that they ever carried weapons.

Hamid brought his face close to Nick's. "Are you a Portugee?" His breath was rich with the scent of cloves.

Nick grimaced at both the question and the overpowering aroma. "I am a London man." As far as he knew, he was the first from his homeland to set foot in this exotic and dangerous country.

All three stared at him, the blank looks on their faces making it plain they'd never heard of London. Nick doubted the word England would mean more to them.

He tried to picture how he must appear to their eyes. He was nothing out of the ordinary at home, a short, sturdily-built man in his twenty-seventh year with broad shoulders, dark brown hair and eyes, and regular features behind a neatly-trimmed beard. Here, however, the paleness of his skin marked him as an outsider just as surely as his clothing did. His complexion had darkened during his travels, from exposure to the sun, but was still several shades lighter than what they were accustomed to seeing.

The scarred man's gaze shifted to the doorway of the house adjoining the garden. "Master!"

They turned as one to watch the newcomer, a man several decades older than themselves, inspect the body. When he had done so, he called to the scarred man, using the name Qadi, and spoke quietly to him. In short order, Qadi departed, several menservants arrived, and Nick was seized and stuffed into a small, windowless chamber. Left there under guard, he was unable to overhear further discussion of his fate.

Nick considered his surroundings. He was in a house typical of those he'd seen since coming to Qazvin. His prison occupied one corner of one of four large porch-like parlors surrounding a smaller private parlor at the center of the house. The door blocking his exit was no more than two thin, wooden leaves folded one over the other like window shutters. He could break through, overcome the guard, and escape into the street through the front of the house, which at best would be open and at worst shut with another fragile sash.

But then what?

Running would be seen as proof of his guilt. He'd be pursued. If they caught him before he could change from his English clothes into Eastern garments and darken his skin, he'd be dispatched without mercy. There would be no opportunity to plead his case before the shah, only a painful and ignominious death.

Nick leaned against the plain plaster wall, prepared to wait for the Master's decision. Well, here he was, he thought, in the land the legendary Tamerlane had conquered, and it was not at all like a play. He felt his lips twist into a wry smile and the smile turn into a grin as he remembered how captivated he'd been as a boy by scenes from *The Persian Knights* acted out on a makeshift wooden stage in an innyard. He'd longed to see the world even then … or at least to run off and join the troupe of traveling players.

Had he chosen the latter course and been in a situation like this, he'd have

been able to call up a puff of smoke and a trap door to vanish through. Instead, after what seemed like hours, the old man's servants came for him. He'd
been granted his wish. They took him to the palace.

†

The audience hall was redolent with rich fragrances – aloe, camphor, saffron,
and frankincense. Large and sumptuous, its walls were colorfully painted and
its floor covered with thick carpets. Impressively bearded royal guardsmen,
armed with fearsome blades and wearing turbans wound around scarlet
uprights, added an exotic overlay of menace to the splendor.

Shah Tahmasp did not match his surroundings. He was a small, wiry man
with a pinched face and dark, haunted eyes. Nick had been told he was in his
forty-fifth year. Although both his bushy whiskers and his hair had been dyed
black, he looked far older.

Tahmasp regarded the captive Englishman with suspicion, then signaled
the old man's servants to release him and dismissed them. Their master remained, though well in the background, to watch the shah solemnly stretch
out one leg.

Nick took a deep breath, grateful he'd been coached in the proper way to
greet the monarch. Dropping to his knees, he kissed the shah's extended foot
with as much reverence as he could muster.

A little murmur of approval greeted the act and he was cautiously wel-
comed, even allowed to sit when the shah did. Praying the rest of the advice
he'd been given was also accurate, Nick perched awkwardly, his buttocks resting on his heels and his knees close together. Such, he had been told, was the
proper position to assume when one wished to show respect for one's betters.
He was careful to keep his toes out of sight, since for a man to let them show
when he sat was considered a great piece of rudeness in this culture.

Nick's mentor, Abd Allah Khan, a sensible, personable fellow Nick greatly
admired, was also the shah's cousin and brother-by-marriage. As such, he had
provided a letter of introduction, which Nick now produced, watching in anxious silence as Tahmasp examined the seals and read the contents.

After another considering look at Nick, the shah ordered rose water brought
in a silver bowl. Nick duly washed his face and hands and, although the pro-
cedure seemed strange to him, dried off by bending over aloe smoke, which
left its scent on his hair and beard.

The interrogation that followed was long, thorough, and, at times, difficult to follow. The Persian habit of choosing the most convoluted way to express a simple thought tested the limits of Nick's command of the language. In addition, the shah mumbled when he spoke. Some of his words were impossible to understand. Nick did not dare offer insult by asking him to repeat what he'd said. Instead he bluffed, giving the answers he thought Tahmasp expected.

On the matter of murder, the shah said little. After a search, a bloodstained knife had been found at the scene, but it had been identified as belonging to the victim. Tahmasp did not accuse Nick of killing the woman in the garden. He was more interested in London, a place he claimed never to have heard of, although he had had dealings with Russia and seemed to understand that Nick had come to Persia from Moscow.

Nick decided against trying explain that he'd been there as a stipendiary with the English Muscovy Company, or how a joint-stock company operated, or even why he'd struck out on his own after traveling as far as Bokhara with his friend, Anthony Jenkinson. With luck, Jenkinson was halfway back to England by now. It had been his plan to return to Moscow, then sail home while Nick investigated opportunities in Persia for trade in silk, spices, and other luxury goods. God willing, in a year's time they would both be back in Moscow.

As chief merchant of Persia, Shah Tahmasp held the monopoly on raw silk. Nick presented him with a pistol inlaid with mother-of-pearl. It had been concealed in his boot. Next came the emerald pendant shaped like a grape, which he'd worn around his neck.

The shah accepted both and waited for more.

Nick hesitated. If he gave away all he had, he'd have naught to bargain with and no means to pay for lodging and food. He chose his next words with care. He wished to convey a complex notion – that he had more of value to offer, but not just yet. He mentioned rubies.

The shah looked momentarily intrigued. Encouraged, Nick asked what Tahmasp wished to acquire from the west. The answer surprised him – London clothes such as Nick wore and also chain mail and suits of armor.

Nick assured him that such things could be provided.

"And a marriage alliance," Tahmasp declared, going on to ask who reigned in Nick's homeland and if there were unwed females in his house.

Nick hesitated. At the time of his departure from Moscow, the last news from England had already been months out of date. Did Mary Tudor rule there with her consort, Philip of Spain? Or had her half sister Elizabeth succeeded her? Or was Elizabeth dead, executed for her refusal to give up the New Religion established by her father and accept the tenets of the church of Rome?

"There are princesses in England yet unmarried," Nick told the shah. That seemed a safe statement. After Elizabeth, several other females stood in line to inherit the throne. Unless Mary and Philip had produced a son.

"Is London home to unbelievers?"

"Those who live there believe there is but one God."

It did not trouble Nick to call that God *Allah*. As far as he could see, Muslims and Christians worshiped the same deity. Abd Allah Khan had warned him, however, that Tahmasp was as extreme in his religious views as any supporter of the Inquisition. If he doubted Nick's expedient statement of faith, the mildest outcome was likely to be a demand that Nick prove he embraced all aspects of Islam by undergoing circumcision.

Abd Allah Khan had taken great delight in providing his honored guest with a detailed description of the process, one very painful for an adult. It was, he'd claimed, commonly a fortnight or three weeks before a man could walk again. The prospect did not bear thinking about.

Nick felt a rush of relief when Tahmasp once more changed the subject. He spoke at great length about a dream he'd had the previous night. Nick soon lost the sense of it, although he did catch the word *rubai*, which he himself had used when speaking of the gemstones he had to trade.

At the end of this oration, the shah fixed Nick with a steely gaze. "If you wish to become a merchant in Qazvin, you must first prove yourself innocent of murder."

Nick swallowed hard. He had no idea how to accomplish such a feat, yet he had no choice but to agree. Bowing low, he murmured, "My hand is on the skirt of the robe of the Shah Tahmasp," the standard phrase Abd Allah Khan had taught him. It meant he depended upon the shah for protection and was no less than the literal truth.

†

A short time later, the shah's guardsmen returned Nick to the scene of the crime. The old man was already there. Once they were alone in one of the parlors, he approached Nick, for the first time coming close enough to the London man for Nick to get a good look at him.

"The woman in the garden," he said, "was nursemaid to my youngest daughter."

He spoke in Italian.

"God's blood!" Nick exclaimed, startled into replying in the same language. "You are no Persian." The fellow's eyes were a bright, sapphire blue.

The old man gestured for Nick to sit on the thick carpet covering the floor. A servant brought refreshments. "I have lived here more than forty years now," he said, "but I was born in Venice. My name is Lorenzo Zeno."

"Nick Baldwin of London, at your service."

"*Cherab?*" He offered a wine of a deep purple color. "It is similar in taste to Muscadine."

Nick shook his head.

"Very wise. The punishment for drinking wine, unless one has permission –" he displayed his, with its special seal "– is to have your belly ripped open on the spot. A long poniard is plunged into you on the left side and drawn round to the back. It is not a speedy death."

Servants offered Nick a choice between a cup of barley water and a drink called sherbet, but he was distracted by his desire to ask Zeno questions. The old man waved them aside.

"By the king's sacred head, you have no time for inquiries into my history. You've two tasks to perform, neither of them simple."

"Two?" Taken aback, Nick almost choked on a swallow of barley water. "I know I must find the real murderer in order to clear my name. What more?"

Zeno grinned. "Tell me, Englishman, what is the meaning of *rubai?*"

"Ruby. The gemstone."

"The ruby that comes from Egypt, a very fine stone, is called *yacut-eeylani*. The rose-colored ruby is *balacchani*. The carbuncle, said to be bred in the head of a dragon, is called the *icheb chirac*, or flambeau of the night. Then there are the *cha mohore*, the royal stone, and the *cha devacran*, the king of jewels."

"And a *rubai?*" Nick was no longer sure he wanted to know.

"A poem of four lines only, of which the first, second, and fourth lines rhyme. It needs no connection to what comes before or after, but a collection of these poems is called a *rubaiyat*. That is what you agreed to give to the shah, after you find the person who killed my servant. An original composition. Verses. Have you any skill with poetry?"

Nick drank deeply of the iced barley water and helped himself to a handful of grapes from a platter that also contained dates and slices of melon. Grammar school Greek and Latin had introduced him to Petrarch and other classic poets, and as a young man he'd written his share of sonnets to a lady's eyebrows, but he'd long since abandoned such flights of fancy for life as a merchant.

"I appear to have overestimated my command of the spoken language of Persia," he admitted. "Poetry aside, I did not understand much of what the shah said when he spoke of dreams. Is it some superstitious belief on his part that dictates the tasks I am to perform?"

"Last night the shah, who sets great store by such things, dreamt of the coming of a poet who would make right a wrong and tell of it in verse."

Nick bit back a groan. He would not, it seemed, even have the freedom to choose his own subject. "Must these poems be written in the language of this land or may I compose in my native tongue?"

"You need not write them at all, only recite the verses."

"In Persian?"

"In Persian. And you must take care to avoid any suggestion of heresy in your words."

As he would in England, also, Nick thought.

"It is safest to begin with religious orthodoxy and a plea for forgiveness of any failings in the lines to come."

Nick contemplated his empty cup. "I cannot compose any poem until I know the identity of the murderer. First I must discover what befell that woman in your garden." Setting aside the drinking vessel, he rose and began to pace. "What alerted those inside the house to what had happened? It cannot have been the cry I heard. Had that been audible, those young men would have arrived before I did."

"A servant reported seeing someone climb over my wall."

"Who are the young men who seized me?"

"My students." A sweep of one hand indicated their surroundings.

Until that moment, Nick had been oblivious to the room's contents. Now he took note of gilded and burnished pages on which miniatures would be painted. Brushes, drawing boards, and a little shell full of silver paint gave further evidence of Zeno's profession. Nick lifted the brush a colorist would use to complete a painting-in-small that had been outlined but not yet filled in. It appeared to consist of a single hair tied into a quill handle.

"Kitten fur," said Zeno.

A memory flashed through Nick's mind at the comment – an animal in flight. "I saw a white cat in the garden just after the murder took place." Frowning, Zeno rose from the rug. "There is no help for it. You must speak with Halima."

Nick had been in the East long enough to know that the women's quarters were forbidden to men outside the family. It was almost as unusual for a wealthy merchant or artisan's womenfolk to emerge from these private rooms to speak to a strange man. In a noble household, such activity would be strictly forbidden. Zeno's daughter Halima, however, was too young yet to be required to wear the veil.

She regarded Nick with undisguised curiosity through eyes as blue as her father's. Nick stared back, equally curious, noting that she wore a long shirt and a vest atop what appeared to be silk, ankle-length drawers. A small cap sat atop hair drawn back and woven into a great many thick wefts. The ends were trimmed with ribbons to make them long enough to reach her waist.

"Marta saw someone in the garden," Halima said in response to Zeno's questions. "One of your students, Father."

"Which one?"

"I do not know." When she shook her head, the fragrance of civet, which here was called *zabad*, wafted toward them. "Marta said only that he appeared to be hiding a small object. She feared he'd stolen something from the house and that when its loss was discovered, the servants would be blamed. She went to retrieve it. She never returned."

"Perhaps," Nick mused, "this Marta surprised the fellow when he came back for his prize. He must have murdered her to keep her from telling anyone what he'd done."

"But why kill over that?" Zeno asked. "A woman's word against a man's —"

"You would have believed her, Father," Halima interrupted. "He must have known that. And she told me what she knew. That's two."

Noticing Nick's puzzled expression, Zeno explained. "The Koran requires the evidence of two women to match the testimony of one man, and even that is not accepted unless a man corroborates it."

"And if it was accepted?"

"The punishment for thieving is amputation of a hand. It is chopped off by repeated blows of a mallet."

"Certes, that would end a man's career as an artist!" To be hanged for theft, England's punishment for stealing any item valued at more than a shilling, was less violent and less painful, but it was more final. "What is the penalty for murder?"

"Killing a man is a capital offense. Murdering a woman is a lesser crime. Although a Muslim man who murders a Muslim woman must be executed, this cannot be done until the woman's guardian pays half of his blood money. This is negotiated with and given to the murderer's family."

"Blood money?"

"The sum the man would be worth if he were to live a normal life."

"There was blood on Bala's fur after Marta was killed," Halima said. "I think he must have been with her in the garden."

"Bala?" Nick asked. "A white cat?"

"A kitten," Halima clarified. "He was accustomed to ride tucked inside the top of Marta's vest."

"A pity he cannot testify." And an even greater pity, Nick thought, that there was not some simple way to narrow their suspects from Zeno's three students down to one.

When Halima had returned to the women's quarters, Nick and Zeno went into the garden to search the area around the rose bushes. "Tell me about those young men," Nick urged him.

"Qadi is the youngest. Only seventeen. He chafes at being given the task of coloring in a whole miniature outlined by a master. He must toil for months illuminating works that will be credited to another artist who spent far less time on the piece."

"How did he get that scar on his face?" Nick was sympathetic to the universal plight of the apprentice but more interested in Qadi's propensity for violence.

"A scuffle with another child when he was ten. He fell against a sharp metal edge."

"Has he a quick temper?"

"No. Nor do the others. Hamid is frustrated only by the requirement that he learn to paint the human form. He believes he will be happy as a gilder, only adding the arabesque ornaments – the designs of flowering vines which are necessary to any painting – and the framing rectangles that isolate text areas."

"And Bihzad? What of him?" The man's fingers had left impressions on Nick's neck.

"Bihzad has a sense of humor that may one day get him into difficulties. He likes to put the faces of prominent courtiers on his figures."

"Would Tahmasp punish him for that?"

"Who can say? Once our king was an artist himself. He appreciated all the pleasures of life."

Nick thought of the sour, stoop-shouldered old man in the palace. "What changed him?"

"Dreams. As you know, he takes his dreams most seriously. They make him moody. In good moods, he enjoys knowing others appreciate pleasures he denies to himself. But when the guilt and responsibility of his position are upon him, he suspects everyone, even those he loves. There are no more court artists. No more court musicians. One dream told Tahmasp to revoke all taxes not justified by religious law. The next day, he remitted all sales taxes and tolls." Zeno's lips twitched. "They have since been restored. But when he decided he would have all his subjects renounce wine and hashish and even sexual congress, since he equates any pleasure with sin, he closed down all the wine shops and brothels."

"Such eccentricity must be difficult for a subject to deal with year in and year out."

"Persia is more to my liking than any of the Italian states," Zeno averred. "I have been content here. Most Persians are open and friendly and would give their own lives before they would harm another."

Nick bent beneath a willow tree to examine a patch of earth in the failing light. It appeared to have been disturbed. "Someone did harm. What are the habits of your three students?"

"Their habits are like any other man's."

Which told Nick nothing. He brushed away a top layer of dirt and uncovered an odd-looking stone. "Bezoar?"

Zeno sighed. "So that is what was stolen. I'd hoped Halima was mistaken. In Persia it is called *padzuhr*."

"Stolen to sell?"

"Or because someone is ill."

Nick nodded. Westerners also knew of its powers. Taken internally or used externally, bezoar was popularly believed to be an antidote against most poisons, including the bites of snakes and other venomous creatures. Some credulous folk even thought it could cure the plague, falling sickness, fevers, and the pox.

"Where are your students now?" Nick asked as Zeno led the way inside. At this time of year, night fell with little twilight. Servants had already lit several tiny, odorless oil lamps.

"I sent them on errands, that we might talk uninterrupted, but they will return soon."

"What is their normal pattern?"

"Bed between nine and ten of the clock. Up at dawn."

"And if you were to give them a day of freedom?"

Zeno's eyes narrowed. "Do you think one of them may betray his guilt by running away?"

"That would be too much to hope for. I intend only to follow them, see where they go and with whom they speak. It may be that I will observe some behavior that will advance my quest, but even if no one does anything suspicious, I will be able to take the measure of each man."

Nodding and looking thoughtful, Zeno approved the plan.

†

In the morning, before the heat of the day came upon them, all three students set out for the *bazarga*. Nick, wearing Persian garments Zeno had found for him, trailed after them past houses of red brick and plaster and into the heart of the city. He moved with greater confidence as they neared the marketplace. Once there, he was certain he would go unnoticed by his quarry. There would be plenty of activity to hide his presence inside the vaulted-over gallery that contained the shops.

Qadi left the group when they came to the turning for the *hamam*. Nick hesitated. He doubted he could pass for a native in there. A pity, he thought with a wry twist of the lips. He'd have liked to bathe, but Moslem men did more than just cleanse themselves in the public baths. They also had all their body hair removed, usually with a lime and arsenic depilatory. He'd be noticeably hirsute in that company. The fact that the other men would all have had other bits removed, bits that did not grow back, would have made him even more conspicuous.

He continued on after Bihzad and Hamid. The former entered one of the shops. A quick glance inside showed Nick a customer accepting silver in exchange for goods he'd brought to sell. Nick frowned. He still had possession of the bezoar stone. Unless Bihzad had stolen something else from Zeno, he had nothing for the shopkeeper.

In order to keep Hamid in sight, Nick remained outside. He could not make out what was being said, but he was near enough to tell the shopkeeper was annoyed with Zeno's student. The young man's voice rose in anger. The other barked a sharp command. Then both adjourned behind a curtain that hid a back room.

In the distance, Hamid was accosted by a veiled woman. No, Nick corrected himself, not just a woman. A *cahbeha*. Her professional status was made clear by the broad embroidered border on her veil. Honest women, Nick had been told, displayed no borders.

But what was she doing out in broad daylight? Abd Allah Khan's instruction had been far-reaching. He'd explained to Nick that such women appeared in a certain place in Qazvin only when night fell.

"Many immoral women," he'd warned, "their faces concealed, stand in a long line and offer their shameful wares. Behind each is an old woman, known as the *dalal*, who carries a cushion and a cotton-filled blanket on her back and holds a lamp in her hand. When a man wishes to come to an arrangement with them, the *dalal* lights the lamp and with this the man sees each *cahbeha's* face and orders the one who pleases him most to follow him."

Shouts from within the shop drew Nick's attention back to Bihzad. The young man stormed out, nearly bowling Nick over as he made his escape. The shopkeeper hurled abuse in his wake, but made no attempt to follow. Nick caught only a few words, but they were sufficient to explain at least some of the animosity. The shopkeeper was Bihzad's father.

Nick remained in the marketplace several more hours, but learned little that seemed useful to him. He did not see any of Zeno's students again until supper, a strained meal filled with surreptitious looks in his direction. They alternated between suspicious and hostile.

After they'd eaten, he met with Zeno in private.

"The only way we can hope to discover the identity of Marta's murderer is to set a trap for the killer," Nick told him.

"How?"

"With a dream, and a trick I learned in the innyard playhouses I frequented in my youth, and the *rubaiyat* I have been commanded to compose. And with the help, I do think, of that kitten."

A scheme had begun to suggest itself when they'd questioned Halima. In the course of the day, Nick had come to realize that the same thing that had almost gotten him killed on the spot, his foreign appearance and strangeness, might be just the thing that could save him. He explained what he had in mind.

Zeno pointed out the flaw in his plan. "It requires that you first compose your poem."

"I will work on it tonight," Nick told him, "and have it ready by morning."

"It is as well, then, that nights in this region and in this season are ten hours long."

†

The wind that came up every evening when the sun went down rattled the shutters and moaned like a tormented spirit. After the first hour, Nick wanted to wail along with it.

He had models to go by – *rubai* Zeno had provided that praised the beauty of a mole on a woman's cheek and the ugliness of having a nose as big as a gugglet – but he would indeed need every second of the darkness in order to complete his task.

The kitten, Bala, proved remarkable soothing to stroke when inspiration waned. The animal belonged to a breed Nick had first seen in Moscow. Highly valued for their long, silky coats, these cats were imported from Turkestan and Persia and sold to Russian noblemen, the only ones wealthy enough to buy them.

With Bala curled in his lap, Nick struggled through verse after verse. He wrote using the English alphabet and spelled Persian words by the way they sounded. He was rather proud of the figure of speech that proclaimed murder had as rank a smell as Muscovy leather, and of his use of the proverb "a black ox trod on my foot" to mean trouble had come upon him. On the whole, however, he knew his *rubaiyat* to be an awkward collection of verses in a flowery foreign tongue he had not yet mastered. Not a single one of the quatrains translated well into English.

By the time Nick finished, it was almost sunrise and the clove-scented candles had burned down to stubs. Persians did love that smell, he thought. Even the bezoar stone carried a trace of it.

†

As he'd promised, Zeno listened to Nick's composition and declared it free of heresy. He found a few errors in meaning. After Nick corrected them, he committed his creation to memory. That done, Nick left Zeno's house to make several purchases in the marketplace. Powder of vernis, he discovered, was more readily available in Qazvin than in London.

By mid-morning, all was in readiness. Zeno had collected the three students in his private parlor to await Nick's grand entrance. The plan was simple – prey on what Nick hoped was a universal fear of the occult. Everyone he knew, whether Englishman, Muscovite, or Hollander, believed in the power of spells and curses. He counted on Zeno's apprentices being every bit as superstitious as their English counterparts.

With as much dignity as he could counterfeit, he advanced into the room. Striking a pose, he began to recite his *rubaiyat*, the tale of a powerful western magician who called up the restless spirit of a murdered woman. There had been a witness, the verses claimed, to Marta's death, a kitten called Bala. With the help of Nick's spell, Bala would be the instrument of Marta's revenge.

He had concealed the small white feline in one of the hidden pockets of his doublet. With slight of hand with flint and steel and the powder of vernis, he produced a flash and a cloud of smoke at the moment when it would have the best dramatic effect. Seconds later, the haze cleared, revealing Bala in Nick's arms. Around the animal's neck hung the bezoar stone.

The theatrical trick startled all three students, but there was an added flicker of guilt in one pair of dark eyes. Thank God! Nick thought, and flung Bala directly at Hamid.

The young man scrambled backward with a cry of alarm. Covering his head with his arms to ward off attack, he began to babble. "Keep it away, master!" he begged. "Master Zeno, save me!"

"There was blood on your sleeve in the garden," Nick said. "And you had been chewing on cloves. Your breath reeked of them. The scent was on your hands, as well, and came off onto the bezoar stone."

Zeno reached out to his sobbing student, touching his shoulder. "Why, Hamid?"

"A woman," Nick murmured. "The woman in the marketplace."

"For Lilas," Hamid admitted. "She swore to refuse me if I did not bring her its magic."

"There was no need to steal the *padzuhr*," Zeno protested. "I would have loaned it to you, had you but asked."

"She did not wish to borrow it, master. She wants things for her own. She can command a great price, and most of her lovers give her rich gifts besides. She honored me with her favors. All she wanted was the *padzuhr*." At that, Hamid broke into loud lamentations.

Watching him, Nick felt a deep sense of sadness engulf him. He had succeeded in clearing his own name, but he could take no pleasure in this outcome. Nothing the authorities did to Hamid could change the senselessness of Marta's death.

†

Nick went to his second audience with Shah Tahmasp prepared to recite the collection of *rubai* and reap what rewards he could from the completion of his assignment. First, however, he was required to witness Hamid's punishment. The shah had decided to be merciful. Marta's killer would not be executed. Instead, with his own knife, Tahmasp cut off Hamid's lips, nose, ears, and eyelids.

Tahmasp turned next to Nick, running his icy gaze over Nick's Persian garb. "Do you adhere to the religious teachings of the Prophet?" he demanded.

Nick did not quibble over semantics. "I believe there is no God but God," he declared in ringing tones. "Muhammad is God's Prophet and Ali is God's Imam."

A long silence followed this avowal. Then, as if there had never been any question but that he would do so, Shah Tahmasp granted Nick permission to spend the next few months traveling throughout Persia. He would be allowed to negotiate the exportation of pepper, cinnamon, mace, jewels, silks, drugs, and alum. After that, Tahmasp declared, Nick would return to England to carry Tahmasp's royal gift to the English ruler. The shah produced a small, ornately carved ivory box. Within was a wondrous well-carved piece of jade of intense apple green, fashioned into the figure of a horse and measuring no more than six barleycorns high.

†

A week later, dawn found Nick Baldwin mounted on the good Arab horse Tahmasp had given him. Its trappings were of gold and turquoise. Behind him ranged twelve camels and five mules, also gifts from the shah. One of the mules carried yet another royal present, a large tent suitable for use when sleeping in the open.

Lorenzo Zeno, who had insisted Nick remain as a guest in his house during the remainder of his stay in Qazvin, came out to see him off. "I do not believe you will come this way again," he observed.

"It does not seem likely," Nick agreed.

"Halima sends you a parting present." Zeno offered up a basket. From within came feline sounds of protest.

"Bala?"

"Bala. To remember us by."

Nick thought it unlikely he would ever forget this sojourn in Persia, although he intended to try his best to block out the memory of Tahmasp's swift and brutal punishment of Hamid.

As soon as he left Qazvin, his heart felt lighter. True, he would be returning soon to a country where heretics were burnt to death and traitors were hanged, drawn, and quartered, but he understood the complexities of life in England. English law, English political factions, and English religion were familiar to him.

He felt a grin overspread his features as he rode on. At home, he knew how to stay out of trouble. He was, after all, a London man.

A Note from the Author

Nick Baldwin's travels in Persia are loosely based on what really happened there. By 1553, England had an interest in finding a northern route to the wealth of the Indies. This led to trade with Russia, which was then called Muscovy. In 1558, Anthony Jenkinson set out from Moscow on a journey that was intended to retrace the footsteps of Marco Polo. When it took Jenkinson nine months to reach Bokhara, however, and he was told it would take another nine to reach China, he went back to Moscow.

This is the point at which I depart from history and let Nick go off on his own. To reach Qazvin, then the capital of Persia, he follows the route Jenkinson took two years later, crossing the Caspian to Derbent, meeting Abd Allah Khan, king of Shirvan and ruler of the Uzbeg people, then going on to meet Shah Tahmasp. Unfortunately, Jenkinson and the official delegation did not succeed in opening trade between Persia and England. He so offended the shah with his arrogance that at one point Tahmasp threatened to cut off his head and send it to Suleyman the Magnificent.

Lady Appleton and the London Man

"Folk hereabout call him the London Man." Jennet gestured toward the stranger at the far side of the gardens. "That is Master Baldwin."

Even as she wondered how Jennet could identify the fellow with such ease when this was his first visit to Leigh Abbey, Susanna Appleton had to smile at the sentiment behind the ekename. To country-dwellers who'd never traveled farther from their homes than Dover or Canterbury, London was as foreign a place as France or Spain. Wealthy city merchants like Master Baldwin aroused their darkest suspicions, especially when they purchased rural estates from the impoverished heirs of local gentry. Baldwin might now own a goodly parcel of land in Kent, but he was an outsider and would remain so.

"We will wait for him here," Susanna said, coming to a halt in the ornamental garden, a semi-circular space planted with shrubs, flowers, and a few fruit trees. Their visitor had not yet seen them, although 'twas plain one of the servants had told him where to look. The gardens on the south side of Leigh Abbey covered nearly an acre, far more extensive than the ones the monks had planted when the manor was, in truth, an abbey.

On this early August day, in the year of our Lord fifteen hundred and sixty-two, Susanna had suggested a mid-morning walk in pleasant surroundings in order to assure that Jennet, once her tiring maid, long her friend and companion, and now her housekeeper, did not wear herself out with work. Jennet would be delivered of her third child in a few months, several weeks before the second reached the one-year mark.

From a stone bench situated beneath an ancient oak planted on a little knoll, the two women had a splendid view. Susanna watched Baldwin pass through her herb garden and continue his advance between the long rows of parallel beds in the vegetable garden. He looked, she decided, like one of his own sturdy merchant ships under full sail.

Her new neighbor was stocky but not fat, with broad shoulders and surprisingly small feet. When he came closer, Susanna judged that he was a bit

71

shorter than she was, but then she was tall for a woman, a legacy from her father. She'd also inherited his square jaw and his inquiring mind.

Baldwin appeared to be no more than thirty, though his brown hair had some white in it. He had regular features behind a fine beard, but at the moment, having spotted the two waiting women, they were much contorted by irritation.

She rose when he reached the base of the knoll, making her countenance as stern as a schoolmaster's. Why should a man she'd never met be so wroth with her? He seemed to be glowering at Jennet, too.

"Who are you, sir? And what business brings you to my home?"

Taken aback by her challenging stance, Baldwin hesitated, but only for a moment. "Good day to you, madam." He doffed his plumed bonnet, then replaced it with enough force to tell her he could barely contain some powerful emotion. "I am Nicholas Baldwin, your neighbor."

Had he been a dragon, Lady Appleton thought, he'd be breathing fire. She thought his scowling face and snapping eyes would look well on a carved wooden figurehead ... if the piece graced the prow of a pirate's vessel.

"And your business here, Master Baldwin?"

He glanced at Jennet, then quickly back to Susanna. "It might be best if your husband were present."

"Impossible," Susanna informed him. "Sir Robert left five days ago on the queen's business. I do not expect to see him again for many months."

Gentleman, courtier, and sometime intelligence gatherer for the Crown, Sir Robert Appleton was often away for long periods of time. In his absence, Susanna ran his estates. In truth, she managed them even when he was in England. Though it galled Robert to admit it, she was better at such things than he was."

Again Baldwin looked in Jennet's direction, but this time his gaze remained fixed upon her. "I came here seeking this woman, Lady Appleton. I believe your servant stole something that belongs to me. Something of great value."

Deluded as one fit for Bedlam, Susanna thought, until she remembered that Jennet had been able to identify Master Baldwin before he introduced himself. And the look now overspreading the housekeeper's face might indeed be guilt. Jennet's eyes were wide and her skin had lost all color. For a moment, Susanna feared the younger woman might faint.

She should have known better.

Servant she might be, but Jennet had never been backward about speaking her own mind. Hands on her ample hips, she recovered in a trice from her shock at Baldwin's claim and returned his irate stare with one of her own. Her position atop the knoll allowed her to look down her nose at him.

"I never stole anything!" she declared. "I am innocent as a newborn babe."

Had the accusation not been so serious, Susanna would have applauded the show of bravado. Unfortunately, the law was clear. Theft of goods worth more than twelvepence was punishable by execution.

Baldwin looked unconvinced by the heartfelt protest. He shifted his attention to Susanna once more. "I must have my property back, madam. If it is returned to me without further ado, I will not bring charges against anyone in this household. Indeed, I will say nothing more of the incident to anyone."

If the claim that Jennet was a thief had been outrageous, this promise of leniency seemed more so. Master Baldwin, Susanna concluded, had something to hide.

"You are blunt, Master Baldwin," she told him.

"I am truthful, Lady Appleton."

"Why do you suspect Jennet?"

"She was seen in my house a week past, lurking in places she had no business, creeping about in a furtive manner."

"I did but pay a visit to Master Baldwin's cook!"

Susanna motioned for Jennet to remain silent, fearing she might say too much. Jennet did have a habit of listening at keyholes, but that was a far cry from stealing.

"You delayed long in coming here," she said to her neighbor, and met his eyes, unblinking.

Baldwin looked away first. "I did not discover my loss until this morning, but no one else could have taken it. Of all others, including mine own servants, only your own good husband even knew I had this particular object in my possession."

Susanna did not like the sound of that, but for the moment she let it pass. "What object?" she asked. "What does Jennet stand accused of taking?"

"You have no need to know."

Susanna's eyebrows lifted. She had heard that excuse too often from Robert and been obliged to accept it. She owed Baldwin no such obedience.

Under her steady glare, her neighbor's uneasiness grew until 'twas almost palpable. There, she sensed, lay a weakness she could use to advantage.

"I see no constable at your heels," she said. "No justice of the peace."

"You cannot want me to take the matter to law. Think, madam of the consequences."

Beside her, Susanna felt Jennet tremble, vibrating with a mixture of outrage and fear at this reminder of her danger. A convicted felon great with child might delay execution until she delivered, but afterward the sentence would duly be carried out.

"I will not permit such an injustice," Susanna declared. She slipped a comforting arm around the other woman's shoulders. Jennet might be adept at spinning tales and be able to lie without a qualm when necessity demanded, but she was no thief.

Baldwin looked thoughtful. "All I have heard of you, madam, from the vicar and from my servants, indicates you are a practical woman. This matter is easily settled. Allow me to search here at Leigh Abbey for what I have lost. I am certain I can rely upon your common sense to tell you this is a happy solution."

Flattery did not sway her, but neither did Susanna have any logical reason not to allow Baldwin to scour the premises. In truth, she could think of one very good argument in favor of permitting him to search.

"I will make a bargain with you, Master Baldwin," she said. "You may go through the entire house and all the outbuildings, look in any place you think Jennet might have secreted this stolen item. But when you have done, and have found nothing, you must grant me a favor in return."

"What favor?"

"To be taken to the scene of the crime, where you will answer any question I pose about the theft."

Master Baldwin began to sputter a protest, but Susanna was spared the need to argue with him.

"Lady Appleton is the most skilled person in all England at reasoning out the truth of strange events," Jennet declared.

Baldwin did not look convinced, but he agreed to her proposal with a curt nod of assent. Likely he felt certain he'd find what he sought. Susanna was equally sure he would not.

"Shall we start with the stillroom?" She led him back through the gardens and up to the door of that separate building near the kitchen. "You may look, but not touch," she told him.

Baldwin hesitated in the doorway, taking in the sight of drying herbs surrounded by all manner of equipment for distillation and dozens of jars, pots, and other vessels, all labeled and dated. Apparently, he did know of her reputation on herbal poisons. When, after a thorough examination of the rest of the stillroom, his gaze fell upon the black chest in the darkest corner of the room, he did no more than request that she lift the lid.

"The thing I seek is not here," Baldwin admitted when he saw that it was full of papers, all the notes she had made over the course of many years of study.

In Susanna's company, Master Baldwin investigated every nook or cranny of Leigh Abbey, combing kitchen and bake house, snooping in the servants' quarters, and the stables, too. He found nothing, and at length the only room left to be searched was the study.

"A pleasant chamber," he remarked, taking in the hearth with the marble chimney-piece, the east-facing window, and the small, carpet-draped table holding crystal flagons and Venetian glass goblets. Susanna did not offer him refreshment. She had no desire to encourage him to linger.

A second table was heavy-laden with leather-bound volumes and the presence of so many books seemed to intrigue Baldwin. One by one he examined them with something bordering on reverence. Susanna did not think he was still looking for the missing object. Simple curiosity drove him now.

A copy of *Variorum planetarium historia*, written in Latin by a French physician and botanist, told him she was literate in more than one language. Then he found *A Cautionary Herbal, being a compendium of plants harmful to the health.* This small volume, printed by Master John Day of London two years earlier, bore only the initials S.A. to identify its author, but Baldwin, having just seen the papers in her stillroom, guessed the truth.

"You wrote this?" he asked.

She nodded. Remaining anonymous had been Robert's idea, not hers. It had allowed him to claim credit for her work.

Without comment, Baldwin abandoned the books and prowled the small room, stirring the rushes with every step to release the scent of the bayleaves strewn among them. He stopped in front of a large engraved map, mounted for hanging, which occupied a place of honor in the room.

Susanna felt herself tense. She forced herself to relax. "Mayhap you would care to look behind the *mappa mundi?*" she asked. "Doubtless there is a hidden panel in that wall."

"This, madam, may be a map of the world, but the term *mappa mundi* properly refers only to written descriptions."

"My husband calls it a *mappa mundi.*"

"Sir Robert is a gentleman who dabbles in seafaring and exploration ... in books and conversation." Baldwin's tone implied he himself was a participant in such things, and therefore an authority.

"Have you finished your search?" She heard the testiness in her voice and that annoyed her nearly as much as Baldwin's attitude.

"Aye, I have done what I set out to do."

"Good. I gave orders some time ago for my mare to be saddled."

A few minutes later, she was perched sideways on her horse, both feet resting on a velvet sling and supporting one knee in a hollow cut in the pommeled saddle, but there was a delay in setting out because Jennet insisted upon coming along and she required the help of two stout fellows to hoist her onto a pillion.

"You hate going anywhere on horseback," Susanna reminded her. "Even when you are not great with child."

"The journey is short," Jennet argued, grasping the waist of the man in the saddle in front of her.

Plainly, she did not intend to be left behind, and Susanna had to admit that she had every right to accompany them. There was little likelihood now that Jennet would be arrested or tried, let alone convicted and executed, since Baldwin had found no proof of her guilt, but neither had he rescinded his accusation. Jennet's honor was at stake.

Baldwin's house was less than two miles distant if one went by way of a footpath that ran through Leigh Abbey's orchards and a small wood and led straight up to his kitchen door. Master and servant alike had often taken this shortcut over the years. But by the road, the distance was nearly double, and because there had been rain during the night, going was slow.

So was pulling information out of Master Baldwin. He still refused to reveal the exact nature of the missing item.

" 'Twas something meant to be presented to the queen," he allowed after considerable badgering on Susanna's part, "to be given to her once certain diplomatic goals have been met. I do but hold it in trust for someone else."

With further encouragement, he was persuaded to talk about his travels. A merchant adventurer, he'd only lately returned from Persia where, to hear him tell it, he'd been the first Englishman to set foot in that far-off land, arriving there a full two years ahead of the merchants of the Muscovy Company. He'd been to the court of Tsar Ivan the Terrible, and that of Shah Tahmasp of Persia, and met someone called Abdullah Khan, King of Shirvan. In all, Master Baldwin had spent six and a half years out of England and come home a wealthy man.

When they at last arrived at his house, Baldwin escorted Susanna and Jennet to a private chamber on an upper floor. From Jennet's look of surprise, and by the way she peered with such curiosity into every corner, Susanna concluded that her housekeeper had not had an opportunity to explore this part of the premises on her earlier visit.

There were many charts and maps on the walls, and the London Man kept other treasures in chests and on tables. The display was comprised of an odd collection of objects, some of which Susanna could not identify.

"Navigational instruments I brought back from my travels," he said, noticing the direction of her gaze. "Your husband found them as fascinating as you seem to."

She was about to ask more about the occasion of Robert's visit when Jennet let out a shriek. Her face was bright red with embarrassment. "I did not think it was alive," she stammered, pointing toward a creature perched atop a silk-covered cushion on the window seat. "And then it opened one eye and stared at me."

"It" was a cat, larger that those Susanna was accustomed to. It was covered with long, white fur.

"His name is Bala," Master Baldwin said of the odd-looking beast. "I brought him back from Persia, too."

Bala continued to stare at them with baleful eyes while Master Baldwin retrieved a small, ornately carved ivory box from a chest and handed it to Lady Appleton. "The queen's gift was kept in this."

"Jewelry," she said. "Of what description?"

"What makes you think it was a jewel?"

"Simple enough. I watched you search Leigh Abbey, saw where and in what you looked. Together with the size of the box, I perceive the object you seek may be contained in a space no bigger than the palm of your hand. Add to that conclusion all you told us of your travels and my deduction is reasonable. Everyone knows that traders carry valuable jewels to exchange for other goods. The first Muscovy merchants took pearls and sapphires and rubies with them, and travelers to the East regularly bring back jasper and chalcedony."

"It is not a jewel, as it happens, but I cannot fault your logic. You are a most ... unusual woman."

"Unusual enough to prompt you to tell me what was stolen?"

Baldwin came very near a smile. " 'Twas a carved stone of great age and beauty. The like has never been seen in England ere now."

"Why do you think Jennet took this ornament?"

"She was the only one with opportunity, unless you wish me to accuse your husband."

He smiled.

Susanna did not.

She'd known for years that her husband had ... flaws. It was possible, though it seemed unlikely, that he had removed something he should not have from Master Baldwin's house.

"I discovered the stone missing this morning," Baldwin continued, "The last time I lifted the lid of this box, Sir Robert stood beside me."

For a moment, Susanna thought she heard something in Baldwin's voice, a hint that it had not been Jennet he'd first suspected, but Robert.

"You did not check to be certain it was still there as soon as he left? How careless of you, Master Baldwin." To avoid meeting his eyes, she crossed the room to the window seat to make a closer inspection of the odd-looking cat. The fur was passing soft to the touch.

Her mild sarcasm had Baldwin blustering. "I had been advised, by someone high in Her Majesty's government, that the head of the household at Leigh Abbey could be trusted."

"Whoever told you that, he's more likely to have meant Lady Appleton than Sir Robert," Jennet blurted.

Baldwin trained his intense gaze on the housekeeper. "You are a strange sort of servant," he told her.

Deciding he'd had enough of a stranger's attentions, the cat Bala abruptly rose and leapt down from his cushion. A moment later, he began to play with a lightweight wooden disk. A checker, Susanna realized. Part of a set.

"I have been looking for that," Baldwin muttered, stooping to retrieve it. "This is yours," he told the cat, and tossed a square of canvas stuffed with pungent-scented catnip toward the center of the room.

Bala ignored the offering.

Susanna smiled. If Master Baldwin was the sort to make toys for a pet, there was hope he might yet learn to appreciate the advantages of individuality in servants and to value intelligence in women. The best way to convince him was to solve the mystery of his missing carving.

"What does your stolen stone look like?"

Still watching the cat, he answered her. "In color it is an intense apple green. No more than six barleycorns high, it has been wondrous well-carved and fashioned into a little figure of a horse."

Jennet would have no interest in such a thing, Susanna realized, but Robert was uncommon fond of horses. After a thoughtful silence, she began to muse aloud. What was most important at the moment was to clear her housekeeper of suspicion.

"Although I see no sign that anyone broke into this room," she said, "you must agree it is scarce secure. The window is an easy climb from the ground. The stone might have been taken at any time since you showed it to Robert. Tell me, was it in this chamber that he inspected the piece?"

"We took the box with us when we went down to the winter parlor near the kitchen, where my cook had set out a modest repast. It was there that your housekeeper was seen, Lady Appleton, though none of my servants thought to mention her presence to me until after I discovered the carving was missing and began to question them."

Master Baldwin led the way to the lower floor, with even Bala following after him, but the cat soon tired of their company and left the winter parlor by way of another open window.

"When is Jennet supposed to have had opportunity to steal the carving?" Susanna asked. "When was the box out of your possession?"

"I left it on the table when I bade Sir Robert farewell. I saw him off, through the front of the house, then returned here to collect the stone."

So, he had not looked again into the box. To clear Jennet, all Susanna had to do was accuse Robert.

Instead she asked for a few days to consider the problem, hinting that the local folk would confide in her, where to Master Baldwin they would plead ignorance. "You are a foreigner in their eyes."

"Aye," he agreed. "A London Man."

✝

"Well, Jennet?" Lady Appleton asked when they were well on their way back to Leigh Abbey. They had sent the horses on ahead with the groom and taken the footpath. No one was in the wood to overhear what they might say to each other.

"I did not take the little horse."

"But you were at Master Baldwin's house the day Sir Robert visited him."

Reluctantly, Jennet nodded.

"And you were in the parlor."

"Aye. How could I not be curious when I heard Sir Robert's voice?"

"So you crept out of the kitchen and hid yourself, so that you might listen to whatever he said to Master Baldwin."

Jennet did not try to deny it. Susanna knew her ways too well. "When they left the little box behind, I wanted to see what was in it. I dashed across the room and opened the lid to peep inside."

"And was the stone there?"

"Oh, aye, but I scarce had time to admire it before I heard Master Baldwin returning. I closed the lid again and hid myself in the alcove behind the wall hanging until Master Baldwin collected his box and carried it away. Then I left his house and came straight home."

So, the carving had still been in the box when Robert left.

"What do we do now, madam? I find it passing unpleasant to be thought a thief."

And she did not like suspecting Robert, but she knew her husband well. Though she could not guess his motive, she accepted that it was within the realm of possibility that Robert had returned to Baldwin's house and stolen the stone from the upper chamber.

She would find the truth, she vowed. She was just not certain what she would do with it when she did.

✝

Sir Robert Appleton had given his wife no reason to expect him to return to Leigh Abbey before he left the country on his latest mission for the Crown, but he was there when Susanna and Jennet reached home. Susanna found him in the study, just lifting down the *mappa mundi* to get at the wall behind it.

"I thought you were to set sail from London," she said as he removed a panel to reveal his accustomed hiding place for small valuables.

"I must cross the Narrow Seas to meet my ship off the coast of France." Leigh Abbey was on the road between London and Dover. To break the journey there was not suspicious in itself, but Susanna could not like this new development.

"You had best make haste," she advised, "before you are arrested."

The glance he shot at her over his shoulder conveyed annoyance. Theirs had been an arranged marriage, and although they managed as well as most couples, nowadays there was little love between them and less liking. "Have you some particular reason to think I will be?"

In clipped sentences she told him of Master Baldwin's visit and his search of the house. She did not, however, mention that it had been Jennet he'd accused of theft.

A furrow appeared in his high forehead, centered between an escaping lock of dark, wavy hair and equally dark brows. Something disturbed him in her report, but she was not certain that meant he had stolen the carving himself. Being accused was reason enough for worry.

"What was in that box was intended as a gift for the queen," Robert said after a moment. "It was to have been given to Her Majesty after the men of the Muscovy Company, with whom Baldwin was associated in his youth, make the first official contact with the Shah. Baldwin's visit to Persia was not authorized."

Susanna waited, letting the silence lengthen until he was driven to fill it.

"The theft of that piece could thwart a political alliance between England and Persia."

"Who would want to do that?"

"You have no need to know."

"I have every need if blame falls on anyone at Leigh Abbey. What was your business with Master Baldwin? Why did he show you the carving?"

"I tell you, madam, that is none of your concern."

As Susanna watched, unable to subdue the anger his attitude provoked, Robert removed a number of oilskin wrapped papers from the opening behind the panel and tucked them into the front of his dark green doublet. Then he reached in again for something smaller, which he likewise tucked away beneath the heavily embroidered velvet garment. She blinked. Had he just palmed the little horse?

She wished she'd looked behind the map before he returned. No woman wanted proof her husband was a thief, but not knowing one way or the other was far worse. Perhaps she had been too clever earlier, diverting Master Baldwin's attention from the map with her sarcastic suggestion that he might find a hiding place behind it. She had not suspected then that Baldwin might have his own doubts about Robert's honesty. Now she realized that by accusing the servant rather than the master, he'd achieved the same end, a search of Leigh Abbey, with far less opposition.

When Sir Robert's hiding place was once more concealed, he approached his wife. "Farewell, my dear," he said, and catching her to him for a rough, parting kiss before she could evade him. "I have no time to deal with our new neighbor. You must take care of the matter as you see fit."

He knew she took seriously the vows she'd made when they wed. She had sworn to obey him. Echoes of his taunting laughter lingered in the room long after he'd gone.

Susanna did not follow after her husband to see him away on his journey. The days were long past when she'd felt obliged to offer the traditional stirrup cup and blessing.

Instead she stared at the map. In her mind, she saw Robert reaching into the wall that second time. To take something small out? Or to put something in?

Master Baldwin had said the little carving was no more than six barleycorns high. She glanced down at her own hand. Strong and work-hardened, the nails blunt, the skin stained with the residue of various herbal preparations, it was large enough to conceal a object that size. A hand half the size could do so. It followed that Robert might easily have concealed the little horse from her just now.

Susanna knew the nature of professional intelligence gatherers, her husband in particular. They tended to complicate matters which otherwise would have been most simple. It would be just like him, she decided, to put back the carving while trying to make her believe he'd removed it. Her mind full of possibilities, she took a step closer to the map.

†

Early the next morning, Susanna once again followed the footpath, this time walking from Leigh Abbey to Master Baldwin's property alone. She paused to examine several likely places along the way, the last just at the point where the path came out of the wood and plunged steeply downward toward the manor house.

Barely a quarter of an hour later, when Master Baldwin joined her in his winter parlor, she handed him the missing horse. His fingers curled tight around the apple-green stone, he waited for her explanation.

"You said, did you not, Master Baldwin, that you left the box containing that stone unattended while you escorted mine husband to the door?"

"Aye, I did."

"And the box was not locked?"

"No. I did not turn the key until I returned. You know already that I did not look inside."

"And Bala, I perceive, is a very clever cat."

"Bala?" He blinked at her in surprise.

"The cat took your little carved stone."

"Bala?" he repeated, thunderstruck.

"I found that carving along the footpath that runs between this house and Leigh Abbey," she explained. "It is small and lightweight. Easy enough for a cat to carry off in its mouth. When Bala tired of it, he must have dropped it there, where it could not be easily seen for the ruts and twigs and leaves."

"I did not search along any path," Baldwin admitted. "I did not realize there was one connecting our two properties until yesterday."

As she'd expected, Susanna thought.

Baldwin abruptly crossed the room to where the large white feline slept atop a carpet-covered table. There was no question in Susanna's mind that the cat could have done what she'd said he had. And she knew that he, in common with all cats, must roam far and wide in search of mice and other prey.

"This cat was well named," Baldwin muttered. "In the language of Persia, Bala means nuisance."

For a moment, Lady Appleton feared Master Baldwin might harm the animal. He picked Bala up and held him at arm's length, but all he did was give him a hard stare. Then, shaking his head, he cuddled him in his arms as he turned to face his neighbor.

The show of affection wrenched at Susanna's heart. She was suddenly very tired of cleaning up after Robert, of allowing him to take the credit for her accomplishments, of letting him shift the blame for his less honorable actions to others. And she had never liked lying.

Did she dare tell Master Baldwin that the carving had been behind the map? That Robert had by stealth entered the upper room of this house and stolen the stone? When he'd believed his theft discovered, he'd shown no remorse, only left his wife, as always, to clean up after him, to "take care of the matter" as she thought best.

Words came out in a rush. "Bala did not —"

"Mean to cause so much trouble," Baldwin finished for her. "I am well aware of that. Perhaps you will allow me to send a small gift to your house-keeper, by way of apology?"

"She would appreciate that, but I —"

This time he held up a hand to stop her. "The end result is the same. Through your involvement, your desire to protect those close to you, I have the carving back. 'Tis best we say no more about it."

The look in his eyes brought to an abrupt end any need to confess. It was a curious mixture of triumph and compassion.

For that brief moment, Lady Appleton and the London Man shared a perfect understanding of the truth.

A Note from the Author

"Persian" cats originally came from Turkey. They did not yet have the flat-faced look associated with the breed today. In the sixteenth century they were a popular export from Persia and Turkey to Muscovy, and although I do not know of any that made the journey to England that early, there is no reason someone associated with the Muscovy Company could not have brought one back with him.

Lady Appleton and the Cautionary Herbal

A horn sounded to announce the arrival of a post boy at Leigh Abbey, a not uncommon occurrence since the manor house stood so near the main road from London to Dover, one of the most traveled highways in Elizabeth Tudor's England. He was gone again before Susanna, Lady Appleton, reached the gate-house, but he had left a package. She eyed it with mild surprise. Although she was in regular correspondence with a goodly number of friends and acquaintances throughout the kingdom, they rarely exchanged anything but letters.

Puzzled, she hefted the parcel. Nothing on the outer wrapping, which was slightly torn, hinted at who might have sent it, but the size and shape left little doubt she'd find a book inside. Her fingers trembled as she undid the string that bound it. The world thought her a widow, but she knew in her heart that her deceitful, traitorous husband still lived. She feared this might be some sort of communication from him.

To her astonishment, the package contained an inexpensive, unbound, fo-lio copy of the volume she herself had written. *A Cautionary Herbal, being a compendium of plants harmful to the health* was the result of many years of research. Susanna had been motivated to compile it by her younger sister's untimely death following the consumption of some harmless-looking berries that had, in fact, been poisonous.

As she retraced her steps to the house, Susanna tried to think who might have sent the book to her and why. It had not, she concluded, come from Sir Robert Appleton, who had disappeared just a year earlier. If he'd wished to communicate, he'd have sent a quite different book. But her relief was tempered by perplexity. That she was the author of this little herbal was no great secret, but on the title page the work was attributed only to "S.A." and her identity, or so she'd always believed, was not widely known.

Since no note accompanied the volume, Susanna carried it into her study and began to turn the leaves, looking for anything written in the margins. She found not a single annotation but she did make another sort of discovery – a jagged edge where a single page had been torn out.

The entries were alphabetical and each had a drawing opposite. The missing text had detailed the properties of hemlock, a particularly deadly poison. In ancient Athens it had been used for state executions.

"Most troubling," she murmured. Still carrying the book, she went to the window to stare out at fields, where the summer ploughing had begun, and orchards filled with apple trees in full flower and the last of the cherries. She found no solace in the peaceful vista, nor did the sight provide any answers.

A jangle of keys warned Susanna that Jennet, her housekeeper, had entered the chamber. She stopped short when she caught sight of her mistress's expression, then crept closer. She had to peer upward to see Susanna's face clearly, for the lady of Leigh Abbey was uncommon tall. She had inherited that characteristic, along with her intelligence, her sturdy build, and the square set of her jaw, from her father. Jennet, although of middling height for a woman, stood somewhat shorter. She was a blue-eyed, pale-skinned, fair-haired, small-boned individual who had gone from slim to plump in the course of giving birth to three children. She had never, in all the years she had served Lady Appleton, been shy about asking questions or expressing her opinions.

"What is the matter, madam? What has happened?"

Before Susanna could answer, Jennet caught sight of the herbal. She had no difficulty recognizing it or perceiving, as anyone in the household would, that it was not one of the copies housed at Leigh Abbey. Those were all bound in expensive hand-tooled leather.

"Someone sent this to me," Susanna said.

"Who?"

"It could have been anyone. It is not difficult to purchase a copy."

Indeed, it had been Susanna's hope when she wrote the slim volume that it would be readily available to all those who needed it. She'd collected information on poisonous herbs for the benefit of housewives and cooks, those most likely to mistake one plant for another and accidentally poison an entire household.

"Madam, what is it?" Alarm made Jennet's voice sharp. "Your face has of a sudden gone white as a winding sheet."

Susanna felt for a stool and sat. "I feared this might come to pass," she whispered as a wave of dismay and guilt swept through her.

She'd realized soon after her book was published than in her effort to do good, she had also gathered together a collection of recipes that could be used by an evildoer intent upon harm. This herbal designed to protect the unwary, in the wrong hands became a manual for murder. Did the package she'd just received mean *A Cautionary Herbal*, compiled in order to save lives, had been used to take one?

Susanna lifted the folio and stared at it, seeking in vain for answers. When she at last put it aside, she was determined to reason out who had sent it to her and why.

The postboy had come from London. She knew that much. And London was also the most likely place for her herbal to have been purchased. But was sending the book an announcement of a crime already committed or a challenge to her to prevent murder? If there was any chance she could do the latter, she knew she had to attempt it.

"We must go to London," she told Jennet. "At once."

†

John Day had printed Susanna's herbal. His premises in London were in Aldersgate. Literally. His printing house was set against the city wall. His shop and warehouse and his lodgings in the churchyard were attached to the gate. From the outside, he did not appear to have much space to conduct business but the buildings extended backward and Susanna knew, from a previous visit, that there was a fine garden hidden away behind them.

There were many such pleasant places in London, did one but know where to find them. On this bright mid-June morning, however, Susanna was only interested in answers. Accompanied by Jennet and one of Leigh Abbey's grooms of the stable, she entered Day's place of business.

The rattle and clash of presses assaulted their ears as soon as they stepped through the door. An inking ball stuffed with feathers brushed the top of Susanna's French hood. She wrinkled her nose at its pungent smell and took note of the location of several more of these offensive objects, which had been suspended from the ceiling in order to be in easy reach of Day's apprentices. A similar stench also emanated from the freshly printed pages draped for drying over lines strung between the presses.

As Susanna searched the huge workroom for Master Day, her gaze took in piles of quartos and pamphlets, already assembled and stacked on tables, and shelves piled high with boxes of movable type. The printer himself, a tall, thin man with a face like a basset hound's, was at his hand press, so engrossed in producing an ornate title page from a finely engraved copper plate that he did not notice Susanna until she called out his name.

At once, he abandoned his task. When she requested that they speak together in private, he escorted her to a comfortable parlor in his lodgings and settled her in his best chair.

"I came here, Master Day," she told him, "hoping you know what persons have of late bought copies of my book."

"I do not keep a record of the names of purchasers, Lady Appleton." With ink-stained fingers, he began to pleat the fabric of his long canvas apron. "And, indeed, my stock for the most part goes to booksellers."

Her question had made him nervous. She wondered why. "You do sell some individual copies. Do you remember if any recent customer behaved in an odd manner? Think, Master Day. Do you recall one who looked furtive? Or guilty? And was there someone, mayhap, who asked you to identify the S.A. who wrote my book?"

"I print many books, madam, and have many customers." The fabric of his apron was now as goffered as a ruff, convincing Susanna that he must know more than he would admit to.

"Well, then," she said with an exaggerated sigh, "there is no help for it. I must withdraw all remaining copies of mine herbal."

As she'd anticipated, Day was horrified by the possibility of lost profit. "You cannot be serious, madam!"

"My work may have been used to do murder, Master Day."

Shock, but no surprise, showed in his features. "Surely the good your herbal may do far outweighs its potential to cause harm."

Although Susanna had reached that same conclusion during the two-day journey from rural Kent to London, she was not inclined to let Day off the hook so easily. "Someone sent a copy of my book to Leigh Abbey with one page missing," she told him. "I believe that person intends to commit murder. Or has done so already. Have you heard of any deaths by poisoning here in London in recent days?"

"Indeed I have not!" Day sounded indignant, but he could not meet her eyes.

"Then mayhap I am in time to prevent one."

Susanna waited, saying nothing more, letting Day's own conscience prick at him. The printer's nervousness increased visibly, causing him to abandon the stool on which he'd been perched and begin to pace. He paused by the window, through which drifted the scents of roses and honeysuckle from the garden below, then turned to glare at his unwelcome guest.

"What profit to save one life at the cost of another?"

"Explain yourself, good sir. I do not wish to bear responsibility for *any* death and I would think you'd feel the same."

"You ask me to vilify a person who has done naught but buy a copy of your herbal."

So he did suspect someone! Elated, Susanna had to struggle to keep her voice level. "No crime has been committed yet. I would have that remain true. But you must see that I need to investigate. If my suspicions are correct, if that torn page means someone contemplates murder, then how can I do nothing to stop it and still hope to live with myself? Give me a name, Master Day. Let me pursue the matter. You have my word that I will be discreet."

Day looked everywhere but at her.

"The book was *sent* to me." Using her most persuasive voice, Susanna rose from her chair and crossed to him to place one hand on his forearm. When he reluctantly met her eyes, she added, "Someone *wanted* me to know ... and to act."

Heaving a heavy-hearted sigh, Day capitulated. "Mistress Drood," he mumbled. "Wife to Ralph Drood the merchant. You will find his house on London Bridge, near the sign of the Golden Key." In his misery, his resemblance to a basset hound increased. "She is his third wife, Lady Appleton. Her predecessors died under most suspicious circumstances."

†

Once more accompanied by Jennet and the groom, Susanna went first to the church of St. Magnus, located near the north end of the Bridge. For some thirty years, all England had been required by law to register births, marriages, and deaths. Some did so more religiously than others but Susanna's luck was in. She found the entries she sought without difficulty. Day had been right. Drood had married his second wife only seven months after burying the first, and had wed the third within a month of the second's demise.

"A most unlucky fellow," said the rector who'd helped Susanna find the records.

"You know Ralph Drood?"

"Everyone knows Master Drood in this parish. He has given most generously to the church."

"A rich man, then?"

"Oh, aye."

Further questioning elicited the information that Drood imported iron, wax, ginger, woad, Spanish asses, herring, beaver, and wine. He exported grain and cloth, and on occasion acted as a moneylender. He had a fine house on London Bridge, five stories high and filled with servants.

"Two maids and a cook among them," the rector bragged, "and Master Drood has property in the country, too."

"Why, then, do you say he is unlucky?"

"Two years ago, he had a wife and son. Then the boy was overlaid and so died."

Overlaid. Susanna winced. Someone had rolled on top of him and he'd suffocated. As a cause of death it was not uncommon, not when an entire family often slept in the same bed. She frowned. This family was wealthy. The child should have been sleeping in a cradle by himself.

"A few weeks after," the rector continued, "the bereaved mother died. Pining for her infant, or so 'twas said."

"Pining," Susanna recalled, had been written down as "cause of death" in the register. It was a useful term, sufficiently vague to account for all manner of symptoms.

"Master Drood remarried without the customary year of mourning," she remarked.

"Aye, that he did. Well, why not?" The rector's defensive tone of voice reminded Susanna that Drood was a generous contributor to the parish coffers.

"And the second Mistress Drood?"

"Stifled to death."

Another ambiguous term, thought Susanna. "Do you mean that someone held a pillow over her face?"

Taken aback by the suggestion, the rector made haste to clarify. "She fell asleep in a closed room after lighting a charcoal stove to keep it warm. That was what the searchers determined."

The searchers were old women who examined bodies in order to report a cause of death to the authorities. They were untrained and ill-paid. Susanna put little faith in their skill. They could easily have made a mistake. More likely, she thought as she thanked the rector for his help and bade him farewell, they had been bribed to accept Drood's version of his wife's death.

†

London Bridge was entirely covered with shops, taverns, and houses, nearly 200 buildings crammed together with room in the middle for carts, horses, and pedestrians to pass. At either end, one could see that a river flowed beneath the structures, but once upon the bridge it seemed to be just another long street.

For that Susanna was grateful. The mere sight of choppy water could make her queasy. She'd taken the precaution, en route from Day's premises to St. Magnus, of taking a preventative made of ginger root and peppermint.

An elderly maid answered the door at Master Drood's impressive dwelling. She led Susanna into a parlor, then took Jennet and the groom off to the kitchen. Jennet already had her instructions. She was to question the servants while her mistress spoke with Mistress Drood. Later, they would compare notes.

Left alone to wait for her hostess, Susanna took stock of her surroundings. The room was lushly furnished with turkey carpets and heavy, ornately carved furniture. One oak chest in particular attracted her attention. The front had been inlaid with other woods in a design meant to depict the exterior of some elaborate building. Nonsuch, perhaps, the palace King Henry had built after destroying the village that had previously occupied the site.

She strode closer, curious to inspect the details. Too late, she realized that the open window above the chest looked directly down into the Thames. Swallowing hard, she backed away. Foolish, she chided herself, to grow so overwrought at the mere sight of the river below. But she did not go near the casement again.

"Lady Appleton?" a meek voice inquired. Mistress Drood was a pale-faced mouse of a woman in rose-color taffeta too fine for her station. She was also rather older than Susanna had expected her to be. She looked frightened.

"Mistress Drood, I have come here to help you."

This comment seemed to surprise Mistress Drood. "I do not understand you."

"I believe you sent this to me." Susanna produced the herbal, which she'd brought with her in a pouch.

Mistress Drood's eyes widened, making it clear to Susanna that she recognized it, but she was still loath to admit anything. "Why would I do that?" she asked.

"Because I compiled this herbal. The initials S.A. represent Susanna Appleton."

"I did know that," Mistress Drood acknowledged.

"How?"

Flustered, the woman wrung her hands and kept her eyes downcast. "Master Baldwin told us. He supped with us one day last month and mentioned that his neighbor in Kent had written a book. He was mightily impressed by your scholarship, Lady Appleton."

One mystery solved, Susanna thought. Nicholas Baldwin, merchant of London, owned lands adjoining the Leigh Abbey demesne farm. And he did know she was the author of the herbal. She hastily repressed the small burst of pleasure she felt at learning he thought well of her for it. She was not here to garner praise.

"I believe you then bought a copy of my book," she said. "This copy."

Mistress Drood's head lifted. Her eyes were wide. "Oh, no, Lady Appleton! I did not do that."

"You did," Susanna insisted. John Day had identified her and he'd had no reason to lie. "Why?"

Tears welled up in Mistress Drood's eyes. "It was Master Drood's idea. He sent me to the printer to purchase a copy."

"Why?"

"Oh, Lady Appleton. He taunts me with it. He plans to kill me using one of the poisons you wrote about." Mistress Drood began to sob.

It was as she had feared, and yet something about Mistress Drood's tale did not ring true. "Who tore out the page?"

"He did. Oh, he did! And let me see that he'd done it, too. He means to torment me, to make the last days of my life a misery before he acts."

Made even more skeptical of these histrionics, Susanna studied Drood's wife. Most peculiar behavior, she thought, but she could not deny the woman's obvious distress. She led her to the window seat and made her sit, careful to avoid looking out as she did so.

The words barely audible between sobs, Mistress Drood admitted to sending the herbal to Leigh Abbey and added that she'd done so because she wanted Susanna's help.

"But you sent no message with it, gave me no hint of who you were or what troubled you."

"I ... I did send a note. It must have fallen out of the parcel."

Susanna frowned. Could a note have become detached? The wrapping *had* been torn.

"Why lie about it, then, when I arrived? If you sent for me, you must have hoped I'd come."

With a lacy handkerchief she'd fished out of one sleeve, Mistress Drood patted her damp cheeks. "I was not thinking clearly. I feared my husband might recognize you. I did not precisely send for you, you see. I wrote to ask what that page contained and to request the antidote for whatever poison was upon it. I ... I thought you would send a reply."

Susanna considered that. "You might have done better to go to Master Day and purchase another copy of my book."

The tears had ceased, but Mistress Drood's voice still had a hitch in it. "I ... I did not dare. Master Drood might have heard of it. Then he'd have acted at once. As it is, I think … I think he is waiting."

"Waiting for what?"

She made a fluttery gesture with one hand. "Midsummer's Eve. Less than a week away."

Nonsense, Susanna thought, but she kept that reaction to herself.

"Ralph Drood killed his first two wives and got away with it," Mistress Drood said. "He believes he can do so again and this time he means to employ poison."

Susanna had no difficulty accepting that Drood had gotten away with murder. Criminals with powerful connections often did, especially those who had sufficient money to pay bribes. What troubled her was the suspicion that Mistress Drood had plans to strike first − to kill her husband before he could murder her.

She felt a reluctant sympathy for the woman. Mistress Drood clearly believed her own life was at risk. Naught but desperation could have driven her to contemplate murder.

The woman did not look capable of harming a flea, but appearances could be deceiving. Even Susanna herself had once contemplated an act that would have brought about another's death. She had found the strength to resist in her deeply ingrained belief that anyone who exacted revenge by murder became as great a sinner as the person who'd committed the original crime.

She frowned at the memory.

Then again, Mistress Drood might be telling the simple truth. Had she sent to Leigh Abbey for an antidote? Perhaps, Susanna thought, that *was* all she wanted − the means to save herself.

"Let us discuss your husband," she said. "What profit to him in your death?"

"Money."

"But he is already wealthy."

"To Ralph Drood, there is no such thing as too much money. He always wants more. That is the only reason he married me. When I'm gone, he can wed yet again, collect another dowry from some poor unsuspecting father burdened with a spinster daughter."

"Can you go back to your father's house?" That might buy time to conduct a proper investigation of Drood's actions.

Mistress Drood shook her head. "My father is as great a brute and bully as mine husband. He'd insist I return. And you need not suggest that I run away to friends. I have considered that. Master Drood would find me and force me to come back. He is too rich and has too many powerful friends. I am doomed, Lady Appleton, unless you can give me an antidote to keep always at hand."

Susanna had powerful friends of her own. One in particular might be able to help her prove it if Drood was a murderer. "How can you be certain your husband killed his first two wives?" she asked. "Both cases were written down as accidents."

"I know they were murders." Mistress Drood spoke with convincing fervor. "He bragged to me of his deeds. He smothered one with a pillow. The other he starved to death."

"The law –"

"The law! Neither sheriff nor justice of the peace will act against him. He has the money to pay the most exorbitant bribe. Please, Lady Appleton. I beg of you. Tell me how to keep myself from being poisoned. What was on that page?"

Susanna sighed. "Hemlock."

"How may I recognize it?"

"The seeds might be mistaken for anise, the leaves for parsley. All parts of the plant are deadly, but the most powerful poison comes from juice extracted just as the fruit begins to form. This usually occurs toward the end of June."

"Around Midsummer Day?" Mistress Drood asked.

"Yes."

"He will no doubt try to give it to me in a drink."

"It has a most bitter taste."

"Could that be disguised by herbs?"

"Perhaps. Hemlock also has a disagreeable odor. A sort of mousy smell."

"And the antidote, should I notice these warning signs too late?"

"There is no sure antidote. There may be some small hope of survival if you empty your stomach at once. Some say that nettle seeds, taken inwardly, can counteract the poison, but I am not convinced they would be of any use. Hemlock is very potent and acts quickly. Few people, Mistress Drood, have ever cared to experiment on themselves, or others, to determine the efficacy of an antidote."

"Would my death look like an accident?" Drood's wife seemed to grow more calm with each bit of information Susanna provided.

"Aye. It well might."

Before Mistress Drood could ask any more questions, the slam of a door below and a series of sneezes alerted them to the return of her husband. "You must go," she whispered, panic evident in every nuance of her voice. "Hurry!

Leave before he sees you, before he hears your name. It will go hard on me if he finds you here."

"Do nothing," Susanna warned as she was hustled out the back way. "Trust me to find a way to help you."

From the street outside, where she waited for Jennet and the groom to join her, Susanna heard Master Drood berating his wife. The words were indistinct, but there was no mistaking his foul temper. It seemed to get worse every time he was seized by a fit of sneezing.

"The cook says Master Drood sneezes for weeks at a time at this season of the year," Jennet remarked, appearing suddenly at her mistress's side.

Inhaling crushed basil might help, Susanna thought, but she felt no inclination to offer that helpful suggestion. "Do the servants think he killed his first two wives?"

"None of them seemed to care if he had. They are well paid and have a roof over their heads and food in their bellies. Their loyalty is to Master Drood, not his wife." Jennet might have said more, but they had reached the end of the bridge, where boatmen waited to be hired.

Susanna had to make a decision.

†

From the upriver side of London Bridge it was but a short ride in a wherry to reach the water stairs at Blackfriars. Throughout this brief journey, Susanna kept her eyes firmly fixed on the shore. Not even her special ginger and peppermint mixture could completely quell the unquietness in her stomach, but at least she did not disgrace herself by being sick. It helped to keep her mind blank. Jennet, accustomed to her mistress's difficulty with travel on water, did not distract her with speech.

Sir Walter Pendennis had his lodgings in Blackfriars, an enclosed precinct in the most westerly part of London. Once it had been a monastery, but in King Henry's reign it had been broken up into shops and dwellings. Near the north end of the former cloister was a door leading to the narrow stairs to Sir Walter's rooms. He lived above what had been the monks' buttery.

"My dear," Sir Walter greeted her when his manservant showed her in. "May I offer you some wine?" He insisted she sit in the comfortable Glastonbury chair he'd just vacated.

"Something restorative would be most welcome." As she remembered from a previous visit, a table by the window held a variety of drink. Sir Walter looked well, she thought, as he filled a crystal goblet for her. If he was a few pounds heavier than when she'd last seen him, he was tall enough and so broad-shouldered that his love of good food had not yet rendered him obese. He served her, then topped off a large, brown earthenware cup with ale for himself.

Revived by a few sips of fine Canary, calmed by the pleasant scent of marjoram flowers and woodruff leaves rising from the rushes underfoot, Susanna sketched out the bare bones of her tale.

"I know something of this man," Sir Walter remarked when Susanna completed a concise summary of the facts as Mistress Drood had presented them.

"That you have heard his name is ominous in itself. Is Drood spy or smuggler?"

He might well be both if Sir Walter took an interest in him. Her old friend was the most prominent of the queen's intelligence gatherers, a man with considerable influence at the royal court. Susanna had decided to speak to him for that very reason, and because she knew he would not mock her concerns, as a constable or a justice of the peace or one of London's sheriffs might.

"I have no proof against him. Only suspicions." Sir Walter absently smoothed one hand over his sand-colored beard, dislodging a crumb of bread. "We want evidence."

"Evidence of what?"

To her surprise, he told her. "Clipping." At her blank expression, he clarified. "Clipping is a form of counterfeiting. For some men, there can never be enough wealth. They adulterate coin of the realm, scraping off some of the gold to sell, and then spend the clipped coins as if they had full value. In a case not long ago a woman clipped twenty half sovereigns, worth ten shillings each, by sixpence a piece."

"And Drood makes a practice of this?"

"Aye. He has done so for some time. Clipping was made a treasonous offense more than a century ago, but a loophole in the law has existed for the last ten years. It has only recently been closed and the Crown has been working ever since to apprehend those who profited in the interim."

Susanna did not need further explanation of Sir Walter's "loophole." She knew already that when the Catholic Queen Mary had come to the throne she'd nullified a great many laws, part of an attempt to overturn all that men of the New Religion had accomplished during the reigns of King Henry VIII and his short-lived son, Edward. As a result, the baby had often been thrown out with the bathwater.

"He is clever, our Master Drood," Sir Walter continued, "but if I can persuade Mistress Drood to help us build a case, we may catch him yet." He gave a wry chuckle. "A pity I cannot simply encourage her to poison her husband before he gets a chance to poison her. That would solve any number of problems."

Susanna gripped the arm of her chair so tightly that she left little pockmarks in the swath of blue velvet flung across it for padding. "How can you joke about such a thing? Murder is never justified! And you know as well as I do that Mistress Drood would at once be suspected if her husband died. At the slightest hint of foul play, she would be arrested for his murder, and tried, and executed, too."

With a courtly little bow, Sir Walter acknowledged her point, then resumed his former pose by the window, one shoulder negligently propped against the frame. "My apologies, my dear. You are right to admonish me. But what, then, would you have me do?"

"Prove Drood guilty of this clipping. As you suggest, Mistress Drood will be inclined to help you gather evidence against him. All you need do is explain the situation to her."

"I can offer her protection, and some sort of reward for her cooperation."

Encouraged, Susanna smiled at him. Clipping would be easier to prove than murder, and it carried the same penalty. "What can I do to help?"

"Go home."

When she started to protest, he held up a hand.

"Mistress Drood has already told you that her husband knows you wrote that cautionary herbal. To involve yourself further will only complicate matters, and possibly place you in danger. Besides, now that you have brought the situation to my attention, you may rely upon me to deal with it in the best manner possible."

Although his reassurances left her far from quiet in her mind, Susanna accepted the argument that she would get in the way of an official investigation. She might even compromise it. "You'll arrest Drood as soon as you can?"

"I swear it."

With that she had to be content, but she had no intention of going home until matters were settled. She returned to temporary lodgings at the Blossom Inn to await developments.

†

"Well, Jennet," Susanna said a short time later, kicking off her shoes and putting her feet up, "we have done a good day's work."

"Yes, madam," Jennet agreed. "Were you still wanting to know what the servants said?"

"We have not yet had the opportunity to compare notes, have we?"

Jennet had overheard Susanna's discussion with Sir Walter, but it was plain she was far from satisfied. In her effort to be brief and to the point, Susanna had left out a good many details. For Jennet's benefit, she now recounted her conversation with Mistress Drood in full. By the time she finished, Jennet was chewing industriously on her lower lip, a sure sign she was troubled.

"What?"

"Perhaps nothing, madam. Servants do like to exaggerate their own importance." She had good reason to know that, being a mistress of the art herself.

"Let me decide. What did you learn from the maids?"

"One of them is an elderly woman named Joan. She came to the household with the first Mistress Drood and stayed on."

Susanna nodded, remembering the servant who had admitted them. "Nothing odd in that."

"She knew who you were. Said she'd been hoping you'd turn up. Said *she* was the one sent the herbal to Leigh Abbey. Said she knew you wrote it because she overheard Master Baldwin say so to Master Drood. Said she'd also heard you were clever at figuring things out."

"Did Master Baldwin say that, too?" Susanna thought it unlikely. He'd not have wanted to explain how he knew.

"Joan said she'd heard that from a certain ... person in Southwark."

"Oh," said Susanna. She did have friends in Southwark ... of the disreputable sort.

"Joan said she does not know how to write, so she sent the herbal without any message. She got the rector of St. Magnus to write your name and Leigh Abbey, Kent, on the wrapping. Said I could ask him, if I did not believe her. Said she hoped you would know what to do about Mistress Drood."

"Mistress Drood says *she* sent me the book." But at first she'd seemed confused about that, Susanna remembered.

"Joan said Mistress Drood bought the book and tore out a page, then discarded the rest. Joan found it. She cannot read, but she could see by the illustrations what the book was about. She thinks Mistress Drood means to poison her husband. Joan is not pleased by that. She fears she'll be turned out once Mistress Drood is in charge."

Susanna's feet hit the floor with a thump. Beset by a terrible sense of urgency, she donned her discarded shoes. "We must go back to Master Drood's house."

If Joan was telling the truth, if Mistress Drood had planned all along to kill her husband and not the other way around, then Susanna's unexpected visit, followed so closely by the one Sir Walter had by now paid, might provoke her to act precipitously.

If murder for gain was Mistress Drood's purpose, it would not suit her to have her husband executed. That would make her a widow, true enough, but in cases of treason the crown seized all the traitor's property. Mistress Drood would be left penniless.

✝

They had most of the city to cross and as it was now late afternoon, progress was slow. The streets were thronged with people hurrying home to sup.

The house on London Bridge was in an uproar by the time they arrived. "My wife! My poor stupid wife!" Ralph Drood danced a little jig as he bellowed the words. There was nothing grief-stricken in his expression.

Neither was he a great hulking brute, as Susanna had imagined. Ralph Drood was a scrawny little man whose most prominent features were a bushy red beard and a nose and eyes made nearly as red by his fits of sneezing.

"We are too late," Susanna whispered to Jennet. "He has already poisoned her."

But there was no sign of Mistress Drood, alive or dead, in the house. Susanna returned to the parlor, this time noticing obvious signs of a struggle. Broken crockery and scattered papers littered the floor. The ornate chest she had noticed earlier, which had been centered beneath the window, had been shoved to one side.

Frustrated beyond caution, Susanna marched up to Drood and grabbed him by the front of his doublet. "What happened to your wife?" she demanded. "Where is she?"

For an instant she thought he would not answer. Then he laughed, a wild, triumphant sound, and pointed to the window. "She fell into the river and is surely drowned. A terrible accident."

"How long ago did this happen?"

"Just now. Just before you came in."

Without another word, Susanna released Drood and ran from the house, calling to her groom to follow. No one had searched the water for Mistress Drood. Why should they? Her own husband clearly wanted her dead. He had, in all likelihood, pushed her out that window. But if she had survived the fall, and if she had managed to stay afloat, there might yet be time to save her. More hope of it, Susanna thought, than if she'd swallowed hemlock.

Susanna put her own chronic fear out of her mind when she reached the end of the bridge. She signaled for a wherry. "Which way would the river carry someone who fell from up there?" She pointed toward the Drood house.

The waterman gestured downstream.

"Row that way, and quickly."

What followed was one of the most horrific journeys Susanna had ever endured. Her stomach in knots, her mind in equal turmoil, she had to force herself to scan the choppy water for any sign of Mistress Drood. All manner of watercraft moved with the tide. Among the larger crafts were barges of the type noblemen used and a "shout" that carried timber.

With the tide going out, Mistress Drood had not been swept into the giant pilings that supported the bridge, but there was plenty of debris in the water that might have been just as deadly. There were also dead dogs and cats and even a dead mule.

How could anything survive in this foul cesspit? Susanna wondered. At just that moment, she caught sight of a hand extending from a rose-colored sleeve and clinging to a piece of driftwood.

They hauled Mistress Drood's limp form into the wherry, but they were too late. She was no longer breathing and they could not revive her.

†

Sir Walter Pendennis was waiting at Drood's house when Susanna returned with the body.

"Can you find enough in a search to warrant his arrest for treason?" Tight-lipped, Susanna watched Walter's face as she waited for an answer.

"I *will* find proof."

His promise gave Susanna little satisfaction. She had failed to keep Ralph Drood from killing his wife. That he would be executed for other crimes would not bring back any of the unfortunate women who had been his spouses.

"Where is he?" she asked.

"In the room from which she fell. He has been drinking heavily since you left."

Drood looked up when they entered, never pausing in the act of broaching a new bottle and slopping wine into his goblet. He drank deeply, then waved the cup in Susanna's direction. "Most excellently spiced," he declared, and sneezed yet again.

Susanna's sense of smell was unimpaired. She had no difficulty identifying the contents of the goblet. Her heart began to beat a little faster.

Sir Walter Pendennis, royal intelligence gatherer, did not seem to notice anything amiss. His men had arrived. Instructing two of them to guard Drood, he led the remainder off to search the premises.

Drood continued to drink.

Susanna did nothing.

She estimated that a bit more than a quarter of an hour passed before Drood complained that his arm had gone numb. A little later, he began to feel pain in his muscles. Within an hour, he was barely able to move. He had lost all sensation in his limbs, as well as the ability to speak.

"Soon," Susanna told him, "you will also be blind, and yet your mind will function perfectly well. You will know what is happening to you. You will retain full consciousness until the last."

Sir Walter came quietly into the room as she was speaking, alerted to what was happening by one of the guards he'd left. "Did he kill the first two wives?"

"I am convinced he did." Everything pointed to it, even if the last Mistress Drood had lied about wanting Susanna's help.

Sir Walter bent over the dying man. "We'll never know for certain. He is past having the ability to speak. He cannot even move his head to nod or express denial."

"Mistress Drood was in no apparent rush to kill him," Susanna murmured, "until you threatened to arrest him and charge him with treason."

Sir Walter did not seem unduly disturbed by the notion. "She miscalculated when she provoked her husband's temper at just the wrong moment."

"She had the poisoned wine ready and waiting when they quarreled and he pitched her out the window. Then he celebrated her death by drinking the wine."

"A fine irony." Sir Walter stared down at Drood's almost lifeless body. "Such a death is just. A murderer should be forced to linger for many agonizing hours, to have ample time to understand that punishment has been exacted for his crimes."

Susanna sighed. She felt remorse, but no pity for the condemned man. "There will be an inquest, certes. I must —"

But Sir Walter held up a hand to silence her. "The searchers will give out that Drood died of a surfeit of drink. And you and I, my dear, were never here."

For just a moment, Susanna wondered if her old friend had done more than ask for Mistress Drood's cooperation. She decided she did not want to know. Neither did she have any desire to make public the fact that her book, written to save lives, could also be used to commit murder.

She had sought the truth. Belatedly, she had found it. Revealing it, she thought with a mixture of resignation and regret, would only make matters worse. Casting a last look at Master Drood before Sir Walter escorted her out of the room, out of the house, out of London, Susanna consoled herself with the only redeeming grace in all this tragedy.

Even without truth, there had been justice.

A Note from the Author

John Day (1522–1584) was a real person. This Elizabethan printer had a print shop, house, and probably a warehouse in the Aldersgate ward of London in the 1560s. Later he had a shop in Paul's Churchyard. Most famous of the books he printed was what was popularly called "the Book of Martyrs." John Foxe's *Acts and Monuments*, first published in 1563, was a runaway bestseller in those days. It detailed the persecution of Protestants by the Catholic Queen Mary.

In the 1570s, Day's stock of unbound works was valued at over £3000 and he had bound stock worth between £300 and £400. To give you an idea of relative wealth, it cost about £500 a year to run two presses, which could produce about two thousand pages. That includes the expense of ink, wages, and overhead. Paper for an edition of one thousand copies cost £350. A halfpence per sheet was the standard price of paper at retail. If Day sold all the copies at twenty-four shillings each, that amounted to a substantial profit.

As often happens when I write one story, something in it sparks an idea for another. I mention the cause of death "overlaid" in this one. Look for it to reappear later in this volume in "Lady Appleton and the Cripplegate Chrisoms."

The Riddle of the Woolsack

England, 1569

"Ho, there!" called a harsh voice. "A word with you."

A rook, startled by the sound, gave a hoarse caw and took flight.

Mark Jaffrey, steward for Leigh Abbey in East Kent, murmured a quiet command to his mount, then turned in the saddle to survey the scene at his left hand. He looked west across fields that undulated gently. Their golden-brown hue was in harmony with the bright, coral-colored leaves of the cherry trees in a small orchard near at hand and the yellow, scarlet, and umber of the wood beyond it. The old woman in dusty black, however, seemed out of place in the picture … and somehow ominous.

Mark patted the neck of his bay gelding, his fingers lingering on the smooth, warm horseflesh. Although he was as impatient as his horse to be off, he stayed put while the stooped, heavily-swathed figure trudged closer. There was nowhere he had to be in any rush. He had been bound for Eastwold, the nearest village, but without any pressing business to conduct there. What had driven him out of the house had been a sudden, fervent desire to escape the gloom that had eclipsed the manor following the departure of its owner, Lady Appleton, for foreign shores.

With Michaelmas just past and the harvest in, accounts had been rendered. It was a fallow time for fields and man alike. Mark knew he should be in the best of spirits. He and his family possessed good health. The estate had shown a profit. Instead, he had been discontent and had spent all this day sunk in a melancholy even the bracing, vaguely medicinal and bitter-sweet aroma of drying hops had not been able to dispel.

An encounter with a stranger would at least break the monotony.

The figure limping his way appeared harmless enough, but he had the sense to be wary. He fingered the pommel of the good, sharp knife he wore at his belt and had a moment's regret that he had not strapped a stout cudgel to the back of the saddle before he left home.

Of late the roads had become infested with beggars and vagabonds. Many of them were tricksters who painted on their sores and pretended to be crippled in order to cozen the softhearted out of more alms. Some traveled in packs, sending the weakest of their number to distract a traveler while the others got in place to attack him.

As steward, it was one of Mark's duties to offer aid to those in real need. He sent the other sort packing, and when sharp words were not sufficient to evict them from Leigh Abbey land, he used hard blows.

A faint odor of peppermint drifted up to him as the woman reached his side and pushed back the hood of her enveloping cloak. He stared down into narrowed eyes and a deeply-lined, scowling face.

"God save you, mother. What is your business here?"

"I came for to see Lady Appleton," the beldame declared.

"Then you made your journey to no purpose. She is gone from home and not like to return for some time."

Months, at the least, Mark reckoned, which was why his wife, Jennet, who was Leigh Abbey's housekeeper, had also been in a foul mood these last few weeks. Jennet had not wanted to accompany their mistress, but she did most bitterly resent being left behind.

Mark started to ease his mount around the old woman.

"Hold!" The crone moved with slow and ponderous steps but spoke with such purpose that it never crossed his mind to disobey. "Who might you be?"

"I am Lady Appleton's steward. I am in charge here in her absence." He grew hot under the old woman's steady scrutiny and the rising breeze did naught to cool his face. Instead it tossed locks of mole-colored hair against ears that were too big for his head, tickling the rims in a most annoying fashion.

"May be you'll do."

Mark frowned. He'd do? He was not certain he liked the sound of that. But before he could turn away and ride off, a hand swollen with age and infirmity closed around the horn of his saddle.

"Three days past, there were murder done."

†

Jennet Jaffrey had just finished setting the maids to work making candles when a groom brought word that her husband had returned to Leigh Abbey and wished to speak with her. Jennet frowned. He'd left but an hour earlier. If he was back already, then something must be wrong.

Her first thought was that there had been word from Lady Appleton. Or of her. Any journey by sea was perilous and after crossing to the Continent their mistress had meant to travel through the Netherlands, where England's enemies held sway. Heart racing, Jennet all but ran to the steward's office, where Mark had sent word he'd wait for her.

He was not alone. A stooped figure all in black stood next to him. Jennet blinked as she recognized the crone. At her sharp, indrawn breath, they both looked toward the doorway where Jennet stood.

"You!" the old woman exclaimed.

She was called Mother Sparcheforde and reputed to be a witch. The last time they'd met, she'd chased Jennet out of the grocer's shop she owned in Dover, hurling a curse after her. Now here she stood, bold as a Barbary pirate, just polishing off a cup of new-made perry.

"Why is she here?" Jennet demanded.

"Now, Jennet –"

"Blessings upon you, Goodwife Jaffrey." There was a malicious gleam in Mother Sparcheforde's eyes as she, too, recalled their previous meeting. On that occasion, Jennet had not revealed either her name or her purpose. She'd visited the old woman's shop hoping to glean information about her daughter, Alys Putney.

Jennet seized the pitcher away from Mark before he could refill Mother Sparcheforde's cup and slammed it down hard on his writing table. The quills in their container rattled against the inkwell and a little of the perry splashed onto an account book, scenting the air with the aroma of pressed pears.

Mother Sparcheford tossed away her empty cup, drew herself up as straight as she could with her widow's hump, and clenched her misshapen fingers around the equally gnarled branch she used as a walking stick. She swung it upward, not to defend herself from Jennet or to strike her, but as if to cast a spell.

Mark stepped between the two women. "Never mind what happened in the past," he said to his wife. "Mother Sparcheforde has come here seeking our help."

"I'd not give her the time of day. Nor to her daughter, neither." To show her utter disdain for both women, as well as her lack of fear – for, after all, Mother Sparcheforde's curse had come to naught – Jennet plopped down in the room's only chair, bouncing a bit as her bottom struck a cushion well-stuffed with wool.

"Jennet, Alys has been murdered."

At Mark's announcement, Jennet blinked in surprise, then voiced the first thought that came into her head. "No more than she deserved."

"Jennet, she was beaten to death." Taking Mother Sparcheforde's arm, Mark guided her to a comfortable padded bench, eased her onto it, then retrieved her cup.

Alys Putney, Jennet thought, had been a venomous creature. Once, when Jennet had been great with child, Alys had given her a vicious shove that had sent her tumbling to the ground. It was a miracle young Rob had been born unmarked.

Mark knew that, but he propped one hip against the corner of the writing table, crossed his arms over his chest, and sent Jennet a stern look. "Lady Appleton believes in justice, even for the unjust. Were she here, she would insist upon accompanying Mother Sparcheforde to Rye, where both Alys and Leonard Putney were of late found slain."

Alys *and* her husband? For a moment, Jennet was bereft of speech.

"Crowner got matters twisted," the old woman muttered. "Must have. Could not have happened the way he says."

"According to what Mother Sparcheforde has told me," Mark said, "the coroner's inquest ruled Alys's death a murder by persons unknown, and further declared that her husband took his own life out of grief."

Jennet frowned. Leonard Putney had been a violent man. People had said for years that he sent Alys out to whore for him, then beat her when she came home. It was not difficult to imagine that he might have gone too far and beaten Alys to death himself, but the rest of the explanation made no sense at all. "Even if Putney killed her, he'd never have taken his own life afterward."

"He'd have felt neither remorse nor guilt," Mother Sparcheforde agreed.

"He might have taken that course to cheat the hangman," Mark suggested.

"There are better ways to escape execution than self-murder." Jennet chewed thoughtfully on her lower lip as she considered the situation. A sympathetic jury might even have ruled he'd acted upon provocation and should not be punished at all for an attempt to discipline his wife. Or he could have avoided trial altogether by hiding her body and saying she'd run off with a lover.

Mother Sparcheforde spoke into the silence. "Sir Robert Appleton abandoned my Alys at his wife's bidding." The old woman's smile was horrible to behold, revealing rotted teeth and blackened gums. "If he had not, my daughter would never have married Leonard Putney. She'd be alive today. I say Lady Appleton owes it to my girl to find out the truth."

Jennet marveled at her reasoning. Alys Sparcheforde, before her marriage to Leonard Putney, had been the late Sir Robert Appleton's long-time mistress. He'd set her up in a house in Dover, only seven miles from Leigh Abbey, all but flaunting his infidelity to his wife.

"She owes you nothing." Jennet glared at Alys's mother.

"I hear things, I do. They say Lady Appleton did put herself at risk to help another unfortunate woman who was once her husband's mistress."

Jennet stifled a sigh. Although Lady Appleton had no obligation to those Sir Robert had wronged, she did seem to make a habit of involving herself in matters that affected their lives, helping those who needed her assistance. She *would* expect Jennet and Mark to look into Alys's death and to do all they could to make certain justice had been served.

"What is it you think we can do?" she asked.

"Go to Rye on my behalf. Say I sent you to run Putney's inn there. Ask questions. Discover whether my Alys was killed by her husband or by someone else, someone who may yet be punished for what he did."

Jennet's eyes met Mark's. The spark of interest there reflected what she felt – the first tingle of excitement at the prospect of an adventure. Each time Lady Appleton encountered trouble, Jennet swore she wanted no part of it, but the sweet taste of a puzzle to solve, a wrong to be made right, was as tempting as Xeres sack and twice as addictive.

When Mark rounded the writing table and took out paper, quill, and ink, Jennet knew he'd decided to do as Mother Sparcheforde asked. Whether he'd take her with him, however, was another matter.

"Where was Alys's body found?" Mark asked.

"In the common room of an inn in Rye called the Woman and the Woolsack. Leonard Putney owned it. Bought it after he sold the Star with the Long Tail in Dover. It belongs to me now."

"How did you come to inherit?" Jennet asked the old woman before Mark could frame his next question.

"There are no other heirs. All that was my daughter's must come to me."

Jennet was not so sure of that. "Are you certain you want to prove Putney killed Alys? If he did, then all his goods and chattels are forfeit to the Crown. You will get nothing."

The old woman looked smug. "If that be the truth, I will not challenge the crowner's verdict. Why should I when my daughter's murderer is already dead? But if both were slain by someone else, I can demand justice for my murdered child and still keep all Alys and her husband owned."

The sound of laughter reached them from the inner courtyard. Jennet's two girls played there with Lady Appleton's foster daughter. Jennet's chest tightened at the thought of what it must feel like to lose a child. And it must be that much worse to suspect that the person responsible was still at large. No matter that something besides maternal affection drove Mother Sparcheforde, Jennet's heart softened toward the other woman.

Mark cleared his throat. "The coroner's inquest ruled that Alys was beaten to death?"

Mother Sparcheforde nodded.

"How did Putney die?"

"They say he stabbed himself. A single wound to the chest."

"Were there any signs he'd been in a fight?"

Before Alys's mother could answer, Jennet interjected a question of her own. "Were his knuckles bruised?"

"I know not," the old woman replied. "You must question the crowner when you get to Rye."

"There will be a record of the coroner's inquest," Mark mused, "but if there is aught irregular about it, they'll not show it to strangers." Of a sudden, his brow creased and his fingers tightened on the quill. "What do you know of your son-in-law's dealings with land pirates?"

Jennet leaned closer, beset by curiosity and trepidation in equal parts. Land pirates were those who disposed of goods illegally brought into the country. According to certain merchants of Dover with whom Leigh Abbey did business, their brethren in Rye provisioned the sea rovers who regularly preyed on Dover shipping.

Mother Sparcheforde seemed reluctant to answer, but at length admitted that Putney might have been involved in the distribution and sale of contraband when he'd owned the inn in Dover.

"Here in Kent sugar and wine from pirate loot are bartered for powder and shot, salt beef, and bacon, then sent by packhorse to London," Mark said. "A profitable business. No doubt a similar trade exists in Sussex."

"There's motive for murder, then." Jennet felt her excitement grow as she considered the possibilities. A falling out among thieves. A rival land pirate seeking to take over Putney's operation.

"There also is danger." Mark set the quill aside and addressed his wife. "Anyone who seeks to investigate a murder ends by threatening other secrets."

"Too late to waver now," Jennet declared. "This riddle must have a solution." Before Mark could object further, out of worry for her safety, Jennet turned to Mother Sparcheforde and took over the interrogation. "What particular enemies had Leonard Putney? Who hated him enough to kill him?"

"Everyone who knew him." Another rusty cackle issued from the black-swathed figure. "Even his own wife."

"Because he beat her?"

"Beat her. Bullied her. Belittled her. And you've only to look at the name of the inn to see how he regarded her. Go to a place called the Woman and the Woolsack," Mother Sparcheforde said with great bitterness, "and you expect the innkeeper's wife to be a whore."

Jennet's sympathy was once again engaged. The old, crude riddle was well known: *When is a woman like a woolsack? When both are stuffed.*

†

Two days later, Mark and Jennet stood staring up at the inn sign. He'd wondered what it would depict. A sack full of wool and a woman being tupped could not have escaped the censure of the church, but there were more subtle ways to suggest the same ribald theme. Leonard Putney's sign showed a woman holding an empty woolsack in one hand and a chastity belt in the other. A large key dangled from the gold chain around her waist.

"Hmpf," was Jennet's only comment.

They went inside.

"Leonard Putney did well for himself." Jennet planted herself in the center of the common room and turned in a circle to survey the premises.

Mark had to agree with her assessment. It was a fine establishment.

"We'll need fresh rushes." Jennet stared hard at the spot where both Putneys had died – just by the door to the cellar, Mother Sparcheforde had said – then shrugged as if to say she'd scrub the floor later. There was only a small bloodstain. Putney had stabbed himself with suspicious neatness.

Apparently undaunted by her knowledge that so much violence had taken place here, Jennet set out to inspect every nook and cranny. Seeing the return of her natural enthusiasm, conspicuously lacking since Lady Appleton's departure for the Continent, Mark put aside his remaining doubts about the wisdom of this venture. He'd already half convinced himself that Putney had killed Alys. Rather than face trial and hanging, he'd committed suicide, for a bully could also be a coward.

This explanation of events pleased him. If it was the correct one, Jennet was in no danger. Mark could look forward to watching his wife enjoy herself while she came to the same conclusion he had.

"The mattresses will want airing, and –" Jennet broke off with a squeak as a section of wall moved under her hand.

"What the devil?"

" 'Tis the devil's work indeed! There is a hiding place here." Jennet poked her head inside, then sneezed.

When Mark brought a candle, they saw footprints in the dust of the narrow passageway beyond the opening. A ladder gave access to the chamber above.

Further exploration of the common room revealed a revolving cupboard, allowing for a rapid retreat into the street, and a door into the adjacent building, bolted from the other side. In addition, the Woolsack's back exit opened onto one of the estuaries that emptied into Rye's tidal bay.

"Convenient for unloading contraband," Mark said. "No doubt Putney dealt with free traders as well as freebooters."

Jennet chewed thoughtfully on her lower lip, as was her wont when she contemplated any perplexing matter. "I have heard the same tales as you — tubs full of smuggled goods buried on the cliffs above coastal towns. Tunnels that run from certain houses into nearby woods."

"The sand and shingle coasts of Romney Marsh, near to Rye, are well suited to such activities," Mark said. "Local merchants can avoid export taxes by sending their wool abroad illegally. And the prospect of importing wine from France or Crete without paying duty on it would appeal to any innkeeper, even an honest one."

They continued their inspection of the Woman and the Woolsack. Leonard Putney's larder contained deep wooden meal-tubs, flour barrels, salting tubs, and earthenware preserving jars. In a storehouse separate from the main building of the inn were quantities of dried, preserved, pickled, and barreled food. And in the cellar, a cavernous space beneath the common room, they found roundlets of ale and several barrels of wine.

"The contents of the inn must have been inventoried at the time of Putney's death," Mark said thoughtfully. "If I ask for a copy from Rye's coroner, it may be I will also find out more about the circumstances of Putney's death."

Jennet agreed this was a sound plan and sent him off in search of that official while she donned an apron and set about disposing of the old rushes.

Mark stopped first at another inn, the Mermaid, which a merchant of his acquaintance had told him was the finest hostelry in Rye. There, he thought, he would find men who knew their way about the town, men who might be willing to set a newcomer straight.

A dozen customers occupied the common room, presided over by a prosperous-looking fellow with an enormous mustache and three gold teeth. "William Didsbury at your service," he said to Mark. "I own this place."

"Then you are a man I am glad to meet." He introduced himself as a distant cousin to Alys Putney, sent by her mother to reopen the inn.

"This is a good town," Didsbury said as he poured Mark a mug of ale. "Our merchant shipping is on a par with that of Bristol and we average more sailings a month than Plymouth or Southampton. In addition, some twenty-five fishing vessels go daily to sea year round and twenty-four more set out in the season for conger and mackerel. Our fish are sent to London the same day they are caught. Freshest of any in England!"

During his short walk along the High Street to Mermaid Passage, Mark had seen one such packhorse train about to set out. Large baskets called dossers had been slung over the back of each beast. He took a long pull of ale, wondering if Didsbury wished to make some particular point.

"There is a forty shilling fine," Didsbury said when he returned from serving another customer, "for accommodating any light person, harlot, whore, or common woman."

Mark frowned. "I do not understand you, Didsbury."

"Your predecessor had a certain … reputation."

"Ah, I see. Do not confuse me with Leonard Putney. I may share his profession, but I do not share my wife's favors with any man."

"Not a dutchman are you?" asked a patron with a shock of bushy white hair. He meant, Mark knew, not a man born in Holland but one with extreme religious views.

Mark considered his answer. If there were smugglers present, he did not want to alarm them. "Just an ordinary innkeeper," he replied after a moment, "but I am curious about the death of the one who came before me."

Several more tankards of ale had to be emptied before the men in the common room began to talk freely, but every one of them seemed to be in agreement as to what had happened. Alys Putney had been killed by an unknown villain.

"A vagabond?" Mark asked. That was what Mother Sparcheforde had been told.

"Or a drunken mariner. 'Twas during the time the ports were closed and the town was overrun with sailors."

"Not her husband? I am surprised he was not suspected of killing her."

"Might have been," Didsbury told him, "had the circumstances been different, but her body was found and the hue and cry raised before Putney appeared on the scene."

Mark wondered how they could be so certain. An easy matter, he thought, to slip out of that inn through one of the hidden exits and return by the main entrance.

"When the mayor's sergeant arrived, he found two bodies instead of one," Didsbury explained. "It seemed clear that Putney found his wife and took his own life in a fit of grief."

Heads nodded throughout the common room. Mark tugged on his ear, thinking hard. No one seemed to be lying, but he had to wonder if any of these men had known Putney very well. Mark remembered the fellow as the sort to keep to himself. "Who found Alys?"

"The ostler," Didsbury told him. "Jack, he's called. No doubt he'll come looking for his old job back when he hears the inn's to reopen."

"My wife fears we'll be murdered in our bed," Mark said, knowing Jennet would forgive him the blatant lie, "by the same killer who attacked my cousin, or by some other vagabond." He drank deeply. "Are there many random killings here?"

The rush to reassure Mark left him more confused than ever. According to the stories he now heard, there were few cases of murder in Rye and in those that did occur arrests were made in good time. Executions, however, were rare. In most cases, the killer pleaded benefit of clergy, was branded, and went free.

Leonard Putney would not have had reason to fear the hangman's noose, or to kill himself. Unless he already bore a brand from some previous crime. It was time, Mark decided, to talk to the coroner.

John Breeds was also Rye's mayor. It was simple enough to find him and procure a copy of the inventory. On other matters, however, he was less forthcoming. Mark's carefully phrased questions about bruises on Putney's knuckles or brands on other parts of his body yielded nothing but evasion. The man was not about to admit he might have made a mistake. He even claimed he still sought the illusory vagabond who'd killed Alys Putney.

"You are a stranger here," he reminded Mark. "Let Rye men tend to Rye business."

†

The morning after Mark's effort to find answers it was Jennet's turn to ask questions. She set off just past sunrise intending to buy fresh fish in the marketplace, make inquiries about the whereabouts of Leonard Putney's ostler, and keep both eyes and ears open for gossip.

When her purchase was wrapped safe in her market basket, she strolled along quayside. The customs office was plainly marked, she noticed, and she wondered how the smugglers dealt with the royal customer. Bribes, no doubt. That was the usual way.

She turned to walk back to the Woman and the Woolsack and let out a startled squeak when she all but ran into a dark-skinned man clad in fantastical garb. The cloth wound around his head and the evil-looking curved sword tucked into the sash at his waist had her eyes widening in alarm and her heart pounding faster. Unable to look away after he passed by, ignoring her, Jennet watched him until he was out of sight.

"Faith!" she murmured when she dared breathe again. "When did Rye turn Turk?"

A soft laugh drew her attention to a woman just letting down the shutter at the front of her shop to form a counter. "They are harmless enough in town," she said as she set out her wares, "but I'd not give odds for your life or your property if you met him at sea."

Jennet moved closer, sniffing appreciatively at the fresh-baked pastries. "Do pirates walk the streets of Rye unchallenged, then? For I swear that fellow sails on a Sallee rover."

"If you've taken over Putney's inn," the shopkeeper said, "you must know already that customer, controller, and searcher all know how to turn a blind eye."

Jennet had but a moment to decide between feigned innocence and a worldly acceptance of such matters. "Toward free trade, yes. But that fellow was surely a pirate."

"The local justices cannot try pirates. Even were they to catch one in the act of robbing a ship in the harbor, they'd be obliged to bind him over to the Admiralty Court." She grinned suddenly, showing a gap between her two front teeth. "Not that it is to anyone's advantage to curtail the activities of sea rovers … so long as they only prey on foreign ships."

Foreign, Jennet supposed, to a citizen of Rye, would include those setting sail from ports in Kent.

She lowered her voice, even though there was no one close enough to overhear. "The Woman and the Woolsack – was it popular with known pirates when Leonard Putney owned it?" That he'd done business with smugglers went without saying.

"It was popular with Frenchmen," the woman said.

Jennet frowned. "Religious exiles?" Was there a motive for murder in that?

Politics? Intrigue? Intelligencers and secret messages in code? The ports had been closed when Putney died. Fear of invasion, she'd heard. But by whom? From where? Pray God, Jennet thought, that Alys and her husband had not been mixed up in that. She and Mark would never be able to sort out the truth if the Putneys had been involved in treason.

A woman came up to buy a loaf of bread, quickly followed by another goodwife. Jennet dug out a ha'penny and made her own purchase. Munching, she watched and waited until the shopkeeper was free, but by then she'd realized that any question she might ask would arouse too much suspicion. Better, she decided, to wait a bit.

"I must get back," she said instead, hefting her basket. "Frenchmen you say? I hope they like fish."

Even more, she hoped they'd have coin to pay for it. If Rye's immigrant population bore any resemblance to the poverty-plagued exiles who'd settled in Kent, they had no extra income to spend at an inn.

She got part of her answer as soon as she entered the Woman and the Woolsack. Putney's ostler had returned, a scrawny lad who had only enough English to understand orders that related to tending guests' horses.

"Did you question him about finding Alys's body?" she asked.

Mark gave her a look. "Unless your French is better than mine, I do not think we will learn anything useful from Jacques."

Jennet sighed, knowing he was right, and set about preparing food to serve their customers. They planned to reopen the inn in only a few hours time.

†

The first person through the door was a tall, broad-shouldered, big-bosomed female with lank yellow hair and a prominent mole on her cheek. She appeared just at noontide and demanded, in heavily accented English, the usual set meal.

"And that is?" Mark asked.

She looked down her nose at him. "A drink, a slice of boiled beef, and a portion of good wheaten bread for threepence."

"You'll have fish," Jennet told her, and served up the fillets she'd cooked. A rich, steamy aroma, redolent of garlic and basil, filled the air.

The common room filled slowly. A man with a shock of bushy white hair was the second person to arrive.

"He was at the Mermaid," Mark whispered to Jennet.

Soon after a chapman came in. "Almeric Horsey," he introduced himself. "What is the price for a room?"

"Twopence for a feather bed," Mark told him, "and another threepence a day if you need hay and litter for your horse."

Bushy-hair glanced up as a tall, thin man appeared in the doorway. "Rowland Weston, the resident undercollector," he muttered under his breath. With a grimace, he swallowed the last of his ale and left.

Mark studied the undercollector, not unduly surprised that he should come into the Woman and the Woolsack. He was taken aback, however, when Weston, after a single drink, produced a blank parchment with the seal of the port already affixed, and handed it over.

"My usual fee is thirteen shillings and fourpence," he said, "but as an introductory offer, I'm willing to exchange this one for a butt of your best imported sack."

When the two men adjourned to a back room, leaving Jennet to serve the inn's patrons, Weston boasted of the fact that he'd borrowed the authentic seal of the port long enough to have a cast made. With this duplicate seal, he'd set up his own private customs house to retail counterfeit cockets and customs clearances.

"I do not believe I have ever dealt with a villain so blatantly corrupt," Mark told his wife that night. He blew out the candle and climbed into bed beside her, glad to be done with the day's work.

Jennet nestled close to him on the featherbed in the inn's best chamber. "So many lawbreakers to choose from! Corrupt officials. Smugglers. Pirates. I must even wonder if Mother Sparcheforde somehow managed to murder Leonard Putney. By witchcraft, mayhap. 'Tis certain she is the one who gained most from his death." She sighed. "How are we ever to sort out the truth? Why, for all we know, there are two murderers."

Mark groaned.

Jennet was silent for a time, but he could almost feel her thinking. "If I'd killed someone in this inn, I'd want to make certain I'd gotten away with it. I'd have to take a look at the new innkeepers. Find out if we are any threat. Living here, we might stumble upon something the coroner's men missed when they made their inventory of goods and chattel."

"Well, then, we have only a few suspects. The murderer is the chapman or the undercollector or one of the Frenchmen." At least a dozen exiles had come in, even Nicholas le Tellier, minister of the French Church of Rye.

"Or the old man with the bushy hair," Jennet murmured sleepily.

"I like the undercollector myself. Mayhap Putney did not pay his fees."

"You forgot to list the Frenchwoman," Jennet said with a yawn.

The only female to come into the inn, she'd made Mark wonder if he'd misunderstood Didsbury's comment about whores. He had not mentioned the innkeeper's remark to Jennet. Now he reached for his wife and planted a resounding kiss on her mouth. "I have not forgot the Frenchwoman," he whispered, "but a bit of effort on your part might make me do so."

"Poor creature," Jennet murmured as she obliged. "If her face were but unblemished, she would be a handsome lass."

Mark did not answer. He had more pleasant matters on his mind.

†

The Frenchwoman came back the following day, again asking for the inn's set meal. As Jennet served her, she found it difficult not to stare at the mole. No doubt it was her imagination, but it seemed to have grown larger.

The woman lingered over her food and was still there when all the other customers had gone.

"A second cup of ale?" Jennet called to her.

"I'd have a word with you instead, now that we are alone."

Jennet glanced into the small room behind the hidden panel. Mark looked back at her, lifting a brow. He was out of sight, having gone into the little chamber to investigate a sound they'd thought might be a mouse.

Jennet shut him in and turned back to the Frenchwoman, heart pounding in anticipation. Whatever the woman wanted, there was no danger. Mark could open the panel from the other side if she screamed. Moreover, there was a knothole in the wainscoting. If he bent over and fixed one eye to the opening, he could peer out into the common room. The position would be passing uncomfortable, but would allow him to keep watch over her.

The Frenchwoman obligingly came closer, taking a stool that gave her a clear view of the entrance. The inn sign creaked as a breeze sprang up, but otherwise all was quiet.

"Will you hire chamberlains and laundresses?" the woman asked.

"With wages so high in Sussex, my husband and I must do all the work of running this inn ourselves," Jennet told her. "Just as the Putneys did."

"*Just* as they did?"

"What little I know of my husband's cousin tells me she did not rely upon selling food and ale for profit."

"You are in favor of making a profit?" It seemed to Jennet that the woman's French accent grew less pronounced as the conversation continued.

"Not the way she did. And yet, what sensible person is averse to becoming wealthy?" Jennet chose her words with care. She lowered her voice to add, "We came to Rye because we heard an inn situated here could ... thrive."

"My husband is an important man hereabout." The Frenchwoman now spoke with the familiar cadence of a native-born Englishwoman, and one gently born, at that. "We will do business with you, as well ... if you meet certain conditions."

"What conditions?" And Jennet wondered why the husband was not here, meeting with Mark.

She got no answer. The chapman returned just then and ended the chance for further private discussion.

"I will return when you have locked up for the night," the woman said, and left.

Mark opened the panel and came out, blinking against the sudden light.

The chapman gave him a curious look, then pulled a slim volume out of his pack. "A book of riddles for a pottle of ale?"

"Too few buyers, friend?" Mark accepted the trade and opened to the first page, chuckling at what he read. "What shines bright of day and at night is raked up in its own dirt?"

"The fire," Jennet answered, impatient with such foolishness.

"What runs but never walks?"

"A river."

"What turns without moving?"

"Milk. Enough!"

Laughing, Mark closed the book

"You are blessed with a clever wife," the chapman said.

A clever wife, Jennet thought, would have looked to see which direction the Frenchwoman took when she left the inn. Although it was doubtless too late, she went out into the street.

The only creature in sight was an old yellow dog.

A sea breeze caught Jennet's apron, making it flap, and caused the inn's sign to groan. She glanced up with a frown, wondering what they might do to stop the annoying sound. The board swung to and fro, but Jennet stood immobile, staring at the painting on the wood.

When is a woman like a woolsack? When she is used to smuggle contraband. The woman on the sign had a key, but it was too big to fit the lock of the chastity belt she held. Jennet's frown turned into a grin. How could she have missed something so obvious? That key unlocked the secrets of this inn. And the painted figure, by her dress a gentlewoman, had a mole on one cheek.

†

As soon as the Frenchwoman entered the common room that night, Mark closed and locked the door behind her.

She fixed him with a basilisk stare. "You have no call to hold me prisoner. My husband is prepared to offer you the same arrangement he had with Leonard Putney."

With a silent prayer that Jennet's solution to the riddle of the Woman and the Woolsack was correct, Mark went to stand at his wife's side. "I fear you are deceived, madam. We did not come to Rye to take Putney's place."

"What do you want, then?" She sounded impatient, but not alarmed.

"The truth about how Alys Putney died."

"Why?"

"For her old mother. She has doubts about the verdict of the coroner's inquest."

"Alys Putney's husband killed her."

"How do you know that?"

"I was there to witness it."

"And did not interfere?"

"Why should I?" She made herself comfortable on the bench beneath the window, regarded them steadily for a long moment, then shrugged. "If he had not killed her, I would have."

An icy finger crept up Mark's spine at her words. Jennet's fingers clenched painfully on his forearm.

"Leonard Putney sent his wife to seduce my husband," the woman continued. "I followed her back to this inn from his bed."

"Putney hoped for greater profits and thought that having his wife play the whore was the way to get them." Jennet exuded sympathy, but Mark's wariness increased.

"When Alys told him she'd failed, that her new lover was willing to enjoy her favors but would offer naught in return but bed sport, Putney flew into a rage. He beat her to death. I saw him do it. And he came after me when he realized I was a witness."

"So you killed him." There was no censure in Jennet's voice. Mark was not sure how he felt.

"I stabbed him," the other woman agreed, "and after Jacques sounded the hue and cry for Alys, I dragged his body out of hiding and left it by his dead wife's side, so that it would appear he killed himself when he found her."

"But he beat her to death," Mark protested. "Why try to hide his crime?"

The woman laughed. "Even if I had not had to strike him down to save myself, we could not have allowed a verdict of murder. If he'd been adjudged guilty, the Crown would have claimed this inn. We would have lost a valuable asset, and provoked an unwelcome interest in the place."

At that moment, the connecting door to the next building, the one that had been bolted on the other side, swung open. The man with the shock of bushy white hair strode into the common room. A wig, Mark realized, as false as the woman's mole, which changed not only size but location from day to day. The face beneath was further obscured by a bristly beard, but more ominous still, he carried a pistol in his right hand, primed and ready to fire.

The woman rose from the bench, smiling at the intruder.

Mark exchanged a glance with Jennet. If her deductions were correct, this was the husband. Further, they were members of the gentry engaged in smuggling. Were they willing to commit murder to hide their crimes? An uneasy silence lengthened as the two couples studied each other.

Jennet broke it. "A second set of owners found dead in the same inn will bring unwelcome attention to this place, as well, and if I could solve the riddle of the inn sign, so can others."

Bushy-hair grinned. "That sign was painted by a previous owner, a fellow who did much admire the lady's ... virtues."

Mark said nothing, wondering what fate Putney's predecessor had suffered. It would be all too easy to kill someone here and dispose of the body in Romney Marsh.

Earlier, Jennet had insisted they could count on the gentry's need for discretion to keep them safe. Mark feared they'd misjudged the situation, lulled into thinking they had only to deal with a lone, unarmed woman.

She spoke next, and without any trace of a French accent. "Goodwife Jaffrey has a point, my dear."

"You told my wife you wanted the truth about how Alys Putney died," said Bushy-head. "Now that you have it, what do you mean to do with it?"

"Leave," Mark blurted.

The man laughed.

"With your permission," Mark added, glancing at the pistol. He cleared his throat. "We have promised to report to Alys Putney's mother, the new owner of this inn."

"She'll do naught to hamper your business," Jennet assured them. "Why should she? And she will not care that you killed Leonard Putney, either. Doubtless she will thank you for making it possible for her to inherit."

The two smugglers exchanged a look Mark recognized. A husband and wife who knew each other well could communicate without words, even when they were at odds.

Bushy-hair lowered the pistol. His smile seemed a trifle less menacing. "Leave Jacques in place as ostler. I'll provide a man to serve as tapster and keep the inn open."

Mark nodded his agreement. "We'll be off at first light." He managed a faint smile of his own. "Mother Sparcheforde is most anxious to hear our report."

It was only after the other couple had disappeared through the connecting door and he heard the bolt slide home behind them, that he dared breathe again.

"That went well." Jennet stepped into his arms, laughing up at him.

She was still well pleased with herself the next morning. As they left Rye behind them, she turned to him with a twinkle in her eyes. "Mayhap we should consider spending a few days away from home every year. I vow I feel most refreshed and invigorated after this adventure, full ready to take on the responsibilities of Leigh Abbey once more."

"A little less adventure next time would suit me better," Mark grumbled. But in his heart he knew she had the right of it. Thanks to their sojourn at the Woman and the Woolsack, his melancholy was well and truly cured.

A Note from the Author

In "Much Ado About Murder," Mark Jaffrey is a groom of the stable and Jennet a tiring maid. These fictional characters married at the end of *Face Down in the Marrow-Bone Pie* and took on greater responsibilities in the household. By the sixteenth century, it was fairly common for upper level servants to be literate. Others were taught how to read but not necessarily how to write.

An estate's steward was the most important position in a sixteenth-century household. Among other things, he managed the demesne farm, bought grain and cattle, supplied the household with all the necessities of daily life, and received and disbursed monies. The housekeeper was in charge of baking, brewing, making white bread and malt, and overseeing the indoor servants.

Records from one sixteenth-century household of approximately the same size as Leigh Abbey list what its servants were paid per annum. The steward received fifty shillings, the housekeeper, twenty-six. The cook, usually a man, was paid twenty shillings a year. A head gardener earned ten shillings and sixpence. The maid of all work was paid six shillings and eightpence. The entire payroll totalled £50 per annum for some twenty-five servants. Food for that household came to £200 for the year.

Lady Appleton and the
Cripplegate Chrisoms

"Goodwife Billings is proved a widow." Nick Baldwin announced.

Susanna, Lady Appleton, looked up from the herbal she'd been reading, a smile of welcome and congratulation lighting up the pale oval of her face. "Excellent. I was certain you would be able to find the correct parish with no trouble.

He sent a rueful grin in her direction and advanced a few more steps into the room, a private parlor on an upper floor of fair, large house near London's Moorgate. It was furnished with considerable luxury – glass in all the windows, floors of Purbeck marble and glazed tile, and thick arras-work hangings. "Aye. On the fifth try."

Light laughter eddied toward him as she rose from a high-backed elmwood chair inlaid with oak. "It might have been worse. There must be a hundred parishes in London." She went to the hearth, where a small pot sat keeping warm on a trivet near the flames, and ladled mulled wine into two goblets. She held one out to him.

"Gramercy," Nick murmured, closing the remaining distance between them. He took deep pleasure in his first sip of the hot, spiced liquid. After a long, cold day spent looking through parish records, both the drink and the heat from the crackling fire sent welcome warmth to his chilled bones.

"You found evidence, then, of the death of Mary Billings's runaway husband?"

Mary, the housekeeper at Nick's Northamptonshire manor, had been abandoned by her feckless spouse several years earlier. She'd heard rumors of his demise soon after, but she'd had no reason then to go to the trouble and expense of confirming them. Only when she'd expressed her wish to remarry and the vicar had refused to perform the rite until she could prove the new marriage would not be bigamous, had the question of when and where Billings died become important. Nick had offered to look into the matter. He'd been glad of the excuse to visit London while Susanna was in residence.

"Billings was buried on the sixth day of November in 1569, more than two years ago, in the parish of St. Giles without Cripplegate. The clerk there has made a fair and notarized copy of the entry in the parish records."

"All's well, then?" Susanna's sharp-sighted blue eyes fixed on his face, studying him with as much intensity as she'd been perusing the herbal when he arrived. She did not wait for him to answer. "There is something troubles you."

It did not surprise Nick overmuch that she could read his mood with such ease. They had known each other more than a dozen years and shared many adventures. If he'd had his way, she'd have long since become his wife, but Susanna refused to remarry and he had learned to content himself with what she would share – her affection, her friendship, her concern, and most of all, her clever, agile mind.

"Well?" Susanna prompted him.

Nick took another strengthening, warming, soothing sip of the mulled wine. "What Mary Billings knew of her husband's life led me to suspect he'd been buried in Cripplegate Ward, for we believed he'd died shortly after having been released from the Compter in Wood Street."

She nodded and drank from her own cup. The Compter, a prison, was used to hold those taken for offenses against city laws.

"Cripplegate contains five parishes. I started with the southernmost church, St. Mary Magdalen in Milk Street. I went on to St. Michael, and there came upon an entry in the register of burials that puzzled me. The cause of death was writ down 'overlaid.' Do you know what is meant by the term?"

Frowning, she set down her goblet. "I fear I do. It means to be suffocated, but in a very particular manner. You know that infants are wrapped in swaddling clothes, bound tightly in order to ensure that the limbs will grow straight?"

"Aye. I've always felt sorry for the child, unable to move."

"More helpless than you know. In theory a baby is unwrapped and washed two or three times a day, but far too many new mothers do not seem to know how to care for their offspring. Or else they do not wish to be bothered."

Nick considered that. Wealthy households employed nurses but poor women too busy to pay attention to their babies simply neglected them. "I fear you have the right of it. I have seen children hooked by the swaddling to a convenient wall or left in the cradle to cry all day."

"Either place is safer than being carelessly placed in the family bed to share sleeping space with several older, larger bodies. An infant 'overlaid' has been smothered because a bedmate rolled over on top of him."

"Not uncommon, then?"

"No, more's the pity. A goodly number of infants die in their cradles, for no apparent reason, but for those who sleep with others, when a cause is sought, it most often found that the mother or the nurse slept unnatural heavy due to drink or illness." She sighed. "Although I've never had any children myself, it is my belief such deaths could be avoided with a small amount of care."

Nick drained his goblet and abandoned it on a round table made of walnut. "How easily could such deaths be arranged?"

Eyes narrowing at his words, Susanna caught her breath. "What have you discovered?"

"Mayhap naught but an odd coincidence."

"And mayhap more. Tell me."

"It was at St. Michael that I first saw the word 'overlaid,' and although I was curious as to what it might mean, I took little notice of it then."

Restless, Nick crossed the chamber to stand at a window, looking out over the garden toward the wall that shielded this property from the sprawling city beyond. He knew Susanna well enough to predict how she'd react when he told her all he'd found. He had debated with himself all the way here. Even if what he suspected was true, naught would be done about it under the law. Only once had he heard of a charge of murder being brought against some-one for the death of an infant, and that had been the case of a mother who'd stuffed her newly delivered baby into a privy and left it to perish. And yet, this was just the sort of wrong that Susanna relished righting. Besides, it went against all Nick himself believed in to do nothing, especially if by inaction he allowed more deaths to occur.

"I'd not have noticed the entry at all had it not been within the time period I'd resolved to search: 12 December, 1570. But there was another oddity about the entry, too. Unlike most, only the name of the mother was given."

Susanna sank down atop the domed lid of a trussing-coffer, a chest de-signed for use while traveling and suitable for storing anything from clothing to muniments to books to grain and bread. "So, the dead child was a bastard."

"Aye."

Most records of burials in parish registers identified the deceased by his profession, or sometimes simply as householder. Dead women and children were almost always listed in terms of their relationship to a man. "John, infant son of John Smith, householder" or "stillborn son of John Smith, carpenter" would not have caught Nick's eye, but "John, base-got son of Jane Johnson" had been another matter.

"I went on to St. Alban," Nick continued, "then St. Mary Aldermanbury, and finally to St. Giles Cripplegate, which lies outside the city walls, half of the parish in the county of Middlesex. At two of the three I came upon similar entries. Three children in adjoining parishes, all dead by cause of being overlaid, all base-got upon the body of one Jane Johnson. I had not thought to do so in the other parishes, but at St. Giles I also inspected the records of baptisms. That child died during the first month of life."

"A chrisom," Susanna murmured, sorrow and pity coloring her tone of voice. The name given to such short-lived infants derived from the fact that the same white chrisom cloth laid over the baby at baptism was customarily used as a winding sheet when only a few weeks separated christening and burial.

"Do you think it possible the mother deliberately killed all three children?"

"Possible? Oh, yes." She'd gone pale, but her chin jutted out at a determined angle and her eyes blazed. "And who knows how many more we will find if we delve deeper?"

He nodded. Her thoughts followed his. "I mean to discover if there are, and find out what happened to Jane Johnson. She may be dead."

"And she may be about to give birth to another child, to kill another infant." Spurred into action, Susanna hopped down from the chest and made her way to a writing table. "Tell me again of the parishes where you found records and the dates given. Then we must determine what other parishes border those in order to widen the search."

"There are, I believe, one hundred six churches in London, in some ninety parishes. Then there are the out-parishes."

"I do not care if there are a thousand! If what we suspect is true, it cannot be permitted to continue and it cannot go unpunished. We must find Jane Johnson and if she is again with child we must keep watch on her to prevent her from taking another life."

†

Three days later, Susanna Appleton's search brought her to the small church of St. Olave. Located in Silver Street, just where it turned to become the north end of Noble, St. Olave's was an unremarkable edifice, but the parish was adjacent to Cripplegate ward and worth the time to search. The clerk, who was the second most important figure in any parish and responsible for keeping the records, was even less impressive. A small, wiry fellow named Lawrence Whitney, he scowled over Nick's request that he remove the parish record book from its locked coffer to allow them to look at it.

"The register is taken out only on Sundays, when the week's new records are added."

"Must I roust a churchwarden, then?" Nick inquired. "I am certain one of them has the second key." This was regulated by law and had been since the time of old King Henry.

They were by now most familiar with the way the system worked. After three days of looking through records and asking for Jane Johnson by name, however, they were no closer to finding more information than they had been at the first.

Susanna hid a smile as Whitney buckled under Nick's steady regard, but the clerk hovered as they went through the entries, as if he feared they would criticize his diligence. Or mayhap his penmanship, for he had a near illegible hand.

"There," Susanna said, pointing to an entry on the page of burials for 1568. Elizabeth, daughter of Jane Johnson, "base got," had been buried on the last day of March. No cause of death was given. Susanna turned to the clerk. "What do you know of this woman?" She tapped the page.

Whitney sidled closer and looked at the name above Susanna's gloved finger. "Jane Johnson? A vagabond."

"She does not live in the parish, then?"

"We do not want such here. She'd have been escorted to the parish boundary and sent on her way." Contempt laced his voice. Bastards were a charge on the parish, all expense and little reward. Those who bore them were held in low regard, unless they would name the father and he could be forced to support the child.

"And the child – how did she die?"

Whitney looked at her askance. "It was close to four years ago, madam. How am I to remember?"

Susanna examined the record of baptisms and found Elizabeth Johnson. She'd been buried three weeks after she'd been christened. Another chrisom.

Further questioning of the clerk yielded nothing more of use and, thanking him, Susanna and Nick continued on to St. Mary Staining and St. John Zachary. They found no mention of Jane Johnson or her base-got offspring in either parish.

"Four children in four years." Nick shook his head. "Is that not enough?"

"But look at the dates," Susanna said, and produced the list she'd made.

St. Mary Aldermanbury – 11 April, 1567
St. Olave – 31 March, 1568
St. Giles without Cripplegate – 5 November, 1569
St. Michael – 12 December, 1570

Nick frowned down at the page. "You think there is a fifth, more recent than the others?"

"Or Jane is even now with child." Susanna pondered what to do. She had already put out word among those few midwives she knew in the city, asking them to notify her if they encountered a woman named Jane Johnson, but it was a common name, the city was large, and midwives were numerous. Susanna was known to some for the herbals she had written, but many others, who could neither read nor write, had no cause to do favors for a visiting country gentlewoman.

In the end, she could only think to revisit the parish where the most recent death had occurred. At St. Michael, the clerk could help them not at all, but he did give them the names of the parish searchers, two old women whose duty it was to repair to the place where a death had occurred and view the corpse, making enquiries and examining the deceased until they could determine what disease or casualty had caused the death. It was their report to the parish clerk that had resulted in "overlaid" being writ down in the register.

The searchers for St. Michael's were two elderly matrons, sisters who lived together in the garret of a sprawling tenement at the edge of the parish. Goodwife Mellon used a stick to help her walk, a slow, ponderous progress. Goodwife Frowley, all skin and bones, flitted birdlike throughout the interview, landing in one spot for a moment, then moving on, head bobbing as she spoke, not in a nod but as if she needed to move it about in order to see everything at once.

"The death of a bastard is a blessing," she informed them when they'd explained their interest in Jane Johnson.

"Nay, sister," Goodwife Mellon objected. "Say not so."

"What? Preserve the child as a charge on the parish?"

"No. No. But it is not such a great sin to procure an abortment. Better the mother prevent the birth of the child altogether."

"Better she do so by not lying with the father," her sister snapped.

Susanna listened to the debate with mixed emotions. She could not help but feel sympathy for a young woman who found herself pregnant and unwed. A clever lass would leave home and go to a parish where she was not known. There she might claim to be a widow. But most girls tried to conceal their plight by a judicious arrangement of aprons and skirts, only to be ejected from their place of employment when they were found out. Pregnant women were an all-too-common sight on the outskirts of villages and towns, where some gave birth alone in a field or hedge, if they could not drag themselves to a church porch. Most, however, were not abandoned when they were "in the straw." Susanna had heard that even vagrant women banded together to help a birth proceed.

"Did she kill her own child?" Nick asked when the searchers gave him an opening.

"It was an accident," Goodwife Mellon said.

"She was in a rare state by the time we got there," said her sister. "I am certain she did not mean the baby to die."

Susanna wondered whether she could trust what either searcher said. Neither dared admit she might have been wrong in declaring the cause of death, even though they disagreed about everything else.

"The woman was simple," Goodwife Frowley murmured thoughtfully. "That's the only reason I recall her at all."

"Nonsense, sister. She was a clever baggage. She did but pretend to be foolish so we'd ask no more questions."

They glared at each other, but neither had more to add.

"Who is the local midwife?" Susanna asked. If she'd delivered the baby, she might remember Jane Johnson and confirm whether she was simpleminded or not. The possibility that she was added a new dimension to the situation. Not child murder but ignorance? Either way, if Jane was with child again, that child was in danger.

The midwife lived nearby, two doors down from the apothecary's sign – a pill resting on a lolling pink tongue – but she was not at home.

"We will return tomorrow," Susanna decided.

"This is women's business," Nick remarked as they made their way back toward the house where Susanna was staying with friends.

She fought a smile. He was brave enough to slay dragons for her, but the possibility of encountering a woman in labor was enough to send him running for the hills. "I will talk to her alone if you wish."

He could not hide his relief.

The next morning, Susanna returned. The midwife was a plump, comfortable sort named Agnes Dane, and she remembered Jane Johnson.

"She has the mind of a child herself." Agnes confirmed. "No sense about men, either."

"Is she a whore?" Most brothelkeepers took care that their women did not bear children.

"Not to judge by the rooms she had." Agnes described the chamber where the child had been born and had died. "Long since vacated," she added. "A poet lives there now."

"Jane bore other children before the one you delivered. All of them were suffocated in their beds."

For a moment, Susanna thought the midwife unmoved, but then she stirred herself. "I have seen this Jane Johnson since then."

"Is she breeding again?"

"May be."

"How far along?" Susanna had no doubt of the midwife's eye.

"The child is due any time now, if I am any judge."

"Did she name the father of the child you delivered?"

"Nay. Resisted all our efforts, she did." Agnes made a dismissive gesture. "Likely she did not know."

"Or she is not as simple as she seemed."

Susanna left the midwife's lodgings more determined than ever to find Jane. It was too late to help the others, but she still had a chance to save this new child.

✝

Just as the church bells tolled nine at night, signaling that lights and fires should be put out, one of midwives who'd heard of Susanna's interest in Jane Johnson sent word that a woman by that name was in labor in the parish of Allhallows, Honey Lane. With Nick's help Susanna found the house in a narrow, dark street.

Jane's screams reached them even before they entered. She lay on a thin pallet, her face contorted with the intensity of her labor. When the pain passed, her features resolved themselves into the vacant stare of one who had given up on life.

Simple? Mayhap she was, Susanna thought, but that did not mean she lacked the power to communicate. "Has she named the child's father?" she asked the midwife.

"Not yet." Her attention fixed on her patient, she paid no mind to Susanna, but when Nick made to enter the birthing chamber she gave him a look over her shoulder that could have turned the sun to ice.

"I will wait below," he muttered, and vanished into the gloom outside. There was an alehouse two buildings along, Susanna recalled, and suspected she'd find him there if she had need of him.

At hand was women's work.

Three tortuous hours passed. The midwife, relentless in her effort to discover who had fathered Joan's latest bastard, denied the straining woman a mother's caudle, the special drink made of spiced wine or ale and given to keep up her strength and spirits. She wanted Jane weak enough to betray her lover, but weakness was not what Susanna saw.

Jane's flailing hand caught the midwife's arm. The midwife yelped in pain and it took Susanna's help to break the hold. Jane had gripped with such force that she'd left red finger marks on the midwife's skin.

"I've known women in the straw to squeeze hard," the midwife muttered, "but this one's got hands as strong as a man's." Her face set with grim determination, she resumed her efforts to goad Jane into telling the truth about her child's father, but she kept her distance from those powerful fingers.

Another half hour passed.

"What if she does not know his name?" No matter what Jane might have done, Susanna pitied her for the suffering she endured in order to give birth. There were herbs that could take away much of the pain and others to ease delivery, but Susanna did not carry such with her and the midwife, if she had them, held them back.

"She knows who he is, I warrant. Just because she is simple does not mean she lacks all sense." The midwife's face was set in a grim expression.

"What if he did not tell her his name?"

"Her lover will have given her some name to call him by, never doubt it."

Susanna had been watching the woman in the bed. Her eyes, open and glazed with pain, widened at the midwife's words. Fear? But of what was she afraid? Penance for bearing a bastard? She would have endured that already, for each of the previous children.

"It may not be mere stubbornness keeps her quiet," Susanna murmured. It was possible Jane was so stalwart in protecting her lover because she lived in terror of what he would do to her if she betrayed him.

Was he an important man in London? Someone who could order her disposed of if she spoke? Or was he simply a bully who'd threatened her often enough that she dared not risk his wrath? Either way, Susanna thought, Jane would not tell them. If she had kept her secret throughout the torture of those previous births, she'd maintain her silence now.

The pains continued for another hour before Jane at last produced a healthy girl child. The midwife tied and cut the umbilical cord, washed the babe, and swaddled her in new linen bands until she was trussed from head to foot. These tasks complete, she handed the newborn child to her mother. Jane smiled at the downy head and cooed and petted the baby.

Concerned for the tiny girl's safety, Susanna moved closer to the pallet. "May I hold her?" she asked, tucking her hands under the small, squirming body.

But Jane would not let go. With frightening ease, she resisted Susanna's attempt to ease the child away from her. Surprised, Susanna's gaze flew to Jane's face, wondering if she knew her own strength. Mayhap she had been wrong. How could such a powerful woman be cowed by a lover?

Another explanation for the deaths occurred to Susanna then. Jane might have killed her own children by accident. Had she hugged them each with such an excess of affection that they'd suffocated?

Vowing to keep a watchful eye on mother and child, Susanna abandoned her attempt to remove the baby from Jane's arms. She'd just turned back to the midwife, meaning to offer to pay her to stay with Jane until other arrangements could be made, when the local vicar arrived.

"Did she give up the father's name during childbirth?" he asked the midwife.

"No. Silent as a monk, that one."

"You were charged with obtaining that information."

"Was I to torture her?" the midwife inquired. "If she did not speak when her time was upon her, she will not."

The vicar's disdain for both Jane and the midwife hardened Susanna's heart against him. He fell lower still in her estimation when he began to rant about the charge this child would be on the parish. "Even if it dies," he grumbled, "it will cost 2s.9d. to bury."

"Enough, sir," Susanna protested. "I will support the child myself if money is all that concerns you."

The vicar, mollified, became effusive in his thanks. Then, duty done, he was about to take his leave when a cry from the baby drew his attention to Jane and he looked well at her for the first time.

"I have seen this woman before," he gasped, "and in similar circumstances! Whore! How many bastards have you brought into the world?"

Susanna prevented him from launching another diatribe by putting her hand on his sleeve. "There is more to this than you know, vicar. *Where* did you see her before?"

Her serious mein and somber tone had as much effect as Susanna's obvious wealth and gentility. He swallowed his outrage and replied in measured tones. "I was previously the curate at St. Mary Aldermanbury."

Where the first baby died. "Will you tell me what you recall of that birth?"

The vicar frowned. "It was my clerk," he said after a moment's thought. "Whitney showed a most unwarranted sympathy for this woman."

"Lawrence Whitney?"

"Aye. These days he is the clerk at St. Olave, Silver Street."

†

Susanna found Lawrence Whitney alone, and for a moment her steps faltered on the stone-flagged floor of the chancel. She'd had the remainder of the night to consider what she should say to him, but now that the moment was upon her, she had second thoughts. True, it was strange that Whitney should remember Jane was a vagabond but not that she was simple. And his interest in her almost five years ago seemed suspicious, but the explanation that had made sense to her in the wee hours of the morning might be dead wrong.

He turned and, recognizing her, scowled.

"Good day to you, Clerk Whitney," she said, and decided to plunge ahead. If she wronged him, she would apologize. "I am come to tell you that you have a new daughter."

Face blank with astonishment, he gawked at her. Then he dropped the communion plate he'd been polishing and his expression changed to one of panic.

"Do not trouble to deny it," she told him with a grim sense of satisfaction. She had been right. He was Jane's lover. "This time Jane Johnson named her child's father."

"She has not the wit to know whether she's had one man or twenty."

"If that is true, sirrah, the more foul your actions in taking advantage of her. But tell me, if all her children were not yours, why go to such pains to hide their mother?"

He started to speak, then appeared to change his mind. Sullen-faced, he settled for glaring at her. Only when the silence between them stretched to unbearable lengths did he blurt out another accusation. "She's naught but a foolish woman. Much to be pitied."

"Foolish? Is that an excuse to have overlaid four young children?"

"What do I care for them? It was better so. She has not the wit to care for them. They'd have become a charge on the parish."

"Not if you married their mother."

"Impossible."

Susanna despised weaklings. The fellow seemed incapable of giving up his mistress, yet he was unwilling to take any responsibility for the children she bore him. He'd rather move her around in the same general area of London, each time into a different parish, so that no one would notice she kept having bastard children and they kept dying.

"You can be required to marry her," Susanna reminded him. "Or do you prefer to sit in the stocks with a notice around your neck saying: 'Lawrence Whitney hath got Jane Johnson with child,' and then parade through this church on three consecutive Sundays wearing a penitent's white sheet and a placard saying: 'Fornicator.' "

"I am already wed." He spat out the admission.

"In that case, the placard will say 'Adulterer,' but having a wife will not spare you the obligation of supporting your child until she reaches her seventh year."

"Think you she will live that long? Such children do not thrive. Not with such a mother."

"All the more reason that you must take steps to protect the babe."

He heaved a deep sigh. "You meddle in matters that are none of your business, Lady Appleton. What will be, will be. It is in God's hands." The pious glance he cast upward was so patently false Susanna was surprised lightning did not streak out of the sky and strike him dead on the spot.

"The laws of God and man alike condemn you, sirrah. And I mean to do more than meddle."

"Report me to the church? Why trouble yourself?"

There was no remorse in him, for he knew as well as she did that no dire punishment awaited him for seducing a simpleminded young woman and repeatedly getting her with child. He'd avoided embarrassment with his machinations, nothing more. Even now, Jane would bear the brunt of the church's censure, not Whitney. He'd do penance and be forgiven.

In frustration, Susanna turned on her heel and stormed out of the church. She had friends. Mayhap one of them had enough influence to force Whitney to support his own child.

This child *would* thrive. Susanna intended to make certain of it. And Jane herself would be removed from her lover's influence. She would make a new beginning.

Susanna's first thought was to fetch Jane and take her into the household where she was at present a guest. Her hostess had no objection, but having birthed two children of her own, she suggested that it might be unwise to disturb a new mother just yet. Instead, Susanna returned to Jane's lodgings accompanied by a maidservant, a quiet girl content to sit in a corner and sew, and bringing with her an ornate wooden cradle.

The next time the exhausted mother awoke, she stared at Susanna in blank incomprehension. Then a smile blossomed on her pale face. "I remember you. You came with the midwife."

Susanna nodded. "Jane," she said in her gentlest voice, "how would you like to live in the country?"

The vacant expression returned, making Susanna wonder if she understood that any other place existed outside the slums of London.

"My friend Master Baldwin has a manor in Northamptonshire, near Rockingham Forest. He raises sheep there to make wool."

"Sheep?" Jane sounded doubtful.

"You need not have anything to do with them if you do not want to. I am certain there is plenty of other work – in the dairy and in the house. You'll have livery to wear and good food to eat. Master Baldwin's housekeeper and the man she is about to marry, who is steward there, will take good care of you and your child."

Tears welled in Jane's eyes. "My babies die."

"Yes, my dear. I know." Susanna moved to sit on the pallet and placed her hand over Jane's cold one. "But this child is different. See, she has her own cradle to sleep in." She set it rocking with her foot. Inside, the swaddled child was awake but not yet restless. A series of knotted bands kept her secured to knobs on the sides of the cradle. Even if it tipped over, the baby would not fall out.

Jane turned her face into the pillow. "It is always the same," she murmured. "I wake up and find them dead. He says I roll over on them in the night. Then he goes away, and the searchers come, and I have to leave the parish."

"Yes," Susanna said. "I have spoken to Lawrence Whitney. I gather that he found you new lodgings every time."

At the name, Jane's eyes widened. Fear? Again, Susanna could not be certain. "Tell me about him, Jane. Do you love him?"

Jane said nothing.

The midwife had been right, Susanna thought. Jane might be simple, but she was not stupid. She had the mind of a child of eight or nine. She was capable of deceit, of stubborn refusal to speak, of great loyalty, no matter how little deserved. But she could also be tricked into saying more than she realized about her own situation.

"This time your friend Lawrence Whitney will allow me to make the arrangements," she told Jane. He had better! "And it will also be my privilege to keep your daughter safe from accidents. You see, Jane. She has her own bed. No one can overlay her."

Still Jane said nothing.

"But we must talk about what happened before," Susanna continued, "so that it will never happen again." It might be beyond Jane's ability to explain what Susanna wanted to know, but there had been four deaths in a row, more than could be accounted accidental. The children could all have had some physical aberration, she supposed, a flaw in the lungs or heart, mayhap, that caused each sudden death, but Susanna still had to consider the possibility that one or more of the deaths had been deliberate murder.

Jane sniffled. "Will I be hanged?"

Susanna's breath stopped. She willed herself to be calm. Why should Jane think that a possibility? Had Whitney accused her of deliberately harming her own children? Had he threatened to report her if she did not continue as his mistress? Was that the cause of the fear she'd seen in Jane's eyes? With an effort she kept her voice level.

"No, Jane. You will be safe with me."

"Even if this baby dies too?" The child had begun to whimper. Susanna freed the infant from her cradle and handed her to Jane to nurse.

"No one will hang you," Susanna promised. She intended to remain with mother and child until they were safe in Northamptonshire. If the infant succumbed, it would not be to a murderous parent.

"He said I must hide. After. He said they'd think I done it apurpose."

"But you did not. You were asleep."

The beatific smile Jane wore as she looked down at her nursing babe vanished when she shifted her gaze to Susanna. Her face became a mask of horror. "The first one, I were suckling."

"In the bed?"

Jane nodded.

A few more questions elicited a clear picture. Jane had fallen asleep with her breast still in the child's mouth. When she'd awakened hours later, the baby had no longer been breathing. Susanna ruled it a tragic accident.

"Did the same thing happen with the next child?"

Jane shook her head. "I were careful, but the baby died anyway."

"You slept soundly and awoke to find your child overlaid?"

Jane frowned. "Seems like I dreamed." She continued to nurse the new infant, stroking the downy head with an absent motion.

"Dreamed what, Jane?"

Her voice puzzled, she murmured, "Pillows."

"You thought there were extra pillows? In the bed with you?"

She nodded.

Susanna leaned forward to take the sated girl child and replace her on her back in the cradle, which was closer to the charcoal brazier, the only source of warmth in the room. She did not take time to tie the strings. A new and troubling possibility sent her rushing back to the pallet to continue her interrogation of Jane Johnson.

"Did you sleep alone those nights, Jane?"

The young woman's forehead wrinkled with the effort it took to work out what Susanna meant.

"Was Lawrence with you?"

Face clearing, Jane smiled, glad to be able to answer Susanna's question. "He said I needed looking after with the new baby."

"So he was with you, each time, when you found your child had been overlaid?"

Tears sprang into Jane's eyes as she nodded.

Jane, Susanna thought, was not a murdering mother, but Lawrence Whitney might well have killed the infants. That explanation made more sense to Susanna than holding Jane responsible for four suspiciously similar "accidents." But what kind of man would deliberately smother his own children?

"Jane," she asked in a tentative voice. "Did Lawrence ever strike you?"

Once again eager to please, Jane bobbed her head. "Said I needed to know my place. Said it were his duty to punish me for what I done."

"For the deaths of your babies?"

"For getting with child."

The words Whitney had spoken earlier came back to Susanna, rife with ominous meaning: *Such children do not thrive.* A chill ran through her. With sudden clarity, she understood that the type of man who would beat his mistress and blame her for being pregnant was also the sort who'd dispose of that child without a qualm.

Would he dare do so again? The risk he might, and try to dispose of Jane, too, had her speaking in a sharp voice to the maidservant, who had fallen asleep in her chair. "Go at once to Billingsgate and fetch Master Baldwin. He must come here at once and bring with him a wagon, that we may take Jane and her child away."

"But madam, it is full dark!"

"Take a torch. Hire a link boy." Susanna thrust several coins at her. "Go quickly."

When the reluctant girl had left, Susanna contemplated the chamber. She had miscalculated. Staying here with Jane once she'd told Whitney she knew he was the child's father had been a mistake. There was nothing in the room to use to defend Jane and the baby if Whitney planned to kill again. Susanna longed for a stout cudgel. Even more, she wished she'd asked Nick to stay here with her.

A pair of sewing scissors was the only potential weapon Susanna had found by the time she heard heavy footsteps on the stairs. She slipped behind the door just as it opened.

Unaware of Susanna's presence, Lawrence Whitney strode straight to Jane's pallet. He seized her roughly by the shoulders. "Jezebel! You betrayed me."

Taught long since to fear his brutality, Jane cowered before his attack, whimpering as she tried to defend herself with words. "I said naught to midwife nor vicar."

"You talked to someone else."

Silently pleading for help, Jane looked past Whitney's shoulder, searching for Susanna. He released her and whirled, an ugly look on his face. "I thought you'd gone."

"You saw my maidservant leave. She will return with Master Baldwin at any moment." Whitney was a coward at heart, Susanna thought. Why else would he come at night when he could enter by stealth? Why else would he wait until he thought Jane was alone? "You have just time to flee before he arrives."

Whitney's features settled into a smile so false no one but an infant would be deceived by it. "How can I go, Lady Appleton? I have a duty here."

"Do you mean to assume your parental responsibilities? Make arrangements for quarterly payments mayhap?"

He glanced toward the cradle. "Ah, yes. The child."

Before Susanna could stop him, Whitney strode to the cradle and with a sudden kick of his leading foot against the rocker, flung the tightly swaddled infant out of her nest and straight toward the glowing coals in the nearby brazier. With a gasp of horror, Susanna rushed forward. Whitney tripped her before she'd gone a half dozen steps. The scissors she'd been holding behind her back flew from her hand and skittered out of reach under the chair.

"No!" Jane lunged from the bed as the linen swaddling bands began to smoke. With bare hands, she beat out the first tiny flames before they could spread.

The newborn screamed, indignant at having been ripped so precipitously from sleep. From the sound of those lusty yells, her flammable wrappings appeared to have protected her from taking harm in the fall. Susanna heaved herself upright to find Whitney, hands clasped to his ears, staring at his daughter through eyes that were wide and frantic.

"Make her be silent!" he bellowed. "Stop that noise!"

Jane stepped away from the baby and put her hands behind her back. Terrorized, confused, she suddenly seemed incapable of any action. The child on the floor wailed louder.

Whitney turned his wild-eyed gaze on Susanna. "This is all your fault. You meddled in matters that were none of your business."

With no more warning than that, he charged, striking Susanna across the face with the back of his hand. The blow sent her reeling into the wall. Pain lanced through her shoulder, joining the agony in her jaw, but she forgot both injuries when she saw that he'd overset the brazier. Within moments, the entire chamber could be afire. Whitney, a gleeful expression on his face, darted toward the door.

"Jane," Susanna screamed. "Save your child."

Staggering a little, Susanna herself ran toward the bed. She grabbed the heavy blanket and flung it atop the glowing coals, hoping to smother the flames aborning. Then, lifting her skirts out of the way, she used her sturdy boots to trample every escaping spark she could find.

The wails of Jane's infant continued unabated. Mercifully, she had been too far from the brazier to be burnt when it toppled over, for Jane had made no move to rescue her. Susanna gathered the baby into her own arms, soothing her with awkward pats and murmurs. Only then did she become aware of the sounds of a struggle behind her.

Jane's hands, those strong hands that had marked the midwife, were clamped tight around Whitney's throat. He staggered, flailing wildly, striking her repeatedly. She did not seem to notice the blows. Nor did she loosen her grip.

Susanna stood and watched as Whitney's face, already red, went purple as his struggles grew weaker. When he dropped to his knees, he took Jane with him, but still she did not let go, not until the man was limp and unresisting as a day-old fish.

Without a backward glance, Jane heaved herself off Whitney's body and reached for her baby. Susanna relinquished the infant, wincing as Jane accidentally bumped against her. Arm and face both throbbed, but she could not give in to the pain yet. First she had to make certain that the villain was dead. She knelt beside the body. No life pounded in the veins. No breath escaped those dead white lips. And all emotion had gone from the bulging eyes.

"He's escaped penance," she murmured, more to herself than to Jane. He would not have to endure the burden of supporting his daughter for the first seven years of her life. Instead he had been punished with a rough justice.

Belatedly, distracted from nursing her child, Jane seemed to realize what she had done. Her jaw went slack. "Will they hang me?"

"No." Susanna spoke with absolute certainty. "I can bear witness to all that happened here. This man tried to kill us – you, me, and your child. You prevented that, Jane. You saved all our lives. You will not be punished. Indeed, I mean to see to it that you are richly rewarded. Mayhap your own little cottage in Northamptonshire," she added, hearing a door slam below stairs and the familiar sound of Nick's voice. "You shall have a maid to help you with the baby and a generous stipend."

Jane made no response. Her attention had already shifted back to her child. The look on her face reflected naught but love and delight.

A Note from the Author

The "bawdy courts" of the sixteenth century grew in importance as the Puritan influence in government increased. They concerned themselves not with criminal behavior but with offenses against the community standard of morality. These ranged from flirting in church to adultery. The ultimate punishment was excommunication, which could lead to imprisonment on the criminal charge of failing to attend church. Most punishments, however, only involved some sort of penance, a subject I'll be touching on again in "Encore for a Neck Verse" and "Confusions Most Monstrous."

The churchwardens of each parish were responsible for detecting offenses and bringing them to the attention of courts set up in each deanery. Every diocese had several courts, each presided over by an archdeacon. It would have been almost impossible for an Elizabethan to avoid a brush with some church court, especially since they also heard "actions of defamation" – cases brought by those who felt themselves injured by gossip in the community or by charges unsuccessfully brought against them at an earlier church court.

Lady Appleton and the Bristol Crystals

July, 1572

The stairs wound upward, narrow, steep, and uneven. Susanna, Lady Appleton had to brace one hand against a crumbling plaster wall to steady herself as she climbed. She was out of breath and her bad leg throbbed steadily by the time she reached the top floor of the George in Glastonbury. It smelt of disuse and mouse droppings.

"A moment," she said to Grace, her young tiring maid. The girl's pretty face was flushed and a strand of dark hair had come loose beneath her coif, but otherwise she showed no sign of exertion. The uncommon hot weather did not affect her as badly as it did her mistress.

The inn had been purpose-built more than a hundred years earlier to house pilgrims visiting Glastonbury Abbey. Susanna supposed those visitors had been more concerned with their spiritual well being than creature comforts, but for many years now, ever since the present queen's father, old Henry VIII, dissolved all the monasteries, the George had depended upon secular patrons for its custom. It seemed odd to Susanna that the innkeeper had undertaken so few repairs. True, Glastonbury was in a remote part of Somerset, but it was on one of the main routes westward from the midlands and what little she'd seen of it as they rode in had suggested a fair-sized market town.

The long, low room in which Susanna and her servant were to sleep, together with any other women spending the night at the George without a husband's company, was better swept but just as stifling as the landing. Narrow windows cut into thick walls, the shutters flung open to reveal the rooftops of the town, let in the only breath of air.

A tiny, tidily-dressed woman already occupied the chamber. She stood on tiptoe on a bench, looking out the far casement at the rapidly gathering dusk. Without turning her head to look at the newcomers, she spoke, her voice soft and melodious. "Lady Appleton, I have been waiting for you to arrive." She hopped down from her vantage point and pattered toward Susanna across the bare planks.

Susanna was certain they'd never met before. The woman stood no higher than Susanna's shoulder and even though Susanna was uncommon tall for a woman, that was surpassing small. Elfin features matched the stature – small chin and nose, narrow face, and ears that were just the slightest bit pointed.

"How is it you know my name, madam, when you are a stranger to me?"

"I am a seer," the little woman said, making the absurd claim in a matter-of-fact voice as she met Susanna's gaze. Her eyes were an unusual clear gray in color.

Young Grace, but newly trained in her duties, abandoned unpacking her mistress's capcase. With the eagerness of a puppy, she tugged at the stranger's sleeve. "Can you see my future? Will I marry well?"

The seer spared Grace a quick, pitying glance. "You are not my concern. It is Lady Appleton I've come to warn."

Susanna felt both brows lift. Ominous warnings from fortune tellers? What had she done to deserve this?

"I see you doubt me." The woman seized Susanna's gloved hand in a surprisingly firm grip and closed her eyes. "You are on your way to Cornwall."

"Easy enough to learn that from the ostler." Susanna tried to pull free but the seer was not yet done with her.

"You go to visit young Rosamond. It has been almost a year since you last saw her but for all that this will be a brief visit. You have allowed only two weeks for the journey, two weeks to visit, and two weeks to return. You do not wish to be absent longer because you have a houseguest – someone recently bereaved."

"You could glean all that by listening to servants' talk." But the woman was exceeding well informed.

The stranger had more to say. "A boy has been following your party since you left Leigh Abbey. He is in grave danger of suffocating in an ill-chosen hiding place."

This ominous prediction set Susanna's heart racing. She had no desire to risk a life. "Where?"

"In the cart with the furnishings you take to Lady Pendennis. He rolled himself into a tapestry. It shifted during transport, making it impossible for him to squirm free."

A quarter of an hour later, nine-year-old Rob Jaffrey stood before Susanna in the torchlit stableyard of the inn. Red-faced and disheveled, he kept his head down to avoid eye contact. He shifted his weight from foot to foot as he awaited her inquisition.

Thankful they'd been in time to rescue him, Susanna moderated her tone. "Account for yourself, my lad. Why did you stow away in that cart?"

She was annoyed with him but she was also very glad to have found him still alive. He was the child of two of her most loyal servants, her steward and her housekeeper. Jennet Jaffrey was also one of Susanna's oldest and dearest friends. She'd have been devastated by the death of her only son.

"I want to see Rosamond." Rob attempted to sound defiant but his high, piping voice defeated the effort.

So that was it. Susanna understood now why he'd stowed away. Jennet did not approve of her son's friendship with Rosamond. The two of them, together with Rob's two older sisters, had shared lessons at Leigh Abbey until Rob had gotten old enough to attend the village school instead.

Susanna acknowledged that the girl she had fostered for six years had been a bad influence on Jennet's son. Rosamond had led him into one scrape after another. But Rob had wept when she'd broken the news to him that Rosamond would not be returning to Leigh Abbey from Cornwall. She lived now with her mother and stepfather. Susanna missed her as much as young Rob did.

At Susanna's side, Nick Baldwin, her neighbor in Kent and sometime lover, fixed the lad with a steely glare. "You deserve a good thrashing. You'd get it if either of your parents were here."

Nick had business of his own in the West Country and had suggested making the journey together. Susanna had not needed much persuasion. Aside from her pleasure in his company, she appreciated the addition of his two stout henchmen to their numbers.

By the way Rob's lower lip stuck out, Susanna judged he felt more put-upon than repentant, and he showed no fear of Nick. "Think of your poor mother," she admonished him. "Jennet must be frantic with worry."

"Mother thinks I've gone to cousins near Dover."

"When did you plan to reveal yourself?" Nick asked.

Rob dared peek at them through his lashes. Susanna fancied he was trying to gauge how much it was safe to tell them. "Soon."

"When you ran out of food?" By the mulberry-colored stain creeping up the back of Rob's neck, Susanna knew she'd guessed well. "Retrieve what you brought with you and go along with Master Baldwin's men. We will talk again in the morning." Simon and Toby would see to it that the lad had something to eat before the three of them bedded down in the stable.

Nick stood beside her, watching the boy walk away. "I wonder how he managed to stay hidden so long? And keep up with us without a horse? Resourceful lad." Reluctant admiration crept into his voice.

"Those are questions for another day. Just now we must send word to Jennet. I fear she may already have discovered he's not where he's supposed to be." She sent a sharp look in Nick's direction. "Do you intend to thrash him *in loco parentis?*"

He shook his head. "The lad is already suffering, afflicted as he is with a most painful ailment."

Alarm shot through her. "What did I miss?" With all her knowledge of herbal remedies, there was likely something she could do to help young Rob.

"There is no cure but time for unrequited love."

"Unrequit –! But he's only nine years old."

"As is Rosamond, but he's been her devoted slave since they first met at the age of three. Consider the situation from his point of view. He feels that if he is old enough to be sent away to school, he is old enough to undertake this journey."

"It is true he is to matriculate at the King's School in Canterbury at the beginning of the next term, but what has that to do with Rosamond?"

"To his mind, they've been separated by cruel fate. Now that he's to leave home himself, what chance will they ever have to meet again?" He took Susanna's arm to escort her back inside the inn.

"They can write each other letters. Indeed, they do already."

At sea with this mad notion of children so determined to be together that one would risk his life to reach the other, Susanna readily agreed to Nick's suggestion that they sup together in the common room before she retired for the night. By the time he'd secured a table, bespoken their meal, and given orders for food to be sent to Susanna's chamber for her maid, Susanna had realized that they had no choice but to take Rob with them on the morrow. She could scarce send him home. They could not spare anyone to accompany him.

"You reward him for his bad behavior by giving him what he wants," Nick said when she told him what she'd decided.

"What else am I to do with him? He and Rosamond can bid each other sad farewells. Then we will return the grieving child to his parents. What a cheerful journey home that will be!"

When Nick produced paper, a portable ink pot, and a quill, Susanna scribbled a brief message to Jennet. Not for the first time, she was grateful her father had seen to it that all Leigh Abbey servants were taught to read. When she'd finished, she used her signet ring and the sealing wax Nick melted for her to secure the flaps of the thrice-folded paper.

He tucked the letter into the front of his doublet. "I will see this dispatched by messenger at first light," he promised. "Do you want to send word ahead to warn Pendennis or shall we surprise him?"

Susanna made a face at him. Warn Pendennis indeed! As if she did not know full well the real reason Nick's journey had so fortuitously coincided with her own. He wanted to see for himself that Sir Walter Pendennis and his wife, Rosamond's mother, had reconciled, visible proof Walter was no longer his rival for Susanna's affections. Men! She would never understand how they could keep a feud going so long after all reason for it had lapsed.

The innkeeper brought bread and butter, eggs, boiled and roast mutton, pigeon pie and a flask of wine. As they ate, Nick asked the question Susanna had been avoiding. "How did you guess Rob was hiding in that tapestry?"

She hesitated, aware of how he felt about those he contemptuously referred to as "figure flingers," but after a moment she told him about the seer. His expression grew darker with every word she uttered.

Containing his anger with an effort, he drained his wine cup and set the vessel down with a resounding thump. "She wants something."

"No doubt."

"You cannot believe she has the sight."

"No more than I believe in love potions or using magic to find missing objects, but I confess I am most curious to hear how she'll explain her knowledge of Rob's presence."

"Have no more to do with her, Susanna."

"I can scarce avoid it when we must share a chamber."

"Then promise me you will be careful. Such people are dangerous."

†

Some time later, when Susanna returned to her bedchamber, she found her tiring maid deep in conversation with the seer. At her mistress's entrance, Grace flushed and sprang to her feet.

"Have you had your fortune told?" Susanna asked. "Or have you been the one answering questions?

The stranger laughed. "I have no need to ask. I simply know. You found young Rob Jaffrey hiding in the cart."

"I thank you for your timely warning."

"And yet you doubt my gift."

"There must be thousands of people who claim to tell fortunes. Certes some few predictions must come true."

"I see I must prove myself." She thought for a moment. "Do you recall the tales your grandmother was wont to tell of the time she spent at court?"

Surprised by what seemed to be a complete shift in subject, Susanna nodded. Her father's mother had been a waiting gentlewoman to the first of King Henry VIII's queens. In her later years, she'd loved to regale the household at Leigh Abbey with stories from those youthful days.

"She talked of the wife of one Robert Amadas," she seer said, "master of the king's jewel house. Mistress Amadas was a woman with a gift. She was much given to prophecy."

Susanna was blessed with a gift of her own, an excellent memory. Although it had been almost thirty years since she'd last heard the tale, she had the story whole within moments. "Mistress Amadas was also much given to hallucinations. And cursed with a sharp tongue. She got into trouble for spreading tales about Sir William Compton's scandalous behavior with Lord Hastings's wife."

"She had the gift of seeing what others could not," the little woman insisted. "And I inherited it from her. I am Elizabeth Amadas."

"Well, Mistress Amadas, do you mean to predict more details of my future? Or mayhap tell me what I am thinking, for you seem to combine more than one skill in this gift of yours."

Responding to Susanna's sarcasm with a glare, the little woman spoke with unexpected heat. "You do not deserve any more warnings." Then, without another word, she disrobed, climbed into bed, and pulled the coverlet over her head to block out the candlelight.

†

In the morning, after she had broken her fast with bread and ale, Susanna called Rob Jaffrey to her. They had the inn's common room to themselves. The others in their party were in the stableyard, preparing to resume their journey.

"You will accompany us to Cornwall," she informed him.

"Thank you, madam. I will not be in the way. You'll see. I'll earn my keep."

"I expect you to do so." His delight made a mockery of her firm voice and fierce expression. "You may begin at once. Go and help Master Baldwin with the horses."

In his hurry to obey he nearly knocked Elizabeth Amadas off her feet.

"Slow down, lad," she cautioned him. "You will do yourself an injury." Ignoring his stammered apology, she entered the common room and addressed Susanna. "Will it convince you of my gift if I am able to tell you something known only to you and Mistress Rosamond?"

"And what would that be?" Susanna asked.

"Your foster daughter does much admire certain stones called Bristol crystals. When she could not persuade her mother to share those she'd been given, she 'borrowed' two. She keeps them in the hidden drawer of the globe in her schoolroom."

Taken aback, Susanna stared at Mistress Amadas. "You know more than I do, mistress."

But Rosamond had spoken of these Bristol crystals in a letter. The glittering stones, also called Cornish diamonds and St. Vincent's rocks, were transparent rock crystal of little value but they were sometimes sold to the unwary as diamonds. Sir Walter Pendennis, Rosamond's stepfather, was a justice of the peace. A case had come before him the previous summer that concerned some of these baubles. He'd sent the malefactor off to gaol, charged with fraud. It appeared he'd then made a present of the evidence to Eleanor, Rosamond's mother.

Susanna frowned. An odd gift. There had been a time when Eleanor prized only the most expensive possessions. She must value these Bristol crystals for some private reason.

She thought over what else Rosamond had said in her letters. Rambling accounts of whatever struck the girl's fancy, they covered many close-written pages. She did not often refer to her mother, although she had provided Susanna with details of Eleanor's difficulty finding a suitable gentlewoman to employ as her companion.

The self-proclaimed seer gasped and clapped both hands over her mouth.

"What is it?" Susanna demanded. "What is wrong?"

Eyes squeezed tightly shut, the tiny woman swayed. Susanna grasped her upper arm to prevent her falling. At once the seer's lids lifted, but her gaze was fixed, as if whatever she stared at lay beyond the ken of mere mortals.

"Elizabeth!" Susanna said sharply, giving her a shake. "Come back."

The gray eyes blinked. "We must help her," Elizabeth whispered. And with that enigmatic statement, she rushed out of the common room.

Susanna hesitated, wondering if she should call for Nick. Then she remembered Rob, who had nearly suffocated. If this situation was as dire as Elizabeth's behavior indicated, they had no time to lose. She hurried after the other woman, reaching her side just as Elizabeth opened the door to an empty chamber and went in. She crossed directly to a wall hanging, twitched it aside, and began to descend the privy stair hidden behind it.

Again Susanna hesitated, but again she followed. The steps were steep, and increasingly uneven as they neared the bottom. The only light was what filtered down through the hanging.

As she went, Susanna fumbled in the pouch suspended from her waist until her searching fingers located the candle stub, flint, and steel she kept there for emergencies. At the foot of the stair, she lit the candle, illuminating a narrow passage. Six cautious paces brought her into a larger, vaulted space. There a single rush dip burned in a wall sconce, casting eerie shadows.

Had Elizabeth Amadas not seemed so agitated, Susanna would have balked at venturing farther into the murky underground room, but the other woman was already groping her way along one side of the cellar. "Here," she whispered. "A servant sent down for supplies. A fall."

Certes *someone* had left that torch burning, but although Susanna listened for groans or whimpers she heard nothing but her own breathing and that of the woman ahead of her.

"In there." Elizabeth pointed to a high stone step below an opening in the wall. It appeared to lead to a room of some sort, mayhap for storing wine, but the entrance was less than three feet high and the interior was unlit.

The hairs on the back of Susanna's neck prickled. She was already turning to retrace her steps, meaning to go for help, when pain lanced through the back of her skull. Stars burst before her eyes. Then there was only blackness.

†

"Where is she, Cowdrey?" Nick Baldwin slammed the innkeeper against the wall and tightened his grip on the fellow's throat. "A gentlewoman does not vanish without a trace unless she's been helped on her way. Tell me what you know and quickly or it will be the worse for you."

Through a red haze, Nick saw his host's contorted face work. Denials. Protests of innocence. Finally a confession to watering the wine. But he could tell Nick nothing about Susanna's sudden disappearance. Half an hour since, when Nick had gone to fetch her from the common room, he'd discovered she was no longer anywhere in the inn. Neither was Rob Jaffrey. A frantic search of every room had roused one unhappy pair of newlyweds from their nuptial bed but had otherwise revealed only inn servants and Nick's own party.

"What of the other woman who shared her chamber?" Nick's voice rose to a bellow and he gave Cowdrey another shake for good measure.

"I know naught of her!" But the brief flash of guilt in his goggling eyes was enough for Nick. He tightened his grip. "A bribe. That is all it was. I swear it. She bribed me to tell your party that I had but one room suitable for women travelers."

"The one she already occupied?"

"Aye."

Nick barely had time to absorb that information before he heard a flurry of activity at the entrance to the stableyard. Rob burst through the gathered servants, eyes wild and chest heaving from the speed of his run. His face was dirt streaked and marred with several small cuts. His clothing was disheveled and likewise dirty, especially at the knees. "They've taken her!" he cried. "They've kidnapped Lady Appleton."

One of Nick's big hands settled on the lad's shoulder, but he kept hold of the innkeeper with the other. "Who has, boy?"

"The seer. We must hurry. They have horses. They're taking Lady Appleton away."

Nick shoved Cowdrey aside. His men had been mounted and ready to go – with Grace on a pillion behind Simon – when they discovered Susanna's absence. "Leave the cart," he ordered now. "Rob, take your mistress's mare." He pointed a finger at the guide he'd hired to help them find the quickest route to the main road into Cornwall. "Do you know all the territory around here?"

"As well as any, sir."

"Then keep up with us. You'll be well rewarded for your service. Which way?" he asked the boy.

Following Rob, they forged a path through Glastonbury's early morning traffic. "There were four men," the lad said.

That explained why he'd not done more than run for help. "How did they get her away?"

"Through a tunnel." By the time he'd explained that he'd stopped outside the common room to listen when he'd heard Rosamond's name mentioned, they'd reached the gatehouse of an old abandoned abbey.

Not far distant from the inn but well-concealed by walls and trees, the ruined buildings covered more than thirty acres. "The tunnel came out there," Rob said, pointing.

Stumbling over his words, he told Nick how Susanna had followed the fortune-teller down a flight of hidden stairs at the inn to enter a cellar where a man with a cudgel had been waiting to knock her on the head.

"Then he and the woman dragged her into the tunnel. I followed them. I was afraid I'd lose sight of her if I went for help." Rob slanted a nervous glance at Nick. He had to swallow hard before he could continue. "They had horses waiting. And more men. Four in all. That's when I left her. To get help."

"You did well, lad." Calling out would have made the villains aware they'd been seen and most likely have lead them to capture Rob. Or kill him. "Was Lady Appleton still unconscious when they rode off?"

Rob nodded. "They tied her onto a pillion, with her hands around the rider's waist so she'd not fall. Then they pulled her cloak around her to hide the ropes."

The image made Nick's blood boil but he contained his anger. Time enough to explode later. "Which way did they go?"

"The road to Meare," their guide said when Rob showed them the direction the riders had taken.

Nick dug his heels into his horse's flanks and set off, the others after him. He hoped they'd shortly overtake Susanna and rescue her, but although he kept a sharp watch all the while, he saw no sign of the party they pursued. They were well away from Gloucester and into rough country before they came at last upon a man herding pigs who'd seen four men and two women pass by on horseback.

Encouraged, they pushed on, following narrow, meandering lanes that seemed to be bearing north and east. Only once, far ahead, did Nick glimpse a plume of dust that might have been kicked up by riders. He turned to the guide. "If those are the villains we seek, where are they headed?"

"They be bound o'er Zomerzet levels, into Mendip."

Mendip, Nick recalled, was a high, rough, rocky area, partially forested but full of cliffs and caves and swallets and underground streams, a landscape containing an untold number of places in which a woman could be concealed.

†

Susanna's awareness of her surroundings returned in fits and starts. The back of her head throbbed. The sting of a dozen cuts and scrapes was so intense it brought tears to her eyes. That she was in constant motion, jiggled and jostled about, occasionally slipping sideways into an even more uncomfortable position, added to her sense of unreality and the aches from the battering her limp body had already endured.

She tried to move and found she could not. Both her wrists and her ankles were tied. The left side of her face pressed into a thick wool surface, the hood of her own cloak. Beneath that layer of cloth she felt something solid yet flexible that smelled of leather and sweat ... and horse. Bewildered, she concluded she was on horseback, riding on a pillion with both arms wrapped around the waist of the man in the saddle in front of her, but she could not think how she'd gotten there.

"She be wakeful." Susanna felt as well as heard the deep rumble of a male voice, since she was tied to him. The rope binding them both bit into her armpits as the horse, cursed with an uneven gait to begin with, began a steep ascent.

As her scattered thoughts regrouped, Susanna made a swift inventory of her situation. Her injuries seemed to be minor, if painful. Too late, she understood that what she'd thought was a room in the cellar of the inn had been a tunnel. Judging by the bruises and scrapes she'd acquired, they'd dragged her through it for some distance.

Listening hard, Susanna heard naught but the clop of hooves, the whisper of leaves, and the occasional murmur of a nearby stream. No voices. No sounds of commerce. Wherever they were, they had left Glastonbury well behind them.

In an attempt to dislodge the hood that had been drawn up over her face and tucked in so that she could see only a sliver of the passing countryside, Susanna moved her head. Pain speared through her, as much from holding her neck in one awkward position for too long as from the blow she'd taken.

"If you struggle, we will have to knock you senseless again," Elizabeth Amadas remarked in a pleasant voice.

Susanna stilled. She had not been gagged, but it was not easy getting words out through muffling layers of wool. "What do you want from me?"

"From you? Nothing. But from your friends, a great deal. You have value to them, I do think. They should be willing to ransom you for a goodly sum."

Susanna digested that information, then asked, "Where are you taking me?"

"To a place where no one will ever find you."

Unenlightened, Susanna fell silent. If she could determine her location, judge how far they'd come from Glastonbury, she might be able to use that information to escape. But concentrate as she might, she could gather only scattered impressions of the route they took. She knew when they crossed stone bridges or forded streams and she could tell the difference between a rough uphill track and the path into a deep valley. Once she smelled wild garlic growing nearby. Another time she caught a glimpse of butterflies in a field. But by and large her senses were of little use.

It was dusk when they stopped. They'd spent the entire day in the saddle. It was impossible to guess how far they'd come, although over such uneven terrain Susanna thought it unlikely they'd covered as much as twenty miles. Ten seemed more probable.

It might as well be a hundred if Nick had no idea where to look for her. That he would try to find her, she had no doubt, but Elizabeth's plan had been a clever one. Susanna had been spirited away without fuss. To those left behind, it must have seemed as if she'd vanished into thin air.

Susanna stumbled when she was untied and lifted from the pillion. Her feet had lost all feeling during the long ride. As she tried to stamp life back into them, she covertly surveyed her surroundings. They'd stopped under cover of trees. The last of the sun dappled the stony, downward-sloping path with shades of gray. It appeared to descend into a narrow gorge.

For the first time, Susanna got a good look at her captors. Elizabeth Amadas had four men with her, rough-looking brutes who'd been mounted on small, sturdy horses. One by one they led their animals toward an outcropping of rock. One by one, three of them disappeared into a hidden cleft.

Before Susanna could see more, the fourth ruffian seized her arm and hustled her after the others. The entrance to the cave was barely high enough to accommodate a riderless horse and the area just inside was passing narrow. The footrest on the pillion scraped against the side as the horse Susanna had been riding moved skittishly into the hillside.

They continued on for some two hundred paces in near blackness, descending all the while down a steep slope before emerging, of a sudden, into the upper level of a cavern. The flickering light of a torch revealed what at first appeared to be an immense void. Above her head, Susanna could not discern a roof. At her feet lay a chasm. To her horror, her captors produced a rope ladder and flung it over the side.

"Climb down," Elizabeth ordered.

Susanna balked at the idea of descending into the bowels of the earth but one glance at the other woman's face told her she that if she did not willingly obey, she'd be hauled down by one of the men.

It was slow going with long skirts to manage. If for no other reason than to keep her mind off the dark pit beneath her feet, Susanna tried to calculate how far she descended. The rungs were set apart by the distance from her knee to her ankle. Seven to a fathom, she reckoned.

Some two fathoms down, the rocks abruptly sheered away from the rope ladder. Susanna froze. With nothing to touch for balance or guidance, she succumbed to a momentary panic. Certain she was about to fall, she would have attempted to climb back up had the way not been blocked by the men coming down after her.

Anxious for solid ground beneath her feet, even if it was the floor of an underground cavern, Susanna resumed her descent. She counted twelve more fathoms and could hear the rush of water from an underground stream before her boot at last touched bottom.

Elizabeth's henchmen brought light with them. She followed, leaving the last man above with the horses. "Light a fire," she instructed, "and find the cookpot."

By the erratic beams of torches made of sheaves of reed sedge, Susanna saw piles of supplies stacked against the cavern wall, sufficient provisions to feed a small band of outlaws for some weeks. The tension in her shoulders eased slightly. It seemed unlikely they would leave her here alone.

The cooking fire flared up, spilling light into dark corners, revealing a river wider than Susanna had expected. Nearer at hand, the glitter of reflected light caught her attention. Curious, she stepped closer. A rock crystal. It could be nothing else, given its resemblance to a diamond.

All around the crystal were spherical balls of a reddish stone. One broke loose as Susanna fingered it. Fragile, so light that she imagined it must be hollow within, it reminded her of an egg. When Elizabeth called to her she slipped it, unseen, into the pouch that still held flint and steel. She'd lost her candle stub in the cellar of the George.

"You mocked my skill as a seer," the little woman taunted her, "and I readily admit that I cozened you, but there *are* those born with special gifts. My husband was a jowser."

The West Country pronunciation confused Susanna for a moment before she realized that Elizabeth meant her spouse had possessed the ability to locate things with the help of a dowsing-rod. "He found water?"

"He found calamine. No one could equal his talent."

Susanna did not reply. She'd never seen anyone work a dowsing-rod but she knew enough about the subject to realize that if a dowser grasped his hazel branch tightly in his fingers and held his arms close to his sides, he could make the rod seem to move of its own volition by pressing his hands together.

She was no expert, but she was widely read, and Walter Pendennis had talked to her a bit about mining a few years back. She remembered that calamine stone could be mixed with copper to make latten and that latten, brass compounded in specific proportions, could be used in turn in the manufacture of ordnance. Deposits of calamine stone, she recalled, were notoriously difficult to locate in England. Most latten had to be imported.

Susanna knew one other thing about calamine, too. Rock crystals were often found near such deposits. When she was allowed a few minutes of privacy in the secluded corner of the cavern set aside as a latrine, she examined the "egg" she'd found more closely. It cracked open when she squeezed it, revealing a half dozen transparent crystals fixed all around the cavity.

†

Susanna was given a pallet and fed. After the meal, Elizabeth produced paper, ink, and a quill. All manner of supplies appeared to have been stockpiled in the cavern.

"The ransom is two hundred pounds, to be gathered and sent to the George in Glastonbury. Write that message. Say also that you are well and will remain so if they obey. Then make a copy."

When both missives had been sanded and sealed – Elizabeth had indeed thought of everything – Susanna sat on her pallet, leaned back against the cushions provided for her comfort, and considered what she knew about her captors.

Elizabeth was clearly in command here, the leader of this small band of villains. Her husband, by the way she spoke of him, was either dead or in prison. What Susanna could not understand was why the woman had chosen her as a victim. And why two hundred pounds? True, 'twas enough to keep a substantial household for a year, but Susanna was wealthy enough that they might have asked for much more.

"How did you learn so much about me?" She allowed a hint of admiration to come into her voice. "You presented most convincing details. I was halfway to believing that you were a seer in truth."

Elizabeth was not immune to flattery. "Diligence, Lady Appleton."

Hoping Mistress Amadas, if that was indeed her real name, would be unable to resist the temptation to boast of her own cleverness, Susanna encouraged her to preen. "You must have intercepted the letter Rosamond wrote about the Bristol crystals, but how did you learn of my impending journey to Cornwall?"

"You are well known in your part of Kent, Lady Appleton," Elizabeth said. "A subject of much speculation."

"Did you follow me when I left, hoping for a chance to arrange an accidental meeting?"

"Oh, no, madam. I left nothing to chance. I knew your itinerary in advance. I thought of everything, even this foolish attempt to coax me into saying more than I should. Sleep well, Lady Appleton. I intend to." With that, as she had at the inn, Elizabeth turned her back on Susanna, curled onto her pallet, and pulled a coverlet over her face.

Susanna dozed fitfully. Although she knew she needed rest if she was to outwit her captors, she also wanted to stay alert long enough to take note of their movements. When she concluded that the guard set on the upper level was relieved at regular intervals, she gave herself permission to drift off, but for a long time sleep eluded her. Dampness pervaded the cavern, making her glad of her wool cloak. Her hand, if she let it stray off the straw pallet, touched stone rough with lichen. And she was uncomfortably aware she was deep beneath the earth. She did not know how miners stood the sensation of being buried alive.

Morning came in the same degree of darkness as the night, harkened only by the stirring of one of Elizabeth's henchmen by the fire. Susanna stretched, winced, and levered herself to her feet, feeling as if she'd aged ten years in a night.

There was bread and ale with which to break their fast. While Susanna ate, Elizabeth dispatched two of her men with the ransom notes.

Why two? Susanna did not care for the logical answer. One to Nick. Another to someone else. To Cornwall? Did the Bristol crystals Walter had given Eleanor have something to do with this? Now that Susanna thought about it, she recalled that Elizabeth had known more about them than Rosamond had written in her letters.

She glanced at the rope ladder as she sipped, then blinked in surprise. No one was paying any attention to it. Or to her. Elizabeth had retired to the makeshift privy. The remaining henchman's attention was fully occupied by his efforts to dislodge crystal-bearing stones.

Susanna set aside her cup and eased to her feet, knowing she'd never get a better chance to escape.

†

Nick Baldwin studied the cliffs surrounding the gorge, pearly, pale grey rock for the most part, although they'd passed outcroppings of red sandstone on their journey. Just at dusk, they'd lost the trail and been forced to abandon the search for Susanna. They'd spent the night in one of the area's numerous small caves, after a colony of bats had left on their nocturnal hunt for food.

A peregrine flew across his field of vision. The birds nested hereabout, as did ravens. And butterflies, he'd discovered, were as common as blue damsel flies. But of the kidnappers and their victim, Nick found no trace. For all he knew, Susanna might be miles away.

No sooner had he entertained that possibility, when two men appeared on the track ahead. Rob's sharply indrawn breath was all the confirmation Nick needed to identify them.

"Pretend to give way," he ordered his men. "Then close in and take them as they ride past us."

There was a moment when all might have been lost. One of the villains reined it, recognition dawning on his bovine features. He'd have turned and fled had Nick not swiftly drawn his sword and borne down upon him with Simon and Toby at his heels. Seeing the desire to strike them dead for what they'd done to Susanna in his eyes, the miscreants gave up without much of a fight.

The message each man carried was enough to condemn him. Written in Susanna's own hand, the notes demanded payment of two hundred pounds. One had been addressed to Nick himself, at the George, the other to Sir Walter Pendennis, Priory House, Cornwall.

"I know these men," Rob said when the prisoners had been trussed up and deprived of their knives. "One I saw along the Harroway, the other after we turned toward Glastonbury."

Nick's hands curled into fists at his sides. Coincidence might account for two separate parties traveling along the ancient long-distance route from Kent to Cornwall, but it defied the odds that these fellows should also have taken the same detour, the ridgeway that bore northeast.

"Two nights past," Rob continued, "the second man and two others slept in the stable, as I did. They sat up late, drinking and dicing and telling tales. That one recounted the story of Cleopatra, who rolled herself up in a carpet in order to meet Julius Caesar. I had heard of the trick at school, but I'd never have thought to hide myself inside Lady Pendennis's tapestry if he'd not reminded me of it."

Clever, Nick acknowledged. And if Rob had not taken the suggestion, they'd no doubt have devised some other scheme to incline Susanna to trust the seer's word. "Did he also roll that tapestry against the side of the cart so that you were trapped inside and near died?"

Rob frowned. "It was not until the cart stopped at the George that the tapestry shifted."

Nick drew the lad aside. "Tell me, Rob – were there others who endeavored to assist you along the way? People who helped you stay out of sight?"

Rob's answers confirmed Nick's suspicions. It seemed likely the boy had been watched over all the way from Leigh Abbey. These villains had known of his desire to be reunited with Rosamond and used it to capture Susanna.

"You are in a perilous position," Nick said, addressing his captives. "Holding a gentlewoman for ransom is a hanging matter."

Sullen silence greeted this statement.

"Fortunately for you, I am not the sort to hold a grudge, and 'tis obvious you do but obey the orders of the woman who employs you. So here is what I propose. You tell me all you know, including the location of your prisoner, and I will petition the queen herself for pardons."

He'd not wager money that they'd be granted, but that scarce mattered. Time was of the essence now. He needed directions and he needed them quickly, in case Mistress Amadas decided a living prisoner was more trouble than she was worth. Now that the ransom notes had been written, she might think she no longer needed Susanna in order to collect the money.

The bigger of the two prisoners turned to Simon. "Is your master a magistrate?"

"Not yet," Simon replied honestly, "but he'll be appointed a justice of the peace by the next quarter sessions. He got the letter about it before we left Kent."

There were no secrets from servants, and for once Nick was glad of it.

The bigger of the two prisoners offered to lead them to Susanna.

"How many more of you are there?" Nick asked a short time later, as they started down a path with delicate scree on either side.

"Two men and the widow."

"Lady Appleton do you mean?"

"Nay, the other one. Jowser's widow. She's the one come up with this plan. She's the one to blame."

"What has she against Lady Appleton?"

"Summat to do with Jowser dying in gaol," the second man said.

"But the woman at the inn was not named Jowser," Grace objected. She and Rob had been hanging on every word.

"Her husband called himself Jowser. That's all I know. He made us call the woman 'mistress.' " He hawked and spat, then grinned. "Had grand ideas, did Jowser, till he got himself sentenced for selling Bristol crystals for diamonds."

Bristol crystals – Rob had mentioned overhearing a reference to such stones in connection with Rosamond. The story still did not make sense to Nick, but at least he could now guess at the connection. "The magistrate in the case, I warrant, was Sir Walter Pendennis."

"Aye."

But further questions yielded no useful information. Their "mistress" had given orders without explanations and paid them well to obey.

After a treacherous passage over on slippery rocks and a stretch of anemone-filled woods, they reached the entrance to a cave. It opened out into a cavern of immense proportions. An empty cavern.

"They 'ood never a-went," the bigger man objected.

"Took the horses, too," Simon pointed out.

Nick's first fear was that they'd killed Susanna and left her body below, but a quick descent and search of the cavern relieved that worry. "Was Lady Appleton bound?" Nick asked when he'd ascended the rope ladder once more.

The fellow revealed they'd untied her, thinking her naught but a woman, and getting on in years at that. He pointed out that Susanna had a limp.

Nick strode into the sunlight, a grim expression on his face. That old injury to her leg would not slow her down if she was determined to get away. She'd escaped. That much was clear. And her captors were doubtless in pursuit.

She'd go up, he thought. Out into the open rather than take the risk of being trapped. And she'd attempt to return to Glastonbury, hoping to find him still there. A rocky prominence rose above him, whence one could see out over the gorge and across all the low-lying Somerset countryside to the south.

"This way," he barked at his troops, and led them into mixed woodland.

Oaks, alders, and willows were native to the Mendips. White banks of ransoms broke the green of the trees. Once, he caught sight of a hare, a sandy, black-pointed creature most unlike his reddish cousins in Kent. Of signs that Susanna had passed this way he found none.

Then they were climbing in the open again. Almost at once, Nick caught sight of a flash of light ahead, then another. As he watched, the bursts continued, coming at erratic intervals.

He was no seer, but as the signal dazzled his eyes, he knew with a certainty that, somehow, Susanna was behind it.

†

Wary of remaining too close to the edge of the cliff, Susanna backed away, the Bristol crystals clutched in one hand. Many-faceted, without being shaped by a jeweler, they were as brilliant as real diamonds but without their inner fire.

She swayed a little in the hot sun. She needed to be in the open so she could see anyone who approached her, but the lack of sleep and the many injuries she'd sustained during the last twenty-four hours had left her weak and dizzy. She felt over-warm. It was only with difficulty that she kept her focus.

It had been a risk using the crystals to attempt to catch Nick's attention. The flashes would also have been clearly visible to Elizabeth Amadas and her henchmen. Susanna had no doubt they were pursuing her. They'd have come after her the moment the guard she'd knocked out revived enough to lower the ladder into the cavern once more.

Susanna would have taken it away with her if she'd had the strength, but it had taken all her energy to haul it up after her, then deal with the guard. Only the fact that he'd been intent on currying his horse, humming to the beast as he worked, had allowed her sneak up behind him, strike him with a rock, and get away. She'd considered taking the horses, but given the terrain she'd decided she'd make better time on foot. Too late, she'd realized she should have driven them off so her pursuers could not use them either.

The climb had been fraught with difficulty. For the most part she'd tried to ignore the dramatic view of the gorge below and concentrate on placing her feet safely on the steep, narrow path that took her up through trees and ferns, boulders and scree to the top of an escarpment. Pausing for breath, she'd looked off to the south, in the direction she supposed Glastonbury must lie. The only habitation she'd been able to make out was a smattering of pudding stone cottages. She'd been considering how to reach them when she'd looked back the way she'd come and there, far below, caught sight of a familiar green cloak. Nick. Searching for her.

Of Elizabeth, she'd seen no sign, but she was certain the other woman was somewhere nearby. Should she stay here, out in the open, waiting for Nick? He'd reach this point eventually, even if he had not seen her signal.

So might Elizabeth, in which case it would seem exceeding foolish to remain where she was, but Susanna was tired, hurting. She lacked the stamina to reach that village. Even though she was aware she was not thinking clearly, might be making a fatal mistake, she chose to walk to the nearest tree, a spindly ash, and sit down in the small pool of shade beneath its branches.

She watched butterflies and grasshoppers, and once caught sight of a roe deer, while enjoying the profusion of herbs and flowers that grew in the meadow.

In the woods, even in flight, she had recognized lily of the valley and Solomon's seal. Now she had time to appreciate others – saxifrage and self heal, blue groomwell and ox-eye daisies. Birdsong soothed her. There were nests nearby – black-tailed godwit, lapwing, redshank, and bullfinches, who went by the local name of "whoops." A kestrel flew past, far overhead. Hunting.

With a start, Susanna realized she'd almost drifted into sleep in the warmth of the summer day. She struggled upright, bracing her back against the bark, just as the first party of searchers emerged onto the gruffy ground at the top of the prominence.

Face livid, Elizabeth Amadas drove her horse straight toward Susanna. She meant, mayhap, to run her down. Susanna willed herself not to flinch. She moved only at the last possible moment, opening her hand so that the crystals her fist had concealed caught the full light of the sun.

Blinded by the sudden glare, the horse reared in panic, throwing its rider. Before Elizabeth could recover, Susanna seized the smaller woman, using every bit of strength she possessed to jerk her erstwhile captor's arms behind her. Holding Elizabeth like a shield, Susanna faced the woman's henchmen, but by then they had no interest in helping their employer. Nick had arrived.

Held close in her lover's embrace a few moments later, Susanna felt a quiet elation fill her. She had survived. Triumphed. She stirred in his arms.

"Let me take care of you. I'll see to everything," he whispered.

She smiled up at him but shook her head. She needed to sleep soon, and for a good long time, and she hoped he'd be beside her when she did, but there was something else she had to settle first. It could not be delegated to anyone else.

Hands bound behind her, guarded by Nick's men, Elizabeth Amadas was not in a good mood. She cursed Susanna and spat at Nick. Standing out of range, they conferred. Nick told Susanna what he'd deduced. She shared with him what little Elizabeth had revealed to her in the cavern.

"But I believe I know the rest," she said, speaking loudly enough for the prisoner to hear every word. "When Elizabeth's husband died in gaol, she vowed to take revenge on Walter Pendennis, who had sent him there. To carry out her scheme, she became part of his household."

"Undetected by him?" Nick asked in astonishment. Sir Walter Pendennis had once been one of Queen Elizabeth's most formidable information gatherers – a master among spies.

"I doubt he knew anything about her. And Elizabeth would have used an alias. But one of Rosamond's recent letters included an account of her mother's search for a waiting gentlewoman. None of them stay long and Rosamond gave no names, but she described several of them. "Tiny as one of the fairy folk," she said of that woman who held the post for the longest stretch."

"You can prove nothing," Elizabeth said.

Susanna met her fulminating gaze. "Shall we take you to Cornwall with us and see if Eleanor Pendennis recognizes you? I do not imagine you were there long, but you would have heard, from servants' gossip if not from observation, that Walter and his wife have a ... tempestuous relationship. You feared that if you kidnapped her, he'd might just let you keep her. You'd get neither ransom nor the satisfaction of depriving him of a much-loved spouse."

Nick swore under his breath.

Susanna ignored him. There was little either of them could do about Walter's continued affection for her. Nor about what the Pendennis household thought of Walter's reconciliation with Eleanor. "You decided that Sir Walter would be more willing to pay for my release than for that of his own wife, and that by killing me after you had the ransom, you could hurt him more deeply than you would if you made him a widower. Mayhap you were correct. I cannot say."

The angry expression on Elizabeth's face had deteriorated into a sneer. Had she intended that Susanna die, her ultimate revenge on Walter for his responsibility in the jowser's death? "He'll suffer for a time," she hissed. "I dispatched one of my men to Cornwall with the ransom note."

"Did you indeed? Then I fear you have made a mistake. Despite appearances, Walter is reconciled with his wife. He'd be far more devastated to lose her than me."

A sly look came into Elizabeth's eyes. "A pity, then, that she is the one behind all that has transpired. Lady Pendennis wants you dead, Lady Appleton. It was her idea to demand you bring her that tapestry and the other household goods in the cart. We planned together how you could be obliged to return to Cornwall, to deliver those things to her yourself."

"I might believe you," Susanna mused, "but you have forgotten about Rosamond." The little girl was the real reason for this visit, and Eleanor knew that better than anyone.

"I forget nothing." It was very nearly a snarl.

"Ah, yes. You are a seer. You know everything."

"Curious, then," Nick murmured, "that she did not realize both her messengers have been captured. They are in a small cave along the trail, securely bound."

When they went to collect them, Susanna discovered the answer to her one remaining question. The smaller of the two men admitted he'd lived near Leigh Abbey for several months, sent there by his mistress to spy on the household. While there he had heard, by chance, some of the old stories Susanna's grandmother had been wont to tell. It had been the tale of Mistress Amadas, the one at the court of Henry VIII, that had inspired Elizabeth Jowser to pose as a fortune teller in order to lure Susanna away from the rest of her party.

"If she does have any skill as a seer," Susanna remarked, after they'd turned their prisoners over to the local authorities in Glastonbury, retrieved their cart, and made their way to another inn for the night, "mayhap she knows already whether she'll end her days in a house of correction or at the end of a rope." Dangerous as Elizabeth was, it disturbed Susanna to think that she might die for her crimes. She had not, after all, killed anyone.

"I do not have supernatural powers," Nick said with a rueful chuckle, "but I believe I can predict the outcome of her trial. She had controlled her temper by the time she came before the justice of the peace. He took one look, saw a delicate little flower of a woman, and did, in an instant, much pity her. By the time she comes before him for sentencing, she'll have him eating out of her hand."

"You think he'll let her go?"

"I would not be surprised," Nick said, "if he ended up marrying her."

A Note from the Author

I've stayed at the George and Pilgrims in Glastonbury. It is reputed to have had, in its early days, a tunnel that led onto Glastonbury Abbey grounds. Unfortunately, if it ever existed, it is there no longer.

Bristol crystals are also called Bristol diamonds, Bristol stones, Bristowes, St. Vincent's rocks, Cornish diamonds, and Irish diamonds, depending upon where they were found. They are rock crystals, usually colorless quartz. In the sixteenth century they were described as "counterfeiting precious stones." The cavern I've described does not exist, but it could. The landscape north and west of Glastonbury is dotted with caverns, caves, cliffs, and old mines.

Encore for a Neck Verse

September 19, 1576

Alarmed by her companion's sudden stillness, Susanna, Lady Appleton, widowed gentlewoman of Leigh Abbey, Kent, looked up from a display of smallwares in front of a Dover haberdasher's shop. To her relief, the strongest emotion showing on Nick Baldwin's beloved face was bewilderment. Whatever had startled him did not present an immediate danger.

"Odd," Nick murmured. "The fellow coming out of that cookshop is the image of Stephen Bourne."

Susanna glanced in the direction of his gaze, although half her attention had already returned to the quill pens she was thinking of buying. A scarecrow-thin man all in gray, even to the feather in his bonnet, stopped to rotate his left shoulder, as if easing some old injury.

"Ho, there!" Nick shouted, advancing toward him.

"Do you address me, sir?" Spoken with a slight stammer, the words carried a suggestion of panic and Susanna thought she saw a flash of recognition in the fellow's wide-spaced brown eyes before he blanked his features.

Mayhap Nick did know him.

"Bourne?"

"Julius Woodward, at your service." Now stone-faced as a gargoyle, his stance almost defiant, Woodward held his ground as Nick approached him.

"I crave your forgiveness. I mistook you for an Oundle man."

"Mappen the fellow looks like me, but Oundle means nowt, nor Bourne, neither. Good day to you, sir. And madam." With an abrupt nod, he continued on his way along Priory Road.

An expression of deep suspicion etched Nick's features as he watched Woodward pass the cemetery attached to the Maison Dieu, a hospital founded centuries earlier for the benefit of pilgrims passing through Dover, and disappear into the cross street by the little chapel dedicated to St. Edmund. "I warrant you will think me mad," he said to Susanna, "but I believe I have just seen a ghost."

"Passing solid for a spirit." She continued to contemplate the items set out on the haberdasher's pentice. Goodman Kelling offered a wide assortment of merchandise for sale, everything from pins and needles to mousetraps. The larger items – curtains, sheets, tablecloths, even shifts and shirts and other bits of clothing – were displayed inside the shop.

"Aye." Nick did not sound convinced.

"It *is* possible for a man to have a double. Or a twin."

"One who denies he's ever heard of the market town of Oundle yet betrays with every word he speaks that he hails from Northamptonshire? Moreover, this Julius Woodward not only resembles Bourne in physical appearance, he favors the same colors. And he has, as Bourne did, what good Northamptonshire men call a maffle."

"The stammer?" She replaced the ornate little dagger she'd discovered between a lantern and a stack of almanacs and chapbooks and gave Nick her full attention.

"Aye. You're quick, as ever."

Nick's admiring smile warmed Susanna. They had been neighbors here in Kent for a long time, and friends, and sometimes more. She knew she was the only woman he had ever asked to marry him. She had turned him down, rejecting not his offer of love but the legal alliance that gave a husband complete control over both the person and the property of his wife. It was not that Susanna did not trust Nick. She simply saw no need to remarry. There were too many advantages to widowhood.

At times her adamant refusal to reconsider resulted in a certain strain between them, but she knew he had no doubt that she cared about him and she did not question his devotion to her. All in all, they muddled along well enough. She was not surprised when Nick escorted her into the cookshop Woodward had just left.

The proprietor sold meat pies and stews, evidently of some succulence, for there were several people waiting to buy. The air was redolent with garlic and onion.

"What reason would your Master Bourne have to hide his identity?" Susanna asked in a quiet voice.

"Bourne, alive, would have much to answer for, if the tale I heard at second hand from my housekeeper is true."

"Goodwife Billings?"

"Goodwife Chappell," Nick corrected her.

Susanna smiled. Through their combined efforts, she and Nick had made it possible for Mary Billings to remarry. Her second husband, Edward Chappell, served as steward at Nick's Northamptonshire estate.

"Time passes far too quickly," she murmured, performing rapid calculations.

How long had it been since they'd found proof Goodman Billings was dead and, as an unexpected result of that investigation, sent a young woman and her newborn daughter to live at Candlethorpe? More than four and a half years! Although Susanna had meant to check on Jane Johnson and her child long before this, she had yet to visit Candlethorpe. Indeed, Nick himself did not spend much time there, preferring his lodgings in London and Whitethorn Manor in Kent, which adjoined Susanna's land.

"Two of your best meat pies," Nick told the cookshop owner, proffering a rose noble, "and information."

The woman's eyes goggled at the value of the coin, but a moment later it vanished beneath a none-too-clean apron.

Nick described Woodward to her, from his long, fitted rat's-color fustian doublet with its close-set buttons, to his scuffed leather boots, to the way he combed his hair forward at the front to form a short fringe over the forehead. "And he has a tuft of hair on the point of his chin," he finished. "Do you remember him?"

"Pencil beard and him all in dull gray? Aye, I know him. Woodward, his name is. He and his wife have a room at Molly Greene's victualing house." The woman grinned, showing a profusion of gaps where teeth had once been. "That's why he's been buying food from me. Molly's the worst cook in all of Kent."

"What does Woodward's wife look like?" Nick leaned a little forward as his interest quickened.

"Slender. Dark-hair. Big eyes."

"Doe-like," Nick murmured.

Susanna sent a sharp look in his direction at the description but refrained from asking questions until they'd left the cookshop. They took with them two savory meat pies and directions to the victualing house where Woodward and his wife had lodgings.

"This Bourne," Susanna said as they walked, munching. "I take it he is supposed to be dead?" The meat pie was very good indeed, tiny bits of shin of beef mixed with herbs and spices and generous chunks of carrot, white cabbage, celery, leeks, and parsnips.

"Murdered, according to Goodwife Chappell."

Susanna felt her eyebrows climb.

"In the same letter, which I received some months past, she also informed me that his killer had been caught. The Assizes are over for the year, Susanna. Those condemned for felonies have long since been hanged for their crimes. If Woodward *is* Bourne, an innocent man was executed."

"Might the man accused of killing Master Bourne have been allowed benefit of clergy?" Susanna was well aware that some convicted felons had escaped hanging by reciting the so-called "neck verse."

"A man who steals may be branded on the hand and discharged if he has his books, as they say, but murder is a crime excluded from the statutory qualifications for grants of clergy." Nick, a justice of the peace in Kent, had made a study of the current laws concerning such things.

Susanna, too, had reason to be familiar with the statutes on murder. But in her experience, bribes could sometimes subvert justice ... or secure it, depending upon one's point of view. "There are exceptions," she reminded Nick. "And pardons." The latter were the only recourse for women convicted of a felony, since women were specifically denied benefit of clergy.

But he shook his head. "I know the two crown judges who ride the Midland Circuit. It is rare they agree on anything. I cannot imagine either, let alone both, acting *ultra vires* to grant freedom to a convicted murderer."

"Then if Goodman Woodward *is* Goodman Bourne, there has been a great miscarriage of justice. A man died for a crime he could not have committed."

"Aye. And it seems to me all too possible that Bourne is alive, for there was never any body found."

Susanna missed her footing on the cobblestones and stumbled. "How can that be? What other proof of murder would a jury accept?"

"Remains." Nick caught her elbow to steady her. "They were discovered in Rockingham Forest. Some animal had been at them, leaving only a few bones and some scraps of clothing, but those bits were deemed sufficient to identify Stephen Bourne."

A passerby, overhearing, gave them a startled look before hurrying on.

Nick ignored him. "Having seen Julius Woodward, I must wonder if that judgment was warranted."

Susanna considered for a moment as she polished off the last of her meat pie, then asked, "Did Bourne have a wife?"

"Not his own. Stephen Bourne was a merchant in Oundle, the market town nearest Candlethorpe. A haberdasher, as it happens. He dealt in the same sort of smallwares Goodman Kelling stocks. As is not uncommon in rural towns, where the great livery companies that regulate such things in London are not so strong, a merchant may offer goods not strictly within his province.

Bourne had long been in competition with one Barnaby Morrison, a mercer by trade, selling shifts and shirts, cloth and clothing, and cheap bone lace. And Morrison, although he styled himself a clothier and sneered at Bourne as naught but a petty chapman, himself sold smallwares in addition to woolen clothing and Italian silks and velvets."

Susanna wiped her mouth with a handkerchief and made a futile effort to remove all the grease from her hands. Nick was engaged in a similar exercise, also fruitless. "So the wife you spoke of was Morrison's?"

"Aye. They both courted her, or so I am told. Morrison married her. When Bourne vanished, so did Clementine Morrison. At first everyone assumed they'd run off together. Then a hogherd made his grisly discovery. Of the missing wife there was no trace. Her husband, to no one's surprise, was arrested and accused of killing them both."

They had reached Goodwife Greene's victualing house, one of more than two dozen such establishments in Dover. Like Dover's inns, they offered beds for travelers at a modest fee.

Goodwife Greene was in her garden, busy hauling wet sheets out of a wicker basket and draping them on bushes to dry. The color of Nick's money persuaded her to tell them all she knew about Julius Woodward and his wife. To Susanna's disappointment, it was very little.

"Pretty little thing, she is," Goodwife Greene said as Susanna helped her spread the last of the laundry over a clump of privet, "but sharp-tongued. Be dunked for a scold, she will, if she be not careful."

"And her husband?" Susanna asked.

"Dour, as the Scots say. They stayed at the Angel when they first arrived. That was late in April, as I recall. A few weeks later, they came to me."

Further questions elicited that Woodward had no visible means of support but no lack of ready money and that, at the moment, both husband and wife were abroad in the town. Another coin overcame any scruples Goodwife Greene might have about letting Nick and Susanna into her lodgers' chamber. Pocketing it, she led the way up a winding stair, smiling all the way.

When Susanna saw how small and bare the room was, she felt a reluctant twinge of sympathy for lovers forced to flee their homes in order to be together. She knew firsthand the difficulties of living in an unhappy marriage, as well as the painful joy of falling in love with someone she could not wed. On the other hand, she'd been faithful to her husband as long as he'd lived. Susanna Appleton believed in keeping vows. If the two living here were Stephen Bourne and Clementine Morrison, they did not.

Nick had not said so, but the determined way he set about searching these lodgings made Susanna certain he believed Bourne had intended that Morrison be blamed for his death and executed. She doubted he'd find proof of his theory here, but she helped him look. If they were right, what Bourne had done amounted to cold-blooded murder.

A chest contained changes of linen and a few other items of clothing, supporting the idea that these people had fled their former lives in haste. Lifting each layer with great care, so that the disturbance would not be obvious, Nick came, at the very bottom, to a packet wrapped in cloth and fastened with a ribbon. When he untied it, a chapbook tumbled out. Nick examined it, then passed it to Susanna.

"*A Warning to Wise Men,*" she read aloud from the title page, "*being an account of unlucky days and what to avoid on them.*" Well-thumbed pages indicated someone regularly consulted the cheaply-bound volume.

Goodwife Greene gave a derisive snort. "I am not surprised he'd have such a thing. Always gloom and doom with that one. Why only last week, when I broke a fingernail and he saw me clipping off the jagged edge, he told me I should have left it be. Bad luck to cut nails on a Friday, he said."

Susanna sent a questioning glance Nick's way, but he shook his head. "I did not know him well enough to say if Bourne was superstitious."

"Every almanac I've ever seen lists unlucky days, and always different ones. A man who believes in all of them would have difficulty finding a safe time to begin a new venture." Had Bourne consulted an astrologer, she wondered, to help him choose the best date on which to disappear?

They replaced the contents of the chest, careful to leave everything just as it had been. The rest of the room yielded nothing of interest.

They went next to the Angel, distinguished from other Dover inns by the fact that it lacked stabling for traveler's horses. No one there remembered anyone named Woodward, nor did a description of the couple spark recollections. Since Dover was the main stopping point for travelers to and from the Continent, hundreds of people had broken their journey at the Angel since April.

By the time Susanna and Nick left the inn, the afternoon was well advanced. They would have to leave Dover soon if they hoped to reach Susanna's home at Leigh Abbey and Nick's house, Whitethorn Manor, before dark. The distance was not great, only seven miles, but an uncommon wet summer and autumn had made a quagmire of the road and now more water dogs filled the sky. The small floating clouds were sure forerunners of rain.

"What now?" Susanna asked. "We've found no proof that Woodward and Bourne are the same man. Would you recognize Morrison's wife?"

Nick shook his head. "All I know of her appearance comes from hearsay. It was Mary Chappell's husband, Edward, who told me she had doe's eyes. He said she was the best looking woman in Oundle, but as far as I know I've never met either Goodwife Morrison or her husband.

"Will you stay in Dover and confront them with your suspicions?"

"To what purpose? Even if I am right, it is far too late to save Morrison's life." Nick gave a bitter laugh. "Indeed, just think what the probable outcome will be if I tell Bourne that Morrison was charged with his murder, convicted, and executed. He will thank me, for I will have done him good service. He can express surprise and horror at the news, abandon his false identity, marry his mistress, and return to Oundle to lay claim to her first husband's estate."

They had reached the inn where they'd stabled their horses. Susanna waited until Nick sent the ostler to saddle them before she asked him what he did plan to do.

"I cannot ignore the possibility that the two of them, Stephen Bourne and Clementine Morrison, are guilty of murder, that they plotted to have her husband blamed for a crime he did not commit. It may be a futile effort on my part, but I intend to go to Northamptonshire and learn all I can about the case. At the least, I may be able to prevent them from profiting from Morrison's death."

"I believe," Susanna said after a long, thoughtful pause, "that I will go with you. I should like to visit Jane and her baby. I am, after all, the child's godmother."

Nick, who was her godfather, seemed amused by this sudden and uncharacteristic interest in little Susanna Johnson but he accepted her decision. During the ride home, they made their plans. If all went well, they could leave Kent in two day's time.

†

A week later, at Stilton, accompanied by a few servants and a packhorse, Susanna and Nick abandoned the main road from London to Stamford and the safe numbers of a larger party for the less well-traveled track to Oundle. It was too late in the day to stop there. Susanna gleaned little more than an impression of houses, church, and market cross before they entered woodland thick with oak and beech.

"This is the Forest of Cliffe," Nick said as they passed a herd of pigs fattening on acorns and beechmast, "part of the Royal Forest of Rockingham. The queen came here once to hunt deer."

"Fallow deer could not reduce a man to a few bones and bits of cloth."

"There are also badgers and foxes and wild boar."

Susanna shuddered. A wild boar, like its domestic cousin the pig, would eat anything.

"If we are correct in our suppositions," Nick reminded her, "the bones discovered in Rockingham Forest did not belong to Stephen Bourne."

"Do you know where the remains were found?"

"Somewhere between Oundle and Southwick. That is Glapthorne." Nick indicated a tiny stone-built forest village surrounded by small patches of arable land. "Southwick lies yonaway, as they say in these parts. Yonder, at a distance, with Bulwick and Candlethorpe beyond."

Susanna studied the terrain. "Bones might have lain unnoticed for months."

"If the hogherd had not stumbled across them, a verderer might have. They are the judicial officers of the Royal Forests. The court that upholds Forest Law is called the swanimote, to which each village sends officers. It meets at King's Cliffe, five miles from here in the valley of the Willow Brook."

"Did justices or foresters investigate? Or neither?"

"By tradition criminal or civil pleas are heard in common law courts even if they originate in the forest," Nick said, "and even if the trial were to be heard in the forest eyre, it would still be the coroner who'd make the indictment. And the accused would still have the right to a trial by jury."

"Who is the local justice of the peace?" Susanna asked.

"I imagine George Lynne of Southwick and Edmund Brudenell of Deene Park, a mile or so on the other side of Candlethorpe, presided over the inquest."

Nick and Susanna reached Nick's manor in late afternoon and received an effusive welcome from Mary Chappell. Jane Johnson's greeting was quieter and her child's shy, but Susanna was delighted with the progress they had made under Mary's care. Jane, who had the mind of a child herself, had learned to use a loom and had woven several beautiful pieces, which she insisted upon showing her benefactor within moments of Susanna's arrival. Jane's daughter, when she was finally persuaded to come out from behind her mother's skirts, proved to be sweet-tempered and very bright. Susanna made a mental note to provide her with tutors as soon as she was old enough for schooling.

"A dimpsy lass and mild as a moon beam, but a handful all the same," Mary

Chappell said of the girl when she'd shooed the others away and taken sole possession of Susanna to escort her to the well-appointed guest chamber where she would sleep. The windows overlooked grazing sheep. Hundreds of them. "You'll be wanting to refresh yourself while the master talks with my Yed'ard."

It took Susanna a moment to translate Yed'ard into Edward, Mary's husband and Nick's steward. Meanwhile, Mary bustled about, checking to be certain there was wash water, expressing her delight that the master would be at Candlethorpe for Pack Rag Day.

"Pack Rag Day?" Susanna echoed in a dubious voice.

"Michaelmas, you'd call it. Four days hence. When the year's service ends and those servants who mean to move on do pack up all their belongings to take away."

A great racket broke out in the courtyard below. Mary rushed to the window and threw the shutters wide. "Stop that wouking!" she shouted. "Waffling cur! Belike he's after one of the cats." When the barking subsided into what Mary called a yaffle, she turned again to Susanna. "I'd fain have you ask if there be summat you're needing."

"I need answers to questions," Susanna confided. "You see, a visit with Jane and her child was not the only reason we came here at this time."

"Twa'n't? Well, you may speak plain to me." Expectation writ large on her friendly countenance, she plunked herself down on the window seat. A moment later a sleek gray cat joined her there and settled in her lap.

"We have come about the murder of Stephen Bourne. What can you tell me of Bourne and the Morrisons?"

Although startled – belatedly, Susanna realized the housekeeper had expected an inquiry of the sort a future mistress might conduct – Mary was willing to recount all she'd heard about Bourne's disappearance and that of Goodwife Morrison. "Fig Sunday, it were. Palm Sunday, you'd say, but it is so called in these parts because it is the custom here to eat figs on that day."

The more she talked, all the while stroking the cat, the easier it became for Susanna to translate Mary's Northamptonshire speech. The cat closed bright topaz eyes and purred accompaniment.

"When the bones were found in the wood," Mary explained, "Goodman Morrison swore his wife killed Bourne and fled in panic, but all the world and Little Billing knows he did it. Morrison was a great gulshing fellow with a blob lip who always looked as if the black ox had trod on his toe."

The world and Little Billing, which Susanna presumed was a local village, also thought Morrison had killed his wife. Enraged by his discovery that she'd run off with Stephen Bourne, he was popularly supposed to have followed, caught, and slain them.

"They do say Bourne were her sprunny when they were young," Mary went on. "He courted her when he was yet an unlicked cub, but they quarreled over summat and when they'd burnt their writings, she married Barnaby Morrison. Belike for spite. She were ever twea faced. Or mappen 'twas for money. He came here from away to take over a cousin's business, but he brought wealth with him."

"Did Morrison beat his wife? Mistreat her in some other way?"

Mary shook her head. Gently she extracted the cat's claws from her apron. "Mind your manners, Greymalkin," she murmured.

"Then I am surprised no one took Morrison's suggestion seriously," Susanna said. "Why not believe the woman capable of murder?"

"Clementine Morrison nettles up, no doubt of that, but why should she kill her lover and leave his body for the animals? A man's a good thing to have along on a journey."

Susanna could not argue with that logic. "So Morrison was arrested and taken off to trial in Northampton."

"Aye."

"Did anyone from here go to the trial or to see him hanged?"

"I warrant Sir Edmund were there." Mary sniffed.

"The justice of the peace?"

"Aye. Married a rich heiress, he did, and was unfaithful to her from the start. Fine example that sets!"

"But he'd have taken an interest in Goodman Morrison?"

"Oh, aye. Morrison is some distant kin to the steward at Deene Park."

Most assuredly, then, Susanna thought, they must pay a visit to Sir Edmund Brudenell on the morrow. In the meantime, having changed her dusty traveling clothes for clean garments and washed her hands and face while Mary talked, Susanna was ready to rejoin Nick.

"Master admires to go awalking," Mary told her when she asked where he might be found. "No doubt he's gone out adoors."

With Greymalkin following in her wake, Susanna located Nick and Yed'ard by the eastern wall. The two men were staring at a distant glow and haze of smoke but Nick smiled when he saw her and bent to scratch the cat's head. He received a nuzzle in return.

"What is burning?" Susanna asked. Her first flash of alarm had already been quelled by Nick's calm composure. It was not a house or, worse, a whole village.

"Stubble in the Fens. It is set alight every year at about this time. It only looks as if the marshes themselves are on fire."

He dismissed Edward Chappell, with detailed instructions for some repairs he wanted made. "Hire a carpenter from Bulwick if you need to for the work on the stable," he said, "and see that there are day men enough to do the plashing."

Susanna studied those hedges she could see, recognizing whitethorn, hazel, crab-apple, and holly. Doubtless Nick meant to have them carefully thinned of their wood and the remaining branches bent double and intertwined so that in the spring the growth would be twice as thick. His extensive flocks of sheep had to be contained somehow.

Nick slung an arm around Susanna's waist as the sun dropped below the horizon. He pointed to the sky. "Watch just there and you'll soon see the shepherd's lamp."

As they waited for the first star to rise after sunset, Susanna summarized what Mary had told her.

"Edward predicted his wife would be splatherdabbing, as he put it. She's a long-tongue of the first order, he says, and would do better to confine herself to her duties as my potwabbler."

Susanna fought a smile and lost. "Was there any detail Mary missed?"

"The location of the bones. Edward says they were in a squeech – that's a wet, boggy place – just halfway between Oundle and Southwick and near the forest track. He also told me that Brudenell is at present away from Deene Park."

"So, we return to Oundle tomorrow?"

"Aye. And until then we can think of more pleasant things. Let us go in and sup. Edward tells me we are to have whispering pudding – that's plum pudding with many plums, as opposed to hooting pudding, in which plums are few and far between – and squab pie."

Susanna wrinkled her nose. "I am not fond of pigeons."

Nick laughed. "You will be pleased, then, to know that there are no birds in a Northamptonshire squab pie. It is made with apples, onions, and fat bacon."

†

On the way to Oundle the next day, Nick and Susanna stopped once, at the squeech Edward Chappell had described. There was nothing to see.

It was not yet noon when they crossed the north bridge over the Nene and entered the market town. Nick pointed out Morrison's house, now claimed by the Crown. It had been seized and its contents inventoried, but as yet no one had moved into the shop or the lodgings above. The windows were boarded up, the doors locked.

They located the constable, a glover named Josias Rutter, hard at work in his shop, for constables were chosen from the citizens of the town to serve for one year. He continued to cut a piece of cheveril, the soft and flexible kid-skin used to make fine gloves, as he answered Nick's questions. His replies added nothing to their knowledge except the fact that the remains had been identified as Bourne's by the bits of rat's-color cloth found with them.

"He did favor dull gray," Rutter said, shaking his head over Bourne's preference.

And still did, Susanna thought, recalling the man they'd met in Dover.

"It is not an uncommon color," Nick protested. "There must have been more to tell you the remnants were Bourne's clothing."

"How else would they have got there?" Rutter asked. Before Susanna could give in to the temptation to tell him, he added, "There were a bit of a glove too, one of mine own making. No other glover in the county makes stitches in just the same way I do."

Faced with this unshakable conviction that the remains had therefore been Stephen Bourne, Nick offered Susanna his arm with the intention of escorting her out of Rutter's shop.

"Han ye no desire to see the bones?" the glover asked.

"You have them here? They were not sent to Northampton for the trial?"

"The cloth were ta'an, but they did leave the bones with me." Rutter set aside his knife to rub his hands together, an avaricious gleam in his rheumy eyes. "Accounted a wonder, they bist. 'Twill cost ye ha'penny a peep to look at them."

When they had left the glover's shop, Susanna and Nick exchanged an ironic look. The broken and discolored bones they'd been shown were not human. "Cow?" she asked.

"Or mayhap deer. Not Bourne. That much is certain."

"A clumsy attempt, all in all, to make Bourne appear dead."

But it had worked. On the journey back to Candlethorpe, Susanna and Nick discussed what to do next. That the trick had been Bourne's own doing seemed likely. How else would the easily identified cloth and bit of leather have gotten there?

"He wanted to be certain no one would search for him," Susanna concluded.

"Yes," Nick agreed, "but was there another, more sinister motive? Was the goal all along to have Morrison executed?"

"We will know soon," Susanna predicted. "If that was the plan, Clementine will reappear to claim Morrison's estate. She'll have to show that Bourne is alive to do so, since upon his conviction for murder, all Morrison owned was confiscated by the Crown. They will both come. Why not? As you suggested in Dover, they can claim that blame falling on Morrison was a tragic mistake. They were only two lovers, desperate to be together."

The church would have something to say about that aspect of the situation. They would be censured for adultery, made to do penance before all the congregation. But Morrison, it seemed, had been wealthy, and his wife was his only heir. Clementine and Bourne would likely consider public humiliation a small price to pay if at the end of it they got their hands a goodly inheritance.

"Shall we travel to Northampton tomorrow and see what we can learn of the trial?" Nick asked.

"Aye. If Sir Edmund Brudenell has not yet returned to Deene Park."

But with the dawn came news that brought them back to Oundle instead. Stephen Bourne had arrived in the market town just after Nick and Susanna rode out. Not only was he alive and well, but he'd brought his new bride with him.

"Married as soon as they heard, he said." While Nick and Susanna broke their fast, Mary repeated all she'd learned from the peddler who'd come from Oundle to mend the pots. "And he admitted to leaving cow bones in the forest to be found. The searchers were supposed to think wild animals had eaten them both. Then they took theirsels off to London and beyond."

"How did they hear Morrison was dead?"

Susanna had to repress a sigh when Mary told them it was being recognized in Dover that had prompted Bourne to contact one of Clementine's kinsmen in Oundle. He'd been passing quick to sent back word of Morrison's fate, Susanna thought. Indeed, when she considered the matter, there had not been time enough for a letter to travel from Dover to Northamptonshire and a reply go back, let alone for Bourne and Clementine to receive that news and decide to make the journey here themselves. And when had they managed to secure a special license and marry? It would have been well nigh impossible to have the banns called three times in Dover if they'd waited to wed until someone here confirmed Morrison's death. To Susanna's mind, that meant they'd known all along that he'd been executed. Meeting Nick had done naught but push their plans ahead a bit.

"And so the new-made widow at once wed her lover," Nick muttered. "A happy ending for a tragedy."

"It weren't called so here!" Mary declared. "By my life, here be much wickedness!"

"Back to Oundle?" Susanna asked when Mary had stalked away.

"Aye."

†

Morrison's house in Oundle was no longer boarded up, though the shop was still closed. Through an open door, Susanna studied Clementine Morrison, now Clementine Bourne, as she gave orders to two harried-looking servants. The woman had a striking appearance and was most forceful in her manner. The slaps she dispensed along with her commands did not appear to be necessary to hasten packing.

Bourne came out of the alley next to the shop just as Nick and Susanna were about to announce themselves. "You!" he cried, goggling at Nick.

"Are you Julius Woodward today?" Nick inquired in a polite voice, "or Stephen Bourne?"

Overhearing, Clementine dispensed with witnesses by sending the servants to the upper floor and drew Nick, Susanna, and Bourne into her hall. "Master Baldwin, I presume? And this, then, would be Lady Appleton, your lover. You are both well known in Dover. One might even say notorious."

Former lover, Susanna thought. *And I am here on a visit to my godchild.* Aloud she said nothing and caught Nick's arm to forestall his angry reaction. Clementine's challenge cut too close to the truth.

"Why did you come here?" Bourne stammered out the question.

"Curiosity," Susanna said before Nick could speak. There was no way these two could know they'd been asking questions. Let them think it coincidence that they'd all ended up in Northamptonshire at this time. "When we met in Dover, you did not appear to know it was safe to return."

"A letter arrived soon after," Bourne said. The stammer intensified along with his nervousness.

"Someone knew where to write to you? Knew you were alive?"

"Clementine's cousin. She'd written to ask him what happened after she left. She made no mention of me."

Another lie, Susanna thought, but they'd seen the hole in their story and attempted to fill it. "A cousin in Oundle?"

"Peterborough," Clementine said. "You might ask him yourself, but he's just left on a long voyage."

Convenient, Susanna thought, and difficult to disprove.

Clementine strode to the door and flung it wide. "If your curiosity is satisfied now, madam, I'd fain have you leave. We have much to do before we depart again on the morrow."

A voice spoke from the street beyond. "I fear that will be impossible, madam, until you have answered certain charges laid against you."

Bourne lost every bit of color in his face. Clementine whirled to face the speaker, her eyes narrowing. "You are not the constable. What is it you want, sirrah? What charges do you mean?"

Susanna repressed a sigh. Bourne had expected to be charged with murder. She was certain of it. But Clementine could not be so easily tricked. The two men at the door were churchwardens, come to inform the newly married couple that because, before their nuptials, they had committed the sin of adultery, they must now come before the church courts. They would be ordered to do penance.

Susanna should have felt sympathy for the other woman, having once been threatened with similar charges before a church court herself. But she had never betrayed a husband, not by making a cuckold of him, or by devising a plot that would take his life. And Clementine did not react with remorse or shame to the churchwardens' claims, only irritation that she would not be permitted to leave town as soon as she wished.

Bourne's whining voice followed Susanna and Nick as they slipped away. "You should not have insisted on beginning the packing this morning, Clementine. I told you this was one of the unlucky days."

†

With remarkable speed, Clementine and Bourne were taken before the archdeacon and sentenced to do penance in church. "A generous bribe could not reduce their sentence," Susanna remarked when she heard of it, "but it no doubt hastened their public humiliation. Once that is complete, they can be on their way."

"October 7th," Nick mused. "That is this coming Sunday."

"Penance is not enough, not when they've done murder. There must be a way to get them to confess to more than adultery."

"If there is, we must think of it quickly, before they leave Oundle."

"The seventh day of October," Susanna repeated. "I seem to recall something about that date. Have you an almanac?"

Nick produced one open to the list of unlucky days, but Susanna surprised him by thumbing through the little volume in search of something quite different. "As I thought," she murmured. "There is an eclipse of the moon that night. It should last from nine o'clock until just past one in the morning. I believe I know a way to trick Bourne into confessing what he and Clementine did to Morrison."

The sound of approaching riders interrupted her before she could share her idea with Nick.

"Sir Edmund Brudenell, accompanied by a liveried servant," he announced after a glance into the courtyard below. A few moments later, cloaked and gloved, the two men were shown into Nick's parlor.

"I hear you have been asking questions about Stephen Bourne and Barnaby Morrison," Brudenell said as soon as Nick had presented Susanna to him. He was a confident, prosperous looking fellow somewhat past his fiftieth year.

Nick summarized what they'd discovered and their conclusions. Then, before Brudenell could comment, Susanna detailed the plan she'd been about to outline for Nick.

At first Brudenell looked skeptical, but by the time she'd finished a faint smile curved the corners of his thin mouth. He swivelled his head to locate his servant. "Morrison, come here!" At their startled looks, the smile broadened. "You will have heard my steward was kin to the accused?"

Susanna studied the thin, unhealthy looking man with the Brudenell sea-horse crest on his sleeve. He shambled forward at his master's command. Although he kept his head tucked in like a turtle, she could make out a lower lip so full it seemed to hang down over his chin – the "blob lip" Mary Chappell had spoken of. Apparently, like the big ears that ran in some families and the prominent teeth that descended through others, this was a Morrison trait.

"You heard what they told me," Brudenell said to his man. "It seems only right that you should help them avenge the wrong done to Barnaby Morrison."

"To play on Bourne's superstitious nature," Susanna said, "all you need do is let him think you are your cousin come back from the dead."

"I am nowhere near the fine figure of a man her husband was when Clementine left him," Morrison objected.

A great gulshing fellow, Mary Chappell had called him. In other words, fat. "Well, then," Susanna said, "you must stuff your clothes with straw, for 'tis clear you are the best one here to impersonate Barnaby Morrison's ghost."

†

On Sunday, Susanna and Nick attended evening prayers at the church in Oundle. The penitents stood on two stools in the middle aisle near the pulpit, clad in white sheets, bareheaded, barefooted, and holding white rods. As they had twice already that day, at morning and afternoon services, Bourne and Clementine confessed to the sin of adultery.

Susanna watched Bourne's face as he stammered out the intimate details and asked God's forgiveness. To judge by the dark circles under his eyes, he had not slept well. Did he feel true remorse? Or simply regret being caught?

Clementine maintained a haughty demeanor throughout her penance. Unbeaten, unbowed, unrepentant, she voiced her confession by rote, looking neither left nor right. She might be forced to endure humiliation, but she saw no reason to be humble about it.

The decision of the archdeacon's court required that both of them remain on their stools for the remainder of the service and stay in the church after the rest of the congregation had gone home. Sir Edmund's influence had been instrumental in arranging that. They would not be permitted to leave until just before nine, and then only to be taken to what they'd been told was the unmarked grave of the man they had wronged.

Susanna, Nick, and Morrison were in place in the boneyard well before Bourne and Clementine came out of the church. In truth, there was no grave. Those executed in Northampton were buried there as well. But Bourne and Clementine did not know that.

Susanna's plan was simple. Just as the eclipse of the moon began, Morrison's "ghost" would appear in the churchyard, accusing Bourne from beyond the grave. If the haberdasher was as superstitious as everyone seemed to think, he should panic and blurt out the truth.

The penitents, still in their white sheets, arrived on schedule, accompanied by Sir Edmund Brudenell, the vicar, and two churchwardens. At first everything went according to plan. Barnaby Morrison's kinsman appeared in the moonlight, convincingly rotund. Both Bourne and Clementine gasped when they caught sight of a face with a blob lip.

"Get you gone, Barnaby!" Clementine shrieked. "You are dead and must stay in the ground. Can you do nothing right?"

"You were never satisfied," Morrison shouted back, "not even when I tried my best to please you."

Susanna stiffened. That was not what he'd been told to say. But a moment later, he returned to the plan, accusing them of the crime, relating all the details Nick and Susanna had worked out.

Bourne broke down, haunted by his own guilt. "Yes. Yes," he sobbed. "It is as you say."

"Be silent, you fool!" Clementine's shrill voice nearly drowned out Bourne's words. "You did nothing."

The "ghost" turned on her, advancing with gloved hands outstretched. "Aye. It was you, Clementine. Your plan. Your hatred. And you are the one who must suffer for it. Prison is bad, Clementine. Hanging is worse. And a woman who plots her husband's death will be burnt for it."

He was too close! Afraid Clementine would be able to tell this was no ghost, Susanna started forward, but before she could intervene, Clementine attacked. She rushed at Morrison with a cry of rage, clawing at his face.

He dodged the raking nails, bringing one arm up to protect himself. Flailing, her fingers caught his glove. When Sir Edmund seized her from behind and pulled her away, the soft leather slipped off in her hand.

Stunned, Susanna stared at the scar picked out by the remaining moonlight. This man was not Morrison's cousin the steward. He was Barnaby Morrison. Alive. Freed because he could read the neck verse. Branded with the letter "M" on his thumb rather than hanged for murder.

For a moment movement ceased as understanding burst upon them all. In heavy silence broken only by the distant hooting of an owl, the eclipse continued, bringing with it the steady diminution of light. The brand dissolved into shadow.

Clementine found her voice first. "How did you escape the gallows?"

It was Sir Edmund Brudenell who answered. "Murder may be excluded from the statutory qualifications for grants of clergy, but without a body, how can there be murder? A jury thought those bones sufficient evidence. The judges were not convinced, and Crown judges do not always feel obligated to respect the distinction between clergyable and non-clergyable felonies."

"But why let everyone think he'd been executed?" Rattled by this unexpected twist, Susanna struggled to make sense of it. It was dark in the boneyard now. One of the churchwardens lit the lanterns he had brought.

"With my wife gone and my business forfeit to the Crown, there seemed little reason to return." Morrison glared at Clementine, still struggling in Sir Edmund's grip. "Then, too, I could guess how that evidence got into the wood. I suspected Clementine would return. I meant to avenge myself upon her when she did." His gaze flicked to Susanna. "I must thank you, Lady Appleton, for showing me the way."

"I knew he'd been freed," Brudenell admitted, "but I agreed not to tell anyone the outcome of the trial. And since he had lost so much weight in gaol awaiting trial and would scarce be recognized by his own mother, we deemed it safe for him to stay at Deene Park. Few people there have much to do with Oundle in any case. The market town of Kettering, which has more to offer, lies in the opposite direction."

Nick, Susanna remembered, had never met Morrison either, even though he did frequent the market in Oundle.

Morrison continued to watch Clementine with an intensity Susanna found unnerving. "You failed, my love," he said in a chilling whisper, "and since Bourne plainly lives, I can prove I did not murder him and thus reclaim my property from the Crown. My suffering is over. Yours has just begun."

Some of her accustomed haughtiness returned. Standing straight in spite of Sir Edmund's restraining hands on her arms, she glared at her tormentor. "And yours will continue as long as you live. We are married, Barnaby. Tied together till death do us part. I swear to you now, before these witnesses, that I will make of your life a living hell."

"I think not." He spoke through gritted teeth. "You will be tried for the attempted murder of your husband. That is petty treason. You will burn."

Still defiant, she sneered at him. "I will go free by reading the neck verse, just as you did."

In that she was mistaken, Susanna thought. The only circumstance under which a woman could plead benefit of clergy was if she had formerly been a nun.

"No!" Morrison bellowed, believing his wife's claim. He charged her like a maddened bull.

Determined that the woman who had tried to kill him should not escape punishment, he seized her by the throat. Before anyone could react, let alone stop him, he had snapped her neck. He dropped the limp body and turned to confront the horrified spectators. "*That* for her neck verse!"

"Fool!" Brudenell muttered. "She could not have used it. Nor can you a second time."

Within moments, Brudenell and the constable led Morrison and Bourne away, both prisoners. They left the churchwardens to deal with the body. But when Stephen Bourne reached the lych gate, he turned to stared, dazed, at Clementine's lifeless form. "This is not how it was meant to end," he murmured.

"You are better off without her," Morrison said.

"Oh, I agree," Bourne said with no trace of a stammer, "but I meant to kill her myself as soon as we'd claimed her inheritance."

A Note from the Author

There were many laws regulating use of the "neck verse" (Psalm 50 in Susanna's day; Psalm 51 in the King James Version and after) and many felonies for which hanging was the accepted punishment. Both local officials and juries, however, tended to make exceptions to the law. Court records for Rye reveal the following crime statistics on hanging offenses for the years 1558–1603:

26 (including 3 accused of murder) fled to avoid arrest or had the charges
    dropped
24 were released when no one appeared to prosecute them in court
48 (including one accused of murder) were acquitted
2 were found guilty but received royal pardons
2 were found guilty but had their sentences reduced to whipping
11 were found guilty but claimed benefit of clergy; these included one case
    in which a plea of manslaughter was accepted and another in which
    the trial jury reduced the charge to "homicide by chance," since it
    took place during a duel with rapiers
9 (including 5 who committed premeditated murder) were found guilty
    and sentenced to death by hanging

An eclipse of the moon did take place on October 7, 1576 and sixteenth-century almanacs did list unlucky days. Most Elizabethans believed in signs and portents, ghosts and witches, and things that go bump in the night. They'd have considered Susanna Appleton a bit odd, and somewhat foolish, for not taking popular superstitions more seriously.

Confusions Most Monstrous

The wedding began in the usual way. The bride, Jocasta Dodderidge, was escorted to the Church of the Holy Cross in a procession that began its journey at her father's house. The bridal party walked from Dodderidge Manor to the village of Kyrton on a carpet of rushes strewn with roses, led by a rosemary bearer carrying a silver bride cup.

Susanna Appleton, delayed by bad roads, arrived just ahead of them. As a guest invited to her kinswoman's nuptials, she had hoped to reach Devonshire days earlier. Instead, she almost missed the ceremony.

The bride was granddaughter to Susanna's mother's brother. A plain young woman of twenty-three, she looked uncomfortable decked out in a kirtle of cloth of silver mixed with blue and a gown of purple velvet embroidered with silver. Her flushed face and the determined gleam in her wide-spaced green eyes drew Susanna's attention. Palpable waves of some strong emotion seemed to radiate from her as she strode along, escorted by two bachelors selected by the groom.

Suppressed excitement? Susanna hoped that was it. Certes Jocasta had not left off any of the traditional bridal accessories. Silver ribbons, the so-called bride laces, had been loosely stitched to her bodice, sleeves, and skirt and tied in true-lover's knots. In her left hand, she carried a garland of gilded wheat ears. After the ceremony, she would place it on her head as a symbol of gladness and dignity, a crown signifying that the bride had steered a virtuous course against evil temptations before her marriage. As further proof of her virginity, Jocasta had combed her hair so that it hung down her back like a veil and she wore a brooch of innocence on her breast. Her only other jewelry was her betrothal ring.

The alternative explanation for the bright color in her cheeks and the militant gleam in her eyes was one Susanna could not like but did understand. Could Cousin Arthur have coerced his daughter into this marriage? It was not uncommon for parents or guardians to arrange such matters for their children, but both parties had to consent.

Susanna studied the groom, waiting on the church porch with Master Atkinson, the vicar, when he stepped forward to meet his bride. Henry Markland had good legs, Susanna noticed, and the sort of physique that looked well in the fashionable peascod-bellied doublet he wore. Shaped like a pea pod, its rigid and unwrinkled shell of crimson velvet extended well below his hips. Although it had decorative buttons down the front, it had been designed to be fastened at the sides, like armor. To preserve the correct shape, the back was lined with stiff canvas, the front with a triangular piece of wood, and the whole of it with stuffing.

The face above this finery sported a short brown beard. A slightly bulbous nose, narrowed grey eyes, and thin brows were shaded by an elaborate, broad-brimmed hat. Susanna judged he was only a few years older than his betrothed. His expression, as he watched her approach, showed neither anticipation nor pleasure.

A flash of memory had Susanna's hands clenching at her sides. At her own wedding many years earlier, Robert Appleton had smiled upon her, his bride. She, foolish girl, had taken it for affection. In truth, what he'd felt was triumph. Her fortune had been about to become his. Taking her person as well had been the price he'd been willing to pay for wealth and position.

Jocasta acknowledged her groom's presence by slanting a quick glance at him from beneath lowered lids. She did not seem nervous, Susanna decided. Nor reluctant. And she could scarce fault Master Markland's somber mein. Marriage was serious business, a commitment for life with no way out short of death.

When Markland took Jocasta's hand to lead her inside the church, the bride maidens followed. One of them, a snub-nosed, yellow-haired young woman, now seemed as agitated as the bride had been earlier. She clutched the chaplet she carried tight against the sprig of rosemary pinned to her ample breast. The garland of gilded wheat she held in the other hand drooped alarmingly as she hurried into the church.

Arthur Dodderidge, the bride's father, came next in the procession, with household servants and friends of the family following close behind. Susanna joined in as they passed her. In their wake, those who had gathered to watch the procession set up a great clamor by beating on drums of hollow bones, saucepan lids, and tin kettles containing pebbles. Noise was supposed to be lucky at weddings. It drove out evil influences and brought good fortune to the marriage.

Inside the church, the formalities commenced as Susanna's cousin bestowed pennies on the poor of the parish. The man chosen to receive the bag of coins grinned and gave it a shake hard enough to make the contents jingle.

A homily on the honorable estate of matrimony came next and the service proceeded without a hitch until the vicar asked, "Wilt thou take this man for your lawfully wedded husband?"

Jocasta spoke in a loud, clear voice. "I will not."

The yellow-haired bride maiden gasped, but an appalled silence engulfed the rest of the assembly. Susanna moved toward the bridal couple, prepared to lend Jocasta her support. She did not understand why the young woman had waited until this juncture to object, but it did not matter. She had the right to refuse an unwanted marriage.

Before Susanna could reach the front of the church, the groom seized Jocasta's hand, gripping it tight enough to make her wince. "Proceed," he said to the vicar. "You heard her say the necessary words."

The vicar cleared his throat. "Yes. Er, you did say 'I will,' my dear."

Just as Susanna opened her mouth to object, Arthur Dodderidge caught her arm and hauled her roughly toward him. "Do not interfere," he warned.

By then the vicar had resumed the ceremony, rattling through the words set out by the Book of Common Prayer at great speed. Arthur thrust his daughter's hand into Markland's and he forced a ring onto her finger. White faced and wide eyed, Jocasta stood like a statue as the vicar concluded the ritual.

"I pronounce that they be man and wife together," he declared, and then droned on for another quarter of an hour, delivering a sermon on the duties of holy wedlock. After sharing his own deathly dull experience in the perils of marriage, he suggested superficial ways in which spouses could become tolerant of and remain faithful to one another.

In other circumstances, Susanna might have approved the attempt, but she was too worried about Jocasta. Blatant disregard of the bride's wishes did not bode well for a marriage. She had every intention of seeking out Jocasta during the wedding feast at Dodderidge Manor. If the bride's reluctance stemmed from more than sudden panic at the thought of giving herself to a man, then Susanna vowed she would help her kinswoman, no matter what church and state decreed.

But there were additional rituals to be gotten through first. The young men of the congregation plucked bride laces from Jocasta's clothing. Everyone drank the health of the bride and groom from a bride cup passed from hand to hand. Then followed the return procession, in which the bride was flanked by two married men instead of by bachelors. Musicians playing joyous music accompanied the crowd and Susanna set off with the rest. She could do nothing yet, but an entire afternoon and evening lay between the wedding and the bedding.

†

At the manor, the bride cake that had been carried to the church and back again was broken over Jocasta's head as she stepped through the door. "Read the future in the pieces," someone called out.

Jocasta's response was so soft that only the groom and Susanna, pressing close, heard her anguished whisper. "They are the broken bits of my life."

For her bridal gift to Jocasta, Susanna had chosen one of the traditional symbols of the married state, a pair of knives contained in one sheath.

Jocasta fingered the blades, each in turn, and her gaze flicked to her new husband before she hung the sheath from her girdle. "This may prove most useful," she said with a crooked smile.

Susanna caught Jocasta's hands and spoke in an urgent whisper. "I will help you if I can. You must not do anything foolish." Murdering a husband was never a good idea, and a particularly ill-conceived notion for the wedding night.

"Too late, cousin. The die is cast." She, too, kept her voice low.

"If you were coerced into marriage, Jocasta. It can be undone."

"It scarce matters now."

"Jocasta —"

"It does not matter, I tell you."

Susanna drew her cousin aside, all too aware of Markland's interest in their exchange. "Was there someone else you hoped to marry?"

Tears pooled in Jocasta's eyes. "Hoped to, yes. His name was Gawen Poole."

"Was? He's dead, then?"

She had no time to do more than nod before her new husband reclaimed her, but she looked so forlorn that Susanna was moved to spirit her out of the great hall at the first opportunity. An hour later, in a pleached arbor in the garden, temporarily safe from prying eyes and stretched ears, she coaxed her cousin into telling her the whole story.

"He sailed on the *Squirrel* last summer. In October the ship put into port in Ireland. The crew was given the liberty of the town and in one of the taverns they discovered a supply of Spanish wine, sufficient proof to any good Englishman of Irish loyalties. A brawl broke out."

"And your Gawen?"

"I was told he was killed in the fighting. They did not trouble to bring his body home."

"You'd have married him?"

"We –" She broke off, swallowed hard, and met Susanna's eyes. "Yes."

"I understand your grief, Jocasta, but you must have accepted Master Markland's suit. Why change your mind at the last moment?"

"Because I do not want to spend the rest of my life with Hal Markland." She gave a bitter little laugh. "Not that he plans to spend much of his time with me. He has a mistress." She nodded toward the yellow-haired bride maiden. "Beatrice Atkinson. Ticey, she's called. The vicar's niece."

"Why did Hal not marry her, then?"

"She has no dowry. Her parents are dead. She serves as her uncle's house-keeper at the vicarage."

"Does the vicar know she's Markland's mistress?" In Susanna's opinion, that seemed an excellent reason to object to the marriage.

"I doubt he realizes she gave herself to him. He did know she wanted Hal for herself. He did not approve. Not only would he lose an unpaid servant, but the community would suffer. The joining of my father's lands and Hal's is good for the village. That is why no one here in Kyrton opposed the marriage, not even Ticey. There is too much to be gained from it."

"Ah, there you are, my dear!" Arthur Dodderidge's booming voice made his daughter jump. "Your new husband awaits you."

As Susanna could see that Hal Markland was surrounded by his grooms-men, all of them quaffing ale at a steady rate, this was patently untrue. Never-theless, Jocasta hastened to obey.

Arthur turned on Susanna, glowering. "Why does she have such a guilty look on her face? What have you been saying to her?"

"She told me she did not want to marry that man." Susanna glared back at him. "How could you let your only child be forced into marriage?"

"I know what is best for my daughter."

Susanna had heard such reasoning from men before. Most of the time it meant there were financial or political advantages to coercing a woman into doing what they wanted.

Arthur sighed. "Try to look on him with unbiased eyes, Susanna. He is our nearest neighbor. He and Jocasta grew up together. They will manage well enough."

She retained her skepticism. "What kind of marriage is it when a man forces an unwilling woman to tie herself to him for life?"

"She suffered a moment's panic in the church. No more than that. And it is none of your concern."

"She is my kinswoman."

"If you were so interested in her welfare, you should have come to Devon sooner. It is too late now."

Susanna took the rebuke to heart. Arthur's wife had died years before. As Jocasta's closest female relative, Susanna should have asked the young woman to come live with her in Kent.

†

During the masque after supper, Susanna noticed that Jocasta was missing. The bride maidens were accounted for, which meant it was not yet time for the bedding ceremony. So was the groom. Although it was possible Jocasta had just slipped out to use the privy, Susanna did not think so. Heeding an unquiet heart, she made her way to her cousin's chamber.

The bride was there, but she had discarded her bridal finery. She had also hacked off her long hair. The knife she'd used was still in her hand.

"Do not look so shocked, cousin," Jocasta said. "Better this than that I use your gift to stab Hal on his wedding night."

The words were lightly spoken but Susanna feared she meant them. As she watched, trying to think what to say, Jocasta opened a chest and took out men's clothing. "These belonged to my brother."

Rowland Dodderidge, twenty when he'd died, had been a victim of the plague of 1571. It had wiped out a quarter of the population of the parish and left Arthur with only a daughter as his heir.

"Being taken for a boy will not protect you from brigands."

"They'll have to catch me first. Besides, I have been practicing how to walk like a man, and swear like one, too. From now on, I will be John Rowland."

Once more bereft of words, Susanna simply stared at her cousin. Dressed in doublet and hose, bonnet and cape, her hair shorn, she made a passable young man, but the disguise would never stand up to close scrutiny.

"Travel in such garments if you must, but take women's clothing with you. When you are safely away —"

"I mean to live as a man," Jocasta repeated. "A woman has no freedom."

"Where will you go?"

"Better you do not know."

"If you can make your way to Leigh Abbey, I will take you in."

"Better that I disappear."

"We will consult lawyers. Since the marriage has not yet been consummated –" Jocasta's expression stopped her. "An examination by midwives would cast doubt on that?"

Jocasta's nod confirmed Susanna's guess. She had given herself to the man she'd loved. To Gawen, who was dead. And if Jocasta could not prove she was a virgin, her marriage to Hal Markland would stand. She would be forced to live with her husband unless he repudiated her.

Hefting a bulging capcase, Jocasta headed for the window. She'd tied a rope to the casement. With reluctant admiration, Susanna watched her cousin straddle the sill. Whether she'd thought this out well in advance or come up with the plan at the last moment, it was clear she'd considered all the angles. It was equally obvious that she could not be dissuaded.

"Wait," Susanna called. From a pocket sewn into the underside of the heavily brocaded fabric of her skirt, she extracted a sum sufficient to pay Jocasta's way to Kent. "Come to Leigh Abbey when you can and we will talk again. You need not stay. I will help you reach any destination you choose."

†

Less than an hour after Jocasta's escape, the bride maidens came looking for her. Giggling, they tumbled into the chamber, ready to strip their friend naked – to show her husband and anyone else who cared to look that she had no flaws or deformities – and deposit her in the flower-strewn bridal bed to await the drunken revelers who'd bring Master Markland. Even in the most restrained version of the custom, wedding guests crowded into the bedchamber to throw stockings at the newlyweds and watch the bride share a sack posset with her new husband. Only after those rituals were complete would she be left alone with him.

"Where is she?" Ticey demanded when she saw that only Susanna occupied the room. Seated on a chest beneath the window, she'd been waiting for them, considering what she should say when they came.

"She needed a breath of fresh air." Rising, Susanna made a vague gesture toward the window. "She has gone out."

"Are you so anxious to see her in bed with Hal?" a second bride maiden taunted Ticey.

"She'll use any excuse to see him naked," quipped the third young woman, reminding Susanna that the groom was sometimes forcibly deprived of every scrap of his clothing before his friends thrust him into the bridal chamber.

Ticey glared at them both.

"Does she need a vial of pig's blood?" the fourth bride maiden asked. "He'll want to show off the sheets in the morning."

It was a practical consideration, but repulsed Susanna all the same. Although she could not approve of young couples marrying without any of the traditional formalities – elopements were fraught with difficulties of their own – she despised this sort of spectacle. It was bad enough on the wedding night, but on the morning after newlyweds were awakened with music and further ribaldry and the husband was expected to show proof he'd success-fully deflowered his bride. She wondered how many unhappy arranged mar-riages might have gotten off to a better start if the newly joined couple had been allowed a little privacy in which to consummate their union.

"Jocasta," she began, "has –"

"Gone." Ticey's voice, high-pitched with astonishment, cut across Susanna's words. She'd opened the chest Susanna had been sitting on and found the rope Jocasta had used to escape.

The confusion this announcement caused continued for some time, and the noise of four young women all talking at once – and saying nothing – drowned out the sound of approaching footsteps. They were unprepared for the arrival of Hal Markland. When he flung open the door and came in, still fully clothed and, to Susanna's surprise, alone, he was greeted first by shrieks of dismay and then by an ominous silence.

"Well? Where is she?" Markland's gaze went at once to the empty bed.

Ticey Atkinson cleared her throat.

"Beatrice? Do you know where she is?"

"She's fled." The suggestion of a smirk accompanied the announcement.

"What did you tell her to give her a dislike of me?" Markland's roar rever-berated through the chamber.

"She's known you all her life," Ticey shot back. "What could I possibly tell her that she does not already know?"

Hal Markland looked stricken and furious by turns. Seizing Ticey's arm, he hauled her into an alcove where they exchanged acrimonious words in a whis-per. Susanna could not make out what they said, but the tone was unmistak-able. Clearly he believed it was something his mistress had done that had driven away his wife.

Before another hour passed, search parties were scouring the countryside, looking for Jocasta. Since Susanna did not tell them how her cousin was dressed, she supposed they were looking for a woman. They'd assume that, hampered by skirts, she'd not get far, even on horseback.

With the sunrise, the men began to trickle back to the manor house, all but Hal Markland. Sober now and discouraged, for there had been no trace of the runaway, they speculated on his failure to return, wondering if he'd found Jocasta, if the two of them were somewhere together.

Then his horse was discovered, tied to a tree in the orchard.

This time Susanna accompanied the men, uneasy in her mind about what might have happened. Hal was not with his bride, of that she was certain. But there was no sign of him in the orchard either. While the others debated what to do next, Susanna searched, her gaze on the ground, looking for she knew not what … until she found it.

Near where the horse had been left was a flattened area, as if a man had lain there, unconscious or dead, for some time. A short distance away, and every few feet thereafter, were small tufts of fleece.

She blinked, remembering the peascod-bellied doublet. If he'd torn it, or someone had pierced the outer layer, it would leak stuffing. But where had he gone that he could not be seen? Shading her eyes, she studied the terrain. Had he inched along under his own power, or been dragged by someone? The only potential hiding place she could see was a nearby thicket.

She found him deep within a circle of raspberry bushes, curled into a tight ball, unconscious. Susanna called out to the rest and bent to examine his injuries. He had a lump on his head and had been stabbed in three places with a small, sharp blade. The wooden triangle used to stiffen the front of his doublet had likely saved his life.

Just as several sturdy servants were about to lift Markland to carry him back to the house, one of his groomsmen found a club. It was stained at one end with blood.

Susanna watched the unconscious man borne away and felt a deep sense of foreboding. His injuries were the result of a deliberate attack. A blow to the head had rendered him helpless so that his attacker could stab him when he was down. That was not self-defense. If Jocasta had done this, it was not in an attempt to escape. No degree of panic could excuse her if she had deliberately set out to murder the man who'd forced her into marriage.

Susanna frowned. Jocasta, as Susanna had last seen her, had not been in a panic. If she'd attacked Markland, she'd meant to. But by the same token, if she'd intended to kill him, he'd be dead. It made no sense that she would stab her unwanted husband, and yet who else had reason to stop his pursuit? Deeply troubled, Susanna followed the litter bearers back to Dodderidge Manor.

†

The song of a lark heralded the dawn, rousing Susanna from a restless doze. A moment later, a rock flew through her open window to land on the floor with an ominous thump.

She scrambled out of bed and stumbled to the window but there was no one in sight. The paper tied to the rock, when examined, proved to be a note from Jocasta. She wrote that she would wait for Susanna in the village church for an hour. She had heard what happened to Hal Markland. She wanted to know if he would live.

Susanna dressed and walked the mile into Kyrton in less than half the allotted time. She passed few people on the way. None paid her any mind but two caught her attention. Although they were some distance away, standing by the garden gate, Susanna recognized them both. Ticey Atkinson was engaged in an animated discussion with the man to whom Jocasta had presented her bag of pennies at the wedding.

The church was quiet and seemed deserted, but Susanna closed the door behind her and softly called Jocasta's name.

"Here." Her cousin appeared from behind the altar, still attired in her brother's clothes. "Does Hal yet live?"

Susanna nodded. "Your father sent for a doctor from Exeter who bled him. Markland drifts in and out of consciousness. He says it was a woman who struck him, first on the back of the calves and then, when he fell, on the head. He cannot remember being stabbed."

"A woman?"

"He seems certain of that, though he claims he cannot put a name to her. Were you hiding in the orchard, Jocasta? Did you attack him when you feared discovery?"

"I heard nothing about what happened to Hal until late last night."

"Where have you been, then? I expected you'd be miles away by now." In her cousin's shoes, Susanna thought, she'd already have crossed the Narrow Seas to France.

"I cannot tell you," Jocasta said.

Susanna felt like shaking her. "Can someone swear you were elsewhere than in the orchard? If they can, bring them forward Jocasta, for there is already talk of sending constables out to look for you."

"I hid with old Mother Coombs. I was safe in her cottage by the time Hal was attacked."

Susanna's relief was tempered by the expression on Jocasta's face, but before she could ask her what was wrong, the vicar arrived.

"Have you no shame?" Master Atkinson gaped at Jocasta in her male attire. "How dare you come into the church in such apparel? You dishonor God by such dress."

Outrage made his face flame and his shouting quickly drew a crowd to the door.

"Send for the constable," Ticey Atkinson said. "I warrant she's the one who attacked poor Hal Markland."

"She did not," Susanna said in a carrying voice. "Mother Coombs can tell you. Jocasta was with her."

This announcement did not have the effect Susanna had hoped for. Two of the men lost all color in their faces. A third crossed himself. Ticey smirked.

"Mother Coombs lives alone in the woods and never comes into the village," Jocasta said in a subdued voice. "Some think she is a witch and fear her."

"A hermit?" Susanna asked.

"A cunning woman, skilled with herbs. She knows how to cure ailments and make healing brews."

"A monstrous woman." The man who'd crossed himself stepped forward to take Jocasta into custody. "She hath is a great horn, ten inches long, growing out of the center of her forehead."

†

Susanna found the cottage in the woods without difficulty, and she had no trouble at all recognizing Mother Coombs. What the constable had called a "horn" was an elongated growth, dark and tough as leather, that hung over the poor old woman's face like a grotesque lock of hair.

To Susanna's shame, her first reaction was revulsion and her second curiosity. Only when she'd mastered herself did she step closer. "I am told you are skilled with herbs. I have some ability in that direction myself."

Mother Coombs mumbled an incomprehensible answer. She kept her head down, and in the murky interior of the house, filled as it was with smoke from the cooking fire and the haze of steam from gently bubbling herbal remedies, Susanna could not make out much of the face besides the horn.

"I am here on behalf of my cousin, Jocasta Dodderidge," Susanna said. "She has been taken to Exeter by the constables and charged with the attempted murder of her husband." If he died, she would burn for it. "I have come to ask you to step forward and confirm that she was with you at the time he was struck down. She says she came straight to this cottage from Dodderidge Manor and stayed until she heard of the attack on Hal Markland." Susanna wondered who had brought word to Mother Coombs, but that question was less important than persuading the old woman to cooperate.

When the hermit turned bloodshot eyes on her visitor, the horn hanging between them was impossible to ignore. "Constables?" she croaked.

Susanna nodded and explained again. "She needs your help."

"A good girl," Mother Coombs said, but to Susanna's dismay, she at once began to gather belongings into a sack. She could not have made more clear her intent to flee rather than face the authorities.

"Wait," Susanna begged. "Stay and help Jocasta and I will consult with the finest surgeons in England on your behalf. No doubt one of them can find a way to remove that growth. You can live a normal life once –"

Mother Coombs's suddenly fierce expression cut short Susanna's plea. "Begone!" she bellowed, pointing at the door. She said more, but Susanna could not catch all the words. The gist of it was that Mother Coombs was certain she would die if anyone attempted to remove her "horn."

Weighed down by a sense of failure, Susanna returned to Dodderidge Manor. She could not persuade anyone to go to the cottage and take Mother Coombs into custody. They were all afraid she'd bewitch them. By the next morning, when Susanna herself returned, the old woman was gone.

Accompanied by the servants she'd brought from Leigh Abbey, Susanna went next to Exeter, eight miles distant from Kyrton. She was permitted to visit her cousin in gaol, where she found Jocasta still wearing her brother's clothing.

" 'Twas my choice." Jocasta attempted a smile but managed only a grimace. "It is warmer than a kirtle." Given the dampness and drafts in the prison, Susanna could see the logic in the decision.

"Hal Markland has been brought here to his own house in Exeter to recover," she told Jocasta. "If he has remembered any more of what happened to him, I've not been told." The flash of relief in Jocasta's eyes came at the positive report on Markland's health, not when she heard he'd failed to accuse her. "You care about him," Susanna said.

"As a friend. I've known him all my life. If I'd been allowed to remain no more than that and he'd been injured, I'd have offered to nurse him back to health, but I have no wish to be married to him."

"I am told the vicar's niece has moved in to see to his needs."

Jocasta frowned. "I am surprised the vicar allowed it."

"He is with her. Markland's house provides a convenient lodging while he pursues his own charges against you."

"My monstrous apparel?"

"Aye."

"A minor charge compared to attempted murder."

"Markland has not said you attacked him."

"But that is what everyone believes. That is why I am being held."

"There is another woman who might have been angry with him," Susanna mused.

"Ticey? But she loves him. She'd never hurt him."

"Are you certain of that? Jealousy can lead to fuddled thinking. If she could not wed him herself, she may have felt no one should have him as husband."

"But I'd already fled."

"She could not be certain you'd stay away."

"It would have made more sense if she'd tried to kill me. She had ample opportunity in the days before the wedding."

"Mayhap that was her true goal," Susanna said, remembering another case in which one spouse had been intended to take the blame for the other one's death. "If you are found guilty of the attack and executed for it, she'll have free rein to marry your widower, if she can first nurse him back to health and convince him to accuse you."

Jocasta was not convinced, but Susanna spent her journey back to Dodderidge Manor pondering how they might prove Ticey the culprit. She arrived just in time to join Arthur for the evening meal.

He appeared to have imbibed a goodly quantity of sherry sack while she'd been gone. "You should have prevented Jocasta from running away," he muttered when they had been served.

"Tied her to the bedpost, mayhap?" Susanna bit into a chicken leg, discovered she'd lost her appetite, and returned it to the trencher.

"The girl's an unnatural daughter. She did this to spite me."

"You forced her into an unwanted marriage."

"A proper child should be willing to sacrifice herself to save her family's estates."

Susanna studied him as she forced herself to eat. He was cup shot, but still capable of giving her answers. When the servants had returned to the kitchen wing, leaving them alone, she abandoned tact. "How close are you to losing Doddington Manor?"

His expression descended from lugubrious into morose but he sounded like a sulky child when he answered. "I invested everything I had in a shipping venture. The ships were lost at sea and their cargo with them. Markland promised to pay all my debts if I gave him Jocasta. What choice did I have?"

"You might have asked me for a loan."

"And what reason had I to think you would give me money? It had been years since I last heard from you."

"We are kin." That would have been enough, but Arthur had the right of it – there was no way for him to have known that she would be generous. Since the one delightful summer she had spent here as a child, she had seen Arthur only a handful of times. She had little idea what either his life or Jocasta's had been like.

"It is too late now." Maudlin, he reached for the sack and refilled his goblet. "She's ruined me. Ruined herself. A woman trying to pass herself off as a man is a monstrous thing. And immoral – revealing her lower limbs that way. What are men who see that to think of her?"

Susanna blinked, surprised that the charge before the church courts appeared to upset Arthur more than the accusation of attempted murder. "In Persia," she informed him, "the women wear breeches and the men, long robes. In that country it is considered improper for a woman to show her face to a man."

Arthur looked affronted by the very idea.

"Besides, it is not as if Jocasta wants to dress as a man all the time."

"Do not be so certain of that. She is always prattling about such things, talking about women who've lived as the other sex for years before being found out. There was one soldier whose gender was not discovered until she was wounded in battle."

Susanna had heard similar tales and also knew of a case that had recently come before the courts in London. A woman had been made to stand in the pillory in her men's attire for public shame and had been committed to Bridewell afterward. She was a prostitute and had dressed herself as a boy as a way of enticing clientele.

"A mankind woman," Arthur lamented. "What did I do to deserve such monstrous child?"

Annoyed by his attitude, Susanna spoke without thinking. "If it is acceptable for a woman to dress in men's clothing in order to travel long distances, then why not all the time?" She shocked herself with the suggestion and Arthur looked horrified.

"It is *never* right, nor is it ever acceptable for a man to dress as a woman!"

"But they do so all the time, on the stage and for holiday revels, especially May Day."

"And they should be punished for it. Never tell me you approve of plays and players."

"I have naught against them."

"Anyone who defies morality should be forced to do penance. That is the only way to stop such monstrous behavior."

"Penance is of little use as a deterrent to those who are truly wicked." Susanna argued, speaking now from personal experience, "and requiring penance of good people who have the misfortune to long for some condition beyond the narrow boundaries of convention does little more than create unhappiness and frustration."

Their exchange might have grown even more heated had Arthur's steward not interrupted to tell him a man named Tom Bickford was at the door and demanded to speak with him.

"Bickford? What does he want?"

"He says he has important information about the attack on Master Markland."

"We'd better see him, then," Susanna said. "Who is Tom Bickford?"

"Bickford is the fellow who accepted the bag of pennies from Jocasta at the wedding."

"Is he?" That meant Tom Bickford was also the man she'd seen talking to Ticey Atkinson just before the vicar found Jocasta in the church.

Bickford's shuffling gait and cap in hand were mitigated by a grin that stretched from ear to ear. He should have been made to wait longer, Susanna realized. His prompt admission had betrayed how desperate they were for a way to help Jocasta.

He wasted no time getting to the point. "Your daughter bought a club from me," Bickford said. "I did not know it at the time, but I sold her the very weapon that she used to strike down Master Markland. For five gold angels, I'll keep silence about what I know."

The accusation, or mayhap the demand for money, restored Arthur to sudden sobriety. "You are a runagate and a scoundrel. Why should anyone believe you?"

"Because it would cost me dear to lie." Still grinning, he turned to Susanna, offering a far-from-humble bow. "Anyone in Kyrton will tell you I have a long history of petty crime. The first charge was living out of service in my home village, but I escaped that by absconding. Later, I was taken up as a vagrant and imprisoned on suspicion of felony, but there was no indictment and I was released. Then a few years later, I was accused of stealing grain but acquitted, and next it was a charge at the quarter sessions for stirring up dissension by my evil tongue."

"Minor offenses," Susanna said, quelling her distaste for the fellow. This boasting would lead somewhere, she was certain.

"Then I was indicted for the theft of two skins worth two shillings but the jury reduced the value of the goods."

"That is not uncommon." If the value of stolen goods was more than a shilling, a man could be hanged for the crime.

"After that the charge was petty larceny and I was whipped. Last year I was indicted for petty larceny a second time, found guilty, and whipped again, and at the next assizes I was indicted for taking some hose and petticoats valued at two shillings. That time the valuation was not reduced. When I was found guilty, I had to plead benefit of clergy and was branded with a T on one thumb."

Susanna doubted the fellow could read, but it was not difficult to memorized the neck verse. *Have mercy upon me, O God*, and so forth. "You will not get off so lightly again," she reminded him.

The grin widened. "And that is why I will be believed. Another conviction, say for perjury, and I'd be hanged."

"But whatever would possess you to sell Jocasta a cudgel?"

"When a fine gentlewoman asks a poor man to do something for her, and offers to pay him, how can he refuse?"

"When did she approach you?" Susanna asked.

"The very night of her wedding day. Creeping off, she was. Escaping by moonlight."

"And she stopped to buy a weapon?"

"Why not?" he asked, all innocence. "A woman traveling alone must have some protection."

"But she was not —" Susanna broke off, her eyes narrowing. "Yes. And still in her wedding finery too. And she'd attract footpads with her good green cloak."

Bickford's vigorous nod betrayed him. He'd not seen Jocasta that night. He had no idea she'd been wearing her late brother's clothing.

"You, sirrah, are a knight of the post. You were willing to lie in court."

"Nay, madam. I have told you the truth?"

"Then why would you sell a weapon to a woman and not notice she was dressed in men's clothing?"

"Men's –!" His astonishment was almost comical.

"Who really bought that club?"

The grin had vanished. When Arthur rose from table and seized the villain by the collar, Bickford lost his last vestige of self-confidence. "I did not sell one at all. You must believe me. It was just that she offered me money to say I had, and I thought I might earn more by promising not to. You cannot begrudge me a little profit. I am a poor man reduced to begging and I've a family to support."

"You took a bribe to lie in court?"

Broken, he nodded.

"Who paid you."

"The vicar's niece. And not even in coin. She promised to give me the gloves Mistress Jocasta gave her for being a bride maiden."

"Release him, Arthur." Susanna gave Bickford one gold angel and sent him off with a warning of what would happen to him if he tried to make more trouble for Jocasta. Then she told Arthur what she suspected about Ticey Atkinson.

"There is no way to prove it," Arthur said, "and I cannot imagine that delicate, sweet-faced girl taking up a fallen tree branch or some such and striking out at a sturdy fellow like Hal Markland. And then stabbing him? No one will believe that."

"You cannot believe *Jocasta* guilty!"

He hesitated too long before denying it, until Susanna despaired of ever reconciling father and daughter. "I am convinced she is innocent. She was with Mother Coombs."

"Why, then, did the old woman run away?"

"Fear of the constables, no doubt. Mother Coombs shuns all company. That is why no one will believe she allowed Jocasta to stay with her."

"Mayhap searchers will find her and persuade her to tell the truth."

"On Dartmoor? I doubt she'll ever be seen again." He made an odd sound Susanna interpreted as a laugh. "You'd best hope she *is* a witch. Only with supernatural powers will she ever find her way back out of that place alive."

"Which is more to be despised," Susanna wondered aloud, "an old woman with a growth on her forehead, a woman in men's clothing, or a woman who tries to kill a man and would let someone else burn for it?"

"All three are monstrous." There was no hesitation in Arthur's reply this time, "but most especially Mother Coombs. How can a horned woman be anything but evil?"

"And I believe the true monster lurks beneath the most pleasing countenance," Susanna said.

But of the three, Ticey Atkinson was the one most likely to escape punishment. For her monstrous behavior, she might even be rewarded with a rich husband. It did not seem fair when Mother Coombs had been driven to flee into Dartmoor and could well die there and Jocasta would, at the least, be obliged to do penance in the local church for wearing men's apparel.

Arrested by a thought, Susanna frowned. Like Tom Bickford, Hal Markland had been ignorant of Jocasta's disguise. What would his reaction be, she wondered, if he were faced with a woman in man's clothing?

†

The following day, Susanna returned to Exeter. When she had arranged for mainprise, promising to pay an exorbitant fine if Jocasta did not appear at the next assizes, she went to the gaol to fetch her cousin. To her surprise, she discovered that Jocasta already had a visitor. Someone she knew well, it seemed, for Jocasta was kissing the bearded and unkempt stranger.

By his manner of dress, the fellow had recently been at sea. "Gawen Poole, I presume?" Susanna said.

The couple sprang apart. "Susanna, is it not a wonder? Gawen was rescued from Ireland when an English ship cruising off the Munster coast got word that an English sailor was stranded in a village on the shore."

"A wonder indeed," Susanna agreed, "and we may see another such if you come with me now to Hal Markland's house."

"Gladly," Gawen Poole said. "I've something to say to that blackguard."

Sending him a quelling glance, Susanna said, "You will do nothing but watch and listen. At present he claims he cannot remember what happened to him, but since it is clear that he's not likely to die of his stab wounds, he may be inclined to listen to reason. I hope to convince him that Jocasta was not the woman who attacked him."

"By now he will have been told I was responsible," Jocasta said.

"Aye, but I am hopeful that is *all* he's been told."

They were in luck. When they reached Markland's town house, the manservant who let them in informed them that Ticey Atkinson and her uncle the vicar had gone out. No one stood guard over Hal Markland's bedchamber.

Susanna entered that room first, followed by Gawen and Jocasta, the latter still in her brother's clothing.

Markland had been dozing, but his eyes flew open at the sound of the door closing. "Lady Appleton," he murmured, recognizing her. His gaze skimmed over the pair behind her without any sign that he knew them. Assuming them to be her servants, he ignored them.

"Master Markland, I trust you are recovering well?"

"As well as can be expected." His lips twisted into a wry grimace. "But what brings you to my sickbed?"

"The hope that you will listen to reason." She motioned Jocasta forward, into the light streaming through the window.

Still Hal Markland did not recognize her.

"You have said that a woman struck you with a cudgel. How could you tell?"

He frowned. "Did I say that?"

She nodded.

"I fear I do not remember." With an absent gesture, he touched the bandage on his head.

"If you have no memory of what person attacked you, it would be wrong to let the authorities charge your wife with the crime."

"I've no intention of pursuing the matter," Markland said in an irritable voice, "but neither do I wish to let someone who tried to kill me into my house."

"Too late for that," Jocasta said, and removed her bonnet.

"Jocasta?" He gawked at her. "What did you do to your hair?"

Exasperation writ large on her features, she stalked toward the bed. "Is that all you can say to me? At least do me the courtesy of cowering in fear. For all you know, I've come here to complete the job of murdering you."

Hal Markland laughed out loud. Then he frowned, examining Jocasta's clothing with an intense gaze. "Is that what you were wearing when you ran away?"

"Yes."

"No one told me." He closed his eyes and massaged his temples. For a moment he said nothing, long enough for the door behind Jocasta and Gawen to open. "I knew a woman attacked me because she had a feminine smell to her. Rosemary. There was a sprig of rosemary pinned to her bosom."

"Rosemary for remembrance," Susanna murmured, struck by the irony.

When Markland's eyes opened he was staring at the two people framed in the doorway, Ticey and her uncle. "Why?" he asked.

"Why what?" Master Atkinson demanded, pushing his way past his niece to glare at Jocasta. "And what is this monstrous woman doing here?"

"She is no monster," Susanna said, "and it is your niece who clubbed and stabbed her lover."

Markland could not take his eyes off Ticey. "It *was* you."

"You deserved to suffer!" she cried. "You did not love me as much as I love you."

"What is this? What are you saying?" The vicar's agitation had him hopping from one foot to the other as he fired questions at his niece.

She ignored him. "I loved you, Hal, and you married *her*. Tell them she attacked you. Let them execute her. If you do not, you will be burdened with her as your wife for as long as you live."

Gawen Poole chose that moment to clear his throat and step forward. Hal Markland stared at him through narrowed eyes. "Poole? You've grown a beard." And then, inexplicably, he began to laugh.

"I confessed the truth to Hal when we were betrothed," Jocasta told Gawen. "It scarce mattered, since we thought you dead."

"Confessed what?" Susanna supposed that it was the fact that Jocasta would not come to her marriage bed a virgin.

Gawen moved close to Jocasta and slid one arm around her waist. "Confessed that we went through a binding form of marriage before I left on the *Squirrel*," he said. "And since I am not dead, she is *still* wed to me. The contract with Markland is invalid."

"Well," Susanna said with relief, "that solves one problem." She turned her attention to the vicar. "Do you still intend to bring charges against Jocasta, Master Atkinson?"

He did not seem to hear her. His gaze was fixed on the bed, where Ticey and Hal were locked in an embrace. "Better to marry than to burn?" Susanna suggested.

"Certes he will marry her. He deflowered my poor sweet girl and she grew deranged with grief when he abandoned her. Marriage is the *only* remedy."

"But she tried to kill him," Gawen objected. "How can you condone that?"

"No one need know of it." A sly look came into the vicar's eyes. "I will not pursue the matter of this monstrous garb, so long as Jocasta Dodderidge swears she will never again wear men's clothing."

"Jocasta Dodderidge never will," Susanna's cousin assured him in a suspiciously reasonable tone of voice.

Satisfied, Master Atkinson turned to his niece and her future husband and so missed the look that passed between Jocasta *Poole* and her spouse.

"We will never be parted again," Jocasta said.

"Never," Gawen agreed.

Of a sudden, Susanna was reminded of another woman who'd dressed as a man. She'd gone to sea with her husband, so the story went, and lived a long and happy life as his ship mate.

Despite her suspicions, Susanna said nothing. She had meddled enough. If Markland could accept an act of violence as proof of love, it was none of her concern. And Jocasta's future? That, too, was out of her hands.

It was time to go home and tend her own garden.

A Note from the Author

The laws on marriage in England were as complex and confusing as those on benefit of clergy and became more so after Henry VIII broke with the Roman Catholic church in order to obtain his own divorce. His New Religion actually provided fewer ways to escape an unhappy marriage. Not only was there no specific provision for divorce, but annulments were harder to arrange. A pre-contract with someone else, however, could invalidate a marriage and an informal exchange of vows, even without witnesses, might be as binding as a church wedding.

In sixteenth-century England, most women did not have a legal existence other than "daughter" or "wife." There were two exceptions. A woman could control her own fate if she was a childless widow or if she had reached the age of thirteen before her father died and she had not yet been betrothed to anyone. Economic pressures, however, usually made it impossible for such a woman to keep her freedom. The moment she married, her husband took control of everything.

There were no feminists in the modern sense in sixteenth-century England, but many Elizabethan women did enjoy a great deal of personal freedom. As so often happens, this created backlash. Pamphlets attacked what they called "the man-woman." Some of these women chose to dress in men's clothing. Others imitated men in other ways, such as working in men's professions. Aspiring to higher education was also criticized and when the Puritans took control of the government during the seventeenth century, they set out to discourage any kind of independent thought in females. It would be the late nineteenth century before women again achieved the same degree of literacy they had in the 1570s.

The other "monstrous" woman in this story, Mother Coombs, is a fictional creation, but the "horn" is real. A display at the Mütter Museum in Philadelphia features a woman who had just such an appendage growing out of the middle of her forehead.

Death by Devil's Turnips

Candlethorpe, Northamptonshire
June, 1577

"Good day to you, Sir Edmund," said Susanna, Lady Appleton.

"Not good at all, Lady Appleton," Sir Edmund Brudenell replied. "Three women are dead and I do much fear I am to blame."

Susanna exchanged a quick, startled glance with Nick Baldwin, whose houseguest she was, before her assessing gaze returned to Sir Edmund. The slump of his shoulders and a bleak expression accentuated the careworn look in his eyes.

"Is this a confession of murder, Sir Edmund?"

Her blunt question surprised him into a bark of rueful laughter. "What a to-do that would cause!"

"Because you have for so long been a justice of the peace in these parts?"

"Not only that. This year I am also high sheriff."

Nick gestured toward the Glastonbury chair he'd vacated when Brudenell arrived. "Sit, Sir Edmund, and tell us what you want of us."

"We are private here?"

"As you see." The upper parlor at Candlethorpe was a bright, open room comfortably furnished and well-warmed by morning sun streaming in through east-facing windows. As Brudenell, reassured, lowered himself into the chair, Nick pulled a bench closer for himself. Susanna remained where she was on the cushioned window seat, the book on her lap forgotten. With one hand she idly stroked Greymalkin, the cat curled up at her side.

She'd first met Sir Edmund Brudenell the previous autumn on her last visit to Northamptonshire. He was a well-to-do country gentleman, Nick's neighbor at Deene Park. An active life with plenty to eat and no chance encounters with deadly diseases or unsheathed blades had left him with the appearance of rough good health. Only the presence of deep creases in his ruddy face and a slight paunch betrayed that he had reached the middle of his sixth decade.

"May we offer you ale?" Susanna asked. "Barley water? Wine?"

"Nothing but your indulgence while I tell my tale. You did much impress me last year, madam, with your ability to solve puzzles and sort out truth from lies. I have need of those skills in this present crisis."

"You said three women are dead?"

The fingers of his right hand curled around the arm of the chair, gripping the knob at the end so tightly that his knuckles turned white. "Aye, and fool that I am, I did not see the connection until the third death. Early this morning the body of a young woman named Maud Hertford, a servant in my household, was found in Prior's Coppice, a remote section of my estate."

"What killed her?" Nick asked.

"She was found lying next to a flowering vine, a few berries still clutched in her hand and more in her mouth. I am reliably informed, by Dr. Roydon of Gretton, that the plant is called the devil's turnip and is surpassing poisonous."

Susanna felt her whole body tense. No wonder Sir Edmund had come to her. He wanted to tap into her extensive knowledge of deadly herbs. She would help him, certes, if she could, but she more than anyone knew how little accurate information anyone possessed about the properties of plants. The herbals she'd studied were full of contradictions.

"I have ruled her death an accident." Brudenell continued, the ironic twist of his lips giving the lie to that verdict. "I had no choice."

"The plant's proper name is bryony and just one berry would have burned her mouth. More would have blistered her throat and brought on nausea and vomiting. They are filled with bitter-tasting juice that has an acrid, unpleasant odor."

"Not self-murder, then," Nick said. Like Brudenell, he was a justice of the peace, accustomed to presiding over cases of unexplained death.

"No," Susanna agreed. "And to ingest a fatal dose she must have eaten a great many of the berries. Forty, perhaps fifty." She could not contain a shiver.

"Were the other victims also poisoned?"

"They may have been, though there was no clear sign of it. A woman named Faintnot Blaisdell died in Rockingham six days ago, the baker's wife. The cause was writ down as planetstruck, her death the result of a seizure. Two weeks before that, Mistress Barbara Ratsey died alone in her lodgings in Kettering. By the time her body was discovered, no one could say what caused her death."

"Does something link these three women together, Sir Edmund?" Susanna had a suspicion but wanted it confirmed.

"I do. Two were former mistresses. The third shared my bed the night before she died." He sounded defensive, as well he should.

Susanna had to fight not to betray her distaste. If a man had to commit adultery, the least he could do was keep his light-o'-loves at a distance from his wife.

Sir Edmund glanced at Nick but found no support there. He returned his gaze to Susanna. "I believe the murderer's intent is to cause me pain and loss. If I have the right of it, killing Lady Brudenell would strike the hardest blow. Lady Appleton, I want your help to protect her."

Incredulous, Susanna stared at him. From what Nick's housekeeper had told her about the Brudenells, Sir Edmund and Dame Agnes had been estranged for years. This sudden concern for his neglected spouse did not ring true.

"What about other mistresses?" Nick demanded. "Have you no fears for their safety?"

"The three who are now dead were the most recent. No others need concern you."

"How recent?" Involuntarily, Susanna's hand clenched in the cat's fur. Offended, Greymalkin stalked off.

"The woman in Rockingham was my mistress five years ago. I'd not seen the one in Kettering for months, though she still lived there at my expense. Maud Hertford was a milkmaid at Deene Park. She'd warmed my bed, on and off, since mid-winter.

"A means to scratch the occasional itch?" Disapproval writ large on his face, Nick failed to keep the contempt out of his voice.

A defiant undercurrent flowed through Brudenell's reply. "I was fond of all of them and treated them well."

"It is generally known you are not so fond of Dame Agnes," Susanna said. "Why suppose anyone would seek to strike at you by harming her?"

For a moment, before he regained control of his emotions, Sir Edmund's eyes blazed with the heat of anger but cold words followed. "If I lose her, Lady Appleton, I lose half my wealth. She has given me no heir. When she dies, her male relatives will challenge my claim to the estates that came to me when we wed, seven fine manors in Lincolnshire, Derbyshire, and Rutland. That being the case, I have every reason to hope Agnes lives a long, long life."

"Assuming your conclusion that Dame Agnes is in danger is correct, what do you think I can do to keep her safe?"

"You know poisons."

"I know how easily they can be slipped into an innocent dish. You need a food taster, Sir Edmund, not an herbalist."

"You might notice something others would miss. A distinctive smell. A wrong texture."

Susanna could feel herself weakening. If a life *was* at risk, how could she not try to help? "In order to be of any use, I would have to stay at Deene Park."

"Nothing simpler to arrange. As it happens, Agnes has already invited a troupe of strolling players to perform for us this evening. You will both join us as my guests and as it will be late before the entertainment is done, what more natural than to offer you a night's lodging?"

"A journey of less than two miles separates Candlethorpe and Deene Park," Nick reminded him.

"A gentlewoman cannot be expected to travel even that distance after midnight." He bestowed a smug smile on Susanna. "I am certain I can trust you, Lady Appleton, to contrive a way to extend your visit."

✝

Dame Agnes, accompanied by a maidservant, was walking in the gardens at Deene Park when Susanna and Nick arrived at mid-afternoon the following day. They had made a brief detour to inspect Prior's Coppice, the scene of Maud Hertford's demise. The plant had indeed been bryony.

Dame Agnes turned at the sound of voices, but the sour expression on her face offered neither warmth nor welcome. A wizened little woman a few years younger than her husband, she used a walking stick to get about. From the way she moved, Susanna guessed that her knees pained her. The maid, by contrast, was a sturdily built countrywoman, plain and pale of face with a wealth of thick black hair stuffed under her cap. She paused a few steps behind her mistress and kept her eyes lowered, but Susanna had the sense that her ears were stretched to catch every word uttered by her betters.

"We will leave you to your flowers," Sir Edmund declared when he had performed introductions, whereupon he and Nick beat a hasty retreat.

An uneasy silence descended. Dame Agnes seemed to be waiting for Susanna to speak first, but Susanna had not the slightest idea what to say to her. The bald announcement that Dame Agnes's life was in danger would entail too many explanations.

Was the woman aware of her husband's infidelities? Susanna assumed she was and would prefer not to have them pointed out to her. She remembered well the agony of knowing that her own husband, the late Sir Robert Appleton, had repeatedly betrayed his marriage vows. Like most women in that situation, Susanna had, for the most part, pretended ignorance.

As Dame Agnes slowly resumed her perambulation of the garden, Susanna realized something else – Sir Edmund had overlooked one obvious suspect. A wife who had finally had enough of his unfaithfulness might well be capable of taking revenge by killing her husband's mistresses.

Dame Agnes paused beside a plant Susanna recognized, though its flowering time was already past. "Cowslip," she said. "Some women sprinkle the blossoms with white wine and afterward distill the mixture to make a wash for their faces." Her pursed lips and narrowed eyes made clear her distaste for this practice. "This cowslip wine is said 'to drive wrinkles away, and to make them fair in the eyes of the world rather than in the eyes of God, whom they are not afraid to offend with the sluttishness, filthiness, and foulness of the soul.' Do you hold with such vanity, Lady Appleton?"

For one slow blink, Susanna maintained her silence. She recognized both the words and the sentiment, but was uncertain why Dame Agnes had chosen to quote that particular passage from Master William Turner's *Herbal*. An expression of her religious beliefs? A test of Susanna's? Or an outright accusation of immorality? She would not be the first to judge Susanna and Nick for their decision not to marry. Careful to keep her voice level, she replied, "I would use a distillation of cowslips to cleanse unhealthy eruptions from the skin."

"A wise answer." Dame Agnes squinted at Susanna. After a long, careful scrutiny, both her voice and her manner softened. "You are older than I expected."

Too old, did she mean, to be a rival for Sir Edmund's attention?

"I have spent many of those years in the study of herbs," Susanna said, "and had the great good fortune, as a young woman, to be acquainted with Master Turner."

Dame Agnes mellowed visibly, her thin lips very nearly curving into a smile. "He was a godly man," Dame Agnes said. "I own other herbals but suspect those written by Papists."

"The ancients are worthy teachers. *De Materia Medica* is more than fifteen hundred years old but it lists over five hundred plants, with illustrations. I find it most useful."

"You read Latin?" At Susanna's nod, Dame Agnes beamed. "I have acquired a copy of Master Mathias de L'Obel's *Stirpium adversaria nova* but when I wish to consult it I am obliged to wait until my husband or my chaplain or my cousin Richard has time to translate for me."

"I am at your service, Dame Agnes. Is there some particular herb you wished to study?"

"Indeed there is." Limping noticeably now, she led the way into the house. "It is called the devil's turnip."

Susanna scurried after her. "Bryony? Why that one?"

Her hostess began a slow ascent of the main staircase, her bad knees obliging her to climb sideways, settling the upper leg firmly on the tread before she brought the lower up to join it. "One of the servants, a foolish girl, poisoned herself by eating of the berries. I wish to know how to avoid future ... accidents."

It was reasonable she would know what had caused Maud Hertford's death, Susanna supposed. The dead woman *had* been part of her household. Dame Agnes's interest in the plant was also natural enough, for in rural areas where physicians were a rarity it was left to the lady of the manor to maintain a stillroom and provide remedies to those who were sick or injured.

When they reached her bedchamber, Dame Agnes sent her maidservant to fetch the herbals. "Before Judith returns," she said to Susanna, "I've a question for you. Do you mean to set things right by marrying Master Baldwin?"

Her grimace rueful, Susanna settled herself in a welter of skirts on a low, wide stool. "I have no plan to remarry at all, but set your fears at rest. Master Baldwin's housekeeper is in residence. There is nothing improper about my stay at Candlethorpe. I am in Northamptonshire to visit my goddaughter."

"Goddaughter?" Dame Agnes could hide neither her surprise nor her curiosity. She inched her own stool closer to that of her guest.

"A young girl named Susanna Johnson. She is five years old and has a lively intelligence. I have long had an interest in education for girls. I hope to provide her with a tutor before I return to Kent."

"Where is her mother?"

"She lives in a cottage on the Candlethorpe estate. Alas, poor creature, she is simpleminded, but she has a good heart. Indeed, she once saved my life."

Dame Agnes looked thoughtful. "So, you are not Nick Baldwin's mistress?"

"We are neighbors in Kent, and friends. I do not share his bed." That he, now and again, shared hers was no one's business but their own.

"Tongues will wag as long as you stay at Candlethorpe, housekeeper or no," Dame Agnes said.

"It is human nature to believe the worst of others."

"I'll not have it," Dame Agnes declared with the air of a woman coming to a momentous decision. "Not when there is a simple way to silence the gossips. You will stay here for the remainder of your visit to Northamptonshire. It will be easy enough for you to visit young Susanna from Deene Park and the child may come to you, as well. I like children and I share your interest in educating them. I have taken in any number of young cousins over the years."

"If you are certain it will be no trouble ..."

"None at all." A pleased expression on her wrinkled face, Dame Agnes turned at the sound of heavy footsteps. Weighed down by massive tomes, Judith had returned.

While Susanna perused Master L'Obel's work, Dame Agnes consulted Master Turner's *Herbal,* which was written in English. "He says that bryony, when laid to with salt, does much relieve old, festering, rotten, and consuming sores of the legs because its properties scour away and dry moist humours. The leaves and roots have a sharp and biting nature. He makes no mention of the fact that the berries can kill."

Engrossed in L'Obel's book, which had been published nearly ten years after her own little volume on poisonous plants, Susanna acknowledged Dame Agnes's information with an absent nod.

"My cousin Richard was good enough to put into English a part of Master L'Obel's explanation of his system for the classification of plants," Dame Agnes said after a moment. "I found it passing clever."

"To develop some means of grouping flora is an excellent notion," Susanna agreed, "although I am not convinced that arranging plants according to the characteristics of their leaves is the best method." L'Obel lumped together clover, wood-sorrel, and herb trinity, three plants that had little in common but the number and shape of their leaves.

"What does he say of bryony?"

"That there are at least two distinct varieties, both poisonous. Both black and white bryony are rampant twining and climbing plants. They send forth long tender branches with rough vine-like leaves and greenish-white flowers. The berries form in clusters and when ripe are red in color."

"Are these berries sweet, to tempt the unwary?"

"No. They have a foul scent and a loathsome taste."

"Then how could that foolish girl eat so many of them that she died?"

Susanna had no answer for her, nor did she understand why Maud Hertford had been found right next to the plant. It should have taken her several long, agonizing hours to die and yet there had been no signs of illness or violent death throes in Prior's Coppice. The last resting place of the body was a mere indentation in the forest floor, in appearance as peaceful as the hollow left by a sleeping fawn.

"How do herbalists know how poison tastes?" Dame Agnes asked. "I should think that to experiment would prove fatal."

"They rely upon hearsay." And often, she silently acknowledged, hearsay was wrong. She had herself once believed all forms of bryony had black roots, thus providing a simple way to tell them apart them from turnips, which they did much resemble in shape. Now she knew better. Only the root of black bryony was black. That of white bryony was white, making the devil's turnips much harder to distinguish from their benign cousins.

"Can all parts of the plant kill?" Dame Agnes asked. Judith, who had made herself all but invisible in a corner, stirred uneasily at the question.

"Yes," Susanna told them, "and neither cooking nor drying kills the poison."

"Is there an antidote?"

"No certain one. Some say galls counteract the effects. And if the victim can be made to vomit up what he has eaten, then there is a chance of survival."

"Did you read all that in there?" Dame Agnes indicated L'Obel's book.

Susanna did not hesitate to lie. "Yes." Closing the volume with a snap, she added, "If your wish is to avoid a repetition of today's fatal accident, then take your entire household out to Prior's Coppice and show them the plant."

Again there was a rustle of fabric from Judith's direction.

"Pull it up and display the roots," Susanna advised, "that all may know what they look like, but have a care to wear gloves. Even the whitish liquid that seeps out of the stem is a most terrible irritant and can cause a rash."

✝

Supper provided an opportunity for Susanna to meet the rest of the household. She went prepared with names and backgrounds Nick had supplied and began by considering them all suspects in the poisonings.

Dame Agnes seated her mother, Lady Neville, on one side of Susanna and put Nick on the other. An older, stouter, healthier version of her daughter, Lady Neville regarded Susanna with skepticism when Dame Agnes informed her that they shared a number of common interests, the study of herbs and the education of girls among them.

"I would like to found a school one day," Dame Agnes added.

"Waste of money," Sir Edmund grumbled, but he subsided when all three women glared at him.

Lady Neville was twice a widow. By her first husband, John Bussy, she'd had but one child, Agnes. She'd given Sir Anthony Neville none and thus been left dependent when he died upon the good graces of her son-in-law.

Two of Lady Brudenell's cousins were also present. Anthony Mears was a sour-faced individual considerably younger than the rest of the company. The other was Richard Topcliffe of Somerby – the Richard, Susanna assumed, who had translated parts of L'Obel's book for his cousin. He was doubly connected to the family. His sister was married to Sir Edmund's younger brother.

The final guest was Dr. Roydon of Gretton, the physician who had examined Maud Hertford's body, a gaunt individual relegated to one end of the high table. Long-winded and opinionated, he seemed determined to deliver a lecture on the four humours as they related to diet. "Too much red meat can produce a harmful superfluity of gross blood in those of a sanguine disposition," he declared, "and avoid raw fruit and raw herbs, whatsoever they be, as well as those that be roasted, boiled, or parboiled."

"What is safe to eat, then?" asked Lady Neville in an irritated voice.

"A little marmalade can comfort the stomach. And warm and moist foods, such as chicken and almonds are the most temperate, closely akin to the ideal humoral state. You may also eat stewed capon, madam, and broth made from the bones, and other types of poultry. But fish, because they live in water, are naturally phlegmatic and hard to digest unless your cook takes great pains to dry them out."

"That man should not be allowed in a sickroom," Lady Neville grumbled as she turned back to her trencher and selected a succulent bit of trout.

"Is he the only trained medical man hereabout?"

"Trained? Hah! My daughter may swear by him, but I say he's no better than the most uneducated quack."

"He did not study at university?"

"If he did it must have been one of those foreign places. Terrible, they are. Turn out naught but Papists."

"The doctor is a recusant?"

This was dangerous ground and Susanna was reluctant to pursue it, but she could not discount the possibility that religion ... and treason ... might be at the root of the three deaths. She prayed they were not. Dealing with jealousy or greed or revenge was much simpler.

Overhearing the words Papist and recusant, Master Topcliffe, who was seated on the other side of Lady Neville, let loose a stream of venom against all Catholics. He fair seethed when he talked of rooting out traitors in their midst.

"Moderation, Richard," warned Sir Edmund Brudenell. Roydon had abruptly fallen silent and now applied himself to his meal.

Topcliffe's glare suggested he believed even his host might have Papist sympathies and it was obvious that he violently opposed letting any vestige of Catholicism remain in England. "The queen's loyal servants cannot sit back and do nothing," he argued. "The Pope is like a great spider, spinning his web everywhere."

Susanna suppressed a sigh. This household, like so many others in the Midlands and North, appeared to be divided by religious differences. Ever since Pope Pius V's excommunication of Queen Elizabeth several years earlier, those loyal Catholics remaining among her subjects had been encouraged to rebel against her. There were many who were not averse to freeing Mary of Scotland from captivity in Derbyshire and putting her on the throne of England in Elizabeth's place. As a result, there was also increasing pressure among the more radical Protestants to report to the authorities anyone who refused to conform to the "new" religion.

But was there cause for murder in that? As Topcliffe railed on, she studied the others. Only one face betrayed wholehearted agreement with his extreme views – Lady Neville's companion. Seated at the table just below the dais, this tall, angular, middle-aged female, Ursula Ratsey by name, listened with rapt attention, nodding at each particular point.

Susanna frowned. The dead woman in Kettering had been a Mistress Barbara Ratsey. Kin to Ursula? She made a mental note to ask Sir Edmund at the first opportunity.

It came as a relief when supper was finally over and the players were called in.

"Lord Derby's Men," Lady Neville whispered as they commenced a performance of *The Wandering Knight*.

The play proved moderately amusing, having little substance and a fair amount of bawdy humor. It also had a dragon made of brown paper.

"I've seen better at a fair," scoffed young Anthony Mears. His voice, over loud, betrayed an inordinate consumption of wine.

Lady Neville gave a contemptuous snort. "Young lout! Mark my words, he'll come to a bad end. It is in the blood." At Susanna's lifted brow, she leaned closer and lowered her voice. "His grandmother was a murderer."

Could it be that simple? Susanna doubted it, but she encouraged Lady Neville's garrulous confidences all the same.

"Jane Bussy was my late husband's aunt," she said. "He told me she killed a man. Had to be pardoned by old King Henry VIII."

But when pressed for details, Lady Neville knew little more than that, leaving Susanna inclined to consider her comments naught but the mean-spirited rambling of a bitter old woman.

Still, she kept her eye on Anthony Mears.

"These cousins," Susanna whispered to Nick, who now sat behind her, "are they the male relatives Sir Edmund spoke of? The ones who stand to inherit if Dame Agnes dies?"

He nodded. "They and one other, John Bussy by name."

Their eyes met and Susanna knew he was thinking the same thing she was – that the three deaths might have been naught but preparation for the murder of the real target. Was Richard Topcliffe capable of such vileness? Was Anthony Mears? Near the end of the play, when the hero of the piece would have slain the dragon, Mears staggered forward, now much the worse for drink, and ran his dagger through the paper, very nearly skewering the player beneath.

"Sit down, Anthony!" Sir Edmund bellowed. "Damned spooney."

Susanna glanced at Nick for a translation.

"A man so drunk he's disgusting," Nick whispered in her ear. Mears was assuredly that! She watched him stumble out, no doubt in search of the privy. Dr. Roydon went after him. Neither returned.

†

The next morning Nick and Susanna left Deene Park with the excuse that Susanna must return to Candlethorpe to assure her goddaughter that she had not abandoned her. In truth they rode to Rockingham, a distance of some three miles through woodlands in which oaks and beeches predominated.

They found Baker Blaisdell in the shop next to his bakehouse. Nick spun a convoluted tale for his benefit, pretending to be investigating the possibility that Goodwife Blaisdell's death had been caused by venison obtained in violation of forest law. No one but the king could hunt animals "of the chase" unless he had purchased a special license, though in practice the inhabitants of forest villages had special privileges and liberties within the wooded areas and a local landowner's right to make inquiries would not be questioned.

Nick ended his explanation with the suggestion that the baker's wife might have eaten the tainted meat of a red deer from the forest.

Blaisdell's eyes narrowed. "*Red* deer? There be nowt but fallow deer in Rockingham."

Nick covered his blunder with assumed arrogance. "Meat is meat. Had she eaten any?"

"Faintnot were ta'en in a planet," Blaisdell insisted. Planetstruck, as Brudenell had said – dead of a sudden, unexplained fit.

The woman's given name suggested that her parents had been advocates of a purer church – plain vestments, no music, even the abolishment of bells. So, it seemed, was Blaisdell. When he launched into a diatribe on the will of God, Susanna slipped outside to inspect the area for flowering vines, but there was no bryony growing nearby.

It occurred to Susanna that bryony could have been ingested in a number of other ways. Women sometimes took the expressed juice of the fresh root mixed with white wine to bring down their courses, though most midwives knew that too much of the medicine could kill and were careful to dispense only tiny amounts. In addition, both fresh and dried roots were used in medicine – in a posset bryony was said to cure shortness of breath. According to the herbals Susanna had studied, fresh roots were collected in autumn and powdered. In that form, she wondered, did bryony lose some of its odor? Enough to allow it to be added to food ... or baked into a loaf of bread?

She had reached the bakehouse. Inside, a gangly, bored-looking apprentice stood in a clean corner shaking flour through a piece of course canvas to remove the bran. As soon as an appreciable amount had collected, another lad swept it up with small broom and a goosewing and took it to be mixed with salt, yeast, and water in a long wooden trough large enough so that two more apprentices could knead the dough using their feet.

A journeyman baker stood at a long table weighing dough that had already been worked into loaves. He sent Susanna a questioning look but did not stop work. By law, bread had to weigh a certain amount both going into and coming out of the oven. Bakers who failed to comply faced public humiliation as well as fines. When he'd finished weighing the loaves, he marked each one with a skewer and left them to rise, then strode to the large, bee-hive-shaped oven, broke open the oven door, which had been sealed in place with daub, and used a long wooden peel to remove freshly baked bread through the small rectangular opening.

"Is all your bread the same?" Susanna asked when the hot loaves had been safely deposited in racks to cool. "I mean the same ingredients. Do you, for example, sometimes add herbs for flavor. Rosemary, or basil, or garlic?"

"Yarbs?" he repeated, giving the word the local pronunciation. "Aye. Mistress were fond of such." He looked away, as if trying not to let his emotions show. "Master weredn't to know."

"Did you bake a special loaf for her that last day?"

He nodded and admitted, under Susanna's gentle questioning, that Goodwife Blaisdell had given him a dried powdered root to knead into the dough. She'd not told him what it was and he hadn't questioned her. Neither had he noticed any odd odor – scarce surprising when the smells of wood fire and baking bread were so strong.

The apprentice who had kneaded the bread had not noticed anything unusual either, and since his feet were swathed, the bryony would not have reached his skin to cause a rash.

More questions, subtle and not so subtle, yielded no further information. Susanna could see for herself that the apprentices would not have noticed much beyond their own exhaustion. They were kept busy every moment heaving sacks of flour, feeding the fire in one oven, clearing the ashes out of another – the baker sold them to make lye – kneading dough, and scouring the trough after each batch came out.

Susanna returned to Blaisdell's shop convinced that someone had provided Goodwife Blaisdell with powdered bryony root and persuaded her it would cure some ailment that afflicted her if she ate it baked in bread. She tried to question the widower about the state of his late wife's health but Nick's interrogation had already exhausted his patience.

" 'Twere her time to be ta'en!" he bellowed, and threw them out of his shop.

†

"Do you suppose he knew he'd been cuckolded?" Susanna asked as she and Nick rode away from Rockingham. "Could he have exacted vengeance upon her and then set out to punish Brudenell by killing the others?"

"The timing's wrong," Nick reminded her. "Five years ago he was not yet married. Besides, the woman in Kettering died two weeks *before* his wife did."

Nick went on to repeat everything Blaisdell had told him about Faintnot's final hours. Susanna sat up a little straighter in her saddle when she heard that Goodwife Blaisdell *had* suffered from shortness of breath. "The local cunning woman told her there was naught she could do to relieve the condition," Nick reported, "or so Blaisdell says."

"Do you suppose she consulted Dr. Roydon. Is Gretton nearby?"

"A mile or so from Rockingham."

"A pity I had no opportunity to speak with Roydon last night. He took the first opportunity to get away from Richard Topcliffe's sermonizing. *Is* he sympathetic to Rome?"

"Who can say?" Nick leveled a warning look in her direction. "In these troubled times, it is not wise to ask."

They met Sir Edmund Brudenell by arrangement beside the Eleanor Cross in Geddington, a village two miles north of Kettering. As they continued on together to the place where the first victim had died, he listened to their account of the visit to Rockingham. "This is a waste of time," he insisted with ill-disguised irritation. "My wife is in danger. You should be at her side."

"I cannot help Dame Agnes if I do not discover all there is to know about the earlier deaths. Tell me, was Barbara Ratsey kin to Lady Neville's companion?"

"Distant cousin by marriage. Barbara was a widow."

"Was Ursula Ratsey aware that Barbara was your mistress?"

"I do much doubt it. They did not speak. A difference of opinion on a matter of religion."

Religion again!. Susanna dearly hoped there was no motivation for murder there, but she did not discount the possibility. "Your wife's cousin Topcliffe supports radical reform. Does your wife?"

"All the family does. That was part of the reason I stopped visiting Barbara. To have Topcliffe find out about her ..." Suddenly he gave a bark of laughter. "Too much to hope *he* is our murderer! Still, there is a nice symmetry to it – eliminate one or two Catholic sympathizers and lay claim to the Bussy inheritance, all in one fell swoop."

†

Brudenell had paid for Mistress Ratsey's lodgings for the entire year. No one had disturbed anything in the three upstairs rooms since the body had been removed. "Her personal belongings should have gone to a nephew, but he is currently abroad." Brudenell hesitated, then admitted he was at the English college at Douai.

Another Catholic! Susanna exchanged a worried glance with Nick. Douai trained missionaries, sending them back to their native land to encourage recusants to celebrate mass in defiance of the law.

Nick threw open the window shutters, letting in light and fresh air. It had

been three weeks since Mistress Ratsey's death and no attempt had been made
to clean the place afterward. Wrinkling her nose against sour smells, Susanna
studied an abundance of furniture, luxuriously appointed. Atop an oaken table,
she found the remains of a poultice, the wrappings still smelling faintly of
bryony.

"There is your murder weapon," she told Sir Edmund. "Bryony poultices
are beneficial to remove a thorn or mend a broken bone, but if this was applied to a wound or an open sore it would release a deadly poison into the
body."

At the other end of the table, she found something else, a bit of spilled
candlewax. In it, showing up with startling clarity, was the imprint of a hand.
When the wax had still been warm, someone had leaned on that spot, leaving
an impression of the heel of a large hand, a thumb, and two long, thick fingers.

"Sir Edmund, did Mistress Ratsey have large hands or small?"

"Very small." She pointed out the spilled wax and he squinted at it, then
held his own hand above the impression. "Smaller than this, of that I am
certain."

"Then this imprint may have been left by her murderer, a killer so intent
upon instructing Mistress Ratsey in the preparation of the poultice that he did
not realize he was leaving evidence of his presence behind."

Dr. Roydon? Brudenell himself? Another, newer lover?

A spot on the heel seemed to hint at a callous – someone who worked
without gloves. But Susanna's gaze kept returning to the thumbprint. Thoughtfully, she studied the pattern of whorls and lines preserved in the wax. She
lifted her own hand and studied her fingers, noting both similarities and differences. Was it possible these ridges, spirals, and loops could be analyzed and
categorized like L'Obel's leaves? There did seem to be distinct patterns.

"Nick, show me your thumb."

His markings were not the same as her own, nor did they match those on
the table. Once again her thoughts leapt to L'Obel's theory about families of
plants. If certain characteristic patterns ran in families, might they not be able
to narrow down their list of suspects?

Taking her little eating knife, Susanna carefully pried up the wax and wrapped
it in a cloth Nick found in one of Mistress Ratsey's chests. As she worked, she
shared her thoughts with Nick and Sir Edmund. "If I can make wax impressions of the thumbs of all those we suspect of killing these women, I may be
able to match one of them to this."

"How will that prove him a murderer? More than one person must have the same pattern. And no doubt the lines in fingers change with time, as those in faces do."

"I am not so certain of that, Sir Edmund," Nick interjected. "You know I traveled to Persia some years ago. There all documents are impressed with thumbprints. I assumed the practice to be based on superstition, that the Persians believe personal contact with the paper it is written on makes a contract more binding, but it is possible officials also use the thumbprints to verify identity."

"Do you mean to say no two people's fingerprints are exactly alike? Such a thing seems impossible."

Susanna had to agree, and yet she was intrigued by the possibility.

Impatient to return to Deene Park and begin making wax impressions, she had to force herself to stay in Kettering long enough to conduct a thorough examination of the dead woman's rooms. She found nothing more to indicate how Barbara Ratsey had died or who had killed her, but did unearth a rosary hidden behind a panel in the wainscoted wall.

†

They arrived back at Deene Park to find the place in an uproar.

"You must come at once, Lady Appleton." Eyes wide with panic, voice hoarse, Judith burst into the stableyard just as Susanna dismounted. She seized her arm with bruising force. "Summat is wrong with Lady Brudenell."

With Nick and Sir Edmund following close behind, Judith all but dragged Susanna into the house and up the stairs. They had reached Dame Agnes's bedchamber before Susanna was able to free herself from the other woman's ham-handed grip.

She was relieved to find Dame Agnes upright and in apparent good health. It was anger that showed in her expression, not fear, when she caught sight of her husband in the doorway. "Murderer!" she cried. "You knew I'd find that packet of gingerbread. You thought I'd eat it all, to deprive you of your favorite sweet. You tried to kill me!"

His face blanched at the accusation. Acting swiftly, Susanna closed the door, shutting both Brudenell and Nick out.

"What has happened?" she asked, turning to Dame Agnes.

Brudenell's wife thrust a small box full of thin, crisp, gingerbread wafers into her hands. "You saved my life, Lady Appleton. If I had not gone to take a look at the bryony plant in Prior's Coppice, I'd never have recognized the scent."

Susanna lifted a wafer to her nose. The smell of the devil's turnips was unmistakable.

"My husband tried to kill me," Dame Agnes said.

Susanna regarded the box in her hands, then slowly lifted her head and let her gaze linger on the closed door. She saw again the look on Brudenell's face. "I am not so certain of that. Where did this come from?"

"It was in the parlor. I assumed Edmund bought it on one of his trips to Kettering. We are both fond of –" She broke off, swaying. Judith caught her shoulders and eased her toward the bed.

"You had best lie down," Susanna said. "You've had a shock."

Bitter words issued from beyond the bed hangings. "Oh, yes. A shock. That mine own husband should want me dead. That is a shock indeed. He hates me. He has for years. Now he's doubtless found someone else he wants to marry. That's it. I am certain of it. He wants me dead so he can take a new wife."

"You have no proof of that."

"He's not been a faithful husband all these years."

"That would be reason for you to kill him, not the other way around." Susanna stopped herself on the verge of telling Dame Agnes that three of those former mistresses were now dead of bryony poisoning.

Agnes shoved Judith aside – no mean feat with a lass a strong as that one! – and sat up against the bolster. "He wants me dead!"

"Does he profit if you die?"

Dame Agnes took stock, as Susanna had hoped she would. "Edmund might be free to remarry if I died, but he stands to lose a great fortune, the estates that came to him when we wed. I have three male cousins. Once I am dead, any one of them might take him to court to challenge his right to keep the manors I inherited from my father."

Two of those cousins were presently in residence at Deene Park. Susanna considered them in turn. Anthony Mears, the lad Dame Agnes referred to as her heir, was a bold, boasting fellow, loud and lewd, thoughtless and impulsive. Would he have had the patience to poison three women in the hope of making Dame Agnes's death look like just one more in a series of crimes? Was it proof of violent tendencies that he'd stabbed a brown paper dragon? Then there was Richard Topcliffe, self-styled "queen's servant." He had never said precisely what it was he did in royal service, but Susanna suspected he might be an intelligence gatherer, as own her late, unlamented husband had been. Topcliffe had a fiery temper and an obvious intolerance toward those faithful

Catholics who refused to compromise their faith by attending worship serv-ices conducted according to the *Book of Common Prayer*, but was he the sort of man who'd kill his own cousin for an inheritance?

When Dame Agnes finally submitted to Judith's ministrations and allowed herself to be put to bed, Susanna went in search of Nick and Sir Edmund. She located them in a room on the east of the courtyard. Brudenell stood with one hand braced against an elaborately carved and painted mantelpiece. As she approached him, Susanna saw that it bore the date 1571 and the motto *Amicus Fidelis Protexio Fortis* – a faithful friend is a strong bulwark.

"I knew this would happen if you went haring off and left my wife alone," Brudenell complained. "I brought you here to protect her."

"And so I did. She recognized the smell of bryony and did not eat of the gingerbread because of my warning. But you overlook one crucial fact, Sir Edmund. The gingerbread was not intended for Dame Agnes. It was meant for you."

Susanna produced the box, handing it first to Nick, then to Sir Edmund.

"There is so much bryony in it that no one could miss the smell. Only a fool would eat of it. I do not believe your wife was the target," Susanna con-tinued. "Nor were you meant to die. There are two explanations that make more sense. One is this – someone wants to frighten you into thinking your life is in danger."

"And the other?"

"You are meant to be charged with murder and attempted murder. You are the link between the three dead women. Your estrangement with your wife is widely known. What simpler solution than to arrest you?"

"And when conviction and execution follow," Nick murmured, "whoever is behind this will still have achieved the goal of Sir Edmund's death."

Sir Edmund scowled, fingering the seahorse crest on his signet ring. "Who would go to so much trouble? And why?"

"Someone who does not know you'd lose financially by Dame Agnes's death. Unless this is a diabolical plot by one of her cousins, I think we will find the answer in your own past. Have you enemies, Sir Edmund? Men who would like to see you dead? And what of those you've dealt with in the law? You have been a justice of the peace for many years. You have sent men to their deaths. A kinsman seeking revenge may be behind this."

"It takes two justices to condemn someone to die, and a trip to the Quarter Sessions or Assizes. I have not been solely responsible for any man's –" He broke off, a bemused look on his face. "There *was* a case, perhaps six years ago, after which a member of the condemned man's family threatened my life."

"What were the circumstances?"

He thought for a moment. "A vagabond, Jasper Redborne by name, stole several horses and was hanged for it. He swore he had a twin who would avenge him and when, a few days after his execution, I found a cock, beheaded, in the center of my Great Hall, I suspected Redborne's brother had left it. Shortly after that I was accosted in an alley in Northampton. I'd have ended with my throat slit had the watch not come along and forced the fellow to flee."

"You're certain your attacker was Redborne's twin?" Nick asked.

"Oh, yes. He told me so. 'This is for Jasper,' he said, just as he was about to use his knife on me.

"Would you recognize him if you saw him again?" Susanna asked.

But Sir Edmund shook his head. "Never got a good look at him. He was muffled in a hooded cloak. He even spoke in a harsh whisper to disguise his voice. After that he vanished and since he did not trouble me again, I quite forgot the incident till now."

"It he was a twin, he'd look like Jasper Redborne," Nick said.

"Not necessarily," Susanna warned. "Not all twins are identical."

"And after all this time," Sir Edmund admitted, "I cannot remember what Redborne looked like. It would be easy enough to disguise even a familiar face by growing a beard or shaving one off."

"If this second Redborne is responsible for the poisonings," Susanna said, "then he has been here for a while, unrecognized. A stranger would not be able to leave a box of gingerbread in the house without someone noticing, nor would he know that Sir Edmund favored the sweet."

"How are we to unmask him?" Sir Edmund asked.

"With the help of the thumbprint we found at Mistress Ratsey's lodgings," Susanna said.

†

The next day, after Nick left for Northampton to search the court records of the trial of Jasper Redborne for clues, Susanna busied herself making wax impressions. She did not explain why she wanted them but since she started with the servants, no one questioned her until she'd worked her way up to Ursula Ratsey. Lady Neville's woman refused to let Susanna anywhere near her. Then Judith refused. Topcliffe looked at her askance and stalked out of the room. Doctor Roydon backed away muttering about witch's tricks and wax poppets.

"What ails him?" she wondered aloud as she pressed Lady Neville's thumb into warm wax.

"He says he encountered such things on the Continent." Her eyes, avid with curiosity, contradicted the air of disinterest she tried to convey.

"When was he out of England?" Susanna asked. "I took him for a local man."

"Not by his speech. He settled in Gretton but two years past."

Armed with that knowledge and a new theory, Susanna sought out Sir Edmund. He had avoided her all day, and had not yet had his thumb impressed in wax.

"You must stop what you are doing," he told her, "or I will be obliged to charge you with witchcraft."

"I thought you wanted a killer brought to justice!"

"I want to prevent more deaths, but this is not helping." The desperate expression on his face gave her pause. He was more determined than she'd thought to avoid having his secrets come out.

"Sir Edmund, every print I've made has been different. That bodes well for our chances of identifying this villain by matching the lines on his thumb to those in the wax from Mistress Ratsey's lodgings. Two men have refused to cooperate. There is your wife's cousin Topcliffe –"

"A man who has influence with those who advise the queen. A word from him could cause me all manner of trouble. Disgrace. Loss of position. He already suspects me of sympathizing with recusants."

In the last two years, the queen's policy on dealing with recusancy had changed. Where once local officials had been in charge of enforcing attendance at church and fining those who missed Anglican services a shilling a week, now everyone was required to attend church or risk imprisonment. A census of recusants in each diocese had been ordered by the Privy Council. Those who continued to resist faced ever-increasing restrictions. If they were not actually put in gaol, they were made to post bonds to appear in court when summoned. They were also forbidden to have guests frequent their homes, lest they foment rebellion. Accusations, legitimate or otherwise, about Brudenell's conformity could cause him untold harm.

"I think it more likely Dr. Roydon is the culprit," Susanna said in a soothing voice. "Could he also be the twin who threatened you?"

Her suggestion startled Brudenell, but his initial look of surprise was quickly replaced by a pensive frown. "You truly believe the killer's thumbprint will match the impression you found?"

"I do. And if you will let me make an impression of your thumb, that will persuade everyone else that there is no harm in it."

"And if you find a match? How will you explain where you got that bit of wax to compare it to?"

"You are a justice of the peace and sheriff, Sir Edmund. You cannot let murder go unpunished simply to save yourself embarrassment. No one need know Barbara Ratsey was a recusant."

Defeat and resignation in his eyes, he conceded her point. "The entire household gathers to sup. There, before them all, I will allow you to make an impression of my thumb and urge anyone who has not yet complied to do so at once."

†

After supper, to the accompaniment of a great deal of grumbling and muttering, Susanna made impressions of Sir Edmund, Topcliffe, and Dr. Roydon. She compared each one to the wax impression she'd carefully preserved and brought back from Kettering ... and *none* of them matched.

Roydon had been Susanna's chief suspect, the one most likely to be the twin who'd sworn to take revenge upon Sir Edmund. As she continued to make wax impressions, she heartily wished Nick would return from Northampton with more information. She was missing something obvious, but what?

And then, as she pressed Ursula's thumb into the wax, she belatedly realized that a twin could be a woman. Not Ursula. Her family history was well known. But someone at Deene Park. Someone whose presence she had overlooked.

"Judith next," she said, searching the Great Hall for Dame Agnes's maidservant.

"Go on, girl." Dame Agnes, impatient, shoved Judith toward the small table where Susanna sat with her dabs of wax.

Face gone pale as whey, Judith turned and fled, only to be caught by Nick, who had entered the hall unseen while Susanna was busy with Topcliffe and Roydon.

"Redborne's twin was a female," he said, studying Judith with intense interest. "She'd be five and twenty now."

Susanna blinked. That meant Jasper Redborne had been hanged for stealing horses at nineteen. No wonder his sister had been outraged.

Struggling, Judith was forced to approach the table. "I've done naught!" she wailed.

"Then place your thumb on the wax and prove it," Susanna said. *And prove or disprove my theory*, she added silently.

Judith thrust both hands behind her back.

"She is doubtless a Papist," Topcliffe said. "It is her superstitious nature makes her think the devil will rise up and take her the moment she presses her thumb into the wax."

Eyes wide with terror, Judith turned to stare at him. "I am no Papist."

"What are you then, Judith?" Susanna asked in a gentle voice. "It is not your place to seek vengeance. Such things must be left to God." She caught the woman's hand and pressed her thumb into the wax.

Convinced by Dr. Roydon's raving and Topcliffe's taunts that the wax had some occult power to reveal guilt, Judith broke down completely. "He killed my brother!" she sobbed. "I wanted him to suffer."

Sir Edmund acted quickly, calling for Nick to help him convey her to the privacy of the room east of the courtyard. Susanna joined them there a few minutes later, bringing with her the two wax impressions. No one else was allowed in.

"They match perfectly," she said. "This woman killed Barbara Ratsey."

Judith seemed to have lost all desire to deny her guilt. Indeed, she appeared to take pride in what she had done. Her confession left Susanna feeling stunned and sick.

Judith Redborne had planned her revenge for years. She had been in service in a wealthy household in London when she got word of her brother's arrest. She'd stolen a goodly sum of money from her employers and run away, intending to bribe her brother's jailers to set him free. She'd arrived in Northampton too late. In her pain and anger, she'd struck ineffectually at Sir Edmund, but when she'd almost been caught, she'd devised a new plan.

With the stolen money she'd settled in Rockingham and befriended the woman who was then Brudenell's mistress. When he'd tired of Faintnot and taken up with Barbara Ratsey, Judith had found a way to become Barbara's friend too. After knowing Judith for years, both women had been willing to trust her when she recommended remedies for their ailments, but she had waited until she'd taken employment at Deene Park, close to Dame Agnes, before she acted.

"You fool!" she spat, turning a venomous gaze on Sir Edmund. "You did not even realize there had been murder done. I had to kill that poor cow,

Maud Hertford, and stuff more poison berries in her mouth after she was dead before you noticed."

"Did you mean Sir Edmund to be blamed?" Susanna asked.

"I wanted him tried and executed, as my brother was, but I wanted him to suffer first. Dame Agnes was never in any danger. Her death would not have troubled him at all."

"Save for the loss of income," Susanna reminded her.

"I did not know about that, not until after she discovered the gingerbread." Judith's eyes went to the box on the table, where Sir Edmund had left it the previous day.

"What's to be done with her?" Nick asked.

Sir Edmund looked unhappy. "She will be tried at the next Assizes and she will hang, at the least. Burn if she's found guilty of trying to kill me, since I am her master."

Neither man paid any attention to the prisoner as they discussed the ramifications of revealing the sordid details of the case. "It need not all come out," Nick said. "The charge of attempting to poison you is enough to condemn her."

Susanna alone had her eyes on Judith when she heard that she'd face death by fire and realized that she'd be given no further opportunity to cause Brudenell harm. She'd be kept in isolation in a dungeon until her trial and even then she could be prevented from speaking out. Sir Edmund had power in these parts. Judith knew that all too well.

"Not by fire," she muttered under her breath.

Only Susanna heard.

She made no attempt to stop Judith from taking matters into her own hands. By the time she had consumed the last gingerbread wafer, she was in severe pain. She died during the night.

In the parish register the death of Judith Redborne, maidservant to Dame Agnes Brudenell, was writ down as "death by devil's turnips."

A Note from the Author

This story came about because I realized Susanna had made a mistake in identifying the properties of devil's turnips in the novel *Face Down Before Rebel Hooves*. It isn't surprising that she'd be confused. The "experts" of the sixteenth century often were. I wrote a short piece called "Death by Devil's Turnips" for the Lady Appleton Newsletter, *Face Down Update*, in which I explained the error she'd made and why she'd made it. Then I took copies of that news-letter to the annual Bouchercon mystery conference. When people there started asking me if "Death by Devil's Turnips" was a new Lady Appleton story, I realized it would have to be. The title was just too good to waste.

As for Susanna's discovery of fingerprints, the story itself contains much of the history of that science prior to the sixteenth century. I'm certain there were others who made the same observations Susanna does here. Some of them may even have been English gentlewomen with an expert knowledge of poisonous herbs.

Chronological Summary of Published Books and Stories in the Face Down Mystery Series

"The Body in the Dovecote" (1552)
Murders and Other Confusions
"Much Ado About Murder" (1556)
Much Ado About Murder, 2002
Murders and Other Confusions
Face Down in the Marrow-Bone Pie (1559)
hardcover: St. Martin's Press, 1997
paperback: Kensington Mystery, 2000
"The Rubaiyat of Nicholas Baldwin" (1559)
Alfred Hitchcock's Mystery Magazine, September 2001
Murders and Other Confusions
Face Down Upon an Herbal (1561)
hardcover: St. Martin's Press, 1998
paperback: Kensington Mystery, 2000
"Lady Appleton and the London Man" (1562)
More Murder They Wrote, 1999
Murders and Other Confusions
Face Down Among the Winchester Geese (1563)
hardcover: St. Martin's Press, 1999
paperback: Kensington Mystery, 2001
"Lady Appleton and the Cautionary Herbal" (1564)
Alfred Hitchcock's Mystery Magazine, March 2001
Murders and Other Confusions
Face Down Beneath the Eleanor Cross (1565)
hardcover: St. Martin's Minotaur, 2000
paperback: Kensington Mystery, 2001
Face Down Under the Wych Elm (1567)

hardcover: St. Martin's Minotaur, 2000
paperback: Kensington Mystery, 2002
Face Down Before Rebel Hooves (1569)
    hardcover: St. Martin's Minotaur, 2001
    paperback: Kensington Mystery, 2003
"The Riddle of the Woolsack" (1569)
    Murders and Other Confusions
Face Down Across the Western Sea (1571)
    hardcover: St. Martin's Minotaur, 2002
"Lady Appleton and the Cripplegate Chrisoms" (1572)
    Alfred Hitchcock's Mystery Magazine, June 2003
    Murders and Other Confusions
"Lady Appleton and the Bristol Crystals" (1572)
    Murders and Other Confusions
Face Down Below the Banqueting House (1573)
    forthcoming in trade paperback, Perseverance Press, 2005
"Encore for a Neck Verse" (1576)
    Murders and Other Confusions
"Confusions Most Monstrous" (1577)
    Murders and Other Confusions
"Death by Devil's Turnips" (1577)
    Alfred Hitchcock's Mystery Magazine, December 2003
    Murders and Other Confusions

Other Mysteries:

Deadlier Than the Pen, A Diana Spaulding Mystery (Pemberley Press, March 2004)

Nonfiction:

Wives and Daughters: The Women of Sixteenth Century England (Whitston Publishing Company, 1984)
Making Headlines: A Biography of Nellie Bly (Dillon Press, 1989)
The Writer's Guide to Everyday Life in Renaissance England (Writer's Digest Books, 1996)

Novels for Children and Young Adults:

The Mystery of Hilliard's Castle (Down East Books, 1985)
Julia's Mending (Orchard Books, 1987)

The Mystery of the Missing Bagpipes (Avon Camelot, 1991)
Someday (Belgrave House, 2002) ebook only

Romance Novels:

That Special Smile, Bantam Loveswept #913
Tried and True, Bantam Loveswept #895
Sight Unseen, Bantam Loveswept #883
Relative Strangers, Bantam Loveswept #860
Sleepwalking Beauty, Bantam Loveswept #835
Separated Sisters, Silhouette SE #1092 (w/a Kaitlyn Gorton)
Love Thy Neighbor, Bantam Loveswept #825
Hearth, Home and Hope, Silhouette SE #942 (w/a Kaitlyn Gorton)
Winter Tapestry, Harper Paperbacks, 1991
Firebrand, Harper Monogram, 1993
Echoes and Illusions, Harper Monogram, 1993 (reissued 1996)
The Green Rose, Harper Monogram, 1994
Unquiet Hearts, Harper Monogram, 1994
Cloud Castles, Silhouette IM #307 (w/a Kaitlyn Gorton)

Other Short Fiction:

"How Chester Greenwood Invented Earmuffs," *Highlights for Children*, January, 1984
"Runaway," *Primary Treasure*, September 27, 1985
"The Reiving of Bonville Keep" in *Murder Most Medieval* (Cumberland House, 2000)

Short Non-fiction:

"Controlled Lighting at the Blackfriars Theatre," *Renaissance Papers*, 1972
"Proposal for a Survey of Oral Literature Course," *Notes On Teaching English*, May, 1974
"Gladys Hasty Carroll," in *First Person Female American* (Whitston Publishing Co., 1980)
"Patriots in Revolutionary Nova Scotia," *D.A.R. Magazine*, February, 1983
"Kids Love a Mystery," *Mystery News*, July/August 1991
"Law and Murder in Late Medieval England," *Medieval Chronicle*, May/June 1994
"Twenty-Two Days Wide and Nineteen Days Long," *Medieval Chronicle*, January/February 1995

CRIPPEN & LANDRU, PUBLISHERS

P. O. Box 9315
Norfolk, VA 23505
E-mail: info@crippenlandru.com
www.crippenlandru.com

Crippen & Landru publishes first editions of short-story collections by important detective and mystery writers. Most books in the regular series are issued both in trade softcover and in signed, limited cloth-bound with either a typescript page from the author's files or an additional story in a separate pamphlet.

☞This is the best edited, most attractively packaged line of mystery books introduced in this decade. The books are equally valuable to collectors and readers. [*Mystery Scene Magazine*]

☞The specialty publisher with the most star-studded list is Crippen & Landru, which has produced short story collections by some of the biggest names in contemporary crime fiction. [*Ellery Queen's Mystery Magazine*]

☞God Bless Crippen & Landru. [*The Strand Magazine*]

☞A monument in the making is appearing year by year from Crippen & Landru, a small press devoted exclusively to publishing the criminous short story. [*Alfred Hitchcock's Mystery Magazine*]

CRIPPEN & LANDRU, PUBLISHERS

The following books are currently (July 2007) in print in our regular series; see our website for full details:

The McCone Files by Marcia Muller. 1995. Trade softcover, $19.00.
Diagnosis: Impossible, The Problems of Dr. Sam Hawthorne by Edward D. Hoch. 1996. Trade softcover, $19.00.
Who Killed Father Christmas? by Patricia Moyes. 1996. Signed, unnumbered cloth overrun copies, $30.00.
My Mother, The Detective by James Yaffe. 1997. Trade softcover, $15.00.
In Kensington Gardens Once by H.R.F. Keating. 1997. Trade softcover, $12.00.
Shoveling Smoke by Margaret Maron. 1997. Trade softcover, $19.00.
The Ripper of Storyville and Other Tales of Ben Snow by Edward D. Hoch. 1997. Trade softcover, $19.00.
Do Not Exceed the Stated Dose by Peter Lovesey. 1998. Trade softcover, $19.00
Renowned Be Thy Grave by P.M. Carlson. 1998. Trade softcover, $16.00.
Carpenter and Quincannon by Bill Pronzini. 1998. Trade softcover, $16.00.
Famous Blue Raincoat by Ed Gorman. 1999. Signed, unnumbered cloth overrun copies, $30.00. Trade softcover, $17.00.
The Tragedy of Errors and Others by Ellery Queen. 1999. Trade softcover, $20.00.
McCone and Friends by Marcia Muller. 2000. Trade softcover, $19.00.
Challenge the Widow Maker by Clark Howard. 2000. Trade softcover, $16.00.
Fortune's World by Michael Collins. 2000. Trade softcover, $16.00.
The Velvet Touch: Nick Velvet Stories by Edward D.. Hoch. 2000. Trade softcover, 19.00.
Long Live the Dead: Tales from Black Mask by Hugh B. Cave. 2000. Trade softcover, $16.00.
Tales Out of School by Carolyn Wheat. 2000. Trade softcover, $16.00.

Stakeout on Page Street and Other DKA Files by Joe Gores. 2000. Trade softcover, $16.00.

The Celestial Buffet by Susan Dunlap. 2001. Trade softcover, $16.00.

Kisses of Death: A Nathan Heller Casebook by Max Allan Collins. 2001. Trade softcover, $19.00.

The Old Spies Club and Other Intrigues of Rand by Edward D. Hoch. 2001. Signed, unnumbered cloth overrun copies, $32.00. Trade softcover, $17.00.

The Sedgemoor Strangler by Peter Lovesey. 2001. Trade softcover, $19.00.

Adam and Eve on a Raft by Ron Goulart. 2001. Signed, unnumbered cloth overrun copies, $32.00. Trade softcover, $17.00.

The Reluctant Detective by Michael Z. Lewin. 2001. Signed, numbered clothbound, $42.00. Trade softcover, $17.00.

Nine Sons by Wendy Hornsby. 2002. Trade softcover, $16.00.

The Curious Conspiracy by Michael Gilbert. 2002. Signed, numbered clothbound, $42.00. Trade softcover, $17.00.

The 13 Culprits by Georges Simenon, translated by Peter Schulman. 2002. Trade softcover, $16.00.

The Dark Snow by Brendan DuBois. 2002. Signed, unnumbered cloth overrun copies, $32.00. Trade softcover, $17.00.

Come Into My Parlor: Tales from Detective Fiction Weekly by Hugh B. Cave. 2002. Trade softcover, $17.00.

The Iron Angel and Other Tales of the Gypsy Sleuth by Edward D. Hoch. 2003. Signed, numbered clothbound, $42.00. Trade softcover, $17.00.

Cuddy — Plus One by Jeremiah Healy. 2003. Trade softcover, $18.00.

Problems Solved by Bill Pronzini and Barry N. Malzberg. 2003. Signed, numbered clothbound, $42.00. Trade softcover, $16.00.

A Killing Climate by Eric Wright. 2003. Trade softcover, $17.00.

Lucky Dip by Liza Cody. 2003. Signed, numbered clothbound, $42.00. Trade softcover, $17.00.

Kill the Umpire: The Calls of Ed Gorgon by Jon L. Breen. 2003. Trade softcover, $17.00.

Suitable for Hanging by Margaret Maron. 2004. Trade softcover, $19.00.

Murders and Other Confusions by Kathy Lynn Emerson. 2004. Signed, numbered clothbound, $42.00. Trade softcover, $19.00.

Byline: Mickey Spillane by Mickey Spillane, edited by Lynn Myers and Max Allan Collins. 2004. Trade softcover, $20.00.

The Confessions of Owen Keane by Terence Faherty. 2005. Signed, numbered clothbound, $42.00. Trade softcover, $17.00.

The Adventure of the Murdered Moths and Other Radio Mysteries by Ellery Queen. 2005. Numbered clothbound, $45.00. Trade softcover, $20.00.

Murder, Ancient and Modern by Edward Marston. 2005. Signed, numbered clothbound, $43.00. Trade softcover, $18.00.

More Things Impossible: The Second Casebook of Dr. Sam Hawthorne by Edward D. Hoch. 2006. Signed, numbered clothbound, $43.00. Trade softcover, $18.00.

Murder, 'Orrible Murder! by Amy Myers. 2006. Signed, numbered clothbound, $43.00. Trade softcover, $18.00.

The Verdict of Us All: Stories by the Detection Club for H.R.F. Keating, edited by Peter Lovesey. 2006. Numbered clothbound, $43.00. Trade softcover, $20.00.

The Archer Files: The Complete Short Stories of Lew Archer, Private Investigator, Including Newly Discovered Case Notes by Ross Macdonald, edited by Tom Nolan. 2007. Signed, numbered clothbound, $45.00. Trade softcover, $25.00.

FORTHCOMING TITLES

The Mankiller of Poojeegai by Walter Satterthwait.

Thirteen to the Gallows by John Dickson Carr and Val Gielgud.

A Pocketful of Noses: Stories of One Ganelon or Another by James Powell.

Quintet: The Cases of Chase and Delacroix, by Richard A. Lupoff.

A Little Intelligence by Robert Silverberg and Randall Garrett (writing as "Robert Randall").

Attitude and Other Stories of Suspense by Loren D. Estleman.

Suspense — His and Hers by Barbara and Max Allan Collins.

Once Burned: The Collected Crime Stories by S.J. Rozan.

Hoch's Ladies by Edward D. Hoch.

Valentino: Film Detective by Loren D. Estleman.

Funeral in the Fog and Other Simon Ark Tales by Edward D. Hoch.

14 Slayers by Paul Cain, edited by Max Allan Collins and Lynn F. Myers, Jr. Published with Black Mask Press.

Tough As Nails by Frederick Nebel, edited by Rob Preston. Published with Black Mask Press.
You'll Die Laughing by Norbert Davis, edited by Bill Pronzini. Published with Black Mask Press.

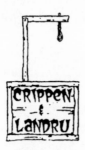

CRIPPEN & LANDRU LOST CLASSICS

Crippen & Landru is proud to publish a series of *new* short-story collections by great authors who specialized in traditional mysteries. Each book collects stories from crumbling pages of old pulp, digest, and slick magazines, and most of the stories have been "lost" since their first publication. The following books are in print:

Peter Godfrey, *The Newtonian Egg and Other Cases of Rolf le Roux*, introduction by Ronald Godfrey. 2002. Trade softcover, $15.00.

Craig Rice, *Murder, Mystery and Malone*, edited by Jeffrey A. Marks. 2002. Trade softcover, $19.00.

Charles B. Child, *The Sleuth of Baghdad: The Inspector Chafik Stories*. 2002. Cloth, $27.00. Trade softcover, $19.00.

Stuart Palmer, *Hildegarde Withers: Uncollected Riddles*, introduction by Mrs. Stuart Palmer. 2002. Trade softcover, $19.00.

Christianna Brand, *The Spotted Cat and Other Mysteries*, edited by Tony Medawar. 2002. Cloth, $29.00. Trade softcover, $19.00.

William Campbell Gault, *Marksman and Other Stories*, edited by Bill Pronzini; afterword by Shelley Gault. 2003. Trade softcover, $19.00.

Gerald Kersh, *Karmesin: The World's Greatest Criminal — Or Most Outrageous Liar*, edited by Paul Duncan. 2003. Cloth, $27.00. Trade softcover, $17.00.

C. Daly King, *The Complete Curious Mr. Tarrant*, introduction by Edward D. Hoch. 2003. Cloth, $29.00. Trade softcover, $19.00.

Helen McCloy, *The Pleasant Assassin and Other Cases of Dr. Basil Willing*, introduction by B.A. Pike. 2003. Cloth, $27.00. Trade softcover, $18.00.

William L. DeAndrea, *Murder — All Kinds*, introduction by Jane Haddam. 2003. Cloth, $29.00. Trade softcover, $19.00.

Anthony Berkeley, *The Avenging Chance and Other Mysteries from Roger Sheringham's Casebook*, edited by Tony Medawar and Arthur Robinson. 2004. Cloth, $29.00. Trade softcover, $19.00.

Joseph Commings, *Banner Deadlines: The Impossible Files of Senator Brooks U. Banner*, edited by Robert Adey; memoir by Edward D. Hoch. 2004. Cloth, $29.00. Trade softcover, $19.00.

Erle Stanley Gardner, *The Danger Zone and Other Stories*, edited by Bill Pronzini. 2004. Trade softcover, $19.00.

T.S. Stribling, *Dr. Poggioli: Criminologist*, edited by Arthur Vidro. 2004. Cloth, $29.00. Trade softcover, $19.00.

Margaret Millar, *The Couple Next Door: Collected Short Mysteries*, edited by Tom Nolan. 2004. Trade softcover, $19.00.

Gladys Mitchell, *Sleuth's Alchemy: Cases of Mrs. Bradley and Others*, edited by Nicholas Fuller. 2005. Trade softcover, $19.00.

Philip S. Warne/Howard W. Macy, *Who Was Guilty? Two Dime Novels*, edited by Marlena E. Bremseth. 2005. Cloth, $29.00. Trade softcover, $19.00.

Dennis Lynds writing as Michael Collins, *Slot-Machine Kelly*, introduction by Robert J. Randisi. 2005. Cloth, $29.00. Trade softcover, $19.00.

Rafael Sabatini, *The Evidence of the Sword*, edited by Jesse Knight. 2006. Cloth, $29.00. Trade softcover, $19.00.

Erle Stanley Gardner, *The Casebook of Sidney Zoom*, edited by Bill Pronzini. 2006. Trade softcover, $19.00.

Julian Symons, *The Detections of Francis Quarles*, edited by John Cooper; afterword by Kathleen Symons. 2006. Cloth, $29.00. Trade softcover, $19.00.

Ellis Peters (Edith Pargeter), *The Trinity Cat and Other Mysteries*, edited by Martin Edwards and Sue Feder. 2006. Trade softcover, $19.00.

Lloyd Biggle, Jr., *The Grandfather Rastin Mysteries*, edited by Kenneth Lloyd Biggle and Donna Biggle Emerson. 2007. Cloth, $29.00. Trade softcover, $19.00.

Max Brand, *Masquerade: Ten Crime Stories*, edited by William F. Nolan, Jr. 2007. Cloth, $29.00. Trade softcover, $19.00.

FORTHCOMING LOST CLASSICS

Mignon G. Eberhart, *Dead Yesterday and Other Mysteries*, edited by Rick Cypert and Kirby McCauley.

Hugh Pentecost, *The Battles of Jericho*, introduction by S.T. Karnick.

Victor Canning, *The Minerva Club, The Department of Patterns and Other Stories*, edited by John Higgins.

Anthony Boucher and Denis Green, *The Casebook of Gregory Hood*, edited by Joe R. Christopher.

Elizabeth Ferrars, *The Casebook of Jonas P. Jonas and Others*, edited by John Cooper.

Philip Wylie, *Ten Thousand Blunt Instruments*, edited by Bill Pronzini.

Erle Stanley Gardner, *The Exploits of the Patent Leather Kid*, edited by Bill Pronzini.

Vincent Cornier, *Duel of Shadows*, edited by Mike Ashley.

Phyllis Bentley, *Author in Search of a Character: The Detections of Miss Phipps*, edited by Marvin Lachman.

Anthony Abbot, *The Detections of Thatcher Colt (and Others)*, edited by William Vande Water.

SUBSCRIPTIONS

Crippen & Landru offers discounts to individuals and institutions who place Standing Order Subscriptions for its forthcoming publications, either all the Regular Series or all the Lost Classics or (preferably) both. Collectors can thereby guarantee receiving limited editions, and readers won't miss any favorite stories. Standing Order Subscribers receive a specially commissioned story in a deluxe edition as a gift at the end of the year. Please write or e-mail for more details.

Printed in the United States
202020BV00003B/70-126/A

9 781932 009217